Like
THERE'S NO
Tomorrow

A Novel

by

Camille Eide

With love
+ Joy,
Camille Eide

Ashberry Lane

"I literally read *Like There's No Tomorrow* in one sitting. A strong but troubled Scottish hero, an American heroine with a secret, and a cast of dynamic supporting characters all come together in this page-turning romantic debut. Camille Eide writes with abandon, depth, and emotional fortitude. Don't miss this sublime novel!"
—LESLIE GOULD,
#1 Best-Selling and Christy Award-Winning Author

"Camille Eide writes with such warmth and honesty, it's nearly impossible to remember that the characters populating this engaging novel aren't real. *Like There's No Tomorrow* offers wisdom, laughter, and lovely, poignant moments from Glasgow, Scotland to Central Oregon, and will steal your heart from the moment you read the first page."
—CINDY KELLEY,
Screenwriter, Author of *Traces of Mercy*

"Camille Eide's writing infuses the reader with honeysuckle from the roads of Oregon to the crofts of Scotland, and with the sweet infusion comes a gentle love, built from heartache and fear, but paved with hope. Ms. Eide's debut novel is rich with characters who have learned that obstacles don't mean an end, but a new beginning. Dare yourself to be steeped in tea and wonder when two hurting people learn where true love leads."
—LINDA S. GLAZ,
Literary Agent, Author of *With Eyes of Love*

"Tender and heart-wrenching, Camille Eide's debut novel brings home the eternal truth that no one knows what tomorrow may bring. With characters and dialogue that sparkle, *Like There's No Tomorrow* will weave its way into your heart and not let go. Beautiful, and the first of many novels, I hope, from this gifted writer."
—CARLA STEWART,
Award-Winning Author of *Stardust* and
The Hatmaker's Heart

"Camille Eide's *Like There's No Tomorrow* will tug your heartstrings as well as tickle your funny bone. The characterization is delicious, and I thought of my own BFF as I fell in love with two elderly Scottish sisters who renewed my faith in a better day ahead."
—SANDRA D. BRICKER,
Author of *Live-Out-Loud* Fiction for
the Inspirational Market

"This tender love story captured my heart. It's a perfect blend of drama, humor, and romance topped off with delightful characters that will stay with you long after you've closed the book. This may be Camille Eide's debut novel, but she is no novice at storytelling. *Like There's No Tomorrow* is one of my favorite reads of the year. And Camille is on my short list of favorite authors."
—BONNIE LEON,
Author of *The Journey of Eleven Moons*

"There's nothing more satisfying than a book that makes you rejoice when love is found, obstacles are overcome, and God's grace is accepted. *Like There's No Tomorrow* meets these criteria and more. Highly recommended!"
—GAYLE ROPER,
Award-Winning Author of *An Unexpected Match*
and *Lost and Found*

Dedicated to the One who stands beside me in the fire

"But blessed is the one who trusts in the Lord, whose confidence is in him. They will be like a tree planted by the water that sends out its roots by the stream. It does not fear when heat comes; its leaves are always green. It has no worries in a year of drought and never fails to bear fruit."

Jeremiah 17:7-8

CHAPTER ONE

Glasgow, Scotland

Ian MacLean had spent the last two years feeding chickens, hiding the kitchen knives from his mule-headed grannie, and questioning his sanity.

But if his luck held out, all that was about to change.

Feeling lighter than he had in months, Ian crossed the street, climbed into the old farm truck, and looked back at the row of flats he'd just left. Beyond the building and to the west, the lights of Glasgow cast a golden glow against the night sky.

Ian slipped the key into the ignition, let his hand drop, and studied the windows of his sister's flat. When had he last felt so free?

His talk with his absentee brother-in-law had succeeded. Davy had not only come home, but he was home to stay—he'd given Ian his word. Ian could still see the look on his sister's face when her husband walked in the door. Claire's stunned silence proved that she could actually hold her tongue when she fancied.

Ian started the truck and smiled. All in a day's work.

Aye, he'd only meant to help Claire's family, but in doing so, he'd also lifted a huge weight from his own shoulders. Not that Claire or her kids were a burden. Ian loved his nieces and nephews as if they were his own, and as long as he drew breath, they'd never go hungry. But more than food, those kids needed security and stability. They needed their da.

And now, Davy was home.

Ian tapped the pedal to bring the truck's idle down to a low grumble. Only one obstacle to his freedom remained: Maggie

1

MacLean. But if his luck held out and all went as planned, he would soon be free of his daft grannie and her mind-numbing nonsense. Free to explore a world of possibilities. Free to write that series of feature articles that would take him to remarkable, far-away places.

But then, any dull place would do—as long as it took him away from Kirkhaven.

Ian glanced at the envelope tucked in the cracked visor above him. Mailing the latest letter to Aunt Grace was all he had left to do. The sooner it arrived in Oregon, the sooner his great-aunt could move back home to Scotland and take charge of her errant sister, Maggie.

And the sooner Ian could get on with his life, shackle-free.

Juniper Ranch, Central Oregon

In spite of the never-ending drama and the occasional runaway, Emily Chapman couldn't have designed a more perfect job for herself. The kids living at the Juniper Ranch group home were so starved for love that they weren't picky about who supplied it, and she had plenty to give. Plus, they were so desperate for normalcy and stability that they didn't have time to think about anyone else.

Which worked out great for Emily. The last thing she needed was anyone worrying about her.

The first of May appeared warm with its clear skies and dazzling sun, but in reality, even with the sun shining, the chill of Oregon's high desert often kept the young teens inside when they weren't doing chores or critter duty. Today's sun had heated the sand and desert flora enough that pungent aromas of sage and juniper filled the air.

She tapped on the parlor window and got Chaz and Brandi's attention. "Hey," she hollered through the glass. "Who's up for a game of volleyball?"

Chaz grimaced and poked his glasses higher on his nose. It would take something more complex than a ball to pull him away from the computer.

Brandi shot up from the couch. "I'm in," she shouted. "As long as I'm captain."

Emily smiled. Yeah, an outdoor game was definitely in order.

She rounded up all seven girls and five boys and led them down to the makeshift volleyball court—little more than a sand pit surrounded by sagebrush—and divided the kids into two teams. Eleven-year-old Hector opened with a serve while Emily worked the sidelines.

A few minutes into the game, her phone vibrated in the pocket of her jeans. She pulled it out and stole a peek at the screen.

Jaye. Naturally. Who else would it be?

Since Emily still had a half hour left of her shift, she tucked her phone away and kept her eye on the volleyball. Her hiking boots kicked up dust and sand as she moved along the sideline, reminding her to toss her old cross-trainers in the Jeep before her next shift.

Brandi lunged toward the net and nearly ate dust, but got beneath the ball just in time.

"Awesome dig, Brandi! Way to go!" Emily silently prayed that God would give Brandi a sense that she mattered and was loved, no matter how troubled her life was. Maybe a little pride in a game well played would add something positive to the older girl's attitude.

Emily watched the game, counting the hits. As she clapped for a clean spike, her pocket hummed again. Getting two texts in a row wasn't good, especially when Aunt Grace was home alone. Emily pulled out her cell phone.

Nope. Just another message from Jaye.

She shook her head.

Commandment Number One in the *Jaye Benson Book of Love, Life, & Death*: when Jaye had a new boyfriend, no one would rest. Especially not the Best Friend.

"Come on, guys. Don't forget to set it up first, then hit." Once the ball was back in play, she viewed the first text.

Just found out Wrangle has a friend! He's totally hot! Probably!

"Probably ...?"

The volleyball sailed out of bounds and disappeared into the sagebrush surrounding the makeshift court. While one of the boys retrieved the ball, Emily scrolled to the second text.

3

I told Wrangle 2 tell him u love line dancing & 4x4s. We'll pick u up @8.

"What?"

The ball sailed toward her. Emily caught it, stuffed it in the crook of her elbow, and double-checked the screen with a groan. "Please tell me you did not just set me up on a date," she muttered. "Especially with some guy you haven't even met."

The phone buzzed yet again.

& it's not a date. It's group fun night. Note the word FUN. And NOT A DATE.

Fabulous. Jaye's idea of a "group" consisted of Jaye and Wrangle, plus Emily and some "totally hot" stray cowboy.

Apparently Jaye had forgotten her promise to lay off the scheming after the last blind date. She didn't understand. But then, it wasn't her fault. Emily hadn't tried very hard to make her friend understand why she had no intentions of marrying and, therefore, wasn't interested in dating. After a lot of prayer and thought, Emily had decided to keep her reasons to herself.

At least for now. It was better for everyone that way. Easier.

It took a few seconds to register that the teens were hollering for the ball.

"Sorry, guys." She lobbed the ball back into play, then powered off the phone and stuffed it into her pocket. Taking a deep breath, Emily refocused her attention on the game. She didn't have time to battle demons that might not even exist.

Right now, these kids needed her.

Twenty minutes later, the afternoon heat had warmed her skin, stirring up an occasional whiff of her favorite honeysuckle scent as she paced the sidelines. The heat had also turned her long, brown curls into a dark, clingy mop. She pulled her hair back and secured it into a ponytail.

"Emily!" The call of her name drifted across the compound from the main house.

"Down here," she yelled back.

But whatever the answer, it was lost as a red pickup barreled up the driveway, spitting gravel and stirring up clouds of dust in its wake.

4

Jaye.

The red Ford Ranger skidded to a halt at the edge of the staff parking lot. As Jaye climbed out, truck engine still running, someone near the house called Emily's name again—her boss, who was hurrying down the path. Sue Quinn looked uptight, even more than usual.

"Emily!" Jaye huffed as she climbed the sandy trail to the volleyball court. "Your phone is off!"

"Weird, huh." Emily grinned. "Maybe that's because some days I actually *work*—"

"Em!" Jaye gripped Emily's biceps. "You gotta go home. Your Aunt Grace—"

"What?" An icy current raced through Emily, numbing every nerve. "What happened? What's wrong with Aunt Grace?"

"Your house is on fire!"

"*What?*"

Kids came running, some of the girls squealing, others yelling at them to be quiet.

"Is she hurt?" Emily breathed. "What happened? What's going on?"

Jaye shook her head, heaving as she caught her breath. "I don't know. Your phone was off so I came straight—"

"Emily!" Her boss's clipped voice cut through the commotion as she jogged up. "There's been some kind of emergency. Fire and paramedic crews were sent to your house. I brought your keys."

Molten fear ignited in her gut. Emily caught her car keys with a shaking hand, turned, and ran for her Jeep, sprinting down the dirt path as fast as her numb legs and stiff boots would allow.

Is Aunt Grace hurt? Is she in danger? Oh, God, let her be okay.

The prayer sent another wave of numbness through her limbs, but she sucked in a deep breath and forced her legs to move faster. All she could think of was her great-aunt trapped in the little blue house, perhaps now ablaze with crackling flames. As she reached the edge of the gravel lot, she could almost feel the flames licking at her heels. The crunch of her footfalls quickened across the gravel.

✝✝✝

Let her be okay ... Please, God, let her be okay ...

Flashing red lights blinked like buoys in a sea of sand and sagebrush from half a mile away. When Emily turned onto Salt Flats Road, she spotted the sheriff's car in front of the house along with the emergency rigs. But as she neared the house, the flashing stopped. Uniformed EMTs worked at the back of their ambulance, locking compartment doors. A couple of firefighters reattached something to the fire truck.

No crackling flames. No smoke. No sheet-covered stretcher.

Still, Emily couldn't breathe. As she braked, the Jeep ground to a stop in the gravel, sending up a cloud of dust. She dashed up the steps and across the covered porch.

A thick, noxious blend of odors met her at the doorway, setting her heart pounding.

"Aunt Grace?" Inside, Emily took a quick glance around the front room and found her great-aunt snuggled up in her favorite corner chair.

A uniformed fireman stood nearby while the EMT on the loveseat beside Aunt Grace packed up a medic kit.

Grace's soft, wrinkly face drew wide with a smile as Emily came near. "Ooh, here ye are dearie. Such a kind lass. Did ye bring the mail? We'll be getting a letter from Maggie and Ian today."

That was good for a partial sigh of relief. "Are you okay?" Emily touched her aunt's thin shoulder, then bent over the little white-haired woman and kissed the top of her head. "What's going on? Have you been baking?"

"Aye. Lemon cookies for tea to go with Maggie's letter." The old woman nodded, leaned closer, and whispered, "But I'm afraid I misplaced my spatula."

Oh, Lord, not again. Emily glanced at the fireman, a guy from their church.

He greeted her with a nod and glanced down at Aunt Grace, his drawn brow deepening his look of uncertainty. "You ... might want to start by looking in the kitchen."

Emily let out a pent-up breath and forced a smile. "Good idea, Brad. Thanks." She smiled into the old woman's clouded eyes, once the color of autumn sky. "I'll be right back."

In the kitchen, another fireman with a clipboard tossed her a nod and kept writing.

She recognized him too, one of Jaye's recent crushes.

The pungent smell of burnt cookie and melted plastic stung Emily's nose.

On the counter, a few dozen lemon shortbread cookies stood stacked in tidy rows. The oven door hung open. Inside, a batch of charred cookies rested peacefully, including what was left of the missing spatula, partially melted at a weird angle in the middle like some kind of eclectic pop art. Though every window was open, a gray haze hovered near the ceiling. Aunt Grace's favorite Nottingham lace curtains fanned the acrid odor with the help of a gentle breeze.

Emily rubbed her tingling nose. After a last glance around the kitchen, she returned to the front room.

"Did ye find it?" Grace asked, still whispering.

"Yes, I did." Emily couldn't help a faint smile at her great-aunt's concern that someone might discover she'd lost a kitchen utensil. Never mind nearly burning down a house. "It's right where you left it."

"Ah, good. Thank ye, dearie." Her soft Scottish brogue and cheerful smile returned.

No harm done.

This time.

CHAPTER TWO

Emily's phone had been oddly silent. Duh—she'd forgotten to turn it back on. She powered it up.

Thirteen messages and voicemails, mostly from Jaye.

Emily dialed her friend, but before the call went through, the red Ranger pulled up out front.

Seconds later, a breathless Jaye burst into the house with Emily's tote bag and a string of questions that began with how Aunt Grace was doing and ended with which firemen had come out on the call.

Emily tossed her bag onto a chair. "I'm sure Wrangle will be glad to hear you got all the important details."

"What? It's a small town." Jaye smoothed her magenta bangs aside. "That was a totally standard question. And by the way, chica, no answer on the double da—I mean group fun night—counts as a yes."

"Yes?" Aunt Grace smiled up at Jaye. "Ye'll stay for tea? I made lemon shortbread."

"Scottish shortbread? Seriously? Of course I'm staying." Jaye grinned and linked an arm with Aunt Grace as the old woman rose slowly to her feet.

As Emily fell into step beside them, she tried to catch Jaye's eye, but her friend wasn't taking the bait. Jaye was busted for the blind date and she knew it. They'd be having a talk later.

Aunt Grace smiled up at each of them. "Ooh, this is lovely. We'll have tea and read Maggie's letter together."

Emily sucked in air between her teeth. "I'm not sure if there *was* a letter from Scotland today." She darted to the chair for her tote bag and shuffled through the contents for the mail she'd tossed in on her way to work. She sorted through bills and junk and spotted it: the prized envelope, complete with extra postage and airmail stamps, a Scottish postmark, and addressed in Ian MacLean's usual block print. Emily took it into the kitchen and waved it like a winning lottery ticket.

Aunt Grace was already making tea for "The Reading."

"Amazing." Emily aimed a smile at Jaye. "I have no idea how she knows."

Grace heated water, while Emily set out a serving tray and collected cream, sugar, and spoons.

Jaye snatched up the envelope and studied it. "MacLean. Hmm. Such a good, strrrrong Scottish name," she said in an exaggerated burr. "So what kind of property do they have in Scotland, these relatives of yours? A manor house? A castle? Ooh—a gothic castle with secret passageways."

With a laugh, Emily tucked napkins under a saucer on the tray. "Well, first off, they're Aunt Grace's relatives, not mine. Secondly, it's a small farm in the lowlands. And third—"

"Wait—you're not part of the MacLean clan?"

"Nope, sorry." She laughed again at the pouty look on Jaye's face. In a small way, she shared her friend's disappointment. Though Emily had no roots in Scotland, the idea of being part of a clan had always appealed to her. Clansmen—and women—must feel a deep sense of history, of family. Of belonging.

"Oh, dear—" Aunt Grace squeaked.

Emily dropped what she was doing and rushed to her aunt's side.

The teakettle Grace held in her good hand had dribbled hot water.

Emily held her breath as the old woman slowly poured the rest of the boiling water into a teapot.

When Grace finished without mishap, she turned and beamed a smile up at Emily. "Did ye hear, Emmy? Ian sent a letter."

"Yes, I heard." Emily smiled down at her aunt's wrinkly face. Even though her mind was sometimes a bit fuzzy, Aunt Grace was still a kind, gentle soul.

Jaye filled a rose-patterned plate with some of the pre-burn cookies. "Who's Ian?"

"Maggie's grandson." Grace sighed. "Such a dear, kind mon. And so dependable, watching over my sister Maggie and her farm. Poor laddie."

"Really? Why 'poor laddie'?" Jaye's eyes lit up. Typical drama junkie.

Emily carried cups and saucers to the tray. "She probably means because he's widowed. But I think it happened a long time ago. In fact," Emily said, turning to her aunt with a laugh, "I don't think he would consider himself much of a *laddie*, Aunt Grace. He's old enough to have traveled all over the world. And in one of his letters he called himself a hermit."

Jaye's eyes widened. "*This* could be seriously cool. Or ..." She made a lizard-tongue face and shuddered.

Emily paused with a teacup in each hand. "What?"

"I mean, like what kind of hermit are we talking about? A fat, hairy, old Friar Tuck, or a gorgeous Johnny Depp The Writer in a cabin?"

Warring images from *Robin Hood* and *The Secret Window* sprang to Emily's mind. "So those are our only options? Not that it matters—"

"Oh, it matters, Em. You need to know what you're dealing with."

Aunt Grace turned to Jaye. "Ian is a writer." She nodded. "A very good one."

"Hey, all right." Jaye grinned. "Johnny Depp in a cabin."

"I saw that movie, Jaye. He was a homicidal psycho."

"Tsss." She tossed the comment aside with a wave of her hand. "A *gorgeous* psycho."

Emily shook her head.

"What?" Jaye threw her an innocent look. "I'm just sayin'. Are you sure Ian isn't your third cousin twice removed or something?"

Checking to see if her aunt was listening, Emily lowered her voice. "Grace was my great-uncle Thomas's second wife. I'm not related to her, her sister, or any of her relatives."

Jaye shrugged a sigh. "Bummer. You could've at least gotten a haunted castle out of the deal."

When tea was ready, Aunt Grace shuffled to the small front room and settled into her chair. Jaye carried in the teapot and placed it on the coffee table while Emily brought the tray of cups, cookies, cream, and sugar. She set Grace's saucer with her cup and cookie on the end table.

The old woman slowly unfolded a napkin with her left hand and laid it across her lap. Her right hand remained curled against her abdomen in a permanent upward turn as though she carried an invisible handbag everywhere she went.

Jaye plopped down on the braided rug and sat cross-legged while Emily sank into the pillowy-soft loveseat and tucked her feet beneath her. As she pulled the band from her ponytail and shook out her hair, she caught Aunt Grace watching her. Emily kept a straight face and unfolded the letter. "Okay, Aunt Grace, are you ready?"

"Aye. Read it aloud, please, dearie."

Emily chuckled. She always read the letters aloud. As she smoothed out the folded pages, Ian's familiar handwriting broadened her smile. She looked forward to these letters from Grace's sister almost as much as Grace did, especially now that Ian wrote them on Maggie's behalf. His writing always conveyed a quiet sort of charm and subtle humor.

And Grace seemed pleased that Ian wrote the letters now because he gave a more accurate report of what Margaret Agnes Buchanan MacLean was really up to.

Sometimes a little too accurate.

Emily read the letter. "Dear Aunt Grace & Emily, we just read your last letter and Maggie insists I reply at once, as usual. She says you're very welcome and she's relieved to know you'll now have a proper cup of Scottish tea. I imagine you have perfectly good tea in America, but Maggie won't hear of you drinking it, so if you do, please don't mention it." Emily raised an eyebrow at the other two women.

"Ooh, no." Grace shook her head. "We won't mention that."

Jaye lifted her teacup in a toast and followed with a loud slurp.

"In answer to your question," Emily read on, "yes, Maggie approves of the new minister. She says he's 'a wee rickle o' bones,' but since the woman is nearly blind, I'm afraid to ask how she knows that."

"Och, Maggie!" Grace dropped her cookie.

Emily bit her lip and focused on the page. "So to fatten him up, she bakes a pie for him every Saturday. Which means I stay close to the house and keep an eye on what might end up in the pie before it goes into the oven. But, what I miss, I miss, and if the minister is as godly a man as she claims he is, he won't flinch at finding a chicken feather or a lock of Maggie's hair in it."

Jaye wrinkled her nose and mouthed *ewww* at Emily.

"Ooh, aye, Maggie loves to bake," Aunt Grace said with a nod. "She's happiest when there's a full house to feed."

"Yummy, I can just imagine." Emily winced, then read on. "This year's berry crop is off to a great start, maybe our best one ever. As long as Maggie doesn't get any more ideas about hauling the berries down to the village in the old farm truck. I still don't know—"

Emily skipped over "how she didn't end up in the loch" with a peek at Grace and read the next line.

"Don't worry, Aunt Grace. Since I was finally allowed to move up from the cottage to the farm house, your sister has found it harder to put her hands on things that get her into trouble. Things like truck keys and butcher knives. Do you remember the incident with the estate agent's car?"

Aunt Grace nodded solemnly.

"Well, as far as Maggie knows," Emily continued, "the axe has mysteriously gone missing too. All that to say Scotland is now a much safer place to visit."

"Such a good, kind lad." Grace sighed.

"Yeah. Good old *Johnny*." Jaye's eyebrows danced.

Emily answered with an eye-roll. "Speaking of visiting, Maggie is pleased that Grace has made such excellent progress after the stroke. Since she's doing so well now, Maggie is in desperate need for Grace to come ho—"

Home? A gasp slipped out as Emily paused on the word. Holding her breath, she skimmed over the rest of the letter. Ian wrote that Maggie eagerly awaited Grace's arrival in Scotland and that he would do whatever was needed to help Aunt Grace make the move.

"What? What else does it say?" Jaye asked.

Emily could only shake her head vaguely as she read the last paragraph to herself. There was plenty of room in the house for Grace, and Ian would gladly move out of the house and back into the old cottage. He repeated Maggie's insistence that Grace come home soon—the sooner, the better. She looked up.

Grace seemed content to sip her tea, but Jaye frowned and held out a hand for the letter.

"We need more tea, Jaye. Come help me." Emily rose and headed to the kitchen while Jaye scrambled up from the floor and followed.

Once they were in the kitchen and out of earshot, alarm deepened Jaye's frown. "What's wrong? What did he write?"

Emily shushed her and handed the letter over. As Jaye scanned the last lines on the page, Emily peeked around the doorway and checked on her great-aunt.

When Jaye finished, she locked eyes with Emily. "So?"

"So?" Emily spoke in a tight whisper. "Did you see what it said? Maggie wants Grace to move to Scotland."

"Yeah, I saw that. So?" Jaye looked genuinely confused.

Which set off a little burst of panic in Emily. She shouldn't have to explain it to Jaye, of all people. "Isn't it obvious? She's eighty-six. She can't just pack up and go tearing off to another country."

Frowning, Jaye looked at the letter again. "Sounds like Maggie really needs her. Maybe she should go. I mean, they're sisters and they haven't seen each other in a long time."

Mouth agape, Emily stared at her friend.

"Come on, think about it, Em. The sooner Aunt Grace is back with her real family, the sooner you can pack up the selfless-caregiver routine and start thinking about yourself."

"*Real family?*" Adrenaline forced her words into a hot whisper. "She's *my* family too."

"I thought you said she was like your step-aunt or something."

"That's not the point." Her pulse kicked up a notch. "Family is about more than blood. She was there when I needed her. She's been like a mom to me for the last thirteen years and I owe her. She depends on me now, and I'll do whatever it takes to keep her safe. Traveling halfway across the world is totally out of the question."

Jaye pinned her with a wide-eyed stare.

"I don't expect you to understand, Jaye. But trust me. I know what's best."

Her friend's left brow arched. "Best for whom?"

Aunt Grace. Who else? A sudden tightening in her throat made swallowing hard. She frowned.

After another brief scan of the letter, Jaye handed it back. "I get it."

"You do?"

"Yeah. Since your mom died and your dad will barely speak to you, Aunt Grace is all the family you have."

It was hard enough to force visits on a dad who clearly didn't want them. But for her best friend to point it out was like chucking salt in the wound. She hoped the rush of heat in her face didn't look as red as it felt. "Jaye, that's not—"

"Emmy?" Aunt Grace's gentle, creaky voice carried from the other room.

"Listen, Em. I know you mean well and all, but she's entitled to—"

"The absolute best possible care." Stiffening, Emily sneaked another peek around the doorway. Grace was brushing cookie crumbs from her lap. Emily drew a deep breath and expelled it along with whatever Jaye was implying. "And that's why traveling overseas is totally out of the question."

"Seriously?"

"Jaye, she's not strong enough to make a trip like that. Think about it. The risk of getting sick multiplies with travel, especially for the elderly. It's dangerous. At her age, even a simple cold could be ... you know ... fatal." Clearly Jaye didn't know what it meant to hold someone's life in her hands. The weight of being solely responsible for another person was something Jaye had never borne. But Aunt Grace's health and welfare were things Emily didn't take lightly.

Maybe one day Jaye would understand.

"Emmy?" Grace called out again. "Are ye getting paper so we can write back now?"

"Yes, I'm coming." Emily leaned close to Jaye and whispered, "I really do feel sorry for Maggie, but there is no way Aunt Grace is moving to Scotland."

CHAPTER THREE

A fine Scottish fog, rising from the twisting burn below, blanketed the braes beyond the farm and settled over the glen. Ian stared out the kitchen window at the spreading mist as fragments of the conversation he'd just had echoed in his ear. When he heard himself say the words aloud, it finally sunk in.

He was going to the States.

It was only for a week, but it would be a seven-day holiday from Maggie and her pigheadedness. And if that last letter to Aunt Grace had done its job, then she would soon be coming to Scotland to keep her sister sensibly occupied. Hopefully, for good.

Ah, the freedom *that* would give him.

It was possible, as long as everything worked out. And so far, things were coming together. He'd booked his flight for the following Friday. He had also spoken with his editor at *The Master's Call* magazine and confirmed the deadline for the first article in the special feature series.

Out of the mist, the post truck ambled along Craig's Hill Road. It stopped at the MacLean's mailbox and moved on. With any luck, the mail included a letter of reply from Aunt Grace and her live-in companion, Emily. And if he were very lucky, the letter would include the date of Grace's arrival.

He strode down the drive. This long-awaited venture was finally becoming a reality. His first assignment was a follow-up story on the woman whose biography he'd written. A week in Oregon would give him enough time to talk with Janet Anderson again and journal her work on the streets of Portland. Not only would it provide him with the material he needed for the story, it would give him the chance to reconnect with the woman who had prayed him through the darkest time of his life.

Janet was probably in her mid-fifties by now, as five years had passed since they had last met. It would be good to see her again, and yet … Janet's friendship would always remind him of how they first met—at his wife's funeral. Regardless of what memories a visit with Janet would stir up, he still wanted to talk with her, to know if she ever gave in to bitterness, which she had every right to do. And more than anything, he wanted to know if she still believed in turning the other cheek.

Because it certainly hadn't done *him* a sorry bit of good.

At the mailbox, he drew out an envelope bearing a US postmark. Out of habit, he brought it to his nose. Same faint, sweet, flowery scent. Ian smiled again. Things were falling into place. He'd brave old Maggie's ire and read the letter on the spot instead of waiting for her and her precious tea. She'd never know.

During the climb back to the house, he drew out the letter. The pages, written in Emily's loopy cursive, also carried a hint of the delicate scent. He scanned through the letter for dates and times of arrival.

Nothing.

He went back to the beginning and read each line. When he got to the last paragraph, he froze.

> *We would like to thank Maggie for the generous offer to come to Scotland. But regretfully, Grace must decline. A trip overseas is just not possible. Please accept our heartfelt apologies. Your invitation was very thoughtful and much appreciated.*
>
> *Yours as always,*
> *Grace and Emily*

Ian came to a halt on the walk a few feet from the house and reread the letter, frowning. *Decline*? A weird throbbing pulsed in his temples. From the reports in recent letters, Grace was healthy now. Was she ill again? Or was she showing a streak of her Buchanan blood? Based on previous letters, neither one made sense.

He stormed into the house and took the stairs two at a time, rounded the wooden newel post, and went into his room. He pulled his mobile phone from his pocket as he paced the floor. Should he ring Grace for an explanation? Or—

It just so happened ...

His trip to the States the following week would take him to Oregon. If Grace wouldn't come to him, then he'd go to her.

How far was Juniper Valley from Portland? He could deal with that after he wrapped up his work with Janet. All he needed to do now was add a few days to his trip and then ring Grace's house to let them know when he would arrive. He would meet with the old woman face to face.

Ian stopped pacing, took a cleansing breath, and blasted it out.

Something wasn't right. There was another reason for the refusal. Emily's wording was too polite, as if she were hiding something. The letters he'd exchanged with these women for the past two years proved Grace wanted to come home—that was a dead cert. He could see the white-haired pair reading his latest missive over their tea, a homesick Grace blethering about the virtues of her homeland to her kind ,old friend.

Could he have been wrong about his great-aunt? Perhaps her polite companion had been "editing" Grace the same way Ian had "edited" Maggie. Maybe in truth, Grace was as stubborn as her sister. Or more stubborn, if such a frightful thing was possible. What would a meeting with such a woman accomplish?

The thing to do was catch Aunt Grace by surprise. That way neither she nor her companion would have time to come up with any more polite excuses or refuse to see him.

He scanned the letter again, but the sound of a sputtering motor and grinding gears followed by rubber skidding across dirt snapped his attention to the bedroom window.

What in the—He pushed back the curtain, held his breath, and listened.

No. She could *not* have found the key.

But as he watched the circular drive below, the green, weathered farm truck lurched past.

With Maggie at the wheel.

Ian flew down the stairs, burst out the front door, and raced down the walkway. By the time he spotted Maggie again, she was more than twenty metres away.

The brake lights didn't even flicker as the truck swerved down the drive.

"Maggie, stop!" Bolting into a dead sprint, Ian picked up speed on the downhill slope.

The truck continued but moved slowly enough that he was able to narrow the gap. At the rate she was going, he could still catch the little fugitive at the bottom of the drive where it met Craig's Hill Road.

But when the truck reached the intersection, it pitched sharply to the right without slowing and continued on.

"Stop!" He had no idea how Maggie kept the truck on the road, but she did.

Apparently, she was headed for town.

He rounded the corner, feet pounding the packed dirt.

The bridge spanning Dumhnally Burn loomed ahead, but Maggie was far more likely to miss the narrow bridge than she was to cross it. Which meant she was going to tumble off the bank and toss herself *and* the old truck into the burn.

Chest pounding, he kicked out longer strides. Yelling was pointless.

The truck lumbered along.

Ian focused all his energy on the driver's door on the right. He caught up and worked to keep a steady pace alongside. With one hand, he latched onto the door handle, and with the other, he grasped the window frame. Mid-run, he sprang and pulled himself up onto the running board.

Maggie grunted. The truck bounced over a bump and she jerked the wheel to the left.

"Maggie, don't—" Ian's grasp on the handle slipped. Grabbing the window frame with both hands, he steadied himself, then reached through and took hold of the steering wheel.

The truck bounced over grassy mounds at the left edge of the road, knocking his hand away.

He reached again and yanked the wheel right, back toward the road. "Stop the truck, Maggie. Now!"

"No!"

The bridge loomed closer. The truck drifted off the left edge of the road again and bounced into the grass.

Maggie corrected hard to the right, throwing Ian off balance.

His foot slipped. He clung to the window frame with one hand, grasped the edge of the truck bed with the other, and held on.

Her correction shot them too far. The truck bounded off the right side of the road, bouncing over clumps and grassy mounds, and headed straight for the bank.

God, I'm not letting go, so You'd better stop this thing. For her sake. Bracing both feet on the running board, Ian gripped the edge of the window.

They neared the bank.

He reached for the key and yanked it out.

The engine sputtered and so did the old woman, but the silent truck coasted on.

"Brake!" Ian grabbed the wheel with both hands and pulled it toward him, hard.

The truck curved right and, though it slowed, kept rolling.

Please ...

He cranked the wheel as far as it would go, bringing the truck parallel with the edge of the bank. The left front wheel dipped, lifting a rear wheel slightly off the ground.

Ian leaned back and held his breath. He could open the door and try to pull Maggie out before it went down, but shifting his weight even a little could send it over.

The truck hovered there, teetering slightly as water gurgled over rocks below. Then the truck tilted back with a jumble of squeaks and settled down, still.

Heart hammering and chest heaving, Ian stepped off and leaned back against the cab. He slid down to the running board and sat, his weight an added measure of balance. Sweat trickled from his head and soaked through his shirt.

The tick of the cooling engine and the cadence of his rapid breathing were amplified by the sudden hush that settled over the glen.

"Give it back," Maggie muttered.

A burst of fury made his temples throb. Ian shot up, spun round, and yanked the door open. "Get out."

"No." Her gnarled hands clamped the wheel.

His pulse thumped in his head. "Where did you think you were going?"

"To the village."

"I said I'd take you when I finished booking my flights, then, didn't I?"

Her hazy eyes narrowed in his direction. "I dinna need ye. I've been going to town on my own since long before ye were born."

"Maggie." His jawed clamped tight, forcing a growl out through his nose. "I don't have time for this."

"Dinna fash yerself, laddie. I was doing perfectly fine before ye came along."

"Fine?" His jaw dropped. "You were headed straight over the bank!"

"I meant before ye came here to *live*." The scowl on her face deepened. "I dinna ken why ye're here."

That makes two of us. "Because you're blind, you're a menace, and you can't take care of yourself."

A wounded look passed through the scowl, just briefly. Then her cheeks burst into blotchy little tomatoes, her lips forming a tight, straight line.

She *was* a menace. But he still felt a slight twinge for saying it. "Come out."

"No." Knobby fingers gripped the wheel harder, turning white.

"If you don't stop this—" he bit back a far more choice word "—childishness, I won't bring your sister home."

"Humph!"

If he had to drag her out, he would, and it wouldn't be pretty.

Suddenly, she loosened her grip and scooted toward the bank.

Truck metal squeaked.

"Don't move!" Ian stepped on the running board to balance the weight. "Get out this side."

Grumbling about it being her truck, Maggie clambered down.

21

Ian climbed in before she could change her mind, backed the truck away from the bank, and headed toward Craig's Hill Road.

One glimpse of the old woman's scowl and it hit him: Like the old truck moments before, his plans to leave the country had just come to a dead stop.

Something had to be done about Maggie.

In the privacy of the old cottage, Ian tugged out his mobile, held his breath, and rang the only person whom Maggie would ever allow to stay, the only person whose nerve equaled hers.

His sister answered on the second ring, a good sign. Now to sound patient as he waded through Claire's usual chatter before making his request. After a polite amount of time, he brought it up.

"Sorry," Claire said. "We've got plans for that week. Davy and I are taking the kids on a holiday to Loch Lomond. I always knew there was an upside to unemployment."

"Can't you take her with you then?"

"Ha! Nice try. We're going waterskiing. Can't you just see her tearing off across the loch like an angry goose?"

Aye. All too well.

"Besides, we're staying with friends. I can't just show up with my old grannie, now can I?"

Ian ran his fingers through his hair and expelled a long, hissing breath.

"Why don't you take her with you to the States?" Claire snickered. "Now that would be loads of fun. I'm sure she'd fancy that."

"Maggie won't go near a plane."

"Well ..." Her hesitation stretched longer and thinner with each passing second. "Oh, come on, Ian. She'll have a lovely, wee time without your sour face. She'll be fine."

"She found the key to the truck, Claire. While I was home. Do you know what she could do with ten days by herself?" He refused to think about it, but the images still appeared. Screaming neighbors, burning farmsteads, maimed livestock. An old truck and an old woman sinking into the loch.

He massaged his pulsating temples.

"You wouldn't be having this problem if you had a wife."

He clamped his lips together as Claire went on about how her single friends had taken a raging fancy to him and how her friend Marion was madly in love with him and was fully prepared to bear him half a dozen children.

We've been over this. A decent woman deserves better.

"I know, I know, that topic is off limits. Though you're altogether daft if you actually believe there is such a thing."

"Such a thing as ...?"

"Off limits."

Ian exhaled.

"Why don't you ask a neighbor or someone from her church to come check on Maggie?"

"What poor, unsuspecting soul do you suggest I send? Nobody could set foot in the door, not if they were coming to check on her. She'd probably run them off with a butcher knife."

A muffled laugh meant Claire had no trouble picturing that.

Ian made a mental note to send all the kitchen knives to Claire's house *with* Maggie.

"So, what're you going to do?"

Ian heaved a sigh. "Either I leave for ten days and pray to God that she doesn't burn anything down, or I cancel my trip."

"Sorry, love. I wish I could help, but this holiday with Davy and the kids ... I can't reschedule, and it would break their wee hearts to cancel. We're long overdue for some family time. You know how it is. I mean—sorry."

"Forget it." He punched the call off and winced. Bad form. It wasn't Claire's fault.

By the end of the week, he had telephoned everyone he knew. As he paced the drive between the house and the woodshed, he stared at his silent mobile. He'd even resorted to ringing a few of Maggie's whist club members. But they were all just as old, likely just as stubborn, and perhaps even more dangerous.

With his trip only days away, he hammered his brain for an answer, but all he could think of was the new minister running down the drive as fast as his bony legs would carry him and Maggie on his heels, glinting blade in hand.

God, what am I doing here?

He stared at the phone as though the Almighty would ring with an answer. He wouldn't, of course. With the way Ian had avoided Him the last few years, God wouldn't have much to say to him.

Maybe pounding his head against the woodshed would help. If nothing else, it might silence the nagging doubts he had about his sanity and why he chose to help a mule-headed old woman who battled him every step of the way.

Maybe she was his punishment.

Aye, maybe this was what ten years of nursing mortal hatred had earned him.

Ian took a deep breath, ran both hands through his hair, and exhaled hard. "Right, then, God. I've done all I can. If You have any sort of plan, it's up to You to do something."

The mobile buzzed in his hand. He nearly dropped it before checking the screen.

Claire Kendal.

"Ian? You're not going to believe this! I can hardly believe it myself, but then I suppose I should."

As she blethered, Ian tried to piece together strings of half-finished sentences on the chance there was something of significance to him. "What are you saying?"

"He got it! Davy got the job we've been praying for. Ha! Isn't that amazing?"

"That's excellent news—"

"He starts next week. Now the girls and I can come out and make jam for the fair with Maggie. She's been after me to teach them."

"What?"

An exasperated sigh. "We had to cancel our holiday, which means I'm free to keep watch on Maggie for you." She snorted. "And *you're* the one who went to college."

Ian's jaw fell and for a moment, he couldn't speak. Something deep, something long buried, broke loose and he burst out laughing, ignoring the affronted silence on the other end.

Claire and her girls would come and stay with Maggie. The old woman would be pleased to have her great-granddaughters come for a visit, and perhaps she wouldn't be too suspicious about Claire taking a sudden interest in helping with the jam for the Kirkhaven Summer Fair.

His sister would have her hands full, without a doubt. He laughed again as he pictured feisty little Claire trying to wrestle the axe away from their eighty-three-year-old grannie. It would be a nearly even match.

As he went inside the house to pack, he dared anyone else to stand in his way.

CHAPTER FOUR

"Emily!" A voice came from the trail behind her.

Halfway to her Jeep, Emily stopped and turned around. "Hey, Hector." She tucked straying tendrils of hair behind her ear and smiled at the brown-skinned boy as he jogged to catch up with her on the path.

He stopped and bent with hands on knees, huffing. "You coming back tomorrow?"

"No, I'm off this weekend. What's up?"

Hector checked out his shoes, shook his head, and looked up. "Nothin'. Just wondered."

Emily studied him for a moment. "Family visit weekend?"

He nodded.

"Okay." She tilted her head for a better look at his face and his nonverbal cues. "Are you worried about it?"

"Naw, nothin' like that. I just wondered if you wanna meet my grandpa, that's all."

Ah. Poor Hector. Even with a mentally unstable mom who'd repeatedly left him with total strangers, no clue if he had a dad, and an uncle who spent more of his time in jail than out, Hector never gave up trying to piece together some kind of a family.

Some would expect him to be hard and angry, yet Hector was one of the sweetest kids she'd ever met. Generous and tenderhearted, he was a boy she wished she could adopt herself, to shield him from further heartache and show him his life mattered.

But she probably shouldn't make those kinds of promises—to a kid or anyone else.

Hope glistened in Hector's eyes.

A deep twinge tugged at her chest. "I would like to meet him,

Hector, but I'm going to be gone this weekend. There's something I need to do. I'm really sorry."

The boy shook his head. "Naw, man, it's cool. Yeah. You probably got a hot date."

With a wink, Emily nodded. "Yeah, a *really* hot date. With a bunch of old people."

He made a face that looked like he'd just found a slug in his Big Mac.

Emily chuckled. "Actually, my great-aunt is away on a beach retreat with her seniors' group from church and I need to go hang with them and ... make sure she's having a good time." *And being safe. And remembering her meds. And not causing herself embarrassment.*

"Aw man, you mean you have to keep teenagers *and* old peoples out of trouble? That's whack. No wonder you got no boyfriend. A'ight. But if you change your mind, you know where I'll be." He started back toward the house, walking backward. "Hey, just so you know, my grandpa's name is Hector too. I mean too like *too*, not number two." He almost tripped on a clump of sagebrush. "*I'm* Hec Two. Hector Emilio Cuevas the Second. Works two ways. Get it?"

"That's cool, Hec." She flashed a double thumbs-up.

"It's like Hec to the second *power*." He emphasized *power* with both hands splayed down like a rapper. Pretty good for an eleven-year-old.

"Yeah, I totally get it." Emily laughed. "See you Monday, Hec Two." She trekked down to the staff parking lot. So many of the kids at Juniper Ranch felt painfully lost and abandoned. Though they were in good care now with Sue Quinn and the other counselors, the loss they'd suffered still pressed in on Emily, making her heart ache.

Lord, being dumped hurts so much. Help these kids get past it. Help me do everything I can to make them feel wanted. Help them know that they matter, in spite of what others have told them. Or not told them.

She dug her phone out of her pocket and checked the recent calls. The last call to her dad was more than a week ago, and he wasn't any happier to hear from her that time than usual. But she'd promised her dying mother, and a promise was a promise, no matter how long ago she'd made it. Or how difficult it was to carry out.

When she reached the Jeep, she hovered a finger over the redial button. First, though, she needed a moment to bolster her heart and mind. Emily leaned her back against the Jeep's warm metal, heated by a full day's sun, and closed her eyes. A gentle breeze blew strands of hair across her cheek, straying from her loosely clipped up-do. She drew in a breath of clean, dry air and let it out slowly, let it carry away the sorrow, the pity. The dread.

He didn't need to hear any of that in her voice.

Emily opened her eyes and caught her reflection in the side-view mirror. She pulled out the clip and shook down her hair. After searching her bag for lip balm, she smoothed it over her dry lips, then shot a practice smile into the mirror. She stared at her dad's number again.

So, what to talk about this time? *Sorry, Dad. I know you can't stand the sight of me, and I have no clue why, but I promised Mom I wouldn't let you pull away after she was gone, so here I am. Again.*

She leaned against the Jeep and, with a deep breath, punched the dial button.

Several rings, a click, a mechanical greeting.

Emily cleared her throat and forced a respectful smile that would hopefully come across in her voice. "Hi, Dad. Just calling to check in. I guess you're not stuck at home grading papers. Hope that means you're out doing something fun."

Something besides the tavern.

She bent a jean-clad knee and rested a boot on the door. "My job is going really well. Juniper Ranch is awesome. I love helping the kids build confidence and skills they'll need to succeed later on their own. It feels good to be a part of that." She closed her eyes.

Her dad used to be happy. Before her mom died. Before both their worlds went spinning blindly off course.

Aiming for more cheer than she felt, she said, "Aunt Grace is still improving. The doc thinks her recovery is amazing. He said the extra therapy we're doing at home is making a huge difference."

A vehicle approached, the cloud of dust stirred in its wake

growing closer gradually, as though the car were moving slowly, uncertainly. Which was not unusual. People often got lost and wound up at Juniper Ranch only to be redirected back to the highway.

Emily brightened her smile. "Well, Dad, I gotta go. I'll talk to you soon." She gathered her nerve with another deep breath. "Love you."

A Honda Civic came into view. The little hatchback slowed to a crawl as it passed her and then stopped.

She punched the call off and stuffed the phone in her pocket.

A tall, dark-haired man unfolded himself from the car. He looked at her, then up at the main house, then back at her.

"Hi. Can I help you?" Emily pushed off from the Jeep.

The man approached with long strides. Tall, broad-shouldered, lean. Comfy, worn jeans and an untucked, button-down shirt. As he came near, the questioning look in his dark eyes startled her.

For a second, she forgot to breathe.

Oh. My. Goodness.

"I hope so," he said. "I'm looking for Grace Clark or Emily Chapman."

His voice sent a shockwave through her. It may have been the rumbling depth, but more likely, it was the Scottish accent. Stronger than Aunt Grace's, but similar. A tingle ran along her nerves.

"I went to their home, but no one was there. The postal clerk said to try here."

Pulse racing, her thoughts whirled. Who was he? What did he want with her and Grace? And why couldn't she tear her gaze from those intense brown eyes?

A slight frown creased his brow. "Do you know where I can find them?"

"Yes." Emily lifted her chin and offered a polite smile. "*I'm* Emily."

✢✢✢

Ian stared at the young woman with the warm smile and sun-spangled hair who stood waiting patiently for him to say something.

There had to be some mistake. *She* couldn't possibly be Emily.

His mind raced back to the letters. There were a number of

29

things he had grown to appreciate about his American correspondent. A natural bond had developed between them. A bond that Ian had shared with a stout, tenderhearted spinster on the downhill side of middle-age.

Or so he'd thought.

A small gust of wind blew strands of hair across her face. She tucked them behind her ear.

Ian caught scent of that sweet, familiar fragrance. It took a moment, although it felt like an eternity, to find his voice. "*You're* Emily?"

She nodded, her little, arched brows rising slightly. "And you are?"

"I'm ..." *At a miserable loss.* "Ian—Ian MacLean." He held out a hand.

"Ian?" Emily's eyes grew wide. "What a surprise!" She shook his hand, but a hint of confusion crossed her brow. She tilted her head and looked past him to his rented car. "Is she—I mean, is Maggie here too?"

"No, it's just me. I've been in Portland this week. On business."

"Oh, I see." Relaxing with a light smile, she nodded. "So how did you like Portland?"

As he answered her questions about his trip, his mind worked frantically to reconcile the Emily he knew from the letters with this woman—this very lovely, young woman—who had apparently been his pen pal for the past two years.

"It's nice to finally meet you, Ian. Aunt Grace will be—" Her smile faded. "Um, actually ... she's not here."

"At the ranch?"

Emily shook her head. "I mean she's gone. She went to the beach on a senior's retreat. They won't be back until Tuesday. When do you leave for Scotland?"

"Monday."

"Oh. I'm so sorry." Frowning, she seemed to be considering how to proceed. "Aunt Grace will be really disappointed she missed you."

Was that true? Or was this Emily's graceful way of covering

for a difficult, old woman? It didn't matter. Either way, he needed to see his great-aunt. But while he tried to focus on finding the absent woman, he couldn't stop staring at the one in front of him. Her hair was most definitely not white, but a rich amber brown that fell in soft, loose waves round her shoulders. Her eyes were the same color, and her mouth—

"We could try calling her," Emily said.

He cleared his throat. "Actually, Emily ..." Her name suddenly sounded like a foreign word on his lips. "If you don't mind, I need to see her. How far is it to the beach?"

Emily stared at him for several long seconds. "About a five-hour drive."

"Five? That's what they said about the trip here from Portland. Is everything in the States always so far then?"

She nodded. "For Central Oregon anyway. Pretty much everything's a long drive for us, unless we're going to Fort Rock or Paisley. Most people think we're in the middle of—"

"Paisley?"

"Yeah. It's about fifty miles from here. You've heard of it?"

"I grew up in Paisley, the one in Scotland. Near Glasgow. It's about fifty miles from us as well."

"Really? What a coincidence." Her words were soft and polite, but a look of unease brewed in Emily's dark eyes. She studied his face for a moment until her dainty eyebrows creased into a frown. "You've come a long way, so naturally you want to ... visit Aunt Grace."

"Right." *Visit.* And get some answers.

She examined him as though searching for something.

He shifted his focus beyond the silent, rocky terrain to the distant highway that snaked through a broad expanse of sagebrush-dotted land. "So if you would point me in the direction of the beach, I'll just go—"

"No!"

"Sorry?"

"Um ... what I meant was ... I'm going there tomorrow. To hang out for the weekend. The seniors have an ocean-side lodge all to themselves and I'm sure there's room for us—" Pink burst through her cheeks. "I mean, if you don't mind tagging along."

"So *you're* going?"

"Yes."

Ian scanned the valley again. Half a day's drive there, a day with Grace, and another long drive back. With *her*. Emily was attractive. Most definitely. Which was, of course, irrelevant.

And the very last thing he needed.

He drew a deep breath of sage-scented air and exhaled. "Right, then. We can go together."

"Good. Great." Emily's eyes said the idea was neither. "I was planning to leave early in the morning. Is that okay?"

"Aye."

"I should warn you, they have lots of activities planned. I'm not sure how many chances you'll get to see her."

He nodded. One chance was all he needed.

CHAPTER FIVE

On her way home, Emily checked her rearview mirror. Ian's rental car followed as she turned onto Juniper Valley highway.

She fought the urge to steal another glance. It wasn't as if she'd never seen a gorgeous guy before. And after all, this was good old Ian, her long-time pen pal. Her good old, long-time, gorgeous pen pal, who would be accompanying her to the beach for the weekend.

No big deal. She could handle it. Even so, good thing he lived far away.

Emily sneaked another peek, although she didn't need to—his face was already burned into her memory. His smile kindled a gentle warmth in his eyes and dimpled the laugh lines around his mouth. His pale gray shirt blazed a sharp contrast to his deep brown hair and eyes, and that hint of dark stubble covering his jaw.

He seemed unpretentious, which was no surprise. From what she already knew of him, he was a kind, witty, intelligent man.

And this kind, witty, gorgeous man with his deep Scottish brogue was going to get Aunt Grace all worked up about going home to Scotland.

Her pulse quickened as she pulled up to the house.

Ian parked beside her and got out. "Sure it's no trouble? You weren't expecting me for dinner."

"Not at all, I insist. Come on in." She led him up the steps. Maybe she should call Jaye to come over and join them—more people, less awkward. But an image of Jaye delighting Ian with her not-so-subtle charms nixed that idea.

Ian followed Emily into the house.

She grabbed a sticky note, jotted down the number of the local inn for him, and headed into the kitchen to start dinner. "You shouldn't have any trouble getting a room. We don't get many visitors in Juniper Valley." She raised her voice so it would carry into the living room. "Sorry, if Aunt Grace were here, you wouldn't have to ..." Frowning, Emily reached for the two plates in the dish drainer while fire rose in her cheeks. She set the plates on the counter and let her face cool. When she turned around, Ian was standing in the kitchen doorway, watching her.

"No problem, I understand." He smiled. "Can I help with anything?"

Emily's heart fluttered. She stuffed the plates in the cupboard. *He smiles and you have heart failure. What is this, seventh grade?* "No, but thanks. I've got some orange chicken, and I'm just adding rice. It's a snap. Make yourself at home."

He took a seat in the kitchen. As he tried to stuff his legs under the café table, the salt and pepper shakers wobbled and toppled over. He set them right, brushed escaped grains off the table, and winced at the floor where the salt and pepper had fallen. He folded his arms and leaned back, rattling the other chairs with his long legs.

Had a grown man ever tried to sit at the tiny table that she and Aunt Grace usually shared? "You know what? The living room might be a little more comfortable."

"No, this is good. Perfect. I'll probably fall asleep right here."

Emily raised an eyebrow.

"You don't believe me?"

"Sure, if you say so." She bit back a smile, started the rice, then took out the chicken and orange sauce and put them on to heat.

Ian fiddled with the salt and pepper shakers. "Are you certain there's nothing I can do to help?"

She faced him, fists on her hips. "All right. If you really want to help, you can make tea. If you know how."

"If I know *how*?" He grabbed the table and steadied it as he stood. "For your information, Scots are *born* making tea. Blindfolded, one-handed, in our sleep."

A slow smile tugged at her mouth. "Excellent." She handed him the tea canister and pointed to the teakettle. "Here's the stuff. I'll get the blindfold."

Ian took the kettle to the sink. He filled it with water, peeking over his shoulder.

She smirked.

He kept his face straight and slipped one hand behind his back.

She chuckled. "Don't worry, I believe you. I'm sure neither of us would last two minutes with Maggie and Grace if we weren't champion tea-makers."

When the food was ready, Emily dished up two plates and arranged them on the table. "I hope this is okay. It's nothing fancy."

"Looks great." He set the teapot in the center of the table and sniffed the food. "Smells fantastic."

Emily bowed her head and asked the blessing, then reached for the teapot.

Ian took up a fork and dug into his food. "How often do you and Grace visit the city?"

"I go into Bend a couple of times a month, but not with Aunt Grace. She's—" Emily clamped her lips and poured tea into Ian's cup. Probably the less said to Ian about Aunt Grace, the better.

"Maggie doesn't fancy the city either. Grace would feel right at home on the farm."

"Farm?" Her hand jerked.

The teapot clanked against his cup and knocked it over, spewing hot liquid all over Ian's plate and splattering his shirt. He shot to his feet and his chair flew back, whacking the cupboard.

Emily jumped from her seat. "Are you okay? I'm so sorry. Did it burn you?" She yanked a towel from the oven door and thrust it at his stomach.

"I'm okay."

"But—"

"No harm done." He blotted at the wet spots on his shirt. "Don't forget that I eat with a blind old woman every day."

"But that was so klutzy of me. Are you sure you're not—?" She winced at the splatter spots on his shirt and jeans, cheeks burning. "Let me ... get you a T-shirt or something."

Ian laughed. "I'm fine, really. And wearing one of your T-shirts would do me far more harm than the tea did, trust me." His face held no sign of irritation.

She relaxed a little. "Well, let me get you another plate at least."

"I won't argue with that."

When they finished eating, Ian offered to help clean up. "I don't like to boast, but I'm top at washing up too."

"I'm sure you are. But I can just do it later." She scraped her plate into the trash. "Sounds like you're good at a lot of things. Maggie must be really grateful to have you living with her."

He hacked out a laugh. "Oh, aye. She tells me every day."

Straightening, Emily studied Ian, unsure how to read his tone. "Does she?"

He set the teacups in the sink, then turned, leaned against the counter, and folded his arms. "Well. Maybe not *every* day."

"Ahh." Emily set down her plate and smiled. This was the droll Ian she recognized from his letters. "Some people have unique ways of showing appreciation. I'm sure Maggie has hers."

"Aye, I'm sure she does." He shrugged. "She must."

Cute and witty. Which is absolutely immaterial. She turned away and wiped her hands on a towel. Restless energy rattled her nerves. "Want to take a walk? It's a long drive tomorrow."

Wincing, he massaged his thighs. "I could use a stretch."

"Great. Just let me change my shoes. I'll be back in a sec." Emily dashed to her bedroom, laced up her Nikes, and hunted for a clean hoodie.

When she returned to the front room, Ian stood near the bookcase, engrossed by the book in his hands. She started to speak, but the look on his face stopped her.

He glanced up and froze, jaw set like stone as though he'd just seen his worst enemy.

"Ian? What's wrong?"

He shoved the book back onto the shelf. Frowning, he fumbled in his jeans pocket and tugged out a car key. "Sorry, it's late. I need to go." He headed for the door.

She darted a glance at the bookcase. "But what—"

"Thank you for dinner," he said, already halfway outside. "I'll be back in the morning." And he drove off.

Mouth agape, she stared after him. A flurry of questions swirled through her mind. She went to the bookshelf and pulled out the book Ian had been holding.

Daniel's Friends Face the Fire. Of all the Bible storybooks she kept in her library for teaching Sunday school, that one was her favorite. The amazing story of faith and courage, as well as the beautiful illustrations, always captivated both herself and the young students year after year.

So what was that all about? Why had Ian suddenly changed his mind about the walk? It didn't make sense. But then, neither did his showing up in Juniper Valley without warning. Which brought up the question that had been eating at her all evening: Exactly why did Ian want to meet with Aunt Grace?

Emily drew a deep breath, exhaled. Without those dark, probing eyes and that smile doing crazy things to her pulse, maybe she could think straight. Maggie wanted her sister to come to Scotland. She must have sent Ian to Juniper Valley to talk Aunt Grace into going. What did Ian hope to accomplish? He couldn't be thinking of persuading his great-aunt to go back home with him now.

Or could he?

His aunt. Ian was a blood relative to Grace, and Emily was not. If Aunt Grace wanted to go to Scotland, he could take her.

I wish Ian MacLean had never come.

CHAPTER SIX

Ian was glad he had come.

On the western horizon, the white-capped Cascade Mountains stood majestic against the clear blue morning sky, promising a dazzling drive over the mountain pass and into the valley beyond. Since Emily had convinced him to leave his ridiculously small, hired car and ride in her Jeep, this drive promised to be less cramped than the one the day before, a definite advantage.

After an hour of driving, Emily started to get stiff and accepted his offer to drive.

He didn't mind. The road ahead, lined with the tallest red-barked pines he'd ever seen, stretched out flat and straight for miles and didn't require him to keep his eyes on it much. Another advantage.

"I can't help wondering why you're spending the weekend with Grace and her friends," Ian said. *Since you're clearly not a doddering old spinster.* "Sure it's not because I needed to go?"

"No, really, I was already planning to go." She leaned back against the seat. "I wasn't exactly sure how I was going to pull it off. But, thanks to you, I have a good excuse for being there now."

"Pull what off?" What had he gotten himself into?

Emily sighed. "It's just a little scheme. To keep an eye on her."

Scheme? Maggie's truck escapade sprang to mind and Ian stifled a groan. Brilliant. Aunt Grace was more like Maggie than he'd thought. Maybe worse.

Emily popped a CD into the Jeep's stereo and U2's Bono crooned that he still hadn't found what he was looking for.

Careful what you wish for, man. You might be better off if you never find it. Ian held his breath, fighting the urge to switch off the song.

Before long, Emily lowered the volume and turned to him. "Maggie is amazing."

Ian grunted. "How do you figure that?"

Emily shrugged. "She does everything around the farm by herself, manages the berries, the chickens and all that. And she's always baking. She sounds amazing."

Try living with her. Ian rubbed his clean-shaven jaw. What was the best way to describe the old woman who impressed Emily and drove him insane? "Maggie needs help, but at the same time, she needs to feel independent. Giving her the help she needs while staying out of her way takes some ... creativity."

"Really? Like what?"

He took a deep breath. "Like the telephone. She won't have one in the house. She complains that estate agents will ring all hours of the day and night. Which is probably true. They come round to discuss turning farms like ours into self-catering crofts. Maggie thinks they can spy on her through the telephone line."

Emily chuckled. "You never know. Maybe they can."

"Well, just between you and me, I needed a land line, so I had one installed to the old cottage. What she doesn't know won't hurt her." He smiled.

She studied him for a moment, then leaned back against the headrest. "You're a very wise and patient man, Ian."

He huffed out a laugh, eyes on the long stretch of empty road. "I'm neither. If I have a scrap of wisdom or patience, it's some kind of miracle." When Emily didn't respond, Ian glanced over.

She aimed a warm smile at him.

That smile captured his attention for several long, heady seconds. He should really look where he was driving before—

A startled deer froze in the road.

Ian hit the brakes and swerved into the left lane.

The deer doubled back, bolted along the shoulder, and bounded into the woods.

Heart pounding, Ian steered the Jeep back into the right lane, took a deep breath, and eased it out slowly. "That was close."

"I'm sorry, Ian, I should have warned you about the deer. That happens a lot out here. Are you okay?"

"Aye. Better than him." Ian aimed a thumb at the spot where the deer had disappeared into the woods.

"Um, actually, that was a *her*." She covered her mouth but a grin peeked out. "No antlers."

"I *know* that. I didn't mean—okay, so this is how you are, then. You're laughing at me."

Emily stopped grinning, her face instantly mortified. "Oh no! I wouldn't—"

"We have deer in Scotland, you know. *Smart* ones. Ours look both ways before they cross the road." He glanced over.

Another smile curved her lips, and she shook her head. "Sorry, but I'm not sure I believe that."

"Nah, didn't think you would." Ian focused on the road, but couldn't hold back a grin.

They drove in silence for several miles. After a while, Emily said, "I keep thinking how strange it is that, even though we just met, it seems as if we've known each other forever."

"I was thinking the same thing. From all those letters. But, I have to admit, I had you pictured wrong." *ALL wrong.*

"I had you pegged wrong too." Emily laughed. "But that was totally your fault."

"*My* fault? How?" Ian kept his eyes trained on the road, but her gaze burned into him. He turned and caught the rising glow in her cheeks. "How did you picture me?"

"I always pictured you ... short and chubby with crazy red hair and a big, bushy beard."

"*What*? How did you figure *that*?"

"Umm." She bit her lower lip. "I'm pretty sure it was something you said in a letter. Something about being a hermit."

The sweet absurdity of Emily sitting at her tiny kitchen table thinking she was writing kind, gracious letters to a hairy little fat man made him burst out laughing.

Emily laughed too, then slapped a hand over her mouth as if she could somehow hold in laughter with her hand.

Ian laughed even harder.

In spite of the hand, her laughter tumbled out and mixed with his. She snorted and gasped, then burst out laughing so hard she could hardly breathe.

Ian laughed so hard he almost had to pull over.

When she could speak, Emily wiped tears from her eyes and said, "Okay, so how did you picture me?"

"I expected you to be a plain, little spinster, tottering alongside Aunt Grace with a bag of knitting or something."

"Close." She chuckled. "Except I don't knit."

Ian stole a glance at her. When Emily laughed, the light in her eyes danced like sunlight on water, stirring up something familiar, something long ago banished and forgotten.

They drove for a while in silence.

Ian slowed to cross a railway track, and as he checked both ways, he sneaked another look at the woman beside him.

She had to know how beautiful she was, didn't she?

He brought the Jeep back up to highway speed.

It made no difference to him whether she knew she was attractive or not. It was not his concern.

Don't be an idiot. You're a man. You're spending the weekend with a warm, kind, attractive woman.

So? It wouldn't be a problem. He was not an animal; he'd proven that. He'd made the mistake of falling into a couple of shallow relationships after Katy, but those had left him feeling so dreadfully empty he'd sworn never to do it again. And over time, as hatred had blighted his heart, he'd vowed never to get involved with anyone. Ever.

And he'd had no problem keeping that vow.

No, you're not an animal. You're a deeply flawed man who has no business getting tangled up with any woman, especially one like this. So just keep your eyes in your head.

As they approached the ENTERING TUMALO sign, Emily's heart sank.

They slowed to pass through the little town.

"My dad lives here," she said quietly. Maybe her dad would be interested to know she was passing through.

Yeah, right.

"You see him often then?"

"Not really." She turned to the window and let the town dissolve in a passing blur.

"But you'd like to?"

"Yes. But ... it's complicated. Losing my mom changed him. He ... has a hard time seeing me."

"Why?"

Good question. She kicked herself inwardly for bringing it up. An old ache inched fingers around her heart and squeezed. What her dad had become was hard to explain and even harder to understand. All she knew was her heart broke for him every time she saw him. "I don't know. Maybe I remind him of her."

Ian blasted a deep sigh.

Like a shot, it hit her—Ian had also lost his wife. How thoughtless of her to bring up a dying wife. Her mind raced to find something else to talk about, anything.

"She was very special," he said quietly.

Startled, Emily twisted around and stared.

"Your mum."

"Oh. Yes, she was. Mom was a very kind, caring woman. She was the best."

"What happened to her, if you don't mind me asking?"

Her fingers clasped together in her lap, as if squeezing them tight would keep the images of finding her mom on the bedroom floor that day from becoming too vivid. She was blue. *Cyanotic*, as Emily had later learned.

Much too late.

"She died of a heart attack. She was thirty-five."

"That must have been very difficult. How old were you?"

"Fifteen." Her throat tightened. Emily had only seen her mom's fainting and tiredness. She hadn't seen the other symptoms that might have pointed to a fatal illness. No one had. What Mom had called "butterflies" were probably heart palpitations. Over the past year, Emily had searched for a possible connection between the sudden, early deaths of her mom and her grandma and pieced together enough of the puzzle to spell it out.

Hypertrophic Cardiomyopathy, a genetic form of heart failure.

"She saw a doctor but the treatment he gave her didn't help. Dad wouldn't accept that, so he took her to more doctors. I think someone told her it was stress and to get more rest." The memory of her dad's increasing frustration and mounting panic sent a sharp pang to her chest. "Dad kept trying, but after a while, Mom made him stop. She was afraid she was—" she forced the words past the sudden constriction "—missing out on my life."

Ian let out a slow breath. "Must have been agonizing for your dad. A man needs to be doing something. He wants to fix what's wrong. Or at least be allowed to try." His lips tightened. "Feeling helpless when someone you love is dying is the worse torture there is. But I suppose you already know that."

Unable to breathe, she nodded. The hollow ache in his words reminded Emily why she was taking no chances on dating. If the disease was hereditary, how could she ever inflict that kind of torture on anyone? "Dad was very devoted to her." Emily swallowed a lump of sadness at the long-forgotten image of her dad so clearly in love. "Mom was always the strong one. Her faith was steady. She prayed every day and leaned on God right up to the end. But Dad lost his faith. I think he felt cheated."

Ian's jaw went suddenly rigid, his lips tight.

Emily stared at her pale, clasped fingers. *Oh, excellent shot, Em. Why not just go in for the jugular now.*

After a few miles of silence, Ian asked, "Do you have any other family?"

"Besides Aunt Grace? No."

"But you and your dad are still a family, right?" He frowned. "He must know how lucky he is that he still has you."

Lucky? He can't forgive me for breathing, so no, he probably doesn't feel all that lucky.

"Time is precious," Ian said. "Once it's gone, you can't get it back."

She kept her eyes on the giant pines picketing the roadside as they whizzed past her window and waited for the tightness in her throat to let up. "I know. You're absolutely right. I should see him more often. It's just ... it's hard to do that when I can see how much it upsets him."

"I was thinking of what *he's* throwing away, Emily. Not you." His voice was quiet. "One day, he'll regret it."

Would he?

Ian drove in silence as another half mile passed. "So let's stop and see him."

She turned to study him. "What? You mean now?"

"Why not?" He glanced at her. "We're here. Why waste the chance?"

We? Emily searched his face, still not sure what he was offering. Did Ian intend to come with her? If so, why? Was he aware of the painful memories a visit with her bitter, widowed father might stir up from his own life? "I don't know, Ian. It's really nice of you to want to help me, but I don't think it's such a good idea."

Ian glanced at her. "What do you have to lose?"

Good question. Could her dad possibly hate her any more than he did already? "I guess I'm more concerned about you."

"Me? Why?"

"My dad is not very friendly."

Ian shrugged. "I don't need a friend."

The steady stream of evergreens counted the miles like a clock ticking off the passing minutes. She took a deep breath, eased it out. "Okay, but why don't we do it tomorrow, on our way back? He's more likely to be home on a Sunday anyway."

"Tomorrow, then." He turned to her with a faint smile. "I think you'll be glad you did."

Emily couldn't help smiling in return as her heartbeat quickened. How many other ways would this man surprise her before the weekend was over?

✥ ✥ ✥

After a couple of hours on the road, a gas station and mini-market offered a welcome break. When Ian returned to the Jeep after paying for a couple of waters and a sack of chips they called *Jojos*, he found Emily had returned from the lav and stood near her vehicle, flanked on either side by two young men. From the look of her, she didn't much fancy their company.

Ian quickened his steps, assessing the men as he approached.

One soft-looking lad, about mid-twenties, grinned like an idiot while his mate, a lean, wiry lad of about the same age spoke to Emily. Both wore jeans, work boots, T-shirts, and ball caps, the latter of which sported a logo that seemed to be a brand of beer.

"You sure there's no party?" the wiry one drawled, close enough to Emily's ear to boost Ian's pulse a few notches.

Emily caught sight of Ian and a look of relief passed over her face.

He took a deep breath. "Hey. Ready to go, then?" He deliberately squeezed between the lad and Emily and tossed the bag into the backseat, catching another trace of her familiar perfume.

The two men moved a few feet away and leaned against the towering four-wheel-drive truck at the next pump.

The wiry one raised his voice. "Arrre ye rrrrrrready, then, wench?" He rolled out a ridiculous, guttural burr.

Bad Scottish imitation. So dreadful it wasn't even close to bad.

The soft one snickered and said something juvenile about what Emily was ready for.

Ian stiffened and glanced at Emily, who, by the look on her face, had clearly heard it. The lads were just being young and stupid. They weren't worth the energy. He brushed it off and gave Emily a nod. "Let's go."

As he reached for her door, one of them raised his voice and said, "So dude—Rob Roy—where are you and the little lassie headed?"

He straightened and caught a hint of unease in Emily. Taking a deep breath, he forced back the adrenaline. "Edinburgh," he said over his shoulder. "Are we on the right road?"

They snickered.

Emily climbed into the passenger seat.

A moan of approval and some whistling followed.

"Duuude, did you see those legs? Hope he can keep at least one hand on the wheel."

Ian froze again, but this time, he let the adrenaline run its full course. He closed her door with a firm click.

Through her window, Emily caught his eye. "Sorry," she said, cheeks aglow.

His jaw tightened. "You've done nothing to be sorry about."

"How do you know that?"

He studied her face. "I know."

Emily searched his eyes, then offered a faint smile.

One of the idiots hooted. "Awww, check that out. I know what she wants. Aw, yeeah."

The other one went on with a description that turned Emily's cheeks even more pink.

Blinding white heat seared through Ian's veins. He leaned in the window and spoke with a quiet calm that surprised him. "Close the window and lock your door. I'll be back."

CHAPTER SEVEN

Stunned, Emily watched the scene unfold like a Chuck Norris movie. Ian marched toward the guys with long, brisk strides, aiming for the thinner one.

The pudgy one wasn't laughing anymore. The thin one stiffened. His mouth twisted into a smirk, but his eyes looked guarded.

Ian spoke in tones too low for Emily to hear. Though he stood with arms at his sides, his stance looked rigid, braced.

Heart racing, Emily held her breath. Ian had put himself in harm's way on her account. She should've found a way to brush them off, should've done something to prevent this.

Ian thrust a thumb over his shoulder in her direction and talked to the thin one, whose expression had gone from wary to angry.

If Ian got hurt, it would be entirely her fault. Emily couldn't stand not knowing what was going on. She cranked her window down.

"—until your giggling, wee mate there doesn't recognize you anymore. Do you understand me now, laddie? Or is my *accent* getting in the way?"

The other man spit out a string of profanities about how he wasn't apologizing to anybody, then told his buddy they were leaving and climbed in the truck. The four-by-four spit gravel and dust as it fishtailed out of the lot.

Ian stared after it as the truck disappeared down the highway, hands clenched into fists. Then he spun and stormed back to the Jeep.

Emily released a gust of pent-up air.

Ian jumped in, slammed the door, and started the Jeep without a word. He threw a glance over his shoulder, pulled onto the highway, and floored it. As they picked up speed, he hissed under his breath.

Emily tried to force away the sickening sensation. She pressed a palm against her churning stomach and took a deep breath. "Sorry—"

"No." He shook his head, eyes on the road. "If anyone should apologize, it's them."

"I know. That was totally inexcusable, the way they treated you."

"Me?" He hacked out a hard laugh. With a frown, his gaze flicked over her and shifted back to the road. "You all right, then?"

"Yeah, I'm fine. It's no big deal." Except for the lingering tingle of alarm that he could have been hurt. At least it had ended without a fight.

"Idiots. They should have apologized to you." His lips clamped tight.

She studied his profile. When was the last time anyone had cared about her like that? And what was she supposed to do with her growing admiration for him?

He turned, frowning. "What?"

"Thank you."

Ian gave her that probing look of his, nodded, and shifted his attention back to the road. He said very little for several miles.

If he kept up this sullen mood, Emily would be a bundle of nerves by the time they reached the coast.

After a few more miles of silence, she turned to him. "Tell me about your time in Portland," she said.

"Ah. Portland is ... weird. Did you know the people there actually take pride in that? Bumper stickers and billboards say 'Keep Portland Weird.' But it's also interesting. College students and coffee shops on every corner. Not a single petrol station— which I found out the hard way."

Emily smiled. "People are meant to travel on foot or by bike downtown. It's an unspoken rule."

Ian puffed out a nose laugh. "Now you tell me. Anyway, I spent the week interviewing an old friend, Janet Anderson."

"For what?"

"I'm writing a series of feature articles for *The Master's Call* magazine. Hers is the first. It's a follow-up to her biography that she and I collaborated on a few years ago."

"You wrote a book? How exciting."

Ian shrugged.

"What's it called?"

"*Worth the Price: The Janet Anderson Story.* Catchy title, eh?"

"Sounds intriguing." She twisted and leaned against the door to get a better look at him. "So tell me the Janet Anderson story."

He took a deep breath. "Janet is a missionary—a rather unusual one. She talks to people on the street about the love of Christ. Gangsters, drug dealers—the kind of people who murdered her husband and son."

Emily gasped. "Murdered? How?"

Ian checked over his shoulder and changed lanes. "Janet's husband and son were part of a street ministry in L.A. They were talking with some gang members, leading them to Christ. Some others from the gang got agitated and jumped them. Both men were stabbed and killed."

"That's awful." She couldn't imagine living with the horror of losing someone to that kind of violence. "How devastating for Janet, both of them being taken at once like that."

"When it first happened, it shook her world. And her faith. But in her grief, she said God spoke to her, gave her a choice. She could keep asking why God would allow such a tragedy, or she could trust God no matter what and go on serving Him faithfully. In time, she chose the latter. But the amazing thing is she didn't stop there. In spite of the way her husband and son died, it became Janet's personal mission to find the men who had taken their lives and share the love of Christ with them. And others like them."

"How incredible. That's like ... the ultimate case of turning the other cheek."

Ian clamped his lips.

"I think that kind of work would be hard for anyone, but especially for someone who'd lost her family like that."

He checked his mirror, glanced over his shoulder, and changed lanes again. "Janet's husband and son believed their message of faith in Christ was worth risking their lives. That message cost Janet almost everything. But she decided the price of their deaths deserved a worthy return, so she picked up where they left off and carried on. That's her story."

"Unbelievable." Janet Anderson sounded like a remarkable woman, someone Emily would like to meet. "So what did you do during your week with her?"

"She has a wee flat downtown, but she spends all her time on the street. I went everywhere she did, journaled her every move, met the people she knows. Had dinner from a tin can under a bridge. There was a lad who didn't want to talk, but she didn't let up. She invited him home for a meal. I didn't think it was a good idea, but Janet said God gives her a special understanding about people, and the lad wasn't dangerous, just lonely. She told him the Lord would never leave him, and, after they talked for a while, he gave his life to Christ."

Emily frowned. "Is she ever afraid? After what happened, especially? I would be."

Ian shook his head. "No, I don't think she is. Somehow, her faith in God has only become stronger through this. She has a saying. 'Faith isn't expecting God to give us good things; it's trusting the goodness of God in the face of tragedy.'"

"Wow." Emily replayed the words, letting them sink in. "She's right, of course. But that's not always easy to live out. A lot of people give up on God after a tragedy." *Give up on God, on family, on your only child ...* "I wish my dad could meet Janet."

"If anyone can understand tragic loss, she can." Ian frowned, as if he wasn't sure that was such a good thing. And yet, he clearly admired Janet's courage, loyalty, and incredible faith. What a rare find in a friend.

"How did you meet her?"

It took a moment for him to answer. "She was a friend of Katy's—my wife."

Emily's cheeks blazed. She should have known.

"She died. But perhaps you already knew that."

"I'm sorry, Ian, I didn't mean to—"

"No, it's all right."

Emily frowned down at her fingers intertwined in her lap. "How long ago?"

"Nine years."

She turned her attention to the passing homes and buildings as they approached the outskirts of Newport. His silence sent a pang that hushed her as well. She wanted to know more, but if he didn't volunteer, she wouldn't ask.

After a while, he spoke. "Katy attended a youth mission training school in Hawaii while I—during our engagement." The last word rattled out like gravel. Ian grabbed a bottle of water, twisted off the cap, and took a drink. "Janet was there doing a series of lectures, and she and Katy became good friends. I didn't meet Janet until ... after." He took another drink, swallowed with a loud gulp. "At the funeral."

The hollow sound of the word sent a dull pain through Emily. She studied his rigid jaw with a sinking heart. *Oh, way to go, Em. Good job brightening Ian's mood.*

As they entered Newport, Ian drew a deep breath. The noon sun dazzled like a jewel set high in the sky.

Driving through the historic Nye Beach neighborhood, Ian caught his first glimpse of the Pacific Ocean. The calm water sparkled, a pleasant surprise. The salty air, stirred by a mild breeze, felt cool but grew warmer by the minute. He navigated the narrow, old streets until they found the Victorian retreat center where Grace's group was staying. It was perched on a small cliff overlooking the beach.

Emily found someone in the manager's office to let her and Ian inside. "I need to check on something. I'll be right back," she said.

Ian tossed his old leather duffel onto a chair and glanced round the main meeting room. Several comfortable-looking couches and chairs furnished one end, dining and game tables the other. A long window overlooking the ocean extended the entire length of the room. He stood at the window and stretched, allowed the blood to flow back into his cramped calves. What an incredible view of the endless, shimmering sea. Definitely a magnificent day.

When Emily returned, she looked guilty.

Ian held back a smile. She was rubbish at hiding what she felt. Hopefully that would never, ever change. "What's up?"

Going a bit pink, Emily bit her lower lip. "I checked to see if Aunt Grace has been taking her medicine. And it looks like she has."

"So that's it, your big scheme?" He cocked one eyebrow. "I thought you had something really twisted in mind, like short-sheeting the beds or switching round all their teeth."

Her laughter bubbled out easily, dissolving her look of guilt. "Really. *That's* what you thought?"

He nodded. "But it turns out you're just a spy."

"The truth is Aunt Grace can be a little forgetful. Which always poses some risk. But she still has her dignity, and I worry about her being embarrassed. I know, I worry too much." She sighed. "Yep, that's my big scheme. Now you're going to say I need professional help."

Ian bent down close and gave her his gravest look. "Emily, you can be free of this deviant behavior. The hardest part is behind you now that you've admitted you have a problem."

Emily chuckled. "Okay. Now you're laughing at *me*. I guess it's only fair after the deer thing."

Her smile was so playful, and she gazed into his eyes with such tenderness that he froze, captive. His heart drummed out a sudden, wild rhythm. They stood so close she could probably hear the hammering in his chest, maybe even see it.

"I promise to check into a program, now that I've—" Her eyes grew wide.

Man, what are you doing? He spun and went to the window. As he stood looking down at the ocean, he could feel her eyes on his back. *What* am *I doing?*

"Maybe we should look around," Emily said quietly. "See if we can figure out what they have planned for the weekend."

He turned round, but Emily was already heading out of the room.

It didn't take long to find the group's itinerary posted in the kitchen. According to the schedule, Grace and her friends were on a guided tour of the lighthouse, then on to a whale-watching tour in the afternoon.

"That leaves us with no choice," Emily said. "Until she returns for dinner, I guess we'll have to console ourselves with all this stunning ocean and miles of beach."

Emily had never seen such a gorgeous beginning of June at the Oregon coast. The water sparkled with a silvery shimmer beneath a cloudless, blue sky. Clusters of people populated the beach in both directions. A tingling sense of excitement crackled all around, as though a collective, pent-up energy had been released into the air.

As Ian and Emily walked along the water's edge in the firm sand, Ian's gaze panned out over the glistening sea. "Miserable way to spend a day."

"I know, right? Breathtaking ocean and clear, blue sky—totally lame."

Ian lifted a foot to model his flip-flops. "Thanks for stopping at the mall. I wasn't thinking of the beach when I packed."

"You could pass for an Oregonian now—*if* you don't speak."

She'd dressed in shorts and layered T-shirts with an Oregon Ducks sweatshirt tied around her waist. The weather could be unpredictable—even the sunniest day in June could turn numbingly cold if the wind picked up.

They headed south along the beach, an endless stretch of sand and driftwood, of kites and dogs, of kids and couples. No work, all play. This was good. She'd been working so long and so hard at building up the kids at the ranch that she'd forgotten to recharge, just to relax.

Emily raised her face to the midday sun, drinking in its warmth, letting it soak into her skin and melt away the last traces of winter. She filled her lungs with the salty air and let out a long, cleansing breath.

"Emily?"

"Mmm?"

"Tell me about Aunt Grace."

A sudden chill chased away the warmth. She stared at Ian. "Why? I mean, what do you want to know?"

He shrugged. "Is she sensible?"

"Yes."

"And what sort of person is she? Is she good-natured?"

Emily frowned. Why did he want to know? He already had a grandmother—he didn't need another one. "Yes. Even with her memory sometimes fading, her character is the same as ever. She's a very kind, gracious woman."

"Is she now?" He slipped his hands in his pockets as he walked. "That's how I always imagined her. From the letters."

A few yards ahead, a young couple threw a stick into the water for a tireless black lab. The dog retrieved it and headed straight for Ian, tail wagging, the stick poking out of his mouth like a dripping cigar. The man shouted an apology, but Ian took the stick from the dog and sent it hurtling down the beach. The dog tore off after it.

Ian tossed a nod at the couple and waved, then turned to Emily. "It was kind of you to stay with Grace all this time."

Was? "Not at all. It's more like repaying a huge debt of gratitude. And not just for me. My mom lost her mother when she was young too, and she spent a lot of time with Uncle Thomas and Aunt Grace." Their footfalls landed in two different tempos on the wet sand. "And later, Grace was there for me when I needed her. She still is. She's always treated me like a daughter."

"So the two of you are close, then." His strides lengthened and he edged ahead.

In spite of her daily running routine, she had to work a little to keep up with him. "Yes, we are. Nothing's changed, even though the roles are sort of reversed now. She needs me. And there's nothing I wouldn't do for her." *Except let you drag her off to some other country.*

Ian nodded. "Good."

With any luck, that was enough to satisfy him. Curling strands of hair blew across her face. Emily tucked them behind her ear. She could ask him what he intended to do once he met his great-aunt, but she was pretty sure she already knew. Her sense of dread grew.

"And is she well now?"

"What do you mean by that?" Her pinched voice sounded childish, even in her own ears, but it was too late to do anything

54

about it.

A hint of confusion creased his brow. "I mean her health. How is she?"

"She's ... as well as can be expected for a woman of her age. And in her condition."

The frown deepened. "What condition?"

She's old. She's not strong. And she's ... old.

They walked in silence for a minute.

Emily's pulse skittered as she prepared herself for the inevitable question.

"Emily, is there something—?"

"Can she make it halfway across the world in one piece? Isn't that what you really want to know?"

Ian stopped walking and stared at her.

Emily stopped too, fully numb with disbelief at what had come out of her mouth. Her throat went dry. She swallowed hard. "I'm sorry, Ian. I don't know where that came from. And I interrupted you. What were you saying?"

But Ian just shook his head slowly, eyes locked on hers.

Emily took a deep breath. "I shouldn't have said that. It's just that I know Maggie wants Grace to move to Scotland and that's why you want to see her, but she can't make the trip."

Folding his arms across his chest, he frowned. "She can't?"

Emily stared at her feet and shook her head.

"Emily?"

For some reason, she couldn't bring herself to make eye contact. "What?"

"Is that true? Or is it something else?"

It *was* the truth. Of course it was. She looked up.

A pair of dark eyes bored into hers. "Are you hiding something from me?" His voice was deep and quiet, not at all what she expected.

Angry tears stung her eyes. *Don't cry! He'll think you're psycho and take her away for sure.* She blinked hard, raised her chin, and looked him in the eye. "I honestly believe it would be too dangerous for her to travel that far."

"*Dangerous?*"

She nodded.

Ian took a long, deep breath, let it out slowly, turned, and took off walking.

She forced herself to move and jogged to catch up.

He strode several yards in silence. "All right, then."

"'All right' what?"

"There's no point in discussing it now, is there? Not without Grace."

"Grace? But she can't ..." A prickle of frustration quickened her steps. "She's not capable of making a sound decision about something like this."

Ian's profile gave no clue to his thoughts. Finally, he stopped and faced her. "Listen, Emily, do you trust me at all? Even a wee bit?"

What was he asking of her? With her feelings such a mess, all she could do was stare into those unrelenting eyes.

"No one wants to harm Grace or threaten her well-being. I'm sure you know that. But I need to talk to her, see for myself. Can you give me that?"

And what would he see? Would he see Grace as Emily did?

God, can I trust this man?

This man—Ian MacLean. The Ian she'd known through years of correspondence. The Ian she'd known as wise, selfless, and caring.

She pulled in a shuddery breath, eased it out slowly. "Okay. But when you talk to her and realize I'm right, will you tell Maggie that Grace can't come?"

Hands on his hips—probably bracing himself for another outburst—he held her in a long, scrutinizing stare, then pivoted away from her and stared at the sea. His torso expanded with every breath. "All right," he said, slowly turning back around. "A ban on the topic until we see her. Deal?"

Relief swept through her. As they walked Emily picked up seashells whenever she spotted whole ones.

Ian began picking them up too, and when he had collected a handful, he blew off the sand and handed them to her.

A dizzy feeling crept over her, making her knees tremble.

Probably just low blood sugar mixed with keeping up with his long strides. She hadn't had time to eat breakfast.

"Hey, are you hungry?" Ian asked. "I'm starving, and I saw something that looked like a chip shop back there." He pointed to a small, shop-lined street just off the beach.

"The Chowder Bowl? Yeah, that sounds really good." Fabulous. Ian MacLean had a talent for reading minds.

CHAPTER EIGHT

"So what was it like growing up in Scotland?" Emily asked. The little bistro table on the boardwalk outside the café offered a good spot for talking over bowls of steaming clam chowder, and gave them a perfect view of the beach and the glittering horizon beyond.

Ian stirred the ice around in his root beer. "I grew up in Paisley on and off. And other places. But Claire and I spent a few summers at the farm with Maggie and my granddad Liam. We helped during shearing season. And for a while, our whole family lived in the old cottage."

Emily took a bite of the creamy chowder. "That must have been fun, all together like that."

The cell phone in her pocket chirped, followed by a vibrating hum.

"Fun? It was cramped. And isolated. Claire and I had to go to secondary in Stirling."

Pulling out her phone, she said, "Secondary? Is that high school?"

He nodded, taking a bite.

Emily checked the screen. Jaye.

Where R U?

Maybe a brief reply wouldn't be rude.

But brief would never cut it with Jaye.

Yet it was brief or nothing. Emily quickly keyed in *At the beach with Ian MacLean* and hit *Send*. Cupping her chin in one hand, she asked, "So how far is it to Stirling?"

He studied his next spoonful thoughtfully. "About a five-hour drive."

Chirp-hum.

58

"Really?" She touched the *view message* button with her thumb, keeping her eyes on Ian. "Wow. That seems like a long way to go to school."

Ian sipped his soda. The faint curve of a smile peeked around his straw.

Instead of exploring what Ian was finding so funny, she glanced down at Jaye's message:

What??!?! Friar Tuck or Johnny D??? Photo!! Now!!

Emily looked up at Ian. An amused smile had settled over his face. Biting her lip, she held her breath and selected camera mode. "So ..." She raised her phone above the edge of the table, tilted it to what she hoped was the right angle, and snapped. "How long did you go to school there?" She sent the picture and stuffed the phone in her pocket.

"About a year and a half. But we moved away before I graduated." He frowned, and it seemed as if he would say more, but instead, he leaned forward and wiped the beads of condensation off his glass. "What about you? You must have happy childhood memories."

"Tons." *If I go back far enough.* "Most from when I was little. I loved to tag along with my mom, especially in the summer when she worked in the yard. Sometimes, I would hide under an umbrella in the corner of our backyard—my secret lookout. I'd lie really still and watch the honeysuckle bushes, waiting for my favorite little visitors."

Chirp-hum.

"Ah. Let me guess. Snakes?"

"Ew, no. Hummingbirds." Emily laughed, ignoring her cell phone. "I had this theory. The hummingbirds came to our yard for magic nectar that came only from *our* honeysuckle. They took it back to the Hummingbird Queen, who used it to make a special kind of perfume."

Ian smiled. "To attract a hummingbird king, no doubt."

"Actually, I believed it gave her the ability to protect her beloved colony. As long as she protected them, her subjects would live forever."

"Forever?" He quirked a frown. "Emily, I hate to tell you this, but—"

"Hey, I was *six*, okay?" Grinning, she flicked a packet of oyster crackers at him. "The honeysuckle scent was really strong on hot days, which was good because I was convinced the birds needed to smell it to find their way to our yard. One day, it wasn't very warm and I was afraid they couldn't smell the flowers and would get lost. Mom joined me at the lookout and we waited together. She whispered, 'They'll find their way, Emmy. Don't worry.' I remember waiting for*ever*—like two whole minutes—and suddenly, a hummingbird appeared. We held our breath. Her wings hummed as she hovered over the flowers, collecting nectar."

"*Magical* nectar." His brows raised in an exaggerated look of correction.

Emily smiled and watched tiny bubbles fizz around the melting ice in her Coke. "Mom spent a lot of time with me. I had no idea those times we spent together would end up being so priceless." She rolled her eyes. "I know, don't say it. I'm horribly sentimental."

"Oh, aye," he said. "*Horribly*. To be honest, I don't know how you live with yourself." His soft chuckle brought a sparkle to his eyes.

Chirp-hum.

Something in the way he looked seized her, something tender. As his eyes held her captive, a surge of warmth welled in her chest.

Whoa, chica. Enough of that.

As Emily poked a spoon around in her chowder.

A shadowy image came to mind—her dad sitting in the dark surrounded by trash and empty beer bottles. Bitter and alone.

She put her spoon down. As it turned out, she wasn't that hungry after all. When she looked up, Ian was staring at his lunch. She pushed her bowl away. "I'm ready to conquer some more beach whenever you are."

"Ready." He nearly sprang from his chair.

As they headed away from the shops, Emily looked back.

Two bowls of world-famous chowder sat cold, hardly touched. Apparently, he wasn't that hungry either.

On the beach, colorful kites emerged on the horizon, drawn by the stiffening breeze. Emily silenced her chirping phone and concentrated on keeping up with Ian's long strides. "Tell me about your nieces and nephews."

Ian drew a deep breath. "Jack is sixteen, a natural-born leader. Douglas is fourteen and dying to be in charge. Kallie is eight and actually *is* in charge. Gets that from her mum. Or her great-grannie, Maggie. And then there's little Hannah, Princess of Faeries and All Things Purple."

Emily glanced up. The smile etched into his profile as he focused on the sand ahead said it clearly. He was crazy about those kids. "Do you see them often?"

"I try to stop at Claire's flat when I'm in Glasgow, and sometimes they come out to the farm. Kallie is always hounding me to—"

Emily glanced up.

His lips were clamped tight.

They walked a few more yards in silence, but the quiet only deepened her curiosity. "What does she want you to do?"

It took a moment for him to answer. "She wants me to paint her some pictures. Like the ones I did for Jack." He scanned the sea's endless horizon as they walked. "Just something I did for him when he was a wee lad. A long time ago."

"Painting? That's a hobby I haven't heard about."

He shook his head. "Not a hobby."

"Really? What then?"

Ian didn't answer. He stooped to pick up a rock from the sand. "I studied art, did some illustrating. For a short time." With a forceful snap, he hurled the rock out to sea.

"Really? That's fascinating." What other secret talents did Ian have? "I didn't know."

He snatched up another rock and kept walking.

"So, you were planning a career as an illustrator?" As the words came out, she winced. *Duh, Em. Why else would he have studied it?*

They walked on for a while in silence. Finally, he said, "I was. But I changed my mind." He chucked the second rock, sending it much farther than the first.

How sad that something from so long past was still hard to talk about.

He glanced over. "But, eventually, I became a writer, which is what brought me here. And for that, I'm glad."

Emily couldn't help but notice even he didn't seem all that convinced.

CHAPTER NINE

As they trekked north along the beach for a while, Ian examined the shoreline. How different it looked from the craggy shores back home.

The tide worked its way out, widening the beach as breaking waves sent sheets of foamy water surging inland. Seagulls soared above them on the breeze, shrill cries sounding like people shrieking. A middle-aged couple strolled past hand in hand, footsteps slapping the wet sand in unison flicking spatters of gritty water behind them.

In spite of little fuel, Ian felt charged. But as the afternoon ebbed with the tide, the gnawing in his stomach increased. Dinner wouldn't come soon enough. "What do you think?" he asked. "Ready to head back yet?"

She pulled out her mobile. "Yeah. Aunt Grace and the others will probably be back soon."

As they turned round and headed in the direction of the lodge, Emily kept her phone out.

What time was it? He glanced over her shoulder and saw his name.

Xplain U & Johnny Gorgeous MacLean @the beach or I'm so crashing your party!

Johnny? Gorgeous? Should he feel flattered or alarmed? Or both? Perhaps Emily would *xplain* in time to derail the party-crashing whomever.

Emily tucked her phone away and pointed. A pair of kids stood braced, daring the bubbling water to reach them. The kids waited as long as they could before running away, squealing as the broken waves swept toward them over the sand.

With a grin, Emily kicked off her sandals and skipped across the shallow surf toward the sea.

Ian slipped off his flip-flops and followed, then gasped at the icy water. "Och! Are you daft? It's freezing!" He hopped from one foot to the other.

"Hey, this is tropical for Oregon." She kicked a good-sized splash at Ian.

He dodged some of it, bent down, and scooped a handful of water at Emily.

She sidestepped and missed most of the scattered spray. "Nice try." She spun and jogged along the glistening water's edge.

He followed, forming plans for revenge.

The plaintive shrieks of seagulls sounded especially odd. Shrill, like—

Whirling round, Ian searched the water.

Emily stopped too, head cocked as if listening, watching the shifting swells. "There!"

Ian scanned the waves and spotted a head and flailing arms.

Emily took off into the ocean, kicking up water as she ran. Then she dove into the surf.

Dashing toward the person, Ian hit the icy water, steeling himself against the shock.

A few yards ahead, Emily surfaced, screaming, "No! Go back! Get help!" and went under.

He pressed on and, waist-deep, he felt the horrendous force of an undertow pulling him down.

Emily bobbed up again and gasped for air. "Get rope—" and then disappeared.

Ian planted his feet in the sand and bent his knees to brace against the back current, but it tore at him with a monstrous pull. *Get Emily—or get help—God, help me!* Ian turned and waved his arms. "Help! Someone's in trouble! Help!"

People farther down the beach yelled.

He turned to find the spot where he'd last seen Emily and the person.

Nothing.

Dear God—

Heart pounding, he yelled, "Emily! Hold on!"

Two men hit the water and ran toward him.

"We need a rope!" Ian yelled at them. "The undercurrent is too strong!" Holding his breath, he scanned the waves for Emily but saw no one. A rush of adrenaline numbed him. *God, help her! Help me get her out!*

He had nothing but himself and two men. More people approached as if ready to help.

Human rope!

Ian shouted to the men, "Link arms, make a chain!"

Others joined them and formed a line. As the two reached Ian, he said, "Keep the line coming out as far as you can and stand fast. I'm going in!" Ian gulped the deepest breath he'd ever drawn and went under.

The current sucked him down to the ocean floor. Dark, murky swirls of cold, sandy water filled his vision and stung his eyes. Panic slammed through his aching chest. He pushed off the bottom and aimed in the direction he had last seen her. He surfaced and sucked in another breath as he scanned the swells.

No Emily.

He went under again. Tumbling against sand and grit, he fought the churning seawater, lungs bursting, arms flung wide, feeling all round. He bumped into a large object.

A person!

He hooked one arm round the person as tightly as he could. With ocean floor beneath his feet, he fought against the current with all his might.

God? Emily? Where are you?

Garbled voices blended with the roar of water as it rushed round them. Hands groped for him from behind.

He tugged the body to his chest while someone grabbed his shirt and shoulders and yanked him up. He cupped the victim's chin, but felt another head at the same time. Two people?

Hands and arms took hold of Ian and pulled hard. He broke the surface again and inhaled a giant lungful of air.

In his arms, Emily gasped for air and gagged, her arms wrapped tightly round a teenaged boy.

The muffled sounds of shouting turned sharp and clear above the roar of water as someone towed the three of them—Ian clutching Emily and the boy—to shore.

"We got 'em, man. Let go, we got 'em!"

Ian's legs braced against the pull of the water. He was standing on firm sand.

People streamed toward them from all directions. Someone took the boy and others pried Emily, coughing and gasping, from Ian's arms.

He grasped for her wrist. "Emily!"

She shook her head and croaked, "We got him. Is he okay?"

Sirens whooped from beyond the beach.

Shivering, Emily tried to walk but staggered.

Ian gripped her shoulders. "Take a breath, Emily. Are you sure you're okay? Breathe, love."

Emily drew a deep breath, coughed a few more times, then bent with hands on knees.

Ian glanced over his shoulder.

A crowd surrounded the boy. Someone worked to resuscitate him. In the distance, paramedics were running toward them.

Ian turned his attention to Emily.

Trembling, she raised her face to him and started to speak, but a sharp breath stopped her. She frowned and laid a palm on her chest.

"What? What is it?"

She stood there for a moment. She seemed to be measuring the rise and fall of her chest beneath her hand.

"What's wrong?"

Wide-eyed, Emily exhaled and shook her head. "Probably just stress. Are you okay?"

Numb and shivering, he nodded.

"Come on, then." She swiped away the hair that clung to her face and tugged him across the sand to where a crowd had gathered round the boy. She dropped to her knees. "Dear God, let him live," she whispered. "Please let him live."

Still shaking, Ian knelt beside her.

A medic pumped the lad's chest, cleared his airway, resumed

compressions.

Emily continued to pray.

Ian watched and waited in a daze, heart racing.

A few teens came crushing into the circle. "Danny!" A girl screamed. "Danny? What happened?"

Some of the early observers kept the kids back as the compressions continued.

After seconds that felt like an eternity, the boy sputtered and retched.

The crowd cheered.

"Thank You." Emily closed her eyes and whispered. "Thank You, God."

Aye. Thank You.

An explosion of cheers and conversation erupted.

"You guys are heroes!"

"Man, that was awesome!"

Shivering violently, Emily turned to Ian. Tears trickled from her eyes, mingling with beads of seawater on her pale cheeks. "You were amazing, Ian. Thank you."

He shook his head. "You saved his life, Emily. You went under and got that lad and didn't let go, even though it meant—" He couldn't say it as his throat suddenly felt too constricted to speak. *You could have drowned. You just risked your life for a stranger.*

She wiped her cheek with the back of a shaky hand. "I knew we were in trouble, and when I saw you coming, I was afraid you'd get trapped too. But you were so quick-thinking with the human chain thing. You saved us, Ian."

"No, that was all you."

She threw him a confused look.

"You said get a rope, so I did."

"Yeah, okay." She sniffled. "If you won't take credit, then I'll tell *my* version of the story to the newspaper. Once it's in ink, you won't be able to deflect the credit with your dorky humor."

Relief rushed from deep in his gut and washed over him. "*Dorky?*"

As paramedics loaded the lad onto a canvas stretcher, one of them asked if he could check Emily out.

"Thanks, but I'm fine," Emily said.

"Hold on." Ian held up a hand to stop the medic and turned to her. "Emily, you need to let them have a listen. Just a precaution."

"I'm good, really."

Ian leaned close, looked her in the eye, and took a deep breath. The tone he felt coming on needed a moment to soften. "*Dorky* humor aside, I don't fancy having to explain to Aunt Grace how I let you get pneumonia. So humor me, eh?"

Emily tried to argue but started coughing. With a lopsided grin, she nodded.

Once she received a passing checkup, and after reassuring the bystanders they were both okay, Ian and Emily headed back to the lodge.

Ian chose a slower pace than usual and kept close watch on Emily.

Her head jerked up. "Did you get his name? I want to check later and see if he's okay."

"Danny, but that's all. Someone will ring, I suppose. Did you give them your mobile number?"

"My—" She pulled a dripping phone from her pocket and groaned. "Oh, man. It's soaked."

"Ah, that's too bad, Emily. No calls from reporters. And no more text updates for your friend." He cleared his throat. "Or photos."

Emily froze, mouth agape. Pink burst across her face.

"Come on." Chuckling, he kept walking. "And by the way ... who's *Johnny?*"

CHAPTER TEN

The church seniors had split into two carpools, and the first group had returned to the lodge by the time Ian and Emily arrived. Grace and the second half were expected to arrive soon.

Chilled, Emily headed straight for a hot shower, then changed into sweats. She found some blankets for herself and Ian. When she returned to the main room, Ian had a snap-crackling fire going in the massive stone fireplace. She introduced Aunt Grace's church friends to Ian.

Though they seemed eager to talk with him, his chattering teeth sent him running to shower.

Cocooned in a thick plaid blanket, Emily watched the dancing flames in a daze and soaked up the heat, breathing in the pungent smell of wood smoke. Grace would be arriving any minute and Emily needed to be there when Ian met her. But if Emily didn't phone Jaye soon, her manic friend would make land like a hurricane.

Emily slipped into the kitchen to use the house phone. It took several rings for Jaye to answer.

Over the sound of squealing children on Jaye's end, Emily gave a brief rundown on why she was at the beach with Ian and promised to fill her in later.

"Um, *yeah* you'll fill me in, and in full detail. Hey, guys!" Jaye shouted away from the phone. "Pelting Auntie Jaye with tots and nuggets is *not* funny!" A groan followed. "Listen, Em. You've got some explaining to do. I didn't think you had it in you."

"What?"

"Playing sly, keeping a drop-dead gorgeous guy all to yourself."

Emily blew out a *pffff!* and peeked around the doorway into the main room, checking for signs of Grace's arrival. "Listen, Jaye, I gotta go. I promise I'll—"

"Promise you won't run off to Scotland and elope till I meet him, okay?"

"Promise. 'Bye."

When Emily returned to the main room, Grace still hadn't appeared. But Ian had returned. Dressed in running gear, he was in the middle of a lively conversation with Gerald, an elderly man from church.

Emily sat on the hearth as close as possible to the fire without singeing her blanket. The quiet moment allowed her to warm up, collect her thoughts, and take in the ocean view.

On the horizon, the setting sun spilled a silvery-orange shimmer over the water. Though warmth had begun to seep back into her body, the deafening roar of seawater and the pounding of her heart still echoed in her ears.

She shivered. The rescue had left her a little shaken, but the thought of Ian heading into danger and risking his life on her account unsettled her more than she'd been in a long time.

From where she sat, Emily observed the two men. Ian seemed engrossed by what Gerald was saying. The old man's hands waved in the air as though describing something immense. Must've been some fish tale. Ian laughed with him several times.

Emily smiled and looked around the room.

The rest of the seniors sat at a table, apparently in the middle of a game. Gerald was the only one not playing. In fact, he'd been sitting by himself, quietly watching the others play when Ian and she had first arrived. Ian must have noticed Gerald all alone and gone straight to him.

How many men would take the initiative to befriend a lonely, old man, especially a stranger? Kindness and patience shone from his handsome smile as Ian listened to the older man.

Warmth flooded through her. Breathless, she watched him, strangely drawn to his every expression and move.

As Ian spoke to the man, he glanced around the room, then held her gaze, a question burning in his eyes.

70

Heart racing, she tore her gaze away. Had he read her mind again? Did he know what she was feeling? She looked out the window and tried to focus on the setting sun, but all she could see was the probing question in Ian's dark eyes.

The door opened and the rest of the seniors entered.

Emily jumped up and rushed to greet Grace.

Ian excused himself from Gerald and joined her.

Her aunt beamed. "Emmy! Have ye come to see the whales?"

"I brought someone who wants to meet you," Emily said. "Ian, this is Grace Clark. Aunt Grace, this is Maggie's grandson, Ian MacLean."

Ian clasped Grace's hand. "I'm pleased to finally meet you in person, Aunt Grace."

Grace squinted up at him without a word.

An uneasy hush fell over the meeting hall.

Emily winced. What if Grace had a memory lapse now?

The old woman's eyes cleared and she nodded. "Aye, Maggie writes me every week. Did she come too?" Her face lit up as her gaze swept around the room.

"No, she stayed home. It's just me."

"Just you?" She stepped closer and tilted her head to peer up at him. A broad smile widened her wrinkly face. "Och! So tall. But such a dear lad." She patted his arm and turned to Emily. "Maggie adores him."

Ian's eyes widened and he shot Emily a quizzical look.

She shrugged. There were some things Aunt Grace just knew.

As they waited for dinner, Grace and Ian fell into conversation about Maggie and life in Scotland, connecting instantly. A steady hail of Scottish brogue overwhelmed Emily with names of places and people and things she'd never heard of.

Grace's eyes glittered with a radiance Emily hadn't seen in years. She quelled occasional bursts of anxiety that Aunt Grace might get too worked up. It would be okay. This was a special treat.

After dinner, the three retreated to a quiet corner near the fire and talked while the others played games. Emily resumed her role as useless spectator since Grace would soon tire after such a long, eventful day.

Actually, in all fairness, Ian did try to include Emily in their conversation. He probably sensed her unease, perhaps realized she felt like an outsider.

But feeling excluded from the talk of their homeland was the least of Emily's worries. Ian's presence had unleashed some kind of youthful energy in Aunt Grace. Insisting they all have another cup of tea, Grace bubbled over with questions and stories about Maggie. The number of things Grace remembered astounded Emily. Real things, things Ian actually knew about.

Yet the more her aunt chattered away with perfect lucidity, the more Emily wanted to stand up and scream.

At one point, Grace leaned closer to Ian. "'Tis such a comfort to know ye're staying there with my sister. But it must get tiresome for ye, dearie. Living on that farm with only Maggie, after ye've traveled all over the world."

Ian drew a deep breath and opened his mouth, but closed it without answering and stared long into the fire. "Aye, I have traveled," he said more to the glowing embers than to either of them. "I've seen a good share of different people and places." He turned to Grace. "A better share than most, I suppose."

Grace let out a sigh and sat back, cheeks flushed.

Emily touched her aunt's delicate hand. "How're you doing, Aunt Grace? Tired? Are you about ready to turn in?"

Aunt Grace smiled at Ian. "Och, no. I'm talking to my great-nephew now." She turned to Emily. "Have ye met Ian?"

"Um, yes, I have." Emily cast a sideways look at Ian, who was downing the last of his tea. Had he caught *that* little chink in her memory?

Grace leaned close to Emily. "And he's a very handsome mon, don't ye think?"

Ian jerked his cup away just in time to avoid spewing a mouthful of tea. He cleared his throat and set the cup down. His gaze didn't leave the cup, but a faint smile creased the laugh line beside his mouth.

"Yes, very handsome," Emily said. *You just said that out loud.*

Ian went still and his cheeks reddened.

Was he annoyed or pleased? Ignoring her own blazing cheeks,

Emily mustered a teasing smile. "But to be honest, I'm partial to fat, little, red-headed men with big, bushy beards."

He threw her a sideways glance. A slow smile spread across his face, then he burst out laughing, drawing stares from across the room.

Emily laughed too—she couldn't help it.

Aunt Grace smiled at each of them in turn. She probably had no idea what was so funny, but that never mattered. With her question answered, Grace seemed satisfied. She announced she was ready to go to bed.

Emily would take the extra bunk in Grace's room and Ian, who said he didn't mind, would get a sofa bed in the main hall.

Ian stood and helped Aunt Grace to her feet.

She patted his arm, thanked him for coming, and said goodnight.

As Grace shuffled away, Ian turned to Emily. "Thank you for bringing me, Emily. Grace is a kind woman. And sensible." He smiled. "I can see why you're so devoted to her."

Yes, but what you haven't seen is her mental instability. The kooky stuff. A ripple of guilt tugged at Emily.

Of course Ian had no trouble seeing her kindness and strength and all the other things that Emily loved about her great-aunt.

Their great-aunt.

Emily brushed so hard her gums hurt and the tooth gel turned to foam. She stared at her reflection in the beveled mirror above the sink. After her rushed hot shower, her hair had dried into wavy clumps and had all the appeal of beached seaweed.

The seaweed hair and red face combo must've looked ravishing when she grinned at Ian and called him handsome.

No. *Very* handsome.

She winced and spit.

That handsome face and those inquiring eyes sprang to mind. Could Ian see how frail Aunt Grace was?

Of course not. And that was the real issue. No one knew Grace's condition like Emily. Not Ian. And certainly not Maggie. Maggie wanted Grace, but did she really *need* her? She had plenty of family to keep her company. Besides, Maggie was partially blind and too old to care for Grace. While Emily was still young enough and strong enough to—

She closed her eyes. She'd come home from school a week after her fifteenth birthday and found her mom lying in a tangle of sheets on the bedroom floor.

Mom was blue, her breathing shallow.

Emily barely remembered dropping her book bag and hitting the floor with her knees. But she would never forget the shrillness of her voice as she screamed for her dad. Or how quickly he had altered afterward; how he crawled inside himself and barred the door against her and God and the rest of the world, seemingly oblivious to the way his only child drifted without compass or rudder, left to navigate life alone.

When Aunt Grace and Uncle Thomas returned from living in Scotland, Aunt Grace became Emily's anchor. Aunt Grace made sure Emily went to church, finished college, set goals for herself, felt loved. Grace Clark always had a soft spot for the wounded— must have been the nurse in her—and carefully preserved the dignity of others. Now that she was the one in need, she deserved no less in return.

Emily hurried down the carpeted hall to the room she shared with her great-aunt. No one knew Grace like she did, and no one owed her more.

Grace was turning back the bedding with her good hand, face flushed and glowing. She straightened and smiled. "Here ye are, dearie. Wasn't that a lovely visit? I would so much like to talk with him again. Such a kind young mon."

"You'll see him again tomorrow." *Will you even remember his name?* Frowning at herself, Emily pulled bedding from the closet and worked on making up a bed.

"He's from Scotland." Grace gazed at the muslin-curtained window. "My home."

Emily chucked a pillow at the far end of her bunk. When she turned, she expected to see Grace crawling into bed, but the old woman hadn't moved.

She just stood there, gazing at the window, silent tears slipping down her dry cheeks.

Emily's heart sank. "What is it?" She rose and touched Grace's shoulder.

Her aunt's drifting gaze didn't register.

"Aunt Grace?"

She must have been back in Scotland, surrounded by cliffs veiled in mist, rolling hills covered in heather, gurgling burns, and lush, green glens.

"I forget things sometimes," Grace whispered. She turned and met Emily's gaze, tapping her chest with a crooked finger. "But some things I never forget. They're in here."

It was true. Aunt Grace had remembered plenty when she talked with Ian. "I know. You must miss it." The soft words caught like splinters in her throat.

Grace looked toward the window. "In my heart, I never left." With glittering eyes, she whispered, "I want to go home."

A steely pang stabbed at Emily's heart. She wrapped her arms around the frail woman, blinded by tears, no longer able to ignore the fact that Grace had long wanted to go.

This wasn't the first time she'd pined for home. Putting her off had been for her own good. Until she was strong enough. But five years had passed since the stroke and, despite ongoing therapy, Aunt Grace had gained as much strength and function as she ever would.

And, if not for Ian, Emily would've kept putting her off indefinitely.

Emily pulled back and examined the wrinkly face of the angel who had loved her like a mother for the last thirteen years. Emily wouldn't hesitate to do anything for her. All she wanted was to see Aunt Grace happy.

Then why haven't you taken her back home?

Because it wasn't safe.

Safe for whom?

Tears burned trails down her cheeks. She wiped them and took a deep, cleansing breath. "It's been a long day, hasn't it? Maybe we should get some sleep."

"Will we see Ian again tomorrow?" The pale eyes brightened.

Emily nodded, gave her a faint smile. "Yes."

Grace's smile dawned like a sudden, glorious sunrise. "Ooh! I'll make us a picnic lunch. We can have it on the beach, after the service. Would ye like that, dearie?"

She gave another nod, swallowing a new lump of guilt. It was so like Aunt Grace to make sure Emily was happy. "Whatever you want, as long as you let me help."

It didn't take long for Grace to fall asleep. To the steady sound of her aunt's breathing, Emily tried to read a chapter in her Bible, but she had a hard time focusing on the words. She finally closed the book with a sigh.

Lord, Ian will probably ask her tomorrow if she wants to move back home, and anyone can see that she aches to go. I should have taken her for a visit. Now they want her there for good. What am I supposed to do? Should I stop him?

Can I?

Emily stared at her closed Bible, but it was Ian's face that filled her thoughts, and that fiery surge of warmth welled up again.

And what about Ian?

She jumped up and paced the tiny room, bare feet moving without a sound across the carpet. At the window, she pushed back the curtain.

A flood of moonlight illuminated the cliff overlooking the beach.

Emily could lose Grace to Ian MacLean, who was not only incredibly kind and brave but also stubborn.

And who, after tomorrow, would be gone.

CHAPTER ELEVEN

5:00 a.m.

The clock above the fireplace had an odd way of ticking faster just before it advanced the hour. Which Ian had discovered firsthand throughout the night. He stared at the ceiling, hands clasped behind his head.

Morning was dawning, but the room was still dark, quiet. The ocean's steady roar continued on as it had during the night, defying rest. Its endless breaking on the sand matched the churning in his heart and mind.

Today, he would talk with Aunt Grace and invite her to come home to live with Maggie. Based on their meeting the night before, nothing about her behavior suggested the move would endanger her. The idea of asking Grace to move didn't trouble him. After all, that was his purpose for coming here, his plan. What he *hadn't* planned on was Emily. Since she was so opposed to Grace's moving to the farm, it was a dead cert she wouldn't be pleased about the one wee matter he'd failed to mention: that he wouldn't actually be living there. He'd have to tell her that part sooner or later.

And why was Emily so passionately opposed? Grace was old and slow, but she and Maggie came from hearty Buchanan stock. No doubt they would be far too busy making mountains of pies and watching morning talk shows on the telly to get into any real trouble. Why the fierce resistance?

Emily seemed like a rational, intelligent woman. Unselfish. And tenderhearted. And very ...

She was so ...

... breathtaking.

Ian closed his eyes and saw her sitting by the fire, silhouetted against deep golden hues of sunset, with that *look* in her eyes—the one that had turned his insides to pudding.

What had she been thinking just then?

He shot to his feet and paced the length of the picture window twice, running both hands through his hair. No. He certainly didn't need the torment of falling for a woman half a world away. He'd already suffered the pain of separation once, and once was too much. Too much waiting, too much valuable time lost. Never again.

Sunlight peeked over the trees on the eastern ridge and danced across the surface of the sea, waking its depths. A forgotten warmth stirred deep in him. So deep and so warm it ached.

Perhaps Emily would come to Scotland.

Think again.

She had put her life and dreams on hold to care for an old woman. Emily's life lay ahead of her, beckoning like a fresh, clean canvas. She deserved a good man, not a hell-bound rotter consumed with buried, blinding hatred.

Ian closed his eyes, held his breath. But it didn't help. In nine years, the antiseptic smell of those hospital hallways had never left his nostrils, and Edward Carmichael's cold, callous face had never faded from his mind.

My daughter will not marry an artist. She's a Carmichael.

Like a good, stupid lad, he'd accepted Edward's terms without question. He didn't care; whatever it took to marry Katy. A few more years of school, a business degree, an internship at McKinley, Carmichael, & Associates.

And then, her father's last-minute addition of one more year.

Probationary period, Edward had called it.

Too late for treatment, the doctor had called it.

In a heartbeat, Ian was back in time, standing in a daze in that hospital lobby, listening as the surgeon spoke in low tones about Katy and his dreadful discovery. Listening to but not hearing his explanation of how invasive her cancer was and his recommendation that she go home and be made as comfortable as possible.

And home she went.

But not with Ian. Not to the new London flat they shared. Not to the young husband desperate enough to do anything and yet able to do nothing. Already agonized by a crushing sense of helplessness, he'd been shoved aside like rubbish. Dismissed.

Edward.

Temples pounding, Ian blasted out a breath as the face of Katy's father taunted his mind. Steely bands rose from his gut and reached out like tentacles that ached to squeeze and squeeze until the face, the man, disintegrated. Edward should've paid for keeping Ian and Katy apart for so long. He should've suffered.

Maybe the beast eating away at Ian's insides was revenge, not hatred. He'd lived with the cold, gnawing urge in his gut for so long he couldn't tell the difference.

If the Bible counted hatred the same as murder, then Edward Carmichael was a dead man. And Ian MacLean stood condemned.

He yanked on running shoes, snatched up his jacket, and fled into the salty mist.

✣ ✣ ✣

Emily's footfalls pounded the packed, wet sand. Hard. Fast. An eerie predawn mist blanketed the empty beach, muffling the sound of water lapping against the shore. Her breaths came quick and steady, but the damp stuff filling her lungs felt like lead. She pressed on, ignoring the weight in her chest.

Lord, I need to make things work out so everyone is happy. I have to—

Wetness trickled from her eye toward her ear, blending with the salty film coating her cheeks. She wiped it and focused on the possible obstacles that lay ahead in the mist.

Ian is going to ask Aunt Grace today, I'm sure of it. Why wouldn't he?

Emily picked up the pace. Maybe she could chase the image of the man and his stubborn, old grannie from her mind. Her pulse thumped in her wind-numbed ears, keeping double time with her pounding feet.

Lord, I need to make it up to Grace. Somehow. I don't know how much longer she has.

A jogging figure loomed out of the mist.

With a gasp, she stopped dead cold. "Ian!"

Ian came to a staggering halt, probably just as startled as she was.

Emily worked to steady her breathing.

He stared at her, chest rising and falling like a bellows, sending out giant steamy puffs.

She pressed a palm against her stomach and tried for a polite smile, but as his eyes roved over face and settled on her mouth, her smile faltered and numbness took over. Why couldn't she breathe when he looked at her like that? The man was clearly unaware that his scrutiny felt like a caress.

He didn't say a word, just stared.

Probably taking in her blotchy face and frizzled hair. She wiped her forehead with a damp sleeve. "How was the couch? Did you sleep okay?"

He tossed up a single nod. "You?"

"Yeah," she lied.

Silence.

He seemed taller than he had the day before, somehow. Larger. Totally determined to do what he came to do.

"Emily, about Grace ... there's something you should know."

He's going to explain what he's about to do.

"I'm—"

"Wait, don't!" Her hand flew up and waved as if she were erasing his words from a chalkboard.

Frowning, Ian pressed his lips tight and waited.

Emily held her breath, gut churning. Not now. She couldn't talk about Grace now. Not with him. "Sorry, Aunt Grace is probably up and wondering where I am. I really need to go." She edged around him without another glance and fled toward the lodge. When she reached the stairs that led up the cliff, what she'd just done to Ian sent a wave of angst crashing hard against her chest.

When had she become such a total jerk?

Maybe she'd just gotten carried away in her desire to protect Grace.

Protect Grace?

No. She'd been protecting herself. Choosing what *she* wanted over Grace and Maggie's wishes. And even her dad's. Maybe she needed to forget the promise she'd made to her mom and leave her dad alone, since that was so clearly what he wanted.

A sharp twinge clenched her chest, followed by a fast flutter. Gasping, she clung to the handrail with both hands.

The fluttering increased, deep and rapid like shoes thumping in the dryer on triple speed.

She doubled over and tried to steady her pulse and her breathing, but a burst of panic sent her heartbeat into overdrive.

She felt her pocket. No cell phone.

Help me, God, I don't want to die now, not all alone, not like this ...

Emily gulped in deep breaths and forced herself to calm down. Light-headed, she slumped onto the step and put her head between her knees.

After some minutes of steady breathing, her pulse slowed, then returned to nearly normal. She stood slowly and took a deep breath. *It's probably just stress.*

Taking it slow, she climbed the rest of the stairs to the lodge. She slipped into the bedroom where her aunt was sleeping, grabbed her duffel, and headed for the shower. When she returned to Juniper Valley, she would make an appointment with the doctor and get herself checked out. Maybe it was time to face the truth, no matter how difficult it might be. And no matter how much distress it would cause everyone who depended on her.

Ian stood at the long window in the lodge's main room, palms pressed flat against the cold glass. Even from here, he could feel the sea churning with energy—fierce, deep, and untamed, the way God created it. He let out a pent-up breath. The thick scent of frying bacon filled the lodge, sending deep jabs to his already rumbling stomach.

"'Tis against the rules, laddie. Ye shouldnae be here."

Ian spun round.

Aunt Grace, in a flannel dressing gown and bare feet, frowned at him. She had a hairbrush tucked askew in the crook of her withered arm.

What? He studied her fixed stare, her eyes clouded as if she weren't fully awake. Maybe she was sleepwalking.

"This is no place for students to footer about. Ye need to go, before the dean finds ye."

"Aunt Grace?" he said in a loud whisper. "Are you awake?"

She shuffled about the room, fluffing pillows and smoothing the furniture one piece at a time. She kept muttering something about "the code," but he couldn't make it out. Surely she would wake soon. Then she took Ian's jacket that he'd draped over a chair and tottered over to one of the windows.

He held his breath.

She proceeded to clean the window. With his warm-up jacket.

His fingers plowed through his already disheveled hair. "Do you want me to get Emily?"

Grace turned and frowned. "Are ye still here, then?"

That was all the cue he needed. He bolted down the hall and knocked on the bathroom door.

After a few seconds, a muffled voice inside said, "Who is it?"

"Ian."

The door cracked open and Emily peeked out, clad in shorts and a pink T-shirt, blotting her long, glistening ringlets with a towel. Alarm creased her brow. "Is something wrong?"

"Sorry, but it's …" He glanced over his shoulder, his voice low. "It's Aunt Grace."

Emily bolted toward the bedrooms, but he caught her gently by the arm.

A cloud of sweet, flowery-scented steam poured from the doorway, enveloping him. "She's all right. She's just a wee bit confused. I think she needs help remembering where she is."

When they entered the main room, Grace was muttering and fixing the blanket on the sofa bed where Ian had lain.

Looking to Emily, Ian mouthed, *What do we do?*

"Give her some time," Emily whispered. She laid a gentle hand on the old woman's shoulder and smiled. "Good morning, Aunt Grace. How are you doing?"

Grace frowned and continued to fix the cushions, starting over where she'd already been. "I need to tidy up here. Thomas is lecturing at the university clinic again, but he'll be back soon. I spoke to one of the students—" She sent a suspicious glance over her shoulder at Ian.

Emily also turned to him, eyebrows raised.

He shrugged.

Grace resumed her tidying. "Thomas needs to finish his research. He's found a connection. It's in the code."

Emily threw another questioning glance at Ian, but he shook his head and turned up empty palms. He must've been absent when they gave out the code.

Turning to Grace, Emily asked, "Didn't Uncle Thomas love coming to the beach? To watch the storms?"

Grace stopped with a pillow clutched to her bosom and looked out the window, beyond the sea. "Aye. There was a fierce storm the first time I saw him." A slow smile spread over her face. "Maggie said I was daft, going to meet that American at the kirk social. She was so jealous." She patted the pillow and surveyed the room with a dazed frown.

"Would you like to sit down for a minute?" Emily asked in a soothing voice.

Grace nodded and let Emily help her onto a couch.

Ian stood mesmerized like he'd been cast in a play and everyone else knew their lines except him. He stepped closer and leaned toward Emily, speaking in low tones. "Can I help? Maybe I could make her some tea." *Tea. That'll fix it. Idiot.*

"Good thinking." She turned to the old woman. "Should we have a little tea now?"

"Aye, there's always time for tea, dearie. But none o' that fancy kind, mind ye." She frowned, then offered up an expectant smile. "Did we get a letter from Maggie today?"

Emily returned the old woman's smile. "Not today." She shot Ian a look before she went on. "Maybe you should get dressed first—I think they're serving breakfast soon, and there's a little chapel service after that."

"Ooh, aye, I must get dressed." She looked to Ian and her eyes lit up. "What do ye say to a wee picnic on the beach after? We can visit more then." She labored to her feet, straightening her little frame as she did, and lifted her face to him. "Would ye fancy that?"

"Whatever you say, Aunt Grace. That's why I'm here." Ian glanced at Emily.

Her brow quirked in a question. She seemed to be waiting for an answer, but he had no idea what the question was. All Ian knew was his brilliant plan was quickly unraveling.

CHAPTER TWELVE

Sunday turned out different from the day before, not as warm, the sea rough and restless.

Ian carried the picnic basket from the Jeep to a picnic table near the sand, inhaling the scent of sea. The salty breeze stirred up a damp fish smell that hung on the air like an old fishing net.

Emily helped Grace unpack the food without saying much.

Aunt Grace served Ian a tiny sandwich on a paper plate. He thanked her and popped it into his mouth, continuing his silent observation of the old woman. She'd worked for over an hour on the picnic lunch, insisting on doing it all herself. How oddly she'd behaved only hours before, and how quickly she'd returned to her right mind. Was it dementia? How often did she have those sorts of *moments*?

And what if Grace had accepted Maggie's earlier invitations to move back home? No doubt he would be dealing with an entirely new problem now, one needing an entirely new solution.

"Are you warm enough, Aunt Grace?" Emily asked.

"Aye, dearie." Grace smiled, then frowned at Ian's empty plate and served him another sandwich. "Maggie is the brave one. Och, she would have fancied that whaling boat yesterday."

"That's a dead cert." Ian disposed of the second mini-sandwich in one bite. Grace probably meant whale-*watching* boat, but there was no need to correct her. Maggie would boldly board either type of vessel. And take the helm.

"But I didn't see any whales. I was too busy holding on."

"What?" Emily set down her cup and stared at the old woman. "What do you mean 'holding on'? How rough was it?"

"Ooh, just some waves, I only had to hold on once or twice."

Grace turned to Ian, her furrowed brow matching the worry in her eyes. "Are ye going to tell Maggie about that?"

Ian knew little of Grace, but he knew Maggie well enough. She detested weakness of any sort. Either Grace feared worrying Maggie, or she was afraid of losing face to her younger sister. There was one way to find out.

"Certainly. I can tell her your whale-boat story, if you like."

"No! Er ... perhaps it would be best not to share *everything* with her." Grace's voice dropped to a near whisper. "About the boat, I mean. I wouldnae want her to worry."

Ian frowned. "You think Maggie will worry?"

"Ooh, dear me." She gave a slow, grave shake of the head. "I'd never hear the end of it."

A sigh escaped him as the full weight of his stupidity sank in. How had he not seen it? Maggie ruled everyone, including her sister, regardless of distance or time spent apart. Grace could no more control Maggie than she could single-handedly win the Battle of Bannockburn. Which, in some respects, wasn't much different.

His brilliant plan to have Grace corral Maggie had made such perfect sense—when he'd first formed it. Now that he'd gotten to know Grace and observed her limitations, his plan ranked as one of the stupidest ideas he'd ever had.

"Now then." Grace aimed conspirator's eyebrows at him. "Do ye have more stories for us about Maggie?"

Ian grunted. "Loads. But perhaps I best not share everything. I'm sure Maggie wouldn't want you to worry."

Grace patted his arm.

Emily frowned hard into her Styrofoam cup, then looked up and met his gaze.

He would speak to her soon, in private, and put her mind at ease about his abandoned plans to invite Grace to move home. No doubt Grace and Maggie would've enjoyed a happy reunion, had Grace been able to come. But happiness alone would not keep Maggie MacLean out of trouble. And Grace was certainly in no condition to keep the old hen under control. Though he respected his great-aunt's dignity and admired her kindness, the day's events had made one thing clear: He would not be leaving Maggie in the care of Grace Clark.

✟ ✟ ✟

Emily finally convinced her aunt she'd had enough wind and it was time to go inside.

As they gathered up the picnic, Grace stopped and turned to Ian. "You know, we might've met sooner, Ian, when Thomas and I went home to work in Glasgow for a wee spell. But Maggie said ye were living in London that year."

"What year was—" Ian stiffened and looked toward the stretch of beach to the north.

Emily took in his profile, the way he held himself, his clenched jaw, and a wave of pity washed over her. That was probably the year his wife died.

After an awkward silence, Ian's attention shifted back to Grace. "Maggie said you and Thomas had worked at the university. So you were only back in Scotland for a short time, then?"

"Aye. It was good to see my homeland again. But I couldnae stay there, knowing poor Emmy was all alone here, without her dear mum." She turned to Emily. "So we came back. I wanted to be here with ye."

Emily stopped packing food and stared at her aunt. "You did?"

Grace smiled. "My home is wherever my heart is, child. And my heart is with ye."

You left your home, moved across the world, for me? Emily held her breath, but that didn't stop the rush of guilt that threatened to choke her.

The old woman patted Emily's hand.

Emily reached around and gave her aunt a hug. In the span of two heartbeats, she knew exactly what she needed to do. She resumed packing the picnic basket, gathering the nerve to back what she was about to say. "So, I guess after your extreme, high-sea adventure, it's a good thing you're going to Scotland by plane."

Ian froze in the middle of taking an enormous bite of chocolate chip cookie. "She is?"

Grace's broad smile illuminated her whole face. "I'm going to Scotland now?"

"Yeah. Well, not *right* now." When her aunt's face fell, Emily

87

winced. "But soon, I promise. I should've taken you for a visit long before now." Her voice faltered. "I'm so sorry."

"Ah, child, dinna worry yer wee head now." Grace patted Emily's arm. "We only come and go as the good Lord wills."

Around his mouthful of cookie, Ian mumbled, "She's coming to Scotland?"

Emily pulled in a deep breath, lifted her chin and nodded. "Yes, we are. For a visit." She waited for his satisfied smile, a victory fist pump, something.

Ian's face darkened into an alarmed frown. *"We?"*

Stifling a yawn, Ian braced himself for the long ride back to Juniper Valley. The balmy weather had drawn a swarm of visitors to the beach, a swarm that was now exiting the coast region simultaneously and funneling into a single lane of stop-and-go on the eastbound highway.

While Emily navigated the road, Ian closed his eyes and let his mind wander. Like the traffic, all his thoughts converged into a single thread. Kind, forgetful old Grace could not solve his dilemma, and there was no one else who would live with Maggie. Ian tried to picture himself traveling the world while Maggie lived alone on the farm.

Fat chance. He didn't have to try to imagine the potential for mayhem. He'd seen it. Most likely, he would have to forget the feature-series job. And worse, forget about leaving the farm for quite a while. His plans rained down round him like a collapsing house of cards. He blasted out a deep breath.

"Tired?" Emily asked.

He glanced at her face.

Her brown eyes twinkled above little, round sunglasses perched partway down her nose, and beneath them a smile dazzled. By the end of their picnic with Grace, Emily's pensive mood had vanished like morning fog in the afternoon sun.

Ian shrugged. "Not much." He fought another yawn and failed.

She chuckled. "Ian, if you want to sleep, go ahead. You'll need all the sleep you can get before your early morning drive to the airport anyway. Lean your seat back. Go for it."

A tempting offer. He drew in a deep breath. "Emily, that odd incident with Grace this morning—what was that?"

Lips pressed tight, Emily shook her head. "Honestly, I don't know. I've been talking to her doctor and he's watching her, but without some extensive testing, he can't say for sure. It could be dementia. He also mentioned—" She frowned.

"What?"

"Possibly the early stages of Alzheimer's." Her voice dropped on the last word.

Alzheimer's? Far more serious than a few bouts of memory loss and, eventually, a wretched end. "Why haven't you told Maggie?"

Emily darted a sideways glance at him, then focused on the slowing fuel truck ahead.

Ian waited. He had learned a number of things about Emily in the past forty-eight hours. Like how careful she was concerning the feelings of others.

"For a while, her doctor thought the memory lapses might be a temporary effect from the stroke. If that was the case, there was no point worrying Maggie for nothing." She checked over her shoulder and changed lanes to pass the truck. "But it's been getting worse, not better. I guess I should've told Maggie sooner. It's just ... so hard to actually say."

"No, I understand." He frowned. "But now you're bringing her to Scotland?"

"Yeah. For a visit."

"How long?"

Emily kept her eyes on the road. "I don't know. Traveling overseas will probably be a drain on her strength. I think we need to stay long enough for her to recover from the trip. And of course, to give her enough time with Maggie and to see everything she wants to see. Maybe a few weeks, if I can get the time off from the ranch. How does that sound?"

Until he found a way to manage Maggie, he wasn't going anywhere. "Fine. But what made you change your mind? Why are you making the trip now?"

Like a soft shadow, something stole over her. A look of

resolution, sad yet peaceful. "I owe it to her, Ian." Her voice softened. "I'm doing it for her—for both of them. I want them to be happy, just like you do. I only hope this visit is enough for Maggie."

"Maggie?"

"Yeah. You've worked hard to care for her and are so thoughtful of her needs." Drawing a deep breath, she seemed to be collecting her nerve. "I've been trying to make Grace as happy as possible, but maybe I was protecting her for the wrong reasons. I've lost everyone else, you know?" She darted a quick look at him and back at the road. Though the sunglasses partially hid her eyes, they didn't hide the sadness in her voice. "It was totally selfish of me not to take her back home."

Something sunk in his gut like a rock. *If you're selfish for fearing Grace's harm, then I'm evil incarnate.* "You're not selfish."

"Yeah, I am. You've gone out of your way to help them be together. I owe it to Aunt Grace to step up and do the same."

Ian stared straight ahead, stunned. His plans had been about helping no one but himself. Perhaps he should confess his real motives on the spot and stop letting her believe lies about him. Make sure she knew what a self-serving jerk he was. And as a bonus, make sure she thoroughly hated him before he left for home.

And how would she respond?

You were going to all this trouble for yourself? You wanted Grace to move across the world to manage Maggie so you could be free to go off on your own?

Well, perhaps *that* particular part of the story could wait until after he'd gone home. At least by keeping it to himself, he would avoid seeing the disappointment in her face.

Not that Emily Chapman's opinion of him mattered.

CHAPTER THIRTEEN

"Do you think your dad will be home?"

Ian's deep voice made Emily jump. He had been quiet for so long Emily assumed he'd dozed off. "On a Sunday night? Yeah, probably." She tore her eyes from the road long enough to sneak a glimpse of Ian's steely profile. Maybe he was having second thoughts. She took a deep breath. "Ian, are you sure you want to do this? If you'd rather not, then I totally—"

"If you want to, then so do I. When a Scot makes up his mind ..." He glanced at her.

"Okay. Just as long as you know he might not be friendly. I hope it won't be too uncomfortable for you."

Ian pushed back his seat, stretched his legs, and leaned back. "Don't worry about me," he said, closing his eyes.

Emily heaved a deep sigh. Why was he doing this? For her dad? Or for her? How typical of him to want to help.

Lord, please help the visit with Dad to go well, for Ian's sake. Soften Dad's heart. Maybe he'll loosen up this time, with Ian there.

She stole a peek at Ian's resting form. A handsome man, definitely. But the qualities that made her forget to breathe and stirred up crazy kinds of warmth came from deep beneath that handsome surface, from the things she could only see from knowing him.

His kindness and strength, his enduring love, his sacrifice for others.

She sneaked one last glance and memorized the look of his slightly parted lips as he snored softly. If he ever found it in his heart to marry again, Ian MacLean was going to make some girl very happy.

Cheeks burning, Emily fastened her eyes on the road.

Ian woke to the smell of petrol and no Emily. From the passenger window, he spotted the faded *Homemade Jojos!* sign he'd seen at this same station the day before. His spine tensed. He visited the lav, and on his way back to the Jeep, he scanned the lot. No big-mouthed dafties lurking about like the ones they'd met the day before.

Only yesterday?

Emily returned to the Jeep with snacks.

"I can drive now if you fancy," Ian said.

She hesitated, then nodded. "Sure, if you don't mind."

As they headed east, Emily pulled drinks from a sack and offered him a choice. "I bet you're glad this gas stop turned out different from the last one."

Ian chose an icy bottle of root beer and focused straight ahead. "Aye."

Emily twisted the cap off and slipped his drink into a holder. "But you handled it well."

A snicker puffed from his nose.

"You don't think so?"

He didn't answer. No good would come from her knowing how ugly it could have been, had he truly *handled* it.

"I guess you were pretty ticked."

"Ticked?" He hacked out a sharp laugh. "A wee bit."

She took a few swallows of her raspberry tea and screwed the cap back on. "Okay. If you had a chance to do it over, what would you do differently?"

Without taking his eyes from the road, he shook his head. "I don't think having the chance to do it over would make a difference."

"Really?"

He reached for his soda and took a long drink.

"Ian, I appreciate that you tried to get them to apologize, but I'm even more thankful that no one got hurt. You stayed so calm. I mean, I know you probably didn't *feel* calm, but you had a lot of self-control. It really could have been so much worse."

You have no idea.

The glowing taillights on the truck in front of them came to a standstill. When traffic began to move, Ian inched the Jeep ahead, his shoulders tense.

Emily said no more—perhaps she'd decided to drop it.

After a few miles, traffic picked up and moved along at a good highway speed and he loosened his shoulders.

"I'd like to hear about it."

"About what?"

"How you got a handle on anger."

How'd you figure that one out? He glanced over and caught her smiling faintly. "Ah. You're laughing at me again."

"No, I'm serious. You say it could have been worse, so obviously you made a real effort, and I'm curious. Because not everyone is able or willing to do that."

Somehow, the Jeep had suddenly gotten far too small. "I'm not sure what you want to know."

"Have you always had that kind of control?"

Ian pulled in a deep breath. With miles of road still ahead, little hope existed for escape. His cheeks puffed with the exhale. "No."

"You've never talked about this before, have you?"

"I have." His hands gripped the wheel. "With Katy."

"Oh. Right." Emily looked to the passing woods.

For a while, neither one of them spoke.

Right. "It began when I was growing up. We moved a lot."

A quarter mile passed before she responded. "Why did you move so much?"

"My da ..." *Couldn't stay sober long enough to pick road litter.* "His drinking always cost him jobs, so we never stayed in one place long. I blamed him, and he knew it."

She didn't answer.

As he followed the curves of road that snaked through towering evergreens, he felt her waiting eyes on him. Oddly, the darkening forest, old and dense like the wooded braes behind the farm, reminded him of the night he and his da nearly came to blows.

And so he told the story, beginning with the family's move to his grandparent's farm. He and Claire started school, where he met

Katy. At sixteen, he'd begun to stand up to his dad's drunken tirades, which came with increasing frequency. And they went round constantly. One night, Claire begged him to leave before someone got seriously hurt. But he had to stay—because of Katy. He tried to keep out of his da's way long enough to finish school, tried to shove the anger down, keep it under control. But that only made it worse.

One night his da told the family he'd found a job in Aberdeen and they would be moving again. Ian's anger rose, paralyzing him. He felt settled for the first time in his life. And he was in love. Moving so far away for a job his da would lose in less than a week was stupid and unfair.

Something inside him had snapped.

Ian could still see his dad's purple face, the spittle flying from his slack, whisky-wet lips. He could still feel the heat of his own young fury.

"All my packed-down resentment erupted, all aimed at him. I was so blind with rage, I was scared of what I might do." *I believe I could've killed him.* Ian drew in a slow, steadying breath, but didn't look at Emily. He couldn't. "So I took off. I ran into the woods and didn't stop running until I was miles away."

"That's good. You got out of there before anything happened. You knew you needed to do something about it."

"Maybe. But I didn't know *what.* Katy had been talking to me about Christ, but I didn't know how much of that I really believed. I stormed through the woods and shouted some nasty things at God. I guess I wanted to see if He was listening. I wanted Him to prove He was real. So I dared God to take away all my anger."

She stopped sipping her Snapple mid-drink. "Are you serious?"

He still could feel the wet grass soaking through his jeans as he knelt near the churchyard, rain hitting his face in the dark, no one round for miles. The scene slipped easily into his mind, like the words of a familiar song. "Then I headed back to the farm, but halfway home, God was *there.* I felt peace wash over me and I couldn't move. When I thought about my dad and all the things he'd done, not a bit of anger came. Just peace. I started walking again, but then it hit me: God did exactly what I'd asked Him to do. I think—" Ian let a cluster of headlights pass while he chose his words. "I think He wanted me to know without a doubt He was real."

"I think you're right." Emily's voice softened. "In fact, I'm sure of it."

His mind replayed things he hadn't thought about in years. How he'd fallen to his knees, muttering incoherent thanks and promises. The look on Katy's face when he told her. The years following that he spent devoted to prayer and Bible study.

"Thank you for telling me," Emily said. "So what about now? Are you afraid your anger is getting out of control again?"

There were things far worse than getting angry. He didn't answer.

"Is it your dad?"

"No. We get on now, from a distance. My parents live in Peru."

"So whatever anger you struggle with now, does it make you doubt God or what He did for you that night?"

"No." He shook his head firmly. God certainly had no use for a man bent on harboring a mortal grudge. "No, I don't doubt God. He can do anything. But I believe there are things He *won't* do, and I can't blame Him for that."

"I know one thing He won't do," she said softly.

He glanced at her.

"He won't give up on you, Ian. He loves you too much."

Ian didn't argue, but a cold certainty sunk in, numbing his gut. He'd have to see that one to believe it.

CHAPTER FOURTEEN

By the time they reached her dad's place, shadows blanketed the compound, cloaking the house and ponderosa pine grove in darkness. As the Jeep rolled to a stop in the gravel, Emily held her breath and searched for signs of life.

Ian studied the house. "Doesn't look like he's home."

True. Not one light shone on the grounds. No pole lights lit the perimeter and no house or porch lights burned. But Emily knew better. She squinted hard at the front room window.

A faint glow came from somewhere inside, maybe the kitchen or a bedroom.

She nodded. "He's in there."

Ian cut the engine. In the sudden quiet, a chorus of crickets burst into crescendo, filling the void.

"Ian, are you sure?"

He rested his back against the door and faced her, but didn't answer.

"Okay, sorry. I'm not second-guessing you, really. I'm just ..." She leaned against the headrest. *Warning you. Because I know what to expect. And because I don't.*

"Emily, if you don't want to do this, we can keep going."

"No, I do." She flipped down the visor and checked the mirror. She'd inherited her mom's big, brown eyes and long, loose curls. She couldn't do anything about the eyes since it was too dark for sunglasses. But the hair ... In two swift moves, she twisted her hair up and secured it with a clip. Checked the mirror again. Maybe this time things would go smoothly. She hoped.

Ian had followed her movements and studied her new look in silence, but he didn't question her. "All right, then. Let's go in."

They climbed the steps to the front door, knocked, waited, knocked again. From where they stood, Emily could see her dad's Suburban parked behind the house. She caught Ian watching her. Straightening, she knocked harder.

The door opened.

At the look on Dad's face, her hope fizzled.

He stood in the doorway and stared at her for several long seconds. Other than a fleeting flash of surprise, his face gave away no emotion.

"Hi, Dad." She forced a bright smile.

"What do you want?"

I'm fine, thanks for asking. How are you ... "We were in the neighborhood. I hope you don't mind us dropping in. Just for a minute."

Dad's gaze shifted to Ian. He gave him a brief once-over with the same impenetrable look. He shrugged, turned, and went inside, leaving them to follow.

Stacks of books, newspapers, dirty dishes, and brown, glass bottles cluttered the dark living room, making the barely furnished space feel more like a cave. A combined odor of stale beer and moldering trash hung in the air.

Emily winced. "Dad, this is Ian MacLean, Aunt Grace's nephew from Scotland. Ian, my dad, Ray Chapman."

"Nice to meet you." Ian held out a hand.

Dad lobbed a glance at the offered hand.

Emily held her breath.

After a moment, he took it without looking at Ian.

"I'm sorry we didn't give any warning." Emily repressed the urge to see if Ian was taking in all the clutter. "We were just heading back from Newport. Ian needed to meet Aunt Grace."

For the first time, her dad looked Ian directly in the eye. "Where are you staying?"

"In Juniper Valley. At the High Desert Inn."

With a frown, her dad just stood there studying Ian. Dad wasn't quite as tall as Ian, but he had a similar build. At fifty-six, he was still lean and strong, but it suddenly occurred to Emily how much he had changed in the last few years. His graying, brown hair reached past his collar, untended like a wild thicket, and his jaw sported more than a weekend's worth of coarse, graying stubble. The lines in his forehead and around his mouth had grown deeply etched, giving him a grim look.

Rough and grizzled, he'd become a stark contrast from the daddy Emily remembered as a little girl.

He crossed taut arms and waited.

Waiting for me to get out of his sight, as usual. Lifting her chin, Emily drew in a deep breath. "Ian leaves for the Portland airport before dawn."

"When's your flight?" Dad said.

"About ten. My plan is to be on the road by three."

Ian seemed calm.

Emily, on the other hand, thought someone had cinched up all her nerves like shoelaces and tied them in a knot. Maybe getting her dad talking about himself would loosen things up a little. "So, Dad, when's your last day at the high school?"

"Two weeks."

"Do you have any plans for the summer?"

He didn't answer but continued to stare at Ian, frown deepening. "How are you related to Grace Clark?"

"Grace is my grannie's sister. So she's my great-aunt, same as she is Emily's."

Her dad shook his head "No. Not the same." He gave a slight nod toward Emily. "She's only related to Grace by marriage. Through the uncle."

She. Emily ignored the pang in her gut. He wouldn't say her name, would hardly look at her. Which was nothing new. But why point out that Emily and Grace were not related by blood? Did he think Ian should now assume responsibility for Aunt Grace?

"Whatever the connection, Emily and Grace seem very close." Ian spoke with a calm, friendly confidence. If he wondered where her dad was going with the topic, he didn't show it.

Dad bent down and stacked piled-up books and papers on the nearest chair. "Better stay close to her. Grace isn't getting any younger. She could die any day."

Emily gasped. The quiet steel of his words sliced through her as she forced back angry tears. *He doesn't realize what he's saying, Em. Let it go.* She didn't look at Ian, but concentrated on keeping her voice from shaking. "You're right, Dad, Aunt Grace is getting older. But she's happy. And I will do everything I can for as long as it takes to make sure she stays that way."

Stiffening, Dad stopped what he was doing.

Ian made piercing eye contact with Emily.

She couldn't guess his thoughts. He had assured her he wanted to come, but maybe he was kicking himself now. *Please, Lord, let something good come from this visit. I have no idea what Mom thought I could do for him, but this is so not working. How can I help pull him out of this cave-dweller life if he won't even look at me?*

Ian's deep voice cut through her thoughts. "No one wants to think about losing those we love." He kept a level gaze on Emily. "Even though it's inevitable for us all. Perhaps it helps Emily to know she's spending as much time with Grace as she can."

Dad spun around, but Emily watched Ian. No matter how things turned out, she loved that he tried.

Her dad looked from Ian to Emily and back to Ian. "You married, MacLean?"

Emily held her breath. *Here it comes ...*

"I'm widowed."

"Widowed?" Pain flashed through her dad's eyes and his face sagged. "When?"

"Katy died nine years ago."

Dad raised trembling fingers to his lips and scanned the room. His eyes lingered on the half-empty beer bottle beside his chair. He walked toward it but then veered toward the picture window overlooking shadowy woods. He stood with his back to them. Moonlight glowed from the window, giving his silhouette an odd film-noir look.

"Any kids?" The question bounced off the glass with a flat echo.

Frowning, Ian nudged a yellowing newspaper with his foot. "No. We discovered her cancer soon after we married."

The quiet regret in Ian's voice stabbed at Emily's heart. What a blow he must have suffered, not only to suddenly lose his wife, but also their dreams for a future, a family.

Ian turned and locked eyes with her.

"What's he doing here?" Dad said, his voice tight.

"I told you. Ian needed to see Aunt Gr—"

"No, *here*. In my house."

Definitely shouldn't have brought Ian. "Dad, I'm just checking in. Like families do."

He muttered something.

"Emily thought it would be good to spend some time with you," Ian said quietly.

Dad spun around and stared at Ian. His body trembled, and for the first time since they'd arrived, his face twisted with emotion. "Were you at your wife's side every day, down to her last breath? Did you watch her die?"

Emily's pulse raced. "Dad, that's enough—"

"As much as ... as I was allowed." Ian's face went rigid.

"And did spending all that time with her help?" Dad's voice fell to a hot whisper. "Did it make you *happier* when she died?"

"Dad!" Emily gasped.

Ian stiffened. "No happier than you were, I suppose." The sound of his quickened breathing filled the tense silence.

"I know why you're here," Dad said, his voice low. "But I don't need your help. And I don't need your parenting advice, since you've never been a father."

A wave of queasiness rolled up from Emily's gut. *Oh, Lord, what was I thinking, bringing Ian here? What have I done?* She went to Ian's side and laid a hand on his arm. "Come on, Ian. Let's go."

Ian didn't take his eyes off her dad. His brow pulled into a deep frown. "Aye, you're right, Ray. I *don't* know what it's like to be a father. But I do know having family who loves you is a rare gift. Only a fool would waste it."

Emily held her breath.

Dad stepped away from the window. For the first time, his full attention rested on Emily. Pain crept over his face. Then, going rigid again, he turned to Ian. "My family is my business, MacLean. Your

100

business is far from here. The sooner you get back to it, the better."

"Your family?" Emily croaked. "*Are* we a family, Dad?"

Dad stiffened briefly, then shook his head and stormed out of the room.

No? And why not? Because she gave up fighting on my account? Because you wish ...

A familiar pain tore through her, ripping open the same old scar. Emily closed her eyes and willed the tears to stay back. Dad was a deeply broken, grief-stricken man. He didn't know what he was saying. He'd lost the ability to care about anyone, including himself.

"Emily?"

When she opened her eyes, Ian stood near, his face a mask of strain. "I'm sorry. I didn't mean to upset him."

She shook her head, bringing up tears in spite of her best efforts to quell them. "It's not you. Let's just go. I'll call him later—"

Dad reappeared, locked his sights on Ian, and headed straight for him.

Ian braced himself and looked at him head on.

Emily couldn't move. *Oh no, God, no, please ...*

Dad came face to face with Ian. "You leave the States tomorrow?"

"Aye."

"Good. You're only wasting your time here."

As they faced off in the crackling silence, Emily sensed something unspoken passing between the two men.

"We're leaving now, Dad."

In three quick strides, Dad was at the door. He held it open.

Ian and Emily followed.

At the threshold, Emily glanced at her dad, hoping for something, though she didn't know what.

He drew back, and as soon as they passed through, the door slammed.

✦ ✦ ✦

By the time they returned to the main road and headed east, Ian's pulse had returned to nearly normal. The traffic on these long, straight stretches of high desert road was nothing but a passing car now and then. After they reached Juniper Valley, he could grab a few hours of sleep before his long drive to the airport.

If he could sleep.

"I'm sorry, Ian. I shouldn't have taken you there." Emily's voice sounded tight.

"You did warn me." *Though 'not very friendly' may have been a slight understatement.* "And don't apologize. You're not responsible for him."

She stared at the road with a dazed look.

"Has he always been like that?"

"No."

Ian tried to imagine Ray Chapman smiling with an arm resting round his daughter's shoulders but couldn't picture it. "When did he change?"

A long silence. "A little while after Mom died."

Grief did strange things to a man, but it didn't explain Ray's behavior toward Emily.

She stared into the dark, but there was little to see.

Perhaps they shouldn't have stopped at her dad's. Since losing Katy, Ian found himself challenging things that kept people apart. Especially stupid, senseless things. But maybe he was wrong. Maybe being with people didn't always fix what was broken.

"He'll see what he's doing to himself and to you, eventually."

"I used to believe that. I used to hope God could help him, but now ... I don't know."

Aye. God can only help a man who isn't beyond help. Some things are too dark. Some roots twist down too deep.

Another quiet mile passed with no sign of another car.

The silence tugged at his chest. "Are you sorry we stopped?"

She shook her head. "No matter what he does, he's still my father, and I love him. I'm just sorry that seeing me bothers him so much."

"Emily, it's not you, I'm sure it's—"

"You saw him, Ian. He can barely look at me." She turned away.

The way she held herself, so stiff and straight, reminded him of the last soldier left on the field, bracing to finish the battle alone. How could a man treat his own daughter that way? She didn't deserve it. In fact, Ray didn't deserve her. Heat seared his veins. "Whatever the reason, it's his choice. He'll regret it."

She faced him. "Are you sure he has a choice?" The glitter in her eyes took on a neon green from the dash lights. "I don't think so. Do you know why he can't stand to see me? I tried to tell myself it was because I remind him of her." She yanked the claw-toothed thing from her twisted-up hair and shook her head, letting the silky waves tumble loose round her shoulders. "But that's not it. He hates me because she's gone and I'm still here. He wishes it had been me instead of her."

Idiot! He smacked the steering wheel hard enough to make his palm sting. Ray Chapman had already broken Emily's heart once, and Ian had just handed her over so he could do it again.

He whipped the Jeep to the edge of the road, spraying gravel into the ditch. Adrenaline surging, he killed the motor and turned to face her. "This is all wrong."

With trembling fingers, Emily unlatched her seat belt. "You know what? You're absolutely right." She scrambled out of the Jeep. "I need some air. Give me a minute."

Emily trudged along the silent road, sandals slapping the asphalt. There wasn't a car or house in sight, nowhere for her to go.

When she'd gone several metres from the Jeep, he jumped out and jogged toward her. "Emily."

She kept going.

He reached her, caught her arm, and turned her round. "Emily, I'm sorry. I shouldn't have made you go there."

Her face was pale in the milky moonlight. "You didn't. It was my choice to see him. And I knew what to expect." Her glistening eyes pleaded. "Ian, it's okay."

"Okay?" Ian caught a sharp breath, stunned. A man shouldn't be excused for wounding others in such a callous, selfish way. A familiar band of fury tightened round his heart, gripping him in its monstrous claw. But the pain in her face gripped him harder. He steadied the thunder in his voice. "No. It's not okay."

She offered a teary little smile and gave his hand a squeeze.

The courage and grace in those eyes clutched his chest so tightly he could hardly breathe. *Fix it, MacLean. Do something.*

"Maybe we could pray," she said.

"Sorry?"

"For my dad."

It took playing her words back a few times before he understood what she wanted. "Right, then."

She took his hands.

He closed his eyes and a moment of quiet passed. Oh. She wanted *him* to do it. What was he supposed to say? How could he pray for the wretched man when he hardly knew how to pray for himself? He cleared his throat. "God, please help Ray not to be such a ... uh ..."

Do it right.

A growl escaped as he exhaled. "Please help Ray get over whatever makes him this way." He swallowed to loosen the anger that threatened to choke him. "I pray he won't have to live with the torment of knowing what he threw away. He's missing out on spending time with someone who loves him very much. Help him see what a priceless gift that is."

A few warm droplets splashed onto their clasped hands.

He drew a deep breath. "And please help Emily know how much You love her. With the sort of love that never grows cold." He had no idea where those words came from, but, somehow, they were right. "Give her peace. Help her feel Your arms round her. In Christ's name, amen."

Without another thought, he pulled her into his arms.

She was in Ian's embrace. And he wasn't letting go.

She closed her eyes and relaxed, savoring the weight of his arms surrounding her.

Ian pulled her closer, held her tight. His heart pounded against her cheek like a caged wild thing.

Numbed by such tender strength, she soaked up his warmth, felt it radiate through her. She'd not been held this way for quite some time and it felt so good, so right.

Like an exile being welcomed home.

I could stay here forever ...

Emily lifted her face. Ian's dark eyes blazed into hers. Without thinking, she whispered his name.

His gaze fell to her mouth, sending a tingle through her lips as though they'd been touched. His chest rose and fell in rapid succession.

As he lowered his face to hers, she could barely breathe. His warm breath bathed her lips, sending her heart racing as he came closer.

Then, without warning, Ian let her go like a hot iron and stumbled several steps back.

Emily staggered to steady herself.

Plowing a hand through his hair, Ian scowled at the ground. "Let's get you home," he said, his voice tight.

The remaining miles ticked by like a silent countdown clock. Though they'd been on the road nearly an hour, she could still feel the impression of his enveloping arms. That roadside embrace had left her dazed. Not only because of the way he'd pulled her close and held her, but also because of the intense craving it had stirred in Emily. Regardless of what his intentions had been, she would have kissed him. Caught up in the pure bliss of the moment like a starved stray, she'd forgotten herself. She was too sensitive, too vulnerable. She would have to be more careful in the future.

Whatever that was at the side of the road, it definitely wouldn't happen again. It couldn't.

They reached Emily's house a little after 11:00 p.m. Ian followed Emily to the door, started to speak, but stopped. A thick silence hung between them.

As they stood on the porch, a warm desert breeze rose and fell in gentle gusts, brushing strands of hair lightly across Emily's face, but the storm brewing in Ian's dark eyes captured her full attention.

She trembled and drew a shaky breath. "Doesn't look like you'll get much sleep."

"I'll catch up." He examined a chip on the wooden porch post. "I didn't sleep at all last night." He frowned as soon as he said it.

"Neither did I." Her cheeks burned, but in the dark, maybe he wouldn't see. "Will you do me a favor and call when you get home?

So we know you made it okay?"

He nodded.

"I'm part lifeguard, part worrywart. Can't help it." She offered a light smile.

His eyes fell to her mouth and lingered, then he looked away.

Did he know what she was thinking? What would he say if she told him she'd never been kissed? *No, Em. Don't.* Her heart thumped so hard he could probably hear it.

Ian faced her again, his eyes dark as a hurricane. "Emily, when we stopped on the side of the road, when I—"

She sucked in a sharp breath, chest hammering.

He looked out over the dark valley. "I want to apologize. That should never have happened."

Right, I agree. Yet the grim set of his profile sent her heart plunging to her stomach. Her gaze fell to the wooden slats between their feet as she fought the tightness in her throat. She lifted her head. "There's no need to apologize, Ian. I'm not—"

His grim look had deepened to one of anger.

Why?

The visit with her dad had left her feeling broken, probably sending off distress vibes. Ian had responded to that by reflex. Against his will.

I messed up. The thought zapped across her nerves, numbing her.

Ian cast a brief look in her direction but wouldn't meet her eyes. "Good-bye." Without another word, he thundered down the steps and stormed to his car, feet pounding the packed dirt.

The car's engine roared to life. Spitting sand and dust, the Honda tore out of the drive.

She fumbled with her house key and barely made it inside before the dam burst.

CHAPTER FIFTEEN

Emily awoke fighting a sea of blankets and gasping for air, heart pounding.

In her dream, the ocean had risen and a gigantic wave had crashed down on her and Ian as they walked on the beach, trapping them beneath tons of water.

By the time she calmed down, all hope of sleep had vanished. She lay awake for hours, in spite of dizzying fatigue. Had she imagined everything? She went over the weekend in her mind again, remembering her promise to Aunt Grace, the visit with Dad, the time she'd spent with Ian. Every word, every gesture.

And being in his arms ... and nearly kissing him ...

No way had she imagined *that*. Or how the embrace had upset him. Had she brought it on?

Emily groaned. Whatever the cause, it was over and done. She couldn't undo it. She tried to go back to sleep, but the dull ache in her chest wouldn't leave. In the predawn hours, when she realized she hadn't prayed about any of it, she did her best to leave it in God's hands. Peace finally came and she fell asleep.

And overslept, making her late for work. Luckily, it was her first time and Sue Quinn didn't hold it against her.

The rest of her workday passed without too much teen drama, giving Emily a chance to refocus, to think about the Juniper Ranch kids and get her mind off things she couldn't fix. When Sue had a free moment, Emily asked about taking a few weeks off to take Grace to Scotland. After work, she raced home and dove into an online search for airfare, thankful to have the house to herself.

Until Jaye showed up at the door. "You *are* home. Bummer. I thought you eloped." Jaye had an imagination bigger than her entire class of kindergarteners combined. And just as prone to earn someone a time-out.

Emily moved aside to let her in. "Really. That's what you thought?"

Jaye blew into the house and headed for the kitchen. "You never called back. What was I supposed to think?" She plopped her bag on the table and pushed her bangs to the side. "I was in total agony all weekend. So? What happened?"

Much had happened. *Too* much.

Jaye hopped up on the counter and snatched one of Grace's lemon cookies from the jar. "Spill it, chica." Eyes wide, she nibbled the cookie like a gerbil. "Tell me *everything* about Ian MacLean."

Warmth spread through Emily at the mention of Ian's name, especially the way Jaye said it. Spinning away from Jaye's scrutinizing gaze, Emily grabbed a couple of Cokes from the fridge and did her best to recount the weekend in spite of Jaye's frequent interjections. She got as far as the roadside embrace.

"Oh, *man*! I knew it. Did you kiss him?" Jaye let off a squeal. "I bet Scottish guys kiss different from Americans, right?"

Frowning, Emily focused on the wall calendar. She reached up and changed the month to June. "I wouldn't know, remember? And no, I didn't."

"Oh, right. Saving that first kiss for your husband. Which doesn't make sense since you're never getting married. Or ... has that changed now?"

Emily stared at the calendar without seeing it. She and her mom had discussed this at length before Emily started high school. Her heart was so sensitive she could become deeply attached to someone by something as simple as a kiss. She'd decided to save that kind of bond for one man.

But that had been a different life, a different time. A hopeful time of dreams before a dark suspicion shadowed her future.

She scanned the dates on the wall for things that might interfere with the Scotland trip. June or July? Their departure date depended on how long it took to get a passport.

"Well?"

"Some people just aren't cut out for marriage, Jaye."

"Right. But those people aren't up for discussion now. Look, check this out." Jaye hopped off the counter, pulled out her phone, tapped the screen a few times, and flipped it around to show Emily. "Yum. Who needs Johnny Depp when you have *this*?"

Against her better judgment, Emily leaned closer for a better look. A slanted, off-centered picture of Ian with an amused smile sent a tingle through her. The photo didn't capture the playful sparkle in his eyes, but she filled that in from memory—no problem.

"See? Didn't I tell you? You just needed to meet the right guy."

Emily resumed her scrutiny of the calendar. "Sorry, Jaye. He's not mine. And I couldn't have him even if I wanted him." Trying to keep her voice from breaking, she described how angry Ian was when he left.

"Wait—he was *mad*? Seriously? It was just a hug. I mean, it *was* just a hug, right?"

"I don't know, Jaye. I don't know what it was." *Yes, I do. It was amazing. Intense and tender and amazing.*

The numbers and squares on the calendar blurred as she traveled back to that moment beside the road. She shook off the memory and downed the last of her Coke. "It doesn't matter anyway."

"Has he called?"

"No, he's flying to Scotland now. He promised to call when he lands in Glasgow tomorrow morning."

Jaye grinned. "Awww, yeah."

"I asked him to call and let us know he arrived okay."

"Oh." Again with the pout. "So that's it? Back to being good old pen pals?"

Emily hunted through a file drawer until she found the folder containing Aunt Grace's passport and checked the date. Grace must have renewed at some point as it was still valid.

"All right, listen, Em. I don't know what's up with you and this crazy ban on relationships, but I *do* know if you let this guy get away, I am never speaking to you again."

Emily cocked a brow at her friend. Jaye not speaking would be something to see.

"I mean it. Listen, I gotta run, but keep me posted." Jaye

breezed out of the kitchen, but halfway through the front room, she spun around. "Whoa, I almost forgot—I need Hector's Fine Arts entry. I have to send them off tomorrow."

"I've got it here. Just a sec." Emily hunted through the stack of papers by the phone and pulled out a large manila envelope with HEC^2 printed neatly in pencil on the flap.

"Let's see it." Jaye pulled the pencil drawing from the envelope and laid it on the counter. "Wow." She drank in every detail. "This is amazing. That kid is definitely gifted."

"Yeah. I'm really proud of him." Emily took the picture and studied it.

Hector had captured a grapevine and branches laden with dew-drenched grape clusters in stunning detail. Fortunately, the school employed a skilled art teacher who not only inspired the students to develop their God-given talents, but also encouraged them to find special ways to use them. Hector clearly had a gift for conveying a simple truth with a beautiful illustration.

Emily stopped smiling and stared. Something about the picture tugged at her memory—something Ian had said—and suddenly, she saw him walking beside her on the beach, throwing rocks at the sea. That image merged with another one and the room began to sway. She dropped the sketch and dashed to the front room, heart pounding. She skimmed through the storybooks on the shelf until her fingers rested on *Daniel's Friends Face the Fire*. She pulled it out, holding her breath.

Title at the top, in large print. Author at the bottom, smaller print. Fingers shaking, she opened the book to the title page.

Title, Author—

Emily gasped.

Illustrated by I. MacLean.

By the time he nudged the rattling truck from the old drover road onto Craig's Hill Road, the sun stood high overhead. To Ian, it felt like 5:00 a.m. He'd traveled more than four thousand miles but the last two couldn't pass quickly enough.

First, he would take a long, swift hike through the wooded braes. That should clear his head. Then, as soon as it was a decent hour in Oregon, he would phone Emily as promised and let her know he'd arrived home.

If he could bring himself to talk to her.

But if Claire was still here, and if Maggie insisted on hearing about his visit with Grace, slipping out to do either wouldn't be easy. Especially with Claire's radar ability to ferret out things he fully intended to keep to himself.

Ian's long trip home had given him loads of time to shake the anger and get his head on straight. But twenty-five-plus hours of travel was far too long to be left alone with his thoughts. A looping mental slideshow of the last few days plagued him.

Her quick, warm smile, the melody of her voice, how sweet she smelled.

How incredibly good it felt to hold her.

And that stricken look on her face when he told her it had been a mistake.

Every time the image arose, chagrin rose with it, in waves. How could he have been so careless? Why had he risked leading her on that way? What was he thinking?

He groaned as the truck bumped along the narrow road. These questions had nagged at the back of his mind all the way home, but the answers remained the same.

Didn't matter and half a world separated them.

Which he should've thought of *before* he threw his arms round her like a drowning man who's suddenly realized he's desperate to live.

Aren't you the poet now? He turned the truck onto the sloped drive and climbed past the cottage, scanning the grounds as he approached the farmhouse. No sign of Claire's car. He pulled up next to the house, killed the motor, exhaled, and stepped out of the truck.

A bleating ewe bolted past him, trailed by Kallie, who packed a worn-out looking kitten under her arm and a determined look on her face.

He groaned. Claire was still here. He could have the decency to feel a pang of guilt for wishing his sister gone after all she'd done for him. "Whoa, Kallie. Where're you going?"

"That lamb's going to pull the cart. We're practicing for the parade." She didn't stop, but chased the runaway toward the front yard.

"Is your mum here?"

"She went to get more jars for the ones that broke," she called over her shoulder as she and her troupe scurried round the corner of the house and disappeared.

Ian hoisted his bags from the truck and headed for the house. But inside the entry hall, he stopped.

Pies—berry, judging by the globs oozing from them—teetered on furnishings in the sitting room on his right. To his left, a mountain of jam-filled jars obscured the kitchen table.

He ventured into the kitchen.

A pot of berry goo congealed on top of the cook stove, and partially burnt chicken feathers and bits of broken glass littered the floor round the stove. Mingled odors he couldn't identify hung on the air, none of them good.

And no sign of Maggie.

She wasn't upstairs when he dropped off his bags in his bedroom, either. The sound of Claire's car brought him back downstairs.

His sister met him in the front hall with Hannah in tow.

"Uncle Ian!" The lass beamed a huge smile.

Ian scooped her up.

She wrapped her arms round his neck. "Where did you go?"

"I flew over the sea and halfway across the world."

"Good to have you back." As Claire headed for the front door, she threw a look over her shoulder. "Even if you *are* sadly in need of a shave."

With a shy grin, Hannah poked a finger at his jaw.

Ian followed Claire outside, tickling his niece with his stubbly chin until she squealed.

At her car, Claire said, "You owe me, little brother. Loads. You can start by giving me a hand." She stopped and looked round, frowning. "Where's Maggie?"

Setting Hannah down, Ian said, "I don't know. I just got here."

Claire opened the rear door of the wagon.

112

Ian reached for a box.

His sister nudged his arm. "Hey."

"Hmm?"

"What's up with you? You look different."

He hauled out two cases and hoisted them up on his shoulder. "*You* try twenty-five hours of driving, flying, and sleeping in airport chairs and let's see if you don't come out looking a wee bit shabby."

"Och! Did I say you looked bad?" She frowned. "Hannah, we should go home and come back after the crabby old bear's had his nap."

Ian carried the jars into the house and set them on the kitchen floor, Hannah trailing his every move.

Claire followed with another box.

He glanced round the room. "So everything went well then?" He held his breath.

"Well?" Claire hooted. "Ooh, aye. *Per*fectly. We sipped tea and had a lovely, wee visit. See for yourself." She waved a hand over the kitchen and fixed narrowed eyes on him. "She insisted on warming the jars on top of the stove, and when they popped, she wouldn't let me pick up the mess. She actually tried to chase me off with a—"

Maggie loomed in the doorway with a shovel in hand.

They all froze.

The old woman stamped mud from her boots. "Is that Ian? Are ye home then, laddie? Did ye see my sister?"

His brow shot up. "Did I have a choice?" He winked at Hannah. "Grace is well. She sends her love."

As he spoke, Maggie tossed the shovel off into a corner, plodded straight to the sink, and filled a kettle with water. "We'll have tea and ye can tell me everything."

"What about the jam, Maggie?" Claire asked. "We've more jars to fill."

"Wheesht, lassie! I don't care a wee pickle about jam now."

Ian glanced at his watch—nearly 6:00 a.m. in Oregon. He cleared his throat. "I've got business to see to. After that, I'll sit down and tell you everything."

Almost.

He ruffled Hannah's hair and headed out the door.

"Och, he just got here. Where does the daftie think he's going?" The crackle in Maggie's voice trailed after him.

He longed to take that hike—he needed to think. But he promised Emily he'd ring as soon as he arrived. He strode down to the cottage, checking over his shoulder more than once to make sure no one was following. In the cottage, Ian checked the phone for a dial tone, pulled out the number, took a deep breath, and dialed.

Emily answered on the first ring. "Ian?"

"Did I wake you?"

A relieved sigh. "Hardly. Did your flights go okay?"

"Fine. Just loads of waiting." He closed his eyes. Her face appeared in his mind.

"That's good. Thanks for calling and letting me know." A long pause, then, "Ian, if you don't mind, there's something I'd like to ask you."

His heart did a crazy drum solo. *Brilliant. Here it comes.* Ian had questions of his own. Purely pointless questions that had only useless answers.

"Why did you stop illustrating?"

What? His mind raced to remember how she knew. "What brings that up?"

"There's a children's storybook in my library. You might have seen it when you were here. *Daniel's Friends Face the Fire.*"

He expelled a long breath.

"I've always marveled at the artwork in that book, Ian. It's so beautiful."

Something twisted deep in his gut, wrenching all the way up to his throat. "Thank you."

"In fact, it's one of my favorites. I had no idea you illustrated it, not until yesterday. Are there others?"

"No."

Silence.

"You'd rather not talk about it?"

Smart cookie. "There's not much to tell." Hopefully, that would be the end of it.

"You started to say something about it when we were on the

114

beach."

His fingers plowed through his hair. What had he said?

"You're such a talented artist, Ian. What an amazing gift—not only for creating such beautiful pictures, but also for bringing a Bible story to life. You should see the kids' faces when I read it to them, the way their eyes light up at the pictures in that book."

Her words hit his gut like a well-aimed boxer's punch.

"I'm sorry, I shouldn't pry. I just couldn't help wondering. I hope I didn't offend you."

He glanced around the dark cottage, as though the empty house might magically produce a way out. "It's a long story."

"Of course. If you aren't comfortable telling me, I understand."

"I ..." He studied the ceiling, marveling at what he was about to say. "It might be best if I wrote it."

"Really? Like an email?"

"A letter. We don't have internet service at the farm yet. I have to get my email when I'm in the village. Kirkhaven is only a few decades behind the rest of the world."

Emily chuckled. "I know the feeling. It took forever to get service in Juniper Valley too. We're so remote we had to wait for satellite."

"Same problem here. But we're getting it soon—"

A squealing Kallie burst into the cottage with a kitten under each arm, followed closely by Hannah, also squealing.

"Whoa, lassies." He pulled the receiver away from his mouth. "What's all this?"

Hannah went first, bottom lip quivering. "My kittlin ran away and she has two and she won't give me one."

Kallie glowered at her sister. "It didn't run away, you let it go. And I told you, you can catch the fat one."

"I don't want the fat one. I want mine or one of yours. You have two!"

"I'm sorry, Emily, just a minute." He turned to his nieces. "Kallie, would you show your sissie how to catch her kitten? Since you're so good at it?"

With a huff, she glared at Hannah. "Come on, then. Don't make so much noise this time." Kallie schooled her sister as they scurried out the door and up the drive.

A soft chuckle danced across the line.

Ian groaned. "You're laughing at me again."

"No, I'm not. That was very diplomatic. And sweet."

Sweet? He grunted. Not high on the list of skills a Scotsman wants to be known for.

"You have a soft spot for those girls. I can't wait to meet them."

"They'll love you." *Rats.* His throat seized up, but too late. The words were out.

A hushed silence fell. "You think so?"

He swallowed hard. "Aye."

Footsteps made Ian turn to settle another round with his nieces, but instead of two creature-laden lassies, one scowling, old woman stood in the doorway, arms akimbo on her sturdy, wee frame.

"Love who? Who's that?"

CHAPTER SIXTEEN

Nothing could keep him from taking that walk now—he didn't care if Maggie came at him swinging a claymore. The braes behind the farmhouse beckoned. He climbed the sloped pasture toward the wooded hills with long, brisk strides. Even if Claire had stayed round and tried to follow, her short legs would have had a hard time keeping up—Ian would have made certain of that.

But by some act of divine mercy, the girls had had a recital and Claire needed to leave. Which probably called for ceremonial thanks of some sort.

In the weeks since Ian last walked this path, summer had made a majestic entrance, robed in vibrant shades of green: deep emerald Scots pine, fair green willow, and slender birch coated in silver bark and drooping with new, bright green leaves. Heather, also green but promising to burst into a rich purple soon, blanketed the hills surrounding the carse.

The crest of the brae offered his first glimpse of the valley and the crumbling remains of the old Kirkhaven church, the surrounding churchyard, and cemetery. A bit further, the path dropped and leveled out before rising again. He followed the trail and climbed the next knoll. As woodland air filled his lungs, his thoughts drifted back to his conversation with Emily.

She had no idea how hard he'd worked to put that time of his life behind him.

At the top of the second brae, the group of trees to his right caught his eye. He'd walked this path in every season and knew these hills well. During the barren days of winter, the ring of trees stood thin, allowing a partial glimpse of a small glen in its midst. Now, summer foliage and thick undergrowth hid the clearing.

He pressed on, following the path down to the valley floor. Countless times he'd walked this way. But something about the glen drew him, the way it was completely hidden and yet so close. Perhaps on the way back he would make a detour and investigate.

A few more minutes of hiking across the meadow brought him to the old church. Nestled in the lowlands like a natural part of the landscape, the church and yard appeared vacant. But as he approached, a choir of goldfinches chirped a merry old hymn from the balcony of trees surrounding the sanctuary.

Ian stepped over the low fence encircling the cemetery.

Promising Emily a letter was easy. Writing it was an entirely different matter.

He worked his way round to the newer gravestones. To Katy's.

Kathryn Carmichael MacLean.

The dates carved in the stone served as a cold reminder. She was only twenty-three. Sixteen when they met, twenty-two when they were finally allowed to marry.

What a joke. He'd actually believed he could impress Katy's father by asking him for her hand.

Ian could still feel his numbing disbelief when Edward told him what he thought of him and his dreams, his plans for the future. He'd struggled to hide how much Edward's words hurt. Once Ian swallowed his injured pride, he decided the extra time would simply be a delay to their plans, an exercise in patience. They would both look back and the extra years of waiting would seem like nothing.

But those few years turned out to be everything. A silent countdown had already begun.

Ian closed his eyes and saw himself back at university, unaware of the precious time slipping through his fingers. And to what gain? A slight but all-important nod of approval from the high and mighty Edward Carmichael.

In the end, what bit of good had it done him?

He kicked a tuft of dried weeds beside the stone, seeing Edward's face in the deadness. What would he tell Emily?

The truth was he hadn't given another thought to illustrating. He'd lost the heart for it.

Crouching near the gravestone, he grabbed a fistful of long

grass and pulled it up. If he told her the story, she would glimpse the hate that had long infected his heart and mind.

He knelt in the grass and lifted his face skyward. *You could take it from me. Like You did before.* Holding his breath, he waited, listened.

The wind stilled. Even the birds' song paused in expectant interlude. The valley listened.

But no answer.

Looking to the crumbling church, Ian spoke. "So I guess there's no point asking You to help me get Emily out of my mind."

The cool stone absorbed his words.

With a grunt, he stood and brushed grass and dirt from his knees. "Right, then."

As Ian climbed the trail toward home, he planned the letter to Emily. Once the letter was posted, that would be the end of it.

Except for the pending visit from Grace and Emily.

After their visit, then. There would be an end to the Grace-and-Emily chapter, time to move on. But move on to what, exactly? Without a solution to his Maggie problem, he had nowhere to go.

For now, he could submit the articles that didn't require travel. But the Sudanese missionary family, the refugee doctor in Rwanda, the retired university professor teaching bushmen of the Kalahari to read, the people living amongst and serving indigenous people whom *The Master's Call* wanted to highlight—those stories could only be told firsthand.

If only Maggie weren't so pig-headed.

As Ian neared the top of the brae, the ring of trees came into view again. What was the appeal? It was probably nothing but a wild mess of ferns and briars. He left the path and worked his way through the underbrush. It took a bit of doing, but once he cleared the tangle of undergrowth and parted the trees, he stood at the edge of a small, grassy clearing about the size of Maggie's front yard.

A thicket enclosed the little glen, bursting with a riot of dark pink and yellow blossoms that filled the air with a sweet, beguiling scent. Thick trees surrounding the clearing provided a sound barrier, isolating it from the world. Laden with tiny flowers, the thicket seemed to hum with life.

Rich as honey, the heady fragrance made him dizzy. He eased himself down onto the grass and looked round, marveling at his discovery.

Ian inhaled long and slow, breathing in the scent. Something about this place tugged at his memory, stirring something very familiar. Maybe he and Claire had played here as children.

The soft grass looked cool and inviting.

He lay back and closed his eyes. Emily's face came easily to mind, the sun glinting off her hair as they walked on the beach. Her face appeared to him so clearly—the soft blush coloring her cheeks, the light in her eyes when she smiled. And the way she smelled was also clear, as though she was here. In fact—

He sat up and stared at the blooming thicket. This place smelled like Emily.

Either that or he was losing his mind.

Brilliant. So, God, is this Your idea of a joke?

After a week of planning, Emily's Scotland trip hit a snag. She stared at the phone in her hand as if it would explain the conversation she'd just had with her dad.

Grace shuffled into the kitchen and filled the teakettle. "Are ye finished, then? So many calls, child."

"No, not yet." Emily powered up her laptop and searched online to find out how to get a copy of her birth certificate.

Dad swore there was nothing of hers at his house, but it had to be there, stored with the rest of the things she hadn't planned on needing when she went to "help" Aunt Grace and ended up staying on indefinitely.

She needed the birth certificate to get her passport. Why would her dad lie? To interfere? Since when did he care where she went?

The online copy would take weeks by mail. If she made the five-hour trip to Portland, she could get a copy the same day. After that, a passport would take at least three more weeks to arrive. The absolute earliest she and Aunt Grace could leave for Scotland would be mid-July. Which seemed like an eternity.

While the water heated for Grace's afternoon tea, Emily went to the post office. She'd forgotten to check the mail earlier and Aunt

Grace insisted there would be a letter from Maggie. On the drive over, Emily squeezed the steering wheel as the phone call with her dad replayed in her head. When he asked why she needed a passport, she explained about taking Aunt Grace to Scotland.

After a hollow pause, he hung up.

Why should that surprise her? Though she knew better than to expect anything from him, his refusal to help still hurt. But there was no sense letting it get to her. She would get what she needed without his help.

Emily pulled into the post office lot, left the Jeep running, and dashed inside. She sorted through a small stack of mail.

Two letters from Scotland. One was addressed to her and Grace, and the other to her alone. From Ian.

Pulse racing, she studied the familiar script before slipping a finger beneath the seal.

An image arose of Aunt Grace waiting patiently for her return, humming a hymn, and keeping their tea warm.

Emily's eyes flickered over his handwriting again. She heaved a sigh. Grace came first.

She stuffed the letter in her bag and dashed to the Jeep. When she arrived at the house minutes later, Aunt Grace had everything ready. Waiting while her aunt carefully served tea with her good hand tapped into every last drop of Emily's patience. But as she read the regular letter to Grace, she could hear the depth of Ian's voice in the words, and she could see him, his eyes, his smile.

His very real presence on the page stirred things in Emily that made her glance at her aunt more than once to see if she noticed.

The minute tea was cleaned up and put away, Emily slipped to her room, closed the door with a soft click, and pulled the other letter from her bag. She tore open the flap but hesitated. What did his letter for her contain? A repeat of how taking her into his arms had been a mistake? Did it explain things he couldn't say in person for fear of hurting her feelings?

Did she really want to know?

She flopped down on the bed with the envelope. As she drew the letter out, something soft and pink landed on the bed. She gave the letter a shake and a few more daintily pressed flowers fell from the pages.

Honeysuckle?

She examined the petals, brought them to her nose, and smelled. First the flowers, then the letter. Faint but insistent, the sweet scent of honeysuckle clung to the folded paper.

> *June 8*
> *Dear Emily,*
> *I found these flowers in the woods today. They reminded me of you.*

She caught her breath as tears turned the petals into a fuzzy, pink blur. If Jaye were here, she'd be on the floor hyperventilating. Smiling, Emily blinked until she could see.

> *When we spoke on the phone, I promised to tell you about illustrating. And I will. But first, thank you for taking me to meet Aunt Grace. Maggie is pleased that Grace is well-loved and cared for, through there was never any doubt about that.*

> *Onto the story. It starts with an eager, young lad fresh out of school, in love and full of dreams, and ends with a grown man trapped by bitterness.*

> *I always liked to draw. I had an excellent teacher who encouraged me to study art and helped me get into illustrating. There was a time I felt God wanted me to use art to—as you said—bring His word to life. And you were right, it was truly rewarding. But, in order to get Katy's father's permission to marry, I was given a choice: either choose a career that met with his approval or continue on the path of an artist—alone. Katy didn't care about things like that, but I knew it was important to her to honor her father and have his blessing. The decision was entirely mine.*

I put art aside to attend university in London and get a business degree. If I did that, Edward promised me a job at his brokerage, then I would be permitted to marry Katy. So I went to school for three more years, earned a degree, and went to work for him.

Everything went as planned—almost. Edward gave me the job at McKinley, Carmichael, & Associates. But it was on the condition that I would be on probation for one year. Then, at the end of that year, if I'd proven myself, he would give his consent to the marriage. It took four years and loads of patience, but I did everything he asked. The day my 'probation' ended, Katy and I were married.

Unfortunately, the cancer was not as patient. Eight months later, Katy was gone.

Emily covered her mouth to catch the sob, but it only muffled the sound. "Oh, Ian, I'm so sorry. How devastating." Tears spilled down her cheeks. She sat up, wiped her face, and read on.

While I wasted time chasing Edward Carmichael's approval, he sent Katy away to school in Hawaii. He did everything he could to keep us apart. Later, when she was sick, he took over her care and shut me out. I shouldn't have agreed to any of it. But I was young and felt powerless to stand up to a man like him. I can't forget what he did and what he cost me. The more I try to put it behind me, the more I despise him. I suppose those feelings drove away any desire I might have had to take up illustrating again.

Hatred for him has consumed me for a very long

123

time, Emily. I prayed God would take it away and help me get past it. But nothing has changed—I can't seem to let it go. I don't know what else to do.

So that's the story. I'm guilty of things I'm not proud of. Telling you was a risk I took because I knew you would want the truth.

IAN

"Oh, Ian." She leaned back against the wall. The pain in his words tore at her. She pulled her pillow close and laid a wet cheek against its softness. She ached for his loss and his bitter regrets, and yet ... he had shared these deeply personal things with her. He was letting her see into his heart, letting her into his life.

She wanted to respond immediately. But what should she say? That it broke her heart to learn how much he'd suffered and how he still hurt? That she would do anything she could to help?

That she loved him?

She closed her eyes as the truth burned its way straight through her.

Yeah. Maybe she could write *that*.

CHAPTER SEVENTEEN

A faint bleating carried across the brae, a thin remnant of the sound Ian remembered as a lad when the hillside was home to shifting droves of wooly, black-faced beasts.

He lifted another chunk of wood to the block and stood it on end, brought the axe down and split it in two. He gathered the pile of cut wood and wheeled the load into the shed to stack. It didn't take long. Just long enough to mentally kick himself, again, for sending Emily that letter.

Maggie's voice warbled up the drive as he added the last piece to the woodpile. He couldn't make out what the old woman was saying. No matter, he'd find out soon enough.

He returned the axe to its hiding place, headed into the house, and washed up in the mudroom.

The sound of Maggie's shuffling footsteps in the hall grew closer until she stood behind him in the doorway.

"Do you need something, Maggie?" He rummaged for a towel.

"Aye. A new set o' eyes, ye daftie. I dinna ken what to make of this. Two letters from Grace on the same day."

Ian spun round.

Maggie held two envelopes in her knobby hand.

"Can I have a look, then?"

"Ye dinna believe me?" With a grunt, she handed them over.

Both were from Juniper Valley. One bore Maggie's name in Emily's cursive. The other was addressed to Ian alone.

Pulse quickening, he stole a glance at Maggie.

Her dim eyes twinkled. "Now do ye believe me? Ooh, we're double blessed today." Maggie clucked and strutted toward the kitchen. "This calls for *two* pots of tea."

He followed. What could he say? Nothing convincing came to mind, nothing that wasn't an outright lie.

"Maggie, only one of these is a letter for us." He held his breath.

She stopped and turned. "Only one?" Her brow furrowed. "What's the other, then?"

"It's for me. Just something from my trip." Partly true, anyway.

As Maggie went to the sink and filled the tea kettle, Ian pocketed Emily's letter and worked to shove aside some of the clutter on the table.

"Verra strange," Maggie said slowly. "Both smell o' honeysuckle."

Ian stiffened and glanced over his shoulder.

The old woman continued her task, humming some old tune as she loaded a plate of honey buns.

When tea was ready, Ian read Emily and Grace's letter to Maggie.

She grunted at Grace's glowing account of meeting Ian but then cooed at the news that Grace and Emily had booked their trip to Scotland for the fourteenth of July.

A few times, as Emily's voice came through the words on the page, Ian lapsed into silence and read the letter to himself.

Maggie squawked and accused him of holding back about her sister. Finally, after a second reading of the letter and some discussion about Grace and Emily's visit, Maggie was satisfied.

Ian bolted. He dashed out the back door, crossed the field, and tore through the upper gate, aiming for the woods.

A light, steady breeze rustled the trees. Enough sun broke through the grey clouds to cast long shadows like fingers drumming across his path as he scrambled up the brae.

Nearing the glen, he patted his pocket for the letter. He pressed through the brush to the clearing and pulled out the envelope. A sturdy pine near the edge of the glen offered a backrest, and he eased himself down at the base of the tree. The air buzzed with a sweetness that wrapped itself round him.

If her letter carried her flowery scent, he couldn't tell.

He held his breath.

126

June 15

Dear Ian,

Thank you for the flowers! That was so sweet. And thank you so much for your letter. I would have replied by email but I don't have your address. I'm including mine, along with my cell number, if you ever need them.

I hardly know where to begin. First of all, I appreciate your willingness to share your story with me, and I'm touched by your honesty. In fact, I'm honored. You may not think so now, but talking about it helps. It brings things that torment us out of the dark and into the light, and invites God in to heal and restore. So the fact that you shared this with me is a good thing.

Ian exhaled a ragged breath. She wasn't disgusted.

Ian, I can't begin to imagine what that must have been like. I'm so sorry for what you lost and for the devastation you must have felt. Anger would be a natural reaction for anyone. You've asked God to help you, and that's the important thing. I know the Lord heard your prayer. Don't stop.

But I wonder—have you forgiven yourself?

The words pulsed on the page, daring him to stop and consider them.

I know how hard it can be to forgive those who hurt us. Remember looking at the ocean? I am amazed that the God who created all that power and beauty also cares about each of us. I don't know why He does. All I know is His love is immense and

127

unfailing, and has the power to do the impossible.
He loves each one of us, though we don't deserve it.
That includes you, me, my dad. And, as I'm sure
you know, it also includes Edward Carmichael.

The meaning of her words sunk in like a hot, iron fist. He flicked the letter away with a growl.

If Emily thought he should call on Edward for a lovely, wee visit over tea, she needed to think again. God may well love the rotter, but that was *His* problem.

Jaw clenched, Ian stared at the paper, itching to crumple it. When he could stare at it no longer, he snatched it up again.

This might sound crazy, but I wonder what would
happen if you started praying for him? What do you
think? I mean—what harm could it do?

"Ha!"

The single hacked-out laugh bounced off the thicket and echoed back at him.

"What do I *think*?" Staring at the words, he shook his head. And just how did she suggest he pray for the man? There was nothing Ian wanted for him. At least, not the kind of things Emily probably had in mind.

Ian closed his eyes. He could see her now with those delicate eyebrows slightly arched above amber-brown eyes. Her kind, patient smile as she waited for his answer.

God knows your heart, Ian. He knows the depth and
strength of your character and your desire to do the
right thing. He will help you get past this. I believe
it without a doubt.

I look forward to meeting Maggie and seeing you
again. Thank you for your letter. It means a lot to
me.

Love, Emily

He read the letter again, then stared at the closing lines for a long, long time. Finally, he stood and scanned the patch of grey sky above him. Either rain or sun waited beyond the hazy veil, maybe both. Or perhaps a fierce summer thunderstorm, steadily gathering strength.

God only knew.

Ian folded the letter, returned it to his pocket, and worked his way back to the path. When he reached the trail, he turned right and headed northwest, toward the old cemetery.

In the weeks that followed, no letters arrived from Juniper Valley, and Maggie didn't send any. She didn't have time. Kirkhaven's summer fair would take place soon, followed by the visit from Grace and Emily, and Maggie was in a flap to get ready for both.

Which was fine with Ian. He didn't need Maggie poking into his business.

For days, Emily's letter burned a hole in his pocket. He couldn't get her face out of his mind. Her suggestion to pray for Edward was absurd. Chewing on rusty nails sounded delightful by comparison. But every time he read her letter and lingered on the good things she believed about him, he broke out in a cold sweat.

How could she suggest it?

What harm could it do?

Harm wasn't the issue—it was pure, dead *wrong*. On so many levels. So wrong that he finally decided to actually do it. Then he could say he tried and there would be an end of it.

And maybe then he could put Emily out of his mind.

A few days later, he went down to the old cemetery. He stared at Katy's gravestone for the longest time and asked himself what he was doing. Thoughts of Edward brought only curses to mind, so he said nothing. *That* had to be worth something. But the effort warranted a job done right. So, through gritted teeth, he said, "God, bless ... the person. Amen."

A few days after that, the fifteen-minute walk to the church gave Ian time to come up with a long list of things God should do about Edward Carmichael, but when he arrived at the cemetery, a sense of God's presence silenced him.

He was there to pray for the man, not list the man's evil deeds.

So he asked God to bless him again, turned round, and trudged home.

After a week of daily treks to the cemetery, Maggie hollered at him from the mudroom as Ian headed out the back door. "Leaving again, laddie? What mischief are ye up to now?"

Considering his options didn't take long. "Praying for my enemies," he said, and slipped out before she could close her gaping mouth.

Something unexpected happened during those daily visits. As he spoke Edward's name aloud and continued to ask God to bless the man, his jaw loosened just a bit.

One summer day in particular, he stayed longer than usual and felt no urge to leave. "How do You do it?" he asked as he knelt in the cool shade. "How can You forgive evil people? How do You not only forgive, but forget? And not only forget, but give evil men second chances?" Lips pressed to a hard line, Ian shook his head. "I could never do that."

Never is a long time. An eternity.

"*You* can give Edward a second chance if You fancy. I can't stop You." He took a deep breath, eased it out through puffed cheeks. "God, I pray—"

Just say it.

"Help Edward seek Your forgiveness, God. Forget about him seeking mine. I suppose I'm asking You to help him do whatever it takes to be right with You."

His prayer treks continued, and a few weeks after he received Emily's letter, Ian made a shocking discovery. He had no idea if his prayers were having any effect on Edward Carmichael, but God had shown up and met Ian each time he went to that place.

Why would God listen to the prayers of a man like Ian MacLean? A man who had once followed Christ and then turned his back on Him? For some reason, during quiet moments at an old cemetery, God had come to him, just as he was, faithless and flawed.

He whispered an apology for his years of wayward indifference, and as he did, something snapped—something cold and heavy and binding—and a warm peace engulfed him. Wanting more, he went home, found the Bible that Katy had given him, and began reading it.

Something else he read repeatedly was Emily's letter. It often ended up in the pocket of his jeans, soft and crumpled from being unfolded, read, folded again, and stuffed back in his pocket. He wasn't sure what he hoped to gain by reading it over again, unless he wanted to make it impossible to stop thinking about her. So he put the letter away in a drawer, only to find it didn't matter.

Everything made him think of Emily.

On the day of the Kirkhaven summer fair, the smell of bacon lured Ian as he descended the stairs.

Maggie's muttering rose to a squawk when he entered the kitchen. "Where did ye hide my griddle? It didn't walk off on its own. Ye'll never see another scone if ye don't produce it."

Extra kitchen work always brought out the charming side of Maggie. She would probably explode with charm when Grace and Emily arrived in little more than a week.

✢ ✢ ✢

A parade kicked off Juniper Valley's annual Fourth of July celebration. It also kicked up a lot of dust.

Emily helped Aunt Grace get comfortable at a picnic table in the shade. As she scanned the crowd on the lawn for signs of Jaye's arrival, Wrangle's truck barreled into the church parking lot, spitting gravel like watermelon seeds.

"Hey—Emily!" Jaye flailed her arm out the passenger window like a manic parade queen on a sugar high. "C'mere, I want you to meet someone."

As Emily jogged closer, Jaye's head bobbed to the rhythm of a Rascal Flatts song thumping from the truck's stereo.

Jaye turned to her companions. "Guys, this is Emily, the one I was telling you about. Em, this is Jake and Jesse. You already met Wrangle. They're from Paisley."

"Hi." Emily shielded her eyes from the sun and squinted, but only saw one of them—the one in a cut-off-sleeve plaid shirt nearly crawling out the window to get a better look.

"I'm Jake." The drawl was attached to a broad set of shoulders that pretty much filled the window. He grinned at Emily and turned to Jaye. "Whoa. You weren't kiddin'."

Jaye slapped at his chest. "Down boy. You too, Jesse. She's taken."

"Jaye—" Emily threw a wide-eyed stare at her delusional friend. Jaye's fantasies were going to get somebody in trouble one day.

"Oh. Sorry. *Almost* taken. He's Scottish."

Ian.

So far, she'd managed to keep her mind off the glaring fact that she hadn't heard a word from Ian in the three weeks since she sent him that letter. She could no longer ignore the sinking feeling that his silence meant she'd said more to him than she should have.

As the festivities wound down and dusk blanketed the valley, the warmth of the day disappeared with the sun. Emily jogged up to the parking lot and grabbed two camp chairs from her Jeep. A chill in the air triggered tiny bumps along her bare arms. When she returned, she set their chairs up at the edge of the "lake," which was really no more than a man-made pond in the center of town. The fireworks that would be launched on the other side would be visible all over the valley.

The chirrup of crickets had grown louder after the sun went down. A mild breeze sent another chill along Emily's skin. She glanced at her aunt. "We didn't bring you a coat, did we?"

"It's not so bad, dearie."

Grace's brave little smile convinced Emily she needed to find something warm for her, and soon. But rummaging amongst their friends' stuff turned up nothing but a smelly, old dog blanket in the bed of the feed store owner's pickup. "Sorry, I should have thought of bringing something warm for you. I'll run home and get a blanket and something hot to drink, okay?"

"But ye'll miss the fireworks."

"I should be back before it begins. It'll only take a couple minutes."

132

Back at the house, Emily hustled to the kitchen, put water in the teakettle, and set it on the stove. She took out Grace's favorite tea and waited, staring at the dainty table where she'd shared countless cups of tea with her great-aunt.

Two women sharing a lonely life over tea.

Emily grimaced. It didn't sound quite so pathetic when she first came to stay with Grace. How long *had* it been? And how long would it continue?

Without invitation, a picture of Ian trying to squeeze himself into a seat at the tiny table came to mind. Was that some kind of sign? Was there no room for anyone but Grace in Emily's life?

As she glanced around the quaint, cozy kitchen, trying to imagine Ian here, a flicker of red on the answering machine caught her eye. She went for a closer look at the blinking number.

Four messages. Odd.

Frowning, she hit play.

A mechanical voice greeted her with a timestamp: *4:14 p.m.*

"Hello, Emily. And Aunt Grace. It's Ian."

Emily gasped. Ian?

"Uh ... Emily, I tried to ring your cell but my call won't go through. Could you ring me?"

Click.

4:17 p.m.

"I meant ring anytime. I'll wait here then. At the cottage."

Click.

5:03 p.m.

"Uh ... sorry, I'm not thinking. It's a holiday there and you're out. Just ring when you get in. No matter what time. There's something I need to tell you."

The rumbling tone of his voice sent a warm shock wave through her. Emily held her breath as the red number *3* changed to a *4*.

8:30 p.m.

"Emily?" The depth of his voice lingered, filling the loaded pause. "Call me."

CHAPTER EIGHTEEN

Three weeks without a word, then four phone messages in one day. What did he need to say that was so important?

She checked the wall calendar.

Ten days until the big green X, the day they would leave for Scotland.

He probably just wanted their travel itinerary so someone could meet her and Aunt Grace at the airport.

But hadn't he said there was something he needed to tell her?

Her pulse quickened as she remembered the depth of his tone.

Oh, no. Something was wrong with Maggie. He wanted to tell Emily before Grace heard about it.

Heart skittering, Emily pulled out her cell, punched the numbers, and got an immediate recording—her plan wasn't set up for international calls. She chucked it, grabbed the cordless phone, and keyed in his number.

As the line clicked through a string of region codes, she checked the time and added eight hours. Should be about 5:20 a.m. in Scotland. Which meant he'd left the first message just after midnight his time and the last at 4:30 a.m. He had been up all night trying to reach her?

Boooo boop.

She couldn't breathe. Elbows on the counter, Emily cradled her dizzy head in her hands.

Boooo boop.

"Emily?"

A thrill zapped across her nerves at the sound of his voice. "Yes, it's me. Is something wrong with Maggie?"

He expelled a long blast of air. Seconds passed before he

answered. "Maggie's fine." His voice sounded deeper than usual, sending her stomach flipping. "I didn't mean to worry you. I guess I wasn't thinking. Sorry."

"What about you? Are you okay?"

"Aye. I mean ... no. I'm, uh ..." A shuddering intake of breath vibrated over the line. "There are things I need to tell you, Emily, but first, there's something I need to know. Do you remember when we stopped that night? Beside the road? When we—I mean, when I—"

A shrill scream blasted from the teakettle.

Startled, Emily lost her grip on the phone and it clattered to the floor. She grabbed it and dashed to the stove, fumbling to get the stupid phone wedged between her shoulder and ear. "Sorry! Hang on." She moved the kettle off the burner, chest thudding like a giant marching drum. "Yes, I remember." *Are you kidding me? How could I forget?*

"I'd like to know how you felt about that."

She closed her eyes and found herself at the edge of the road beneath the dark, velvet sky, melting into Ian's strong, gentle embrace. Drawing a calming breath, she centered her thoughts on the core-rocking truth that had already taken up residence in her heart.

"I mean, when I took you in my arms and nearly kissed you. Because if that was ... unwelcome, then I won't trouble you with the rest of what's on my—"

"I felt like I was home."

A long, breathless silence. "Home?"

"Yes," she whispered.

A steady pulse played on the line.

"Emily." His voice plunged dangerously low. "You fill my thoughts. Constantly."

She tried to breathe, but nothing worked. Her legs were noodles. She reached behind her for something to hold onto as she slid down the doorframe to the floor, phone smashed to her ear. "Really?"

"Aye," he said softly. "I'm in love with you."

Numbing waves of joy engulfed her. She tried to respond, but the words caught in her throat.

The line went still, as though Ian was holding his breath.

Emily closed her eyes and pictured his face. "I love you, Ian. I fell in love with you the day we met." A revelation struck and she added, "No. Long before."

"Ahh." Relief poured from his shaky exhale.

The image of him all alone, pacing back and forth in some tiny cottage, phone pressed to his ear, made her ache.

"Eight days, love. I don't think I can wait that long."

Her pulse skittered at the depth in his tone. Smiling, she gave a soft chuckle. "Ian, I'm sorry, but it's ten, actually."

"*Ten* days?" He growled. "Emily, there are so many things I have to tell you. And there's something very important I need to show you. Alone." He groaned, then another growl rattled the line. "You're sure it's ten days?"

✚ ✚ ✚

Emily barely remembered returning in time to drape Aunt Grace with a blanket before the fireworks started. Barely remembered the next days of gathering things to pack or helping Aunt Grace find mates to her shoes. All she knew was Ian loved her, and the thought of that felt like a drink of pure, cool water after a long, dusty drought. She fumbled through workdays in a cloud and spent all her waking hours thinking of Ian—remembering the weight of his arms around her, his heart beating against her cheek.

Of course, spending all her time dreaming about Ian wasn't helping her get ready for the trip. Though she looked forward to his almost daily phone calls, she made him switch to email before he got a phone bill he would regret.

His emails were short, sweet, and impatient. The things weighing on him most were things he preferred to tell her in person. He couldn't wait to see her.

She wrote back the same.

Tuesday morning, she checked the time for Aunt Grace's Wednesday appointment with Dr. Fletcher and, with a wave of numbing apprehension, remembered her plan to visit the doctor herself. The palpitations on the beach. Her mom's condition. Her *genetic* condition. She pushed the intrusion aside and left for work.

But throughout the day, thoughts of Ian kept bringing her back to what she desperately wished she could forget.

By the time she left work and headed home, she could think of nothing else. The files and studies and links she'd saved on her computer about Hypertrophic Cardiomyopathy. The notes she'd taken. The search she'd begun after that disturbing conversation with her drunken father one night two years ago.

He didn't seem to remember the incident later—he'd been so out of it at the time—but Emily couldn't forget. She'd stopped to see him after a bowling date with the friend of a friend who had just returned from Afghanistan.

Dad was muttering and slurring his words more than usual. Tired of trying to talk to him, she left, but he'd followed her out to the porch, spewing awful things at her. "No more dating. No marriage. Just stay with Grace. Stay out there in the desert."

She'd asked him why he said such things.

"Figure it out yet? You, your mom, your grandma ... ruin a man's life. You can't do that. You'll put him through a living hell." He'd staggered back inside.

Stunned, Emily had decided it was his pain talking and left. She tried to sympathize, but still—what a thing to say to his own daughter. When she asked about it later, he claimed he had no idea what she was talking about. But what he'd said got her thinking and she started digging. Over time, she found sobering clues about the mysteriously early deaths of both her mom and her grandma.

The one mystery she couldn't solve was how much her dad knew. And if he knew something, why hadn't he told her?

When she arrived home after work, she killed the motor but remained in the Jeep, listening to the tick of the cooling engine. She needed to face what she'd been trying to ignore. If she had truly inherited a fatal illness, she needed to know.

But I don't want to know. I love him.

That's why you need to know. If you love him.

Later that night, after Aunt Grace went to bed, Emily went out on the porch, took a deep breath, and punched in her dad's number. As she waited for him to answer, the bizarre reality of what she was doing seized her.

What girl calls her dad to ask if she's dying?

Lord, I wish Mom were still alive. Dad would be happy. Things would be so different.

Click. "This is Ray."

He actually answered? Emily fumbled to speak. "Hi, it's me, Dad."

"What do you want?"

Good question. The sudden dryness in her throat forced her to swallow hard. "I sent you an email. I wanted to make sure you got it."

"What is it?"

"Our travel itinerary. Aunt Grace and I are leaving for Scotland in a couple days. I thought you might want it, if you're interested. Or in case anything happens."

Silence. She could see him, that pallid, weary look permanently stamped on his stubbly face. He always looked much too tired for a man his age. "How long?"

"Four weeks." She paced the length of the porch, gathering her nerve with each step.

The line rumbled as he cleared his throat. "I want to know something."

"Yeah? So do I," she said.

"That guy I met from Scotland—MacLean. Is he the reason you're going?"

"No. I mean, not exactly." *Not originally, anyway.* "Why do you ask?"

He didn't answer.

Emily stopped and braced against the post. *C'mon, Dad, say what you said to me before. Tell me what you know.*

"I'm not stupid."

Wincing at the deadness in his words, she said, "What do you mean?"

"Does he love you?" His voice sounded like gravel.

Yeah, someone loves me, Dad. Finally. A ripple of pain pulsed through her. Every crushed hope and every ache during those lonely, empty years following her mom's death rushed back, caught Emily off guard, sent her trembling. Needing to move, she launched off the porch and headed for the road.

"Emily." His voice wavered. "Does MacLean love you?"

"Yes, he does." She walked faster. "And I love him."

The line went silent.

"Dad, what's this really about?"

"You can't be with him."

"Why?"

"You just can't. Break it off. Now. Before it goes any further."

She stopped and took a deep, bolstering breath. "Dad, is this about me possibly having what Mom had? Do you know anything about that?"

Silence. Except he was breathing hard, as if the conversation had suddenly become too taxing. "Forget MacLean. You'll only hurt him."

The cool steel of his words sliced her heart, sending tart words to her tongue before she could stop them. "Why? Because you don't want to see him hurt, or me happy?"

Thick silence.

Click.

Wednesday morning, Emily drove Aunt Grace in her old, green Buick to Bend for some last-minute shopping before Grace's doctor appointment. Once Dr. Fletcher had taken care of Grace's medication refills, Emily had some questions about what effect their upcoming trip might have on her aunt's health.

Dr. Fletcher appreciated Emily's concerns, but assured her Grace could travel. After he finished discussing Aunt Grace, the doctor smiled at Emily. "And how about you, young lady? Still running?" He leaned closer. "You know what happens if you run too much?"

Emily shook her head.

"Makes it harder for the boys to catch you."

With a smile, Emily shook her head. She'd known Grace's doc long enough to know he was from a generation that had no use for "political correctness."

"You're probably well-prepared for hiking the Scottish hills. I hear the countryside is breathtaking, especially in late summer. You must be eager to go."

"Yes." *At least I was.* "Actually, there *is* a health issue I'd like to ask you about." She glanced at Aunt Grace.

Lips pursed, he nodded. "Grace, Emily and I need to step out into the hall for a moment. Are you okay? Do you need assistance?"

Aunt Grace smiled. "Och, no dearie. I always dress myself."

"I'll be right back, Aunt Grace." Emily followed the doctor. In the hall, Emily asked if he knew about DNA testing for Hypertrophic Cardiomyopathy.

Dr. Fletcher explained that Oregon Health and Sciences University in Portland offered individual genetic testing as well as clinical research studies. "Why do you ask?"

"I think both my mom and grandmother died of HCM and I need to know what the chances are that I inherited it. How soon can I do get tested?"

He hesitated. "Well, it's a process. Initially, it's done to confirm a doctor's diagnosis. It involves screening, preliminary examinations—a number of things." He studied her. "We would need to begin with a full examination. Have you experienced any symptoms? Shortness of breath, dizziness, fatigue, heart palpitations?"

Emily remembered the episode on the beach. "Yes, a few of those."

Frowning, he nodded. "Those can be heart related. They can also be attributed to stress." He patted her shoulder. "Why don't you see me for an exam when you return from your trip? We'll go from there."

She swallowed the tightness in her throat. "I need to know as soon as possible. In Scotland, there's a man ..." She swallowed again, fighting for control of her voice. "It's really important that I know before I leave, if possible. He's already been through ... He's a widower." Unable to trust her voice to finish, she met his gaze. Would he understand?

"Ah." He studied her, nodding. "Okay. Tell you what, Emily. Have a seat in the waiting room with Grace. Someone will call for you in a few minutes."

In the lobby, Emily got Aunt Grace a cup of tea and found a

short story in a magazine to read to her. As she read, her heart whispered a prayer. *Lord, please help the doctor tell me one way or the other so I know for sure. For Ian's sake. But, Lord, please, could You just make me well? So no one suffers? So he and I can think about a life together?*

"Emily Chapman?" A nurse clad in blue waited in the doorway.

Leaving Aunt Grace, Emily trailed after the woman. But instead of an exam room, the nurse led Emily to an X-ray area. She fitted her with the proper gear and guided Emily through the positioning, stepped around the door, and buzzed a few times.

Emily watched the nurse's face for a telltale sign, for something.

The nurse finished up and sent her to Dr. Fletcher's office to wait.

About five minutes later, he arrived with her film. He stuck it on a wall-mounted case and flipped on the backlight.

Holding her breath, Emily stared at it, half expecting to see something weird. It was the first time Emily had seen an image of her own heart. Was it normal? Abnormal?

"Remember, an X-ray is not entirely conclusive, Emily. Now then, this one tells us that your heart is slightly enlarged, which can indicate HCM."

Dizziness hit and Emily gripped the chair arms to steady herself. So it was true. She made herself focus on the doctor's words.

"But it can also be caused by a number of other things. There are some additional tests we can run, but it's not imperative to do them now. Go on and take Grace to Scotland, and I'll see you when you get back. Be sure and make an appointment at the desk before you leave. Okay?"

She nodded. "Thank you."

Enlarged heart ... HCM ...

In a daze, Emily passed the appointment desk, collected her aunt, and escorted her to the sedan. It wasn't until much later, as they neared Juniper Valley, that Emily realized she'd been driving in silence, lost in a numbing cold fog.

"So quiet, dearie. But of course ye're tired." Aunt Grace sighed. "Such a dear lass. All this fuss for such a tiresome, old woman."

Emily shot a quick look at her aunt. "Oh, no. It's no trouble at all, Aunt Grace. I was just thinking."

A jab of guilt stirred her already churning stomach. She'd spent the entire drive home trying to decide whether or not she should tell Ian and hadn't once thought about her dear aunt. How could she tell Grace? Confiding in the old woman would only distress her.

There was one person who would never forgive her if she didn't confide.

When they arrived at the house, Emily slipped outside and called Jaye. She eased into the details of what she'd learned and did her best to soften the news.

"What? You've known about this?" Jaye's voice jumped two octaves. "Emily, why didn't you tell me?"

"I—I didn't want to say anything until I knew more." Emily swallowed hard. If Jaye thought Emily was crying, she would crumble.

"You have to check into the hospital right now and get a full checkup. I mean it, Em. What if, you know, something happens while you're in Scotland? What then?"

Emily squeezed her eyes tight. As much as she loved that her friend cared, her alarm wasn't helping. "Dr. Fletcher doesn't seem too worried if he thinks I can wait a month for a full exam."

She finally convinced Jaye it wasn't necessary to come over and ended the call. The doctor didn't think it was anything to worry about right now. Emily had to hold onto that hope and silence the menacing whisper. *I can't die. What about the Juniper Ranch kids? What about having a home of my own?*

What about Ian?

Emily steeled herself to put it aside for a while and spent the evening helping Aunt Grace fit the new purchases in her suitcases. After Grace went to bed, Emily scoured the Oregon Health and Sciences University website. She found the genetic counseling department and sent a request for information on testing, praying she would hear from someone before Friday. Two more days. She needed at least to make contact and, with any luck, start the process to schedule tests.

Once her message was sent, she looked at the research studies offered at OHSU. She skimmed several articles until she saw a section with the heading *Enlarged Heart*. The article gave a list of tests to determine the extent of tissue damage. The end of the section included a list of other possible causes of an enlarged heart. She read the list twice, focusing on one bulleted point in particular.

Regular exercise—such as running—could also cause a slightly enlarged heart, was considered normal, and posed no health risks.

Emily drew a slow breath and let the information sink in. What if her running routine was all it was? And maybe her little episode at the beach was just stress, like the doctor said.

It was possible.

She read her Bible and slipped into bed, praying as her head hit the pillow. Ian was waiting for her, longing to see her. Her heart ached.

Her dad had a point.

If this turned out badly, Ian would be hurt—again. If her future was uncertain, then she couldn't allow him to continue caring for her. But if nothing was wrong, she didn't want to push him away needlessly.

I need to know, God. Help me know for sure, one way or the other. "Because by Friday," she whispered in the dark, "I'll be in Scotland, no matter what."

CHAPTER NINETEEN

Tapping. No, hammering. Someone must be building a hay barn.

Emily rolled over and squinted at the clock next to her bed.

6:05 a.m. Thursday. She must've been dreaming. But the sound of knocking continued, this time insistent.

Who would come by this early? She grabbed a hoodie, slipped it on over her p.j.'s, and shuffled to the front room. Her hair fell around her shoulders in a riot of loose waves. She tucked some behind one ear and opened the door.

A man stood on the porch.

Emily blinked hard. "Dad—?" She stared at her disheveled father, her fuzzy mind working to register that this was really her dad standing on the front porch for the first time in—ever.

He looked awful, like he'd been drinking. She glanced past him at his Suburban and then looked into his eyes. No, not drunk, but definitely a mess. Distraught.

"What's wrong? What are you doing here?" Her voice cracked with sleep.

Her dad's swollen, bloodshot eyes glanced around the room behind her. "Where's Grace?"

"Sleeping. What's going on?"

"I need to talk to you. Outside." He withdrew to a spot at the edge of the porch and stood with his back to her, facing the valley.

Emily hesitated, then stepped out and closed the door behind her. What would her dad have to say that would make him drive all the way out here at the crack of dawn?

His back swelled as he drew a deep breath. "I wasn't going to tell you, but you've given me no choice. It'll be even worse if I don't." He lifted his face skyward and muttered, "And I don't need

144

any more guilt."

Guilt? Her mind raced, but she held her tongue.

He propped a stiff arm against the post. "Your mom and Grandma Janice both died of a rare type of heart disease. It shows very little symptoms until adulthood. It's fatal." He pulled in another deep breath. "And ... it's genetic."

So you knew about it. All this time. Trembling, she whispered, "Go on."

He deflated. "They inherited it. And so did you."

"What are you saying? That you know this for sure? About me?"

He nodded.

"How could you possibly know?"

"Your great-uncle Thomas told me."

"Uncle Thomas?" Her mom's uncle? "When?" Images from the past jumbled in her mind as she tried to do a mental rewind. "He died eight years ago. And he'd retired from medicine years before that."

"When your mom died, so young and in such a similar way as his sister, Thomas suspected a connection." Dad carefully nudged a flower pot away from the edge of the porch with the toe of his boot. "He researched it with a medical university team, both here and overseas."

That didn't mean anything. Had this research specifically included Emily? She didn't remember anything about it. But then, she'd drifted in a fog after her mom died and very little from those years registered in her memory.

"Dad, I don't understand. He studied it, but what made him think I have it?"

Shaking his head, he said, "I don't remember the details, the genetic science involved was beyond me. He came to me with folders of research notes. Explained how it's inherited and how you would—" He lifted his head skyward, as though he expected someone else to finish the sentence for him.

"Die?" A cold fist struck into Emily's belly, numbing her. Uncle Thomas knew she had it? Did Aunt Grace know too? No. That wasn't possible. "No. He would have told me."

"Wait." Her dad trudged down the steps to his rig, took something from the dash and returned with a stained, wrinkly envelope. Without meeting her eyes, he held it out to her.

She turned it over and stared at the faded word written in the center. *Emily.*

"It's from Thomas. He wanted to wait to tell you because you'd just lost your mom. He thought it would be better to let me decide when the time was right to give that to you."

"The *right* time? And you think *this* is it?"

The image of her mom's pretty, young face as she lay dying flooded her thoughts. Emily had come home from school and heard a faint moan. She hurried down the hall to her parents' bedroom and gasped. Her mom lay in an awkward heap beside the lodge pine bed, covers askew and tangled around her feet, skin blue.

"Mom! What happened?" Emily knelt near her mom's head and reached a hand under her neck. "Let me help you up—"

Mom breathed another weak moan. "No, Emmy." Her eyes fluttered but only opened to thin slits, her breath so faint Emily could barely hear her. The smell of urine was unmistakable. How long had she been lying here?

"Okay, just a sec. Dad's coming, okay? He's out feeding the dogs, he'll—"

Mom's eyes closed.

Emily gasped. "Mom?"

"My sweet, sunshine girl," Mom whispered. Her eyes opened a little, drifted into focus on Emily. "Remember our secret place? We'll share one again, Em. A far … better one. Forever."

The meaning of her words hit Emily like a sandbag, sending a numbing wave through her. "Mom, you're gonna be okay. I'm calling 911." She moved to get up, but another moan held her.

Mom's lips moved without sound.

Emily leaned close.

"Remember … I love you more than life, Em."

Emily whimpered, her panic rising. "I—I love you too, Mom."

"And remember to … help your daddy."

"Help him do what?

"Keep living. Please, Em … promise me."

146

"Okay—yes, I promise."

Mom's eyes closed and, with barely a sound, she breathed, "Ray ..."

Emily's breath came in panicked bursts.

Her dad's boots sounded on the porch and the front door opened.

"Dad!" she screamed.

He was there in seconds. "Jess!" He dropped to one knee and placed his fingertips on the side of her throat. "Emily, call 911!"

Emily stumbled to the kitchen and brought back the cordless phone, punching the numbers as she hurried to the bedroom.

Her dad was still pressing fingers to her mom's neck. Her oddly blue neck. "No, baby, no. Come on!"

Come on, Mom! Please, God!

Dad started chest compressions. The ringing on the other end of the phone line kept time with his steady rhythm.

"C'mon, Jess ... c'mon!" He kept at it, stopping briefly to feel her neck with a shaking hand. His face went pale. "C'mon, baby, please!"

The sight of her strong dad pleading like that sent paralyzing fear ripping through her. She trembled so hard she almost dropped the phone. When the dispatcher answered, Emily sobbed something incoherent about needing an ambulance and then fell silent.

Dad picked up her mom's lifeless body and pulled her to his chest. "No, no, no! Don't do this! Don't do this!" Huge, shuddering sobs shook his entire body.

"Mom?" Emily clamped a hand over her mouth to stop the rising scream and moved toward her mother, trembling at the nearness of her dad's agonized weeping.

He laid Mom on the bed, then pounded the wall, roaring "No!" with each thunderous blow.

Shaking, Emily reached out and touched her mom's unmoving arm.

"She's gone." Dad choked on the words.

Emily burst into tears.

He sank to his knees and pressed his forehead to his wife's. "You should have let me take you somewhere else. We could have kept trying."

"But she said nothing could be done." The words caught in her aching throat.

Dad lifted his head and pushed the hair away from Mom's temple. His face twisted with a mix of pain and anger. "She was tired. Tired of tests. Spending all her time running around, getting the same answers." His face crumpled as he studied her face. "She made me stop, Emily. She—" The words came out tight. "She didn't want to miss out on any more of your life."

Cold crept through Emily, quickening along every nerve and muscle, enveloping her.

Sirens grew louder and bright pink light flickered bigger and higher against one wall until the whole room was a blinking, neon strobe.

Emily could hear those sirens even now as she stood on the porch staring at her uncle's unopened letter. "I didn't just lose her, Dad," Emily said in a choked whisper. "I watched her die. Then I watched you fall apart and shut yourself off. I lost you too." Saying the words touched off a wave of sorrow that hit with hurricane force. She rushed past him and ran down the steps, but her legs buckled. She stumbled and fell to the dirt. Numb, she couldn't move.

As his footsteps approached, the chill of his shadow fell over her.

"Why did you keep this from me?"

He didn't answer.

She looked up, wiping her wet face with her sweatshirt sleeve.

His shoulders sagged under the weight of some unseen burden. Pain twisted his face.

"Why didn't you—" Gasping, she stood up and faced him. "Is *that* why you've been pushing me away?"

He turned from her and looked across the desert without answering. Finally, he spoke, his coarse whisper barely audible. "I can't go through that again." He shook his head. "I can't."

"*You* can't?" She stared at his back. "Because you couldn't stand to lose anyone else, you chose to not love me?" Tears clogged her throat, nearly choking her, as she fought for control.

His frame shuddered and the weight of his pain hit Emily. Seeing her dad cry sent a fresh blast of sorrow through her.

Such crushing burdens they both bore and yet never shared.

She covered her face and wept. When she could finally steady her voice, she spoke. "You said you weren't going to tell me. Why now?"

"I have no choice," he said quietly. "You said he loves you."

Ian.

She tried to breathe, but no air would come. It was as if a giant boulder had landed on her chest and pressed all the air from her lungs.

"He already lost one wife, Emily. I can't stand back and let him walk straight into that again." Dad's body trembled as he turned to her. He wiped his eyes with a shaky hand and met her gaze. "It's a nightmare to watch someone you love more than life slipping away. I lived that hell. I *still* live it. It's a wound that never stops bleeding."

Emily shook her head. "But, Dad, what if—"

"You can't put him through that again, Emily. It'll kill him."

His words swirled around her like dead leaves in a whirlwind. Dizzy, Emily closed her eyes and felt his hands clamp her shoulders.

"Look at me."

She opened her eyes and tried to focus.

"If you really love him, you'll end it. Now."

✢ ✢ ✢

In her room, Emily lay on her back, smeared tears away from her temples, and stared at the envelope.

Creased, smudged, and unopened, it looked as if it had been through battle.

With trembling fingers, she drew out a handwritten letter bearing Uncle Thomas's signature. The letter began with his sorrow at the loss of Emily's mother, and an encouragement to remember the Lord is good, always, and is near to comfort the brokenhearted.

She read on, noting his apology and reasons for not giving her this news himself. When he learned of the disease, Emily was so young. He felt she needed time after the loss of her mother. She read each line slowly until she got to one particular phrase.

Freyer's Syndrome. A rare form of Hypertrophic Cardio-myopathy.

Emily was right about the diagnosis. It even had a name.

The monster that killed her mom and grandma had a name.

And it's going to kill me.

The letter said that after taking part in a study of the disease, Thomas and a research team were able to isolate the mutant gene by performing a DNA test on Emily from a sample of her hair. The test of her DNA was beneficial in confirming the study. And for Emily, the result was positive for Freyer's.

Positive.

Emily forced her hand to hold the paper steady and stared at the word until it blurred. Uncle Thomas said he hoped that when she'd had time to accept the news, she might consider participating in research to help the medical community better understand this rare disease. Perhaps in time, she might see her participation as a way to make something good come from all the suffering her family had endured. Make the pain count for something, turn loss into gain.

So that was it.

Hadn't she prayed and asked God to help her know one way or the other? Here was her answer in bold black and white. If the disease progressed for her the way it had for the others, she might have four to six years. She had no future. No hope for a family. No home of her own.

The time she'd spent with Aunt Grace and the kids at Juniper Ranch had been special, but she'd wanted to see those kids grow up secure and confident, ready to take on the world. She wanted to make a real difference in the life of a child. She'd wanted her life to count.

And so it could. When she returned from Scotland, she wouldn't waste a minute. She would love those kids and help them believe in themselves enough to make a difference with their lives.

But it wasn't fair. What about a life of her own? What about ...

Ian.

"God, why did You let us meet?" Her agonized whisper sounded like someone else, like some other dying woman, not her.

Why had God allowed this amazing man into her life if she couldn't have him? Didn't God know the silent desire of her heart, her deepest longings?

Dragging herself upright, she leaned against the wall with a groan and saw Ian's face. The way his eyes sparkled when he teased her. His kindness and the quiet way he cared for others without calling attention to it. His deep desire to do the right thing. His tender embrace. His spoken words of love to her.

A subtle whisper sneaked in from someplace deep in her heart: Hadn't she waited long enough for someone to love? She'd never dreamed she would meet someone like Ian. Wouldn't a few years with him be better than none?

"No," she whispered, shaking her head with dizzying force. Her dad was right. She couldn't put Ian through that kind of pain and grief again. It would be far better for him if she ended her involvement with him now—the sooner the better.

How would she tell him? She couldn't drop something like this on him by phone or email—it had to be in person. And how would he take the news? She could picture him waiting for her to arrive, eager to share what was on his heart and show her what was special to him.

God, I encouraged him to pray and seek the ability to forgive. Because of me, he is finding healing in his heart. The heart I'm going to crush now.

Maybe she should send him a brief message, to help prepare him a little. But what?

She slid her laptop onto the bed and pulled up her mail server. In her inbox, there was a new message from Ian. Her pulse raced as she clicked it open.

Dear Emily,

I'm thinking about you and what you said. If it's true—if you love me even a little—then I'm the luckiest man alive. But I should warn you about what you're getting. If you could look at my heart, you would see some ugly scars. But if you can look past those, I promise you my heart is whole now, thanks to you. It's yours, so do with it as you please. All I ask is that you take it. And keep it.

Emily, I'm not the patient man you think I am. I love you. I can't wait to tell you in person. I don't know if I can say it right, so perhaps you'll let me show you. It may take the rest of my life to do that properly. I hope you don't mind.

Two days, love. I'm dying here.
Love, Ian

Emily squeezed her eyes tight, but the crushing ache in her chest rushed to her throat. Falling to her bed, she grabbed the pillow to muffle the sobs and cried long and hard until her tears were spent and she drifted to sleep.

When she awoke, her head throbbed. She dragged herself off the bed, shuffled to the kitchen, and found Aunt Grace up and collecting more items to pack.

For their trip tomorrow.

How could Emily handle an entire month with Ian? She could cut the trip short, but that would break Aunt Grace's heart. She'd just have to deal with being near him as best she could.

The decision not to share her news with Aunt Grace came easily. Her sweet little aunt had suffered enough. Apparently Uncle Thomas hadn't told her his findings about Emily either.

Emily followed Grace in a disconnected fog and went through the motions of packing. Movement was an effort, as if sand bags hung from her limbs. As Emily put some of Grace's things in little zipper baggies, it dawned on her. The Juniper Ranch kids and Dad and Ian weren't the only ones who could be affected by Emily's early death.

Grace could outlive her.

She froze and stared at her aunt, a zipper bag in one hand and a tube of toothpaste in the other.

"What is it, dearie?"

"Nothing." Emily shook her head and poked through the pile without seeing. What would another loss do to Aunt Grace? And how would the old woman manage all alone?

"Ye're tired today, child."

"I'm fine." She avoided her aunt's eyes—she had to. There would be no turning to Aunt Grace for comfort.

And with a dull twinge to the heart, it hit her.

Without Grace to turn to, there would be no comforting arms for Emily at all.

CHAPTER TWENTY

Ian's arms ached to scoop Emily off her feet and hold her tight the moment she walked through those doors. But he wouldn't. He would show some restraint.

Maybe.

He and Claire had found a place to sit where they could watch the throng of travelers emerging from Passport Control. Many of the bleary-eyed, dazed souls shuffled like zombies toward Baggage Reclaim, while others greeted loved ones with smiling faces and hugs.

He wanted to see only one face. That warm smile and those amber-brown eyes that couldn't hide what she was feeling. He wanted—no—*needed* to see what was in those eyes.

"Well, at least one of us knows who we're looking for," Claire said above the buzz of people noise. "I'd hate to think we'd walk right past them in the crowd."

Impossible. He grinned like an idiot.

The days since he told Emily he loved her—and she turned him inside out by telling him the same—had gone by painfully slowly. And now, though he'd intended to wait for the right moment to kiss her, he wasn't sure he could.

Emily was likely the kind of woman who would like their first kiss to be special, which meant he would wait for the right moment, the right place. And he had the perfect place in mind. The honeysuckle glen in the woods, where he would ask her to share her life with him. Forever. Just as soon as she had a chance to rest and get her bearings. Of course, if she gave him any sign that he'd figured her wrong and an opportunity presented itself sooner ... well, after all, he *was* a MacLean. He certainly wouldn't hesitate.

"I still can't believe you were going to put them in that musty, old cottage." Claire closed a magazine and tossed it onto a nearby seat.

"Sorry?"

"Did it not occur to you that Grace would have to walk up to the house every day?"

"I suppose not."

"Of course not." She huffed. "Men."

With a sigh, he realized he hadn't thought about much of anything besides the slowly dwindling number of days until Emily would arrive.

"If I'd known you didn't have that downstairs bedroom ready for her, I would have come out sooner and given it a far better scrubbing."

"You did a top job, Claire. It's perfect."

The crowds milled in every direction. Too many people.

Ian stood to get a better view, eyes still glued on the terminal entrance.

"Humph. You still should have told me sooner. I don't mind cleaning. And I certainly don't mind taking them home in my car instead of that beast of a truck. What were you thinking?"

He shook his head. "Glad you thought of that too."

She puffed again. "Someone has to, daft as you've been."

He kept a constant vigil on the newcomers, craning his neck.

There—reddish-brown hair, tucked back on one side.

His heart hammered.

Not her.

He let out his breath.

Claire stood beside him, arms folded. "You're wigglier than a wee lad in church. What's wrong with you?"

The woman I love is about to walk through that door. Ian checked his watch. The boards said their flight had arrived on time. They should have come through by now. He held his breath as another batch of travelers emerged. His studied every young woman and scanned each face that passed by.

"You've lost your mind then, haven't you? I knew it would happen. You've been on that farm too long." Claire turned to him as though a sudden light had dawned. "That's it! You're planning to force them to stay with Maggie so you can escape."

The crowd thinned.

He checked his watch again. They should've been amongst this group. But then, Aunt Grace did move slowly. Maybe he should ask at the ticket counter.

"Aye. You should do it, Ian. I dare you."

"What?"

A few more people entered—a cluster of dark business suits.

Ian blew out a sharp breath.

Claire poked him in the arm, her brow deep in a frown. "Hey, you haven't heard a word I've said. What are you so fashed about? They can't get past us, Ian. They'll be pure exhausted by now."

"Ah, right." Especially Aunt Grace. That would explain the delay.

Two more people emerged, two women—

Emily. His heart raced instantly, right on cue.

"I'd send you on a long walk, if I knew—what? Do you see them?"

Emily had one arm wrapped around Grace and the other arm supporting her elbow and was searching the filled seats in the waiting area.

"Is that them?" Claire frowned. "Who's the young woman?"

"Emily." His smile stretched broad enough to draw stares. He didn't care.

Emily must have heard her name, because at that moment, she lifted her face and caught his eye.

For a second, everyone else in Glasgow International Airport disappeared.

"Ian?" He felt Claire's hot stare boring into the side of his face. "What? Are you and Emily—?"

Ian tuned her out. All that mattered was the two women coming toward him.

Grace faltered and Emily struggled to support the trembling, old woman.

Idiot! He forced his feet to move and bolted forward. As he reached them, he could hear the weariness in Emily's voice.

"You can rest now, Aunt Grace. We're going to sit down right over there." Emily tried to help Grace to a nearby chair, but instead of moving, the older woman began buckling at the knee.

"Let me." Ian reached for Grace, his hand brushing Emily's bare arm.

She pulled back.

He took hold of Grace, helped her to a seat, and gently eased her down. Bending low, he smiled at the old woman. "Hello, Aunt Grace. It's good to see you again."

She gave him a sleepy nod.

He straightened. Emily was close enough that he caught her familiar scent and their gazes locked. "Emily." He smiled. Joy leaped in his chest like a happy, dumb puppy.

Claire joined them and crouched down, level with the older woman. "Hello, Aunt Grace, I'm Claire. I'm pleased to meet you."

Heart thudding, Ian's eyes never left Emily. He reached for her hands, took them in his, and smiled.

And there it was—the look he'd been waiting for. The love shining there nearly knocked him out.

He held his breath and took in everything: the color of her eyes, the soft curve of her cheek, her lips. Leaning close, he smiled and spoke low in her ear, "Welcome home."

She gasped, eyes wide. But instead of the telltale blush, her face paled. She pulled her trembling fingers away.

Claire stepped in. "So you must be Emily. I'm Claire, Ian's sister." She shot Ian a sideways glare, then smiled at Emily. "You two must be exhausted."

Emily looked at the old woman. "Aunt Grace needs to lie down."

"Aye," Ian said. "Let's get you home, then. You can rest as long as you need." He nodded. *Not too long, I hope.*

Emily grew even paler. With a quick glance at Grace, she whispered, "Please excuse me," and hurried off.

Travel fatigue, no doubt. That trans-Atlantic flight was brutal.

"She's ill, poor girl." Claire turned to Ian, concern creasing her brow. "Should I go with her?"

"I don't know." Ian frowned, watching Emily make her way

toward the restrooms. "Let's give her a minute."

Aye. Give her some time to steady her legs and catch her breath, man. Be patient.

But the drumbeat in his chest grew into a wild jungle rhythm as Emily pressed through clusters of travelers and disappeared.

✟ ✟ ✟

Where am I? Aunt Grace?

Layers of fatigue, like blankets of lead, pressed Emily down, hampering her efforts to surface.

She needs me.

"Wheesht!"

"If ye don't go in there, lassie, I will!"

"No, Maggie. Let the poor woman have a lie-in."

Muffled female voices reached down and pulled Emily up through the heavy fog. Her eyes opened to a grayish light that filled the room at an odd angle.

"I dinna care how late in the day it is. No one goes without breakfast in *my* house."

"Och, Maggie, let her sleep."

More shushing pulled Emily's blurry gaze to the door beyond the foot of her bed, but it remained closed.

Creaky footsteps faded away.

She vaguely remembered slipping into this bed, but it had been dark then. She didn't remember this room. The long trip and deep sleep had sent her adrift. But how long ago? What day was it?

Without a clock in sight, Emily looked to her surroundings for something to anchor her, give some sense of her place in time. With clouds filtering the daylight, she couldn't tell what position the sun held in the sky.

A window across from the bed, framed by thick curtains, gave her a view of a steep, green hillside behind the house. Dense patches of evergreens and leafy trees shifted and swayed under the power of a steady breeze.

She inhaled, long and deep. A damp, earthy scent lingered, as fixed a part of the room as the furnishings. Pulling the bed covers close to her chin, she looked around the room.

An old, cushioned chair claimed the corner between the two

windows. The table next to the chair held a reading lamp and a single book, the page reserved with a pencil serving as a subtle reminder for its reader to resume. More books waited in a neat stack on the floor beside the table. At the other end of the room, a wardrobe stood near the door, and next to it, a small chest of drawers. On top of the chest were a Bible, a small box, more books, and an old, framed photo. A thick, plaid quilt covered the bed, beautifully rich in color, soft and well worn. It smelled wonderful, like—

This is Ian's room. Ian's bed.

Emily closed her eyes as the scene at the airport and the drive to the MacLeans' farm came flooding back. Her cheeks burned at the memory. She had known it would be difficult to see him face to face, and she had tried to prepare herself. Yet nothing could have prepared her for the overwhelming love she saw in his eyes and the burst of love she felt in response. She had struggled to hold it back, but lost the battle when she saw the eagerness in Ian's face, the anticipation.

The hope.

Like a panicked child, she'd fled, leaving poor Aunt Grace with Ian and Claire, barely making it to the restroom before she broke down. She had no idea how long she'd hid in the stall, struggling to pull herself together. By the time Claire came into the restroom to check on her, Ian had their bags loaded on a cart and Aunt Grace in a wheelchair, ready to go home.

Home.

The threat of tears stung her eyes and nose. She rubbed it away, pushed the warm covers off, and sat up on the edge of the bed. Her head still felt fuzzy, as though she'd been yanked up through deep water. She waited for the feeling to pass.

Her bags stood near the foot of the bed. But then—Ian had brought them upstairs for her, hadn't he? Much of their arrival was a blur. She had reached a state beyond exhaustion.

But there was one thing she did remember with clarity. When Ian had said goodnight, he'd told her there was something special he wanted to show her as soon as she was rested.

What would it be like to spend a lifetime with such a man?

159

She closed her eyes with a groan. *Why are you doing this to yourself? You know what you have to do.*

"Emily?" The voice from the hall sounded like Claire.

"Yes?"

"Are you hungry? Maggie has been keeping breakfast warm, but there's no hurry."

"Thank you. Claire?"

The door opened. Claire poked her head inside and peered at her. "What is it?"

"Is Aunt Grace up?"

"She was. She had breakfast with Maggie and now she's sleeping again."

"She's okay? I mean, how was she?"

Claire snorted. "She's a sharp, wee cookie. She and Maggie are quite the pair."

"What time is it?"

She cocked her head and studied Emily. "Mm, nearly two, I think."

That late? "Thanks. I'll be down in a minute."

"No hurry, like I said. Take your time."

Claire's footsteps creaked on the stairs.

Emily found her bag, pulled out a pair of jeans and a soft summer blouse, and dressed quickly.

How much did Claire know about her and Ian?

She searched the walls for a mirror.

No clock, no mirror.

She ran a hairbrush through her hair. A soft knock came as she slipped into her shoes.

"Coming." When she opened the door it was not Claire who greeted her, but Ian.

"Hey."

The sound of his voice, quiet and unnervingly deep, sent a tingle through her. His eyes sparkled and the hint of a smile waited at the corners of his mouth.

She tucked her hair back on one side.

"Are you rested now? I mean—did you sleep well?"

She nodded. "But I think I've taken your room."

160

The smile broke loose. "Aye. You have."

Please don't say a word about sharing your stuff with me. Without warning, tears welled up. She looked away. "Would you excuse me? I need to use the restroom."

"Right. Sorry. Lavatory's downstairs. I'll show you."

She blinked hard and followed him to the landing at the end of the hall.

Ian stepped aside to let her go down first. As she started to pass by him, he touched her arm. "Emily?"

She paused on the step, praying he wouldn't notice the tears.

"When you're ready, would you take a walk with me? Just you and me?"

Fabulous. The last thing she needed was to be alone with Ian, but then there was really no point in putting it off—he needed to know. And going for a walk with no one else around was probably best.

The sooner she ended things, the better.

She entered the kitchen and apologized for sleeping so late and causing trouble.

"Trouble? What trouble?" A deep frown creased Maggie's brow above hazy gray eyes. She huffed and puffed as she scraped away bits of goo from the pot. "Ye'll have *hot* porridge in my house and there's nothing troubling about it!" She rinsed the pot and added hot water from a kettle on the stove.

"No, really, you don't have to." Though Emily couldn't remember when she'd last eaten, there was no way she could choke anything down now. She turned to Ian, who smiled from the doorway, and then to Claire, who sat at the table marking dates on jars of jam.

"You'll never win a battle in this kitchen, Emily." Claire tossed a nod at Maggie. "Better get used to it."

Emily took a deep breath. "Thank you, Maggie, that's very kind of you. But if you don't mind, I'd just like to go check on Aunt Grace first."

Maggie spun around with a wooden spoon in hand. "I've already seen to my sister. She was up at dawn. Had a good, hearty breakfast." As she returned to her pot, she muttered, "Which she

161

sorely needed. I dinna ken what ye've been feeding her."

She thinks Grace needs better care?

"Maggie!" Ian hissed her name in warning.

"Och, it's no matter." Maggie threw a handful of oats into the boiling water. Though most of the grain made it into the pot, a healthy dusting of it landed on the floor. "*I'll* put some meat back on her wee bones."

Emily bristled but held her tongue. The old woman stirred the pot as Emily tried to think of something diplomatic to say.

"Don't listen to her, Emily," Claire said. "You've done a top job caring for Aunt Grace."

The breakfast Maggie put in front of Emily could've fed a football team.

Ian pulled out a chair at the table and straddled it beside her.

She swallowed a few bites of porridge, took a bite of a flat cake made from oats, but winced at the heap of bacon and kippers on the table.

Ian caught her eye. "You don't have to eat that." He smiled. "Well, not all of it, anyway." He leaned a little closer. "When you're ready, I'll show you to Aunt Grace's room, so you can check on her."

"Thank you."

"And then we'll take a walk."

She nodded.

And after that, things will never be the same.

CHAPTER TWENTY-ONE

As they climbed the path, a fine, cool mist filled his lungs. He couldn't wait to see her face when she saw it. God must have provided that honeysuckle glen just so Ian would be able to surround her with something she loved. His proposal couldn't fail in a place like that.

But at the tree line where the path grew steeper, Emily was not beside him.

He stopped and turned. "Sorry." He reached out to her. "Here, take my hand."

She stared at his outstretched hand, then into his eyes. She opened her mouth, but no words came.

"What's wrong?"

She drew a sharp breath, still without a word, and he knew. If it didn't matter to Emily where they had their first kiss, it certainly made no difference to him. With a hammering heart, he took a brisk step toward her and pulled her into his arms. Soft, sweet, and trembling—

"Ian ..."

He lowered his face, closed his eyes, and brought his lips close to hers.

"No, Ian, please." She gasped and pulled away.

No? He froze, pulse still racing. He sought her eyes. Not here, not like this—that was it. He hissed out a long exhale. "You're right," he said, his voice unsteady. "This isn't the place. Come on, it's not far." He took her hand and started up the path again.

She trailed in silence, her hand trembling in his.

Patience, man. Almost there. The agonizing wait was nearly over.

But his agony wouldn't end until she accepted what he had to offer.

When they reached the trail into the grove, he led her carefully through the tangle of underbrush, thick from a surge of summer growth. Ian had been through several times in the last weeks and made certain the path to the center stayed clear. "This is it, Emily. I want you to hold your breath and close your eyes."

"Hold my breath?"

"It's a surprise." He took her hand and guided her carefully along the makeshift trail. "Trust me. I've got you."

She stepped cautiously as he guided her through the brush to the grass in the center of the thicket.

"Okay now, open your eyes."

She did. At first, her gaze found him, but then she glanced beyond him, gasped, and turned round. Without a word, she kept turning until she came full circle.

"Can you smell it?"

Inhaling, she nodded. "Honeysuckle. Ian, this place is ..." Mouth agape, she turned again, taking it all in—the profusion of blossoms, the evergreen canopy overhead, the thick grass beneath. When she turned to him again, her eyes shimmered with tears. "It's so beautiful. I can't believe it. The entire place is full of honeysuckle. It's—"

"Your favorite." He smiled. "I know."

Her mouth hung open. "You do?" A tear slid down her cheek.

He took a step closer. "Aye. You and your mum."

She didn't speak, but the question in her eyes was clear enough.

It filled him with a rush of mingled pride and pleasure. "I come here often. It reminds me of you."

Her hand came up to her trembling lips. "It's incredible. Who did this?"

"I don't know." His eyes never left her face. "It may have been here forever, but I only discovered it recently."

Emily shook her head as if marveling at the sight before her. She moved to the thicket and picked a blossom, then brought it to her nose, closed her eyes, and breathed in the scent.

164

"So ..." His voice vibrated low as he moved close to her. "Do you like it?"

Without a word, she turned to him with teary eyes and nodded.

"Good, because I could think of no better place for this." He reached down and took both of her hands in his. "Emily." He cleared his throat and stared at their joined hands, sorting through the words that he'd been rehearsing in his mind. "I want you to know that something miraculous has happened." He drew in a deep breath and lifted his eyes to meet hers. "I haven't always been the man you think I am. For too long, I was weak, bitter, and faithless. But even though I shut God out, He didn't leave me. He helped me do something I believed was impossible. I prayed for Edward, like you said. I still do. I don't know what will happen to him, but I believe *I* was the one who needed those prayers. As I prayed for Edward, God changed me. The hate that consumed me has faded. I have only compassion for him now, and that's a miracle. God helped me to forgive. And He ..." A lump formed in his throat, lodging tight. He frowned at their hands, fighting to keep his voice steady. "He's forgiven me too."

"That's wonderful, Ian," she whispered.

Ian looked into her eyes. "Emily, I thought I'd be chained to that hate for the rest of my life. But those chains fell away. I'm free."

Her glistening eyes darkened.

"I'm free to be a good husband and a good father, and—" He had to lower his voice to keep it from breaking. "I'm free to be the good man you believe I am."

Though her expression didn't change, more tears filled her eyes.

Perhaps she worried that he still held some bitterness. He squeezed her hands. "It's okay, Emily. I'm a changed man. I truly am. God did that. Thanks to you."

"Ian, I—"

"I love you, Emily. With everything in me. You brought my heart back to life, and I'm offering it to you. Forever."

"Please, Ian," she whispered, her voice catching. She wiped the tears slipping down her face. "I need to tell you something."

A terrible tingle climbed his spine.

Trembling, she turned away and pressed her tightly folded arms against her stomach. "I can't ... I can't be there for you the way I wish I could."

"Be where? Emily, I want to marry you. I want to give you a home and a family and everything you—"

"Ian, I can't marry you." Her voice shook. She turned back to him.

All he could do was stare at her face. The echo of her words slapped at his ears like a loose sail in a storm. "*Can't?* What do you mean, you *can't?*"

"Because I ..." She closed her eyes and inhaled slowly.

Ian caught a sharp breath and held his tongue.

"It turns out that I don't have very long to live."

The phrase struck like an icy boulder in the center of his chest, stupefying him. Her words echoed round and round in his head.

"I only just found out for sure. I never would have gotten so close to you if I'd known."

It wasn't true. It couldn't be.

No, no, no!

But her eyes, dark with grief, did not lie. She wiped her eyes and cheeks again. "What my mom had is hereditary. My mom and my grandmother both died in their thirties." She drew a shuddering breath. "And more than likely, so will I."

She shouldn't have run, shouldn't have left him stricken like that. But she couldn't stay. As she answered his questions about the disease, the full weight of her news seemed to hit him, doubling him over.

And, like a coward, she'd run.

Blinded by tears and stumbling over bumps in the path, she kept running down the trail that would lead her back to the house. But she couldn't outrun the image of Ian, so full of hope one minute, doubled over the next like a man who had taken a blow to the gut.

I want to marry you. I want to give you a home and a family and everything—

166

Ignoring the slap of passing branches, Emily ran down the hill through the woods and out into a clearing on the hillside overlooking the farm. When the house came into view, she slowed her steps.

Unhindered by trees, the sky appeared in sullen shades of gray that blocked the sun, draping a shadow like a dull shroud over the house and grounds.

Coward!

Panting, she pressed on. The path took her to a gate leading to the grounds surrounding the house. She passed through the gate, but, instead of going toward the house, she followed the path to some small buildings behind the house. One of them, an ancient woodshed, offered a temporary sanctuary, a place she could let the anguish out.

You encouraged his heart to take a chance, then you crushed it.

Emily stumbled into the shed and burst into tears. She laid folded arms against a stack of firewood and pressed her face into them. Bitter sorrow flowed hard from deep within. She tried to breathe, taking in short, shuddering breaths, but couldn't fill her lungs between the sobs.

Minutes later, or perhaps hours, she turned around and leaned back against the woodpile. She pressed her arms tight against her stomach to break the clenching spasms, to somehow ease the pain. A few slow, deep breaths helped to calm the sobs a little as she wiped her eyes.

Ian's face was so clear in her mind, so full of hope.

And then her dad's face came to mind, grim and hardened by pain and loss.

Would that happen to Ian now?

Tears continued to gather and fall. She tried taking another deep breath, but the sobs regained strength. Her legs wobbled and she slumped to the base of the woodpile.

"Well?" Claire's voice.

Emily covered her mouth.

"No use hiding—I saw you pop in there." Her cheery voice carried from outside as it drew closer. "It makes no difference to me if you two fancy the privacy of the woodshed over the house. I just want to be the first to hear the—" Claire rounded the corner and stopped in the doorway when she saw Emily. Frowning, she scanned the shed. "Where's Ian?"

Emily whispered, "I don't know." She turned away and gave her cheeks a brisk wipe.

"Are you crying?"

The more people knew, the harder it would be on Ian. *Please, God. I don't want to tell her.*

"What happened? I thought you and Ian ..."

Emily squeezed her swollen eyes closed. Ian must have told her he was planning to propose. Who else knew? More people would be hurt.

"What's going on?" Claire came closer and crouched to Emily's level. "Did Ian do something to upset you? The big ox. I'll straighten him out. What did he do?"

"No." Emily shook her head, sniffling. "Ian didn't do anything wrong."

Frowning, Claire studied her for several long seconds. "What is it then?"

Emily pulled in a deep breath. "Ian asked me to marry him." Her voice dropped to a pained whisper. "And I refused."

"You refused?" Claire's tone turned sharp, eyebrows furrowing above dark eyes.

A new rush of tears threatened. Emily turned away from Claire's scrutiny.

"Where is he?"

"I'm not sure," Emily whispered.

"Weren't you with him?"

Emily turned back and met a piercing gaze.

Claire stared at her and then snapped a look out the shed door. When she faced Emily again, her eyes flickered with intensity. "Ian loves you. Why would you refuse him? Is this some kind of game?"

"No."

Claire's red head tilted at a sharper angle. "Do you love him?"

Emily wiped her eyes, swallowing the burning constriction in her throat. "Yes."

Claire shook her head. "Emily, I never meddle in my brother's business, but there's something you should know about Ian. When he lost Katy, it crushed him. For years, he was a very empty, broken man. It killed me to see him like that." Her voice cracked. "I was afraid he'd never love again. Then, by some miracle, something changed. The Ian I once knew came back, full of life and hope. And love. It was because of you, Emily. I'm dead certain of that."

"Claire, please." Quivering, she fought hard to keep from breaking down. She could only speak in a whisper. "Believe me, I never wanted to hurt him."

The fire in Claire's eyes flashed hotter. "But that's what you're doing. You'll break his heart all over again." She leaned close. "You'd better have an incredibly good reason for doing that."

Her tone sent Emily's heart racing. "I have no choice." Her throat cinched up so tight, she could barely force the words out. "I'm dying."

✦✦✦

With hands braced on his knees, Ian caught his breath, heart still hammering from his break-neck sprint from the glen to the old cemetery.

But the cold, vacant church offered him no sanctuary, no relief. No answers.

How was it possible? Again? It had to be a dream. No—a nightmare. Emily dying? She was young and caring, full of life, with dreams of a loving family—a dream shattered before it had a chance to begin.

Just like Katy.

Ian had no idea where Emily went after she left him. All he knew was when the gut-wrenching spasm released him and he could stand up straight, she was gone.

He sucked in a deep breath, stood, and walked over to Katy's grave. Lush, vibrant green grass surrounded the gravestone. The trees around the vacant church burst with life, thick with summer foliage and trilling bird song in tediously cheerful rounds.

Pressed by an unseen weight, Ian dropped to his knees, landing at the place where the tall grass had been worn flat from his prayers for Edward. He took another deep breath. The pungent scent of heather and pine stung his nose. "God ..."

What? What would he ask God to do? Take this from her? Like he'd asked for Katy?

Ian still couldn't believe it was true. But he also couldn't ignore the look on her face in the glen, how hard she fought for control as she answered all his questions and explained more than once about her mom and grandmother, her uncle's test, her dad knowing all along, and her research. And how it wasn't curable.

Why Emily?

Hadn't she always been faithful? Selfless? Forgiving? Hadn't she honored a father who didn't deserve it? Didn't that add years to one's life?

Apparently not. Katy had honored her father too.

He traced a finger over the words etched in cold stone and a flood of images rushed back—Katy's nausea, her restlessness turning to lethargy, how quickly she had slipped away.

Sorrow pressed him, squeezing the air from his chest. All the old feelings returned. The ache that diminished but never went away. That ever-present shadow—a quiet reminder that she was gone but not gone. Always with him, but forever out of reach. And the gnawing regret over the choices he'd made, choices that cost him precious time with her.

Katy's illness had sprung from the shadows without warning. And now Emily faced a similar fate. But she could have been warned. She might have made different choices if she'd been told about her grand inheritance. Why had her father kept silent? He could have spared her.

You mean he could have spared you.

Ian stared at Katy's gravestone. "God, why do You do miracles for some but leave others to suffer? It's not right. You let good ones die young, like Katy and Emily's mum. And now Emily." He raised his face to the sky. "They don't deserve it. But even though I turned my back on You, You did a miracle in me. Why?" Angry tears clogged his throat. "Why me and not them?"

Silence.

"Why are You doing this?"

Birds took flight as his voice boomed across the meadow and faded away. In the stillness, his friend Janet's calm, quiet voice drifted across his thoughts, repeating the words she'd said to him countless times: *Faith believes God is good, not just when things are going your way, but in the midst of tragedy.*

"Good? I'd like to see You prove that," he whispered. "Spare Emily."

Like God had spared Katy?

Ian sprang up and paced among the gravestones, kicking at loose rocks. A small, pointed rock flew up and hit one of the engraved stones. Crouching low, he picked it up and stared at the jagged edges. He closed his hand around it and squeezed until it dug in, sending sharp, stabbing pain. Anger blinded him. He rubbed his eyes with the heel of his hand and studied the gravestones.

Inscribed with names and dates, they marked the length of different lives. Some long, some short. Perhaps God gathered up the best ones for Himself.

"Is that it then? Are You just some selfish, old man?"

Ian didn't really expect an answer to that, and he didn't get one. Nothing but cheery twitters and the brisk, lively smells of summer carried on a mild breeze.

"I'm done here." Ian stood and turned to go, but a surge of adrenaline seized him. He spun round and hurled the jagged rock as hard as he could. The rock hit the silent, old church with a clean *thwack*. The sound echoed, briefly silencing the bird song.

Blind fury drove him back to the darkening trail through the woods.

CHAPTER TWENTY-TWO

Later that evening, Maggie and Grace chuckled in the kitchen over tea, but Emily wavered between the kitchen and the sitting room, her nerves cinching up more with every passing minute.

No one had seen Ian since she left him in the honeysuckle grove. Until he returned, all Emily could do was wait, anxious to know if he was okay. The empty sitting room had grown dark, but she didn't want to go to the kitchen and disturb Grace and Maggie's conversation. Nor did she want to go upstairs and miss Ian's entrance. Out of the two, she chose interrupting the women.

Maggie's voice rattled Emily as she entered the kitchen. "—a wee rickle o' bones, Grace. What do ye feed her?"

"Emmy's a good lass. Always running, running. But she takes such good care of everything."

"Humph."

Emily joined them with a thin smile.

"Here ye are, dearie." Grace pushed a scone Emily's way. "Have some tea."

"Aye," Maggie said. "Ye're too peely-wally."

It had been hours since she'd forced down a few bites of Maggie's porridge. Though her stomach roiled at the thought of food, she needed something. She reached for the scone and took a bite.

Maggie sniffed an empty teacup and squinted into it, then filled it from the teapot, dribbling tea down the side. She offered it to Emily.

"Has he gone back to England now?" Grace asked.

"Who?" A frown creased Maggie's brow.

"Ian." Grace turned to Emily, smiling. "Have ye met Maggie's grandson, dearie?"

The scone suddenly felt like sand in her mouth. What was that about him going to England?

"No, I dinna ken where he's off to today," Maggie said around a mouthful of scone. "Now that ye're home, I don't care a wee pickle if he stays or goes."

Was Maggie serious? It was so hard to tell.

"Ian was very kind to us when he came to the beach, wasn't he, Emmy?"

"Mm-hmm." She sipped tea to wash down the scone.

"Will he be back for dinner?" Grace asked.

Maggie scowled. "Aye. He always comes round when there's food." She set her cup down with a rattle and leaned close to Grace. "Let's take a Sunday drive, eh, Gracie? Just like the old days."

Emily gasped. "Drive? You mean, just the two of you?"

"Aye." The glee in Maggie's raspy chuckle matched her grin. "Dinna concern yerself, lassie."

Emily took a deep breath and let it out slowly. "Isn't it a little late for a drive?" *And aren't you legally blind?*

Maggie turned to Grace. "Come on. Before he comes back."

Oh, Lord, this is not good. Not good at all.

Clearly, Maggie would not be easily dissuaded. Emily didn't think she could tell the older woman what to do, but there was no way Grace was getting into a vehicle with Maggie. Neither one belonged behind the wheel.

Emily forced a smile. "If there's room for me, I'd love to join you." It was a gamble.

Maggie grunted.

"Ooh, aye," Grace said to Emily. "But not tonight, dearie. I'm feeling a bit done in."

Maggie glowered and reached for the teapot. "Tomorrow, then. If Ian stays away."

If Ian stays away.

That might make things easier on both of them, but it meant she wouldn't know for sure if he was okay. It also meant Emily would need to keep a sharp eye on Maggie.

Monday began with bright sunshine and still no sign of Ian. By late morning, Emily couldn't take it any longer. She went outside and headed down the drive. As she neared the cottage, a car turned off the main road and climbed the drive. Emily stepped off the road and onto the grass.

Ian's sister waved as she passed with a wagonload of kids. They continued up the slope and parked next to the house.

Emily trekked back up the drive.

Two teenaged boys and two younger girls piled out of the car, all staring at her.

Claire hollered out a hello.

"Hi, Claire." Emily said. "Is this your family?"

Claire smiled. "Aye. All but Davy. He's working."

The kids continued to stare.

"That's Jack and Douglas," Claire said, pointing at her sons. "Boys, go find your grannie."

The younger boy held Emily in rapt fascination. The other one grabbed his brother's arm and towed him into the house.

"And this is Kallie, who's eight, and this is Hannah."

"I'm five." Hannah demonstrated with her fingers, then plastered herself to her mother's thigh.

Emily held out a hand to each of the girls, smiling. "I'm very pleased to meet you."

Hannah studied Emily from head to toe, her brown eyes wide. "You're beautiful," she said. "Are you a princess?"

Kallie groaned and rolled her eyes. "Och! That's all she ever talks about. She's going to meet a princess. She's going to *be* a princess. She's going to marry a prince." She aimed a glare at her sister.

"Och, Kallie, let your sister dream," Claire said. "It wasn't that long ago all you ever talked about was being a pirate."

Emily met Hannah's gaze. "It's good to have a dream, Hannah. I think you'd make an excellent princess."

A broad smile lit the girl's face. She reached for Emily's hand and led her to the house.

Kallie darted ahead.

Inside, the boys stood over the counter gobbling down

174

whatever Maggie had piled in a heap for breakfast.

"Och! Where are your manners, boys?" Claire said. "Say hello to Emily. She's here from the States."

The older one quickly swallowed a large mouthful, brushed off his hands, and offered one to Emily. "Hello. I'm Jack." His voice seemed strangely deep for a teenager. "Pleased to meet you."

Hannah giggled.

The younger boy stepped forward, brushing Jack aside. "I'm Douglas. Hello." His voice was even deeper.

Kallie frowned at her brothers. "What's wrong with you two? You sound funny."

"Who's that?" Maggie's voice carried in from the back hall. "Jack? Dougie? Are ye staying for dinner, then?" Maggie emerged with two buckets overflowing with berries.

"Is that for pie?" Jack's eyes widened. "Ah, Grannie, I love you."

Maggie scoffed. "Of course it's for pie. But not till after supper. Ye lads run out and get a hen for me."

"I'll do it." Kallie whipped out a wicked-looking dagger from her pocket.

A second later, Emily realized it was plastic.

"Where's Uncle Ian?" Douglas asked. "I want to go fishing."

"Me too." Kallie put her dagger away.

Douglas threw his sister a glare. "*You* can't go. Just us men." He glanced at Emily. "And her, if she fancies."

Maggie frowned. "I dinna ken where Ian is. Go upstairs and get Granddad Liam's pole."

Douglas disappeared, followed by Jack. In spite of the thunder of feet on the stairs, Douglas's loud whisper reached the kitchen. "Did you see the way she smiled at me?"

"I want to see Uncle Ian too," Hannah said. "He said we could draw more pictures next time." She smiled up at Emily. "This *is* next time. Actually, he draws and I color them in."

He's drawing again? Something warm rose up inside of Emily. "I'll bet you're an excellent artist, Hannah."

"I'd like to see Ian too." Claire aimed a questioning look at Emily. "Is he here?"

Aunt Grace appeared in the doorway. When she saw the little girls, a wide smile brightened her face. "Och, bless me! Who are these bonnie lassies?"

As her aunt took a seat at the table and met the girls, Emily spoke quietly to Claire. "Ian hasn't been back, not to the house anyway."

The house shook as footsteps thundered down the stairs, growing louder until Jack and Douglas burst through the narrow kitchen doorway simultaneously.

"Is there a storm?" Grace asked. "Ooh, I love to watch storms."

Claire's hands flew to her hips. "Whoa there, lads, where's the fire?"

"Got it." Douglas shouldered his brother aside and crossed the kitchen, fishing pole in hand.

"Come on, then," Jack said with a grin. "Last one to the burn digs the bait." He disappeared down the hall toward the back door.

Douglas ran after him yelling, "I have the pole! I'm not digging worms too!"

Emily offered to get breakfast for Aunt Grace, but she insisted on doing it herself. After everyone had finished eating, Claire, Maggie, Grace, and Emily pitched in to clean up the kitchen, then went outside with the girls.

The women walked along the edge of the berry field, talking as the girls tried to catch chickens, until the boys returned saying they'd found Ian.

Claire frowned. "He didn't take you fishing, then?"

Jack set the fishing pole down and stood with hands on his hips. "All he wants to do is cut down trees."

"Trees?" Grace asked.

"Aye, for firewood."

Claire frowned at the boys. "You should've stayed and helped him."

"Ma, we tried to help but he didn't want us. He had enough for three winters already, but he wouldn't stop."

"He told us to go fishing without him." Douglas looked glum.

Emily's heart sank.

Maggie muttered some remark about how a bit of hard work

176

would have done the lads some good.

"He asked if the ladies needed anything." Jack shot a glance at Emily. "And he says sorry if he caused any worry."

"Worry?" Maggie snorted. "We're not worried, are we, Grace?"

Aunt Grace smiled. "Ooh, no. They'll catch loads of fish. I'm not worried."

"He can cut down the entire forest as long as he's back for dinner." With a grunt, Maggie shuffled toward the house. "Aye, he'll be back. He always comes round when I cook. Always poking his big nose in it, no matter what it is."

"Not this time." Jack shook his head. "He said not to wait for him." He plucked a berry from a nearby vine and popped it in his mouth. "You won't be seeing Uncle Ian today."

CHAPTER TWENTY-THREE

Tuesday morning, Ian hooked the wood trailer to the tractor, towed it up into the woods, and loaded the pine logs he'd felled the day before. He should have brought the trailer with him in the first place. No matter. At the time, he wasn't thinking about anything but knocking something down.

Repeatedly.

The day before, when he grabbed the chainsaw and fuel can and stormed into the woods, all he wanted was to cut and keep cutting until he ran out of trees. Or petrol. But even if he had an endless supply of fuel and a blade that never dulled, he could have leveled an entire hillside and still not spent his anger or his grief.

Once he filled the trailer with as many logs as it would hold, he hauled the load back down to the farm and stopped at the clearing behind the woodshed. He pulled a log from the trailer and braced it on the cutting blocks. With the chainsaw, he cut it into stove lengths and continued cutting, one log after another. The process was simple, mindless, and repetitive. Not too hard, but enough effort to produce a burn, keep his blood pumping, work up a sweat. Besides, it had to be done. Winter was inevitable. He needed to prepare.

Where would she be when winter came?

Not here. Not curled up next to me and a blazing fire.

He yanked the next log off the stack so hard it rolled away and smacked into the shed. As he brought it back to the blocks, he saw Emily's face and remembered the way she paled as he blethered on with his proposal. He could still hear the tremble in her voice when she told him she couldn't be there for him.

So like Emily. Her future was collapsing in front of her and she was thinking of *him*.

178

He braced the log, jerked the cord, and cut the wood to pieces.

Look at the birds of the air; they do not sow or reap or store away in barns, and yet your heavenly Father feeds them. Are you not much more valuable than they?

"I'm not listening to You." Maybe saying it aloud would discourage any more unwanted input. "I don't fancy Your way of taking care of things."

The way things were turning out, it seemed God had a nomad's life in mind for Ian after all. When old Maggie was dead and buried, he would leave this place. Travel as he had before.

Alone.

As he worked, he kept seeing Emily, her eyes darkened by pain, tears streaking her face.

Who would be with her when she got sick? Grace? Her dad?

A numbing heaviness settled in his chest and spread out in waves, turning his arms to deadwood. The next log didn't come off the trailer as easily as the others had.

"Ah, I see I'm just in time. Can I lend you a hand, Ian?"

Ian propped the log against the trailer and turned round.

Reverend Brown already had his jacket off and was rolling up his shirtsleeves as he climbed the sloped yard to where Ian worked. The grey-haired man offered a bony, outstretched hand as he approached.

Ian pulled off a work glove and gave him a firm handshake. "You're not exactly dressed for wood sap and motor oil." Ian put his glove back on.

Reverend Brown let out a laugh. "I'm not, am I? I should know by now when visiting the farms in my parish to come prepared to work."

"No need for that." Ian walked to the side of the shed, took the cart, and wheeled it back to the pile. "You have enough work as it is. Checking up on absent parishioners must be a tiresome job."

The reverend laughed again, an easy, good-natured laugh. "Aye. We did miss seeing you and Maggie on Sunday. You're quick, Ian."

"So are you." Ian tossed a chunk of wood into the cart. "It's only Tuesday."

Another hearty laugh. "I hope Maggie's not unwell?"

"No. She's strong as a mule. In more ways than one."

That got a knowing smile out of the reverend.

"We have visitors," Ian said. "They arrived from the States late Saturday night. They needed their sleep, so we stayed home Sunday." He frowned.

That's why Emily had been so quiet at the airport. It wasn't jet lag that had her so shaken. She was distressed about telling him. Worried about how he would take her news.

"Maggie's sister, isn't it? I'd heard she and her niece were coming to visit."

"Aye." Ian continued to load the cart.

Reverend Brown stooped and picked up a piece that must have been heavier than he expected, by the look of the veins bulging in his neck.

"Ah, don't soil your clothes, Reverend. I can manage, really."

The minister had already broken into a sweat. He hoisted the piece of wood into the cart with a grunt and smiled. "'Two are better than one. They have a good return for their work.'"

Ian eyed the frail man with a sideways glance. Sometimes a "good return" wasn't the point. He reached down for another piece. "Sounds like a sermon."

"Aye, 'tis. But it was written by a much wiser man than I. It goes on. 'If one falls down, his friend can help him up. But pity the man who falls and has no one to help.'"

Ian tossed the chunk into the cart. "If a man falls, he'll get up on his own—eventually."

"Perhaps. If nothing is broken." The reverend smiled. "Then it says, 'If two lie down together, they'll keep warm. But how can one keep warm alone?'" He reached for another piece and lugged it up to top the load with a grunt. Resting his hands on the last piece, he looked Ian in the eye. "'And a cord of three strands is not quickly broken.'"

Ian hoisted the handles and wheeled the cart into the woodshed.

"I hope to see you next Sunday," the reverend said as he followed, still huffing. "Gathering together, hearing God's word, praying for each other—that keeps our faith strong. We make two good strands when we're all together, holding one another up. And two out of three, it's not bad. It's far better than one."

Inside the shed, Ian unloaded the wood and stacked the pieces against the wall.

The reverend strained with the lifting of each chunk, but he kept a steady pace, sweating as he passed the pieces to Ian. The man didn't say much. He couldn't.

They worked a while longer in silence, but the sermon would certainly resume once the cart was empty. At this rate, it could take the man days to recover and finish making his point.

Ian heaved a sigh. "And the third strand?"

The reverend chuckled. "I'll wager one of your grannie's pies you already know what that is. And perhaps you also know that when you have all three ..." The man swiped his brow with a rolled-up sleeve, hollow temples pulsing. "There's not a thing a man can't do."

Ian stopped and studied him.

The minister was about the frailest man he had ever met. But in that moment, his face beamed with more confidence than the strongest of men.

The reverend handed the last chunk of wood to Ian. "It's been good seeing you so regular at kirk these last few weeks."

With a grunt, Ian chucked the piece to the top of the pile.

Reverend Brown wiped his hands with a handkerchief. "Will you be there next Sunday then? With your family?"

Family. Ian lifted the cart handles, then wheeled it out of the shed and back to the trailer. "I don't know."

"Are they here now?" Reverend Brown called out from behind. "Maggie and the others?"

Ian set the cart down near the cutting blocks. "Aye."

"I'd like to meet them. I need to return your grannie's pie plate." He smiled. "No doubt I'll see it filled again soon. Good to see you, Ian. The Lord bless you." He shook Ian's hand again and walked down to the house.

Ian stared at the empty cart.

Winter would come. There was no stopping it, no avoiding it.

If two lie down together, they will keep warm. But how can one

181

keep warm alone?

He braced the log and reached for the saw, but stopped and stared at the blade, already coated in shavings and beginning to dull. His shock and anger over Emily's news had given way to pain. He supposed the next step—according to the laws of nature or some such rubbish—was to accept what Emily said about dying and let her go.

But even if he could find a way to accept it, it wouldn't change the way he felt about her. Her shadowy future did nothing to lessen his feelings. In fact, the longer he wrestled with the reality of her fate, the deeper his love for her grew.

Was he supposed to simply forget her? Leave her to die on her own?

He knew exactly what she feared on his behalf. But Emily Chapman should not have to face the winter of her life alone.

And she wouldn't—not if Ian MacLean had a scrap of strength in him.

CHAPTER TWENTY-FOUR

By Tuesday, it had become clear that Emily needed to get used to the breakfast-time chaos if she was going to survive the remaining weeks in Scotland. Maggie argued with Grace about every little thing as she made some kind of bread, flour flying everywhere. Grace answered back with a bright, steady smile as she stirred a boiling pot over an old, black cookstove. Emily tried to help, but as an "alien," she was only allowed to watch and learn.

The buzz of a chainsaw drifted in through the window from time to time.

Ian.

Emily let out a quiet sigh. At least he was near and she could assume he was okay. But it also meant he would be coming inside eventually.

Would seeing her be hard for him? Maybe he intended to stay away from the house for the rest of their stay. Which wasn't fair to him. He shouldn't have to avoid his own home.

The sooner she left this place, returned to America, and immersed herself in Freyer's research, the better for them both.

"No, Grace. *I* did all the cooking." Maggie flung a handful of flour onto the counter, kneaded a blob of dough into a circle, and smacked it with a rolling pin. "Ye never lifted a wee finger to cook."

"Och!" Grace chuckled. "I tried but ye never let me near the kitchen."

"Humph. Yer memory fails ye." Maggie slapped the dough rounds onto a baking pan.

"Thomas fancies my cooking."

All that got out of Maggie was a snort. She groped the oven

183

door, leaving streaks of flour along the dark handle, opened it, and slid a pan of rolls inside.

"This porridge is very strange." Grace stopped stirring and peered into the pot.

Emily was not at all sure she wanted to look. "What's wrong?"

"It looks like water." Grace frowned.

With a grunt, Maggie heaved a metal canister from the counter, then shuffled over to the stove. "Because it *is* water, ye daftie."

Emily winced, but Grace only chuckled.

While Aunt Grace continued to stir, Maggie tossed handfuls of oats into the boiling pot. One handful missed and scattered all over the floor.

"I'll clean that up," Emily said. "Where's the broom?"

"Wheesht, lassie." Maggie shoved the oat can across the counter. "If ye want to be of use, go to the mudroom and get a jar of heather honey for the baps."

Emily headed down the hall toward the mudroom. Would she know heather honey when she saw it?

When she reached the end of the hall, the back door opened.

Her heart raced, sending adrenaline like needles along her nerves.

But it was an extremely thin, gray-haired man who entered.

Emily stepped aside to let him in.

Just as he closed the door behind him, a small, brown blur scurried past his feet and darted around in the hall, then ran straight toward Emily.

She plastered herself against the hall coat rack.

The feathery blur squawked and ricocheted down the hall and into the kitchen.

"Och! Here now! What's this?" Maggie's voice rose above the squawking.

Emily peeked around the doorway and then entered the kitchen.

The man followed, stepping around the chicken, which had, by that time, discovered the oats on the floor.

Maggie held out a broom to Emily. "Reverend Brown. 'Tis about time ye showed yerself. This is my sister, Grace. That's

Emily. And that hen," she said, pointing a knobby finger at a small, brown footstool, "can go back outside till it's plucked and ready for the soup pot."

The reverend reached out to shake Emily's hand. "I'm pleased to meet—"

The chicken darted between their feet and made a sudden attempt at flight.

The man jumped back.

"Broom, lassie!"

Emily took the broom from Maggie. "You want me to sweep now?"

"For the bird, ye daftie!"

"Can I do something to help?" The reverend kept a wary eye on the chicken.

"Aye. Ye can start preaching. When the bird falls asleep, we'll toss it back out where it came from."

The man only laughed.

Emily tried to shoo the bird through the doorway with the broom, but the chicken darted around it and continued to peck at the oats.

Grace tapped her wooden spoon against the pot and turned with a smile for the reverend. "It was so kind of ye to bring us a chicken. Will ye be staying for dinner?"

"Chicken? Ah, no, thank you. I've come to say we missed you on Sunday, Maggie. I hoped you weren't ill. But then I learned your visitors had arrived. I hope to see you all in kirk before you return home."

"Och, 'tis no visit." Maggie wiped her floury hands on her apron. "Grace is here to stay."

"What?" Emily stared at Maggie.

"Did ye bring back my pie pot, Reverend?" The old woman went on without missing a beat. "Ye'll not have another pie till ye return it."

"Are ye the new minister then?" Grace asked.

"Aye. And I have brought back your pot, Maggie, just as you asked."

"Reverend, have ye met my nephew, Ian?" Grace smiled.

185

"He's such a kind lad. But I've not seen him since our picnic at the beach."

"Grace!" Maggie huffed. "Are ye daft? Ian brought ye home from the airport three days ago. Do ye not remember now?"

Grace frowned.

Emily watched her aunt for signs she might be getting flustered. If she had a memory lapse, it would only make her confusion—and her embarrassment—worse. "We were so tired when we arrived," Emily offered in a rush. "We barely noticed anything, did we?"

Grace didn't answer.

Emily swept the oats into a pile but continued to watch her aunt in case she started to drift.

The chicken flapped its wings, scattering the oats.

"I have met Ian," the reverend said, eyes still trained on the fowl. "Actually, I was speaking to him just before I came in."

"You saw him? Just now?" Had anyone noticed how anxious she sounded?

"Aye. He's cutting wood behind the shed." The reverend dove suddenly, snatched the chicken, and stood up, holding it out at arm's length with a triumphant smile. "Got it."

"Thank you," Emily said. "I'll get the door for you." She turned to escort him and the bird outside, nearly bumping into the figure of a man in the doorway. "Ian!" She caught her breath, heart racing.

"So he's back then?" Maggie asked. "Well, laddie, ye've decided to honor us with yer presence. And wanting breakfast too, no doubt. Humph. I dinna ken what ye've been eating out there, footerin' about on the braes." Maggie grunted and went to work getting him a plate.

"Ian, ye're back from the beach!" Grace said. "How was it?"

His eyes never left Emily's. "Breathtaking."

She didn't remember his voice ever sounding so deep.

Behind her, the captive fowl made a long, cawing sound.

The reverend hopped toward the doorway with the bird held out as far as his stiff arms would allow. "Pardon me, but I believe this chicken needs to ..."

Ian stepped aside for the man and bird, his expression growing more intense. "Emily, I need to talk to you."

Emily held her breath.

Stunned silence filled the room. No doubt the others were watching her and Ian.

"Will you take a walk with me?"

Whatever he had to say, it obviously couldn't wait.

Ian motioned for her to lead the way down the hall.

Once they were out back, she turned to him, but he kept walking.

"This way," he said, voice low. He guided her along the path away from the house, toward the berry field.

Emily stole a glance at his profile. His expression was hard to read, his attention fixed straight ahead.

He continued in silence. When they reached the fence, Ian stopped and turned to her. His chest rose and fell in a deep, rapid rhythm. He seemed to be struggling for words.

A pang tugged at her heart. *Oh, Lord, please. Don't let him suffer any more, please.*

"I'm sorry, Emily. For what you're facing, for staying away so long. For everything. Please forgive me."

"No, Ian," she whispered, fighting to get the words past the sudden tightness in her throat. "Please don't, you don't need to—"

Ian pulled her into his arms and held her.

Emily closed her eyes, overwhelmed by an unexpected rush of relief. As he held her, she let herself sink into him, suddenly aware of how much she'd ached for this.

He pulled her closer and stroked her hair. "I'm here, Emily. Don't shut me out." His lips brushed her forehead. "I want to spend my life with you, no matter what happens, no matter how long. I'll be there for you."

His words, deep with emotion, sent a tremor through her. There was a reason she shouldn't agree, but at that moment, she had no idea what it was.

His face nuzzled her hair and he inhaled as if taking in every nuance.

The strength of his arms around her and his solemn words

187

worked like a sedative, releasing a sense of calm through her, and she felt herself relax for the first time in days. "Ian—"

"I know what you're afraid of, but I'll be strong. For us both."

Maybe ...

"I love you," he whispered. "Do you love me?"

She nodded.

With a shuddering sigh, he held her tighter. "And you trust me?"

She wanted to see what was in his eyes. When she lifted her face, his lips came down firmly against hers.

In a blinding flash, everything else disappeared.

Her eyes closed as every nerve thrilled with joy at the kiss, the scent and nearness of him, the feel of him, the warmth of his breath. Her lips yielded and pressed into his. Something burst from deep within her, something powerful and new, surging through her like the sudden rush of water from a broken dam.

When their lips parted, she opened her eyes.

He kissed her again, firm and insistent, so full of love and passion and promise. So right. It was as if her soul were melting into his.

Something in the back of her mind tugged at her, tugged hard.

"Wait." She pulled back. It took huge effort, but she tore herself from his embrace and stumbled back a few steps.

"No." Shaking his head, he took a step, closing the gap. "No waiting. I don't want to make the same mistake again. Time is too precious to waste." His voice grew deeper with each word. "Marry me, Emily. Tomorrow. No—today! The minister is here now—"

"Ian, please."

He cupped her face in both hands and kissed her again, his lips seeking hers with such intensity, almost desperation.

Instinctively, Emily reached up and caressed his face.

A moan rumbled from his throat. He slipped a hand behind her head, crushing her lips to his.

Her quickened breathing raced with her pounding heart. *Lord, I love him more than anything, but ...*

Her dad's anguished face came to mind, how he had changed after her mom's death, going from a passionate, caring man to a bitter, tormented one. *If you love Ian, how could you even think of doing that to him?*

She tore herself away. Her breath came in short bursts. "I'm sorry." With every backward step she took, pain ripped through her at the thought of hurting him again. "I can't do that to you. I'm so sorry."

His chest rose and fell with every breath as his dark eyes bored into hers. "Why?"

"You know why. You have no future with me. You get nothing. No family. Nothing but more grief." Tears blurred her vision, clogged her throat. "You have a chance to make a fresh start now. I won't let you throw that away."

He clasped her shoulders with both hands. "I *am* making a start—with you. We'll go through it together. All of it."

She tingled at the strength in his grasp, but shook her head. "You saw what it did to my dad. There's no way I could ever—"

"I'm not your dad." He squeezed her shoulders harder. "Emily, you've got to trust me."

She pulled out of his reach and wiped her cheek with the heel of her hand. "My dad turned away from God and everyone else. I couldn't stand for that happen to you, especially after—"

"After what?" Ian planted his hands on his hips. "Aye, my faith has been weak. Is that what you're afraid of?"

Is it?

"Do you doubt me, Emily? Or do you doubt God?"

"I don't know." Unable to meet the intensity of his gaze, she looked away. "But I know I can't let you give up the life you wanted, the family—"

"That's not important."

"Yes, it is." She looked into his eyes. "It's as important to you as it is to me."

He shook his head slowly, but his expression grew less certain.

"You've suffered so much loss already. Maybe you don't think so now, but—"

"No." His face was a battlefield of emotions. "I know it won't be easy, but that's just it. I *know* what to expect. I'm not letting you go through this alone." He reached for her shoulders again. "I love

189

you, Emily. Whatever I face later will be worth it to see you happy."

"Happy?" Her voice broke. "I've seen exactly what loss and grief does to a man, Ian. How could I be happy knowing I'm doing that to you?" She grimaced at the mental picture of her dad and shook her head. "Please don't ask me to do that."

Ian's gaze fell to her lips. "Emily, couldn't we just—"

"I'm sorry, Ian." She took several steps back. "I shouldn't have ... I'm so sorry." She turned and ran.

"Emily!"

She aimed for the house. But when she reached the back door, she passed it and kept running.

CHAPTER TWENTY-FIVE

Over the next two days, Emily hung around the house and kept an eye on Maggie and Grace. But baking and strolling and chatting over tea did nothing to expend her growing restlessness. With three weeks of their visit remaining, she needed an occupation. And soon. Because even though she'd managed to avoid seeing Ian, she couldn't stop thinking about him and the things he'd said to her out by the berry field.

And that kiss.

Thursday afternoon, the urge to run consumed her. She laced up her shoes and headed out. Just a light jog, she told herself, a slow pace until she got her bearings. And until she saw a doctor and had a better idea of how hard she should be pushing herself.

Beneath a gray sky, the rolling hills and the meadows between took on a dark, dusky, green hue. The scent of pine and heather mingled with the damp air, invigorating her lungs. She followed the road toward town for about a mile until she reached a wooden bridge spanning a large stream, then turned back, not too afraid of running into Ian because he seemed to be avoiding the house.

Even Aunt Grace had noticed. "Where's that nice, young laddie, Ian? He's not still at the beach, is he?"

And Maggie had said, "He probably has an article to send off. He always disappears into his writing cave when he has a deadline."

Every time Emily felt her own concern for him creeping in, she told herself worrying was pointless. She needed to focus on something else. The sooner she could get in touch with the university and schedule her testing, the better. But how? She might have to find the internet café in the village. She'd jog there if she had to.

Later that night, Emily dragged herself upstairs to her room. She closed the door, leaned against it, and looked around.

Spending time in this room—his room—wasn't helping. A clean, woodsy scent lingered here, the same scent that drifted around Ian. She unhooked the window latch and raised the bottom pane, letting in a fresh supply of the same mossy, pine-scented air.

Everything about this room breathed of him. Like oxygen, his presence was inescapable. The clothes in the wardrobe. His things. The way he left his books—angled and marked in such a way as to show his promise to resume.

What was he doing? What was he feeling?

"Lord," she whispered, "I can't stand the thought of him hurting and angry. Please help me know what to do about that. Help Ian forget about everything that happened between us. Help him move on." She closed her eyes. "And help me forget too."

Time for a distraction. A book. Something.

The Bible Ian kept on the dresser would help clear her mind.

She took it down and settled into the chair in the corner. It fell open with ease to the dedication page. The slightly faded inscription had been penned in an elegant, feminine hand.

Emily caught her breath at the words:

To my beloved Ian. My lover,
my rock, my shield.
A noble, humble man of quiet strength,
dearly loved by God.
Philippians 4:13. Never forget.
I love you,
Katy

Ignoring the sudden ache in her chest, Emily focused on the date of the inscription. Nine years ago. She closed her eyes and replayed in her mind what Ian had told her about Katy. His wife had given him this Bible the year she died.

She already knew Katy had been a young woman of faith and character. To Emily, she had seemed more like a sainted icon than a person. But these were the words of a real woman who not only

192

admired and adored Ian, but also loved him. Body, mind, and soul.

A queasy feeling churned in her stomach and she closed the Bible. It felt wrong, like peeking into someone's diary. She stared at the closed cover, but it was too late. The words had singed into her memory.

The queasiness twisted into a sickening knot and stirred up emotions Emily didn't even know she owned. Katy and Ian had obviously been very much in love.

An unrelenting heaviness weighed like a boulder on her chest, and, even though she tried to hold them back, tears came. "Dear God, this is pointless. He's not mine to mourn over."

She opened the Bible to the verse Katy noted in Philippians and read the boldly underlined passage, even though it was a verse she knew well.

I can do all this through him who gives me strength.

She skimmed through the pages, stopping to read other underlined and highlighted passages. At whose hand—Katy's or Ian's?

The notes scribbled in the margins were clearly Ian's familiar block print.

She blew out an exasperated breath and closed the Bible. "Sorry, but this isn't helping."

The books on the table next to the chair were obviously ones he was reading—probably not a good choice either. His study in the next room contained plenty of books which Ian had said were at her disposal, so she rose and went to the hall, tapped on the door, and let herself in. An entire wall of books caught her eye and she aimed for those. She could grab something and leave as quickly as possible. Emily found a few well-worn classics, including her favorite Jane Austen novel.

Again, Ian's or Katy's?

She leafed through the pages. The book would provide a few hours of escape at least. Except—the dutiful Anne Elliot's steady, unfulfilled love for Captain Wentworth … bad idea. She slipped the volume back into place on the shelf, tucked a loose wave of hair behind her ear, and looked around the room.

Filing cabinets topped with stacks of magazines and folders

lined two of the walls. Dated file boxes towered beside them with more folders and magazines piled neatly on top. A framed drawing hung on the wall above the cabinets and, next to it, an award.

Emily moved to get a closer look.

Ian's signature scrawled across the bottom of an illustration from *Daniel's Friends Face the Fire*. In the painting, three men stood together, unharmed amid flames, with a fourth man nearby. A beautiful, inspiring work of art and an award. From a lifetime ago.

Maybe one day his love of art would return.

A computer monitor and keyboard sat lifeless on the desk below the window. A bronze lamp craned over the corner of the desk where several labeled notebooks stood. The window overlooked the berry field to the west of the house. On the wall, a collage of photos covered a whiteboard with captions beneath them.

She stepped closer.

The photos were of the bridges of downtown Portland, Oregon. Most of the photos depicted various people, but one woman, about mid-fifties, was in several of the shots. Probably Janet Anderson, his friend.

Ian was in one of the photos with an arm around her shoulders, posing for the camera with that warm, devastating smile.

Fabulous. Just what I needed to see.

This was the workspace of a conscientious, sensible man. So how could a sensible man offer to throw away the best years of his life on a dying woman? What was he thinking? He couldn't possibly have thought it through.

Out the window, a dimly lit view of the fence at the edge of the berry field brought the last encounter with Ian back to her mind in a rush of vivid detail. His impassioned plea. And that kiss—

That was it. Ian hadn't *thought* any of this through. In fact, he probably hadn't been thinking at all. Physical attraction had blinded his judgment.

It had certainly blinded hers, for one breathtaking moment.

Her cheeks burned at the memory. The crush of his lips on hers, the heat of his skin. Every detail of that kiss came back to her, and with good reason.

It was her first.

And because of her prognosis, it would be her last.

Her eyes stung with the threat of more tears, but she shook the temptation off. No more. She'd cried more in the last two weeks than she had in her entire life.

The voice of reason said there was no point dwelling on it.

"Okay, Em." She spoke aloud, as if that would break the silent grip Ian had on her thoughts. "Time to think about something else."

But Ian had unconsciously taken what she had quietly saved. Her friends had never understood Emily's decision to reserve her first kiss for the man she would marry. Which would have been Ian, if things had been different. But marriage wasn't in God's plan for her after all.

She slumped into the desk chair and massaged her temples, trying to relieve the throbbing tension from the strain of the last few days. In the absence of her voice, stillness filled the room. Summer evenings back home in Oregon's high desert were deeply quiet, just like this.

Home.

The sooner she went home, the sooner Ian could get on with his life and she could get on with hers.

Or what's left of it.

Tears stung her eyes again. She'd never been one to wallow in self-pity. But as the tears continued to well up, she let them come. Why shouldn't she? She had good reason to feel sorry for herself. Several reasons.

"First off, I have a fatal disease," she said to no one. "Secondly, the most amazing man wants to marry me and I can't have him. Third, I'm trying to end things with him, but now he's got me so wound up I can't think straight."

It wasn't fair.

"Lord, why did I kiss him? What in the world was I thinking? And what am I supposed to do for three more *weeks*? Ending it was hard enough, but now ..."

What would it have been like to be his wife? The thought launched a rush of images and sensations she had no business entertaining.

"No." Her whisper cracked the stillness. "See? I knew it. One kiss complicates everything."

Actually, it was three.

"It's not Ian's fault, Lord. I'm sure he's never heard of a grown woman saving her first kiss for her husband." Emily's elbows dug into her knees and she let her forehead fall into her hands. "All I want is to wrap my arms around him and love him with everything I have and forget about tomorrow." She lifted her face heavenward. "God, I can't do this. I can't. I need Your help, please."

Would God help her? It was all her fault. Not only had she let Ian kiss her, but she'd kissed him back. And what about Ian? Had the kiss complicated things for him too?

Emily groaned. She should leave now, go back home this minute. But that wouldn't be fair to Aunt Grace.

Drained and heavy-hearted, she rose, opened the study door, and froze.

Ian stood with his forehead pressed against the door frame, eyes closed.

No. Please tell me you didn't hear that.

Heat surged to her cheeks. Her mind raced for a reply for whatever he might say.

But he said nothing.

She urged her feet forward and slipped past him. As she closed her door, she heard a long, heavy exhale.

Friday morning brought clear, blue skies and a call from Claire inviting everyone to join her and the kids for a picnic and swimming. When Ian delivered the message to Maggie, the old woman launched into a flurry of activity, pulling out picnic baskets before he'd even left the kitchen.

As he walked back to the cottage, he still couldn't decide if he would go or stay behind. He wanted to go along to help. Or, if he were honest, to be near Emily. Because her agonized confession the night before was far from agony for him. Quite the opposite.

He hadn't meant to eavesdrop. He meant to get a book. When he realized she was in the study praying, he started to slip away quietly. But what he overheard seized him, turned him inside out.

It kept him awake most of the night. In the little time he did sleep, Emily visited his dreams in ways that tormented him far worse than his waking thoughts until he finally jumped out of bed, threw on his shoes, and went for a pre-dawn run. It would be best to forget what he'd heard.

He reached for the knob on the cottage door. *Forget what she said? Not possible.*

Ian could either respect her wishes and stay away from her, or take advantage of the situation and double his efforts until she changed her mind. He needed to change her mind. He needed to stay beside her through it all.

He was her first kiss?

The idea sent a ripple of joy and amazement through him, but a wee pang of guilt for taking it without asking nagged at him as well. The least he could do for her was to back off. For now. Besides, that would give him time to think of a new plan.

A MacLean never gave up.

He stayed inside the cottage all morning, working on his laptop, even after he heard Claire's car arrive.

Within minutes, a hail of thumps and giggles rattled the door. Kallie burst in first, then Hannah. "Uncle Ian, we're going for a swim at the loch!" Hannah lunged at him and grasped his hand. "Come on."

"And I'm going to dunk you. You won't get away this time." Kallie gripped his other hand and yanked him as hard as she could.

"Sorry, I'm not going. Maybe next time. I've got to stay here and finish my work."

"No work, not today." Hannah punctuated each word with a shake of her head.

"It's picnic day," Kallie said. "Now let's *go*."

With a sigh, he gave in to their tugging.

They each tucked one of his hands under their arms like the handles of a wheelbarrow and towed him out the door and up the sloped drive.

"C'mon, Hannah, pull harder." Kallie grunted.

As they neared the top of the drive, they came upon the others.

Emily helped Aunt Grace into Claire's estate car.

An instant replay of how soft her lips felt and how sweetly they

197

had yielded to the pressure of his not-so-gentle kiss flooded his senses.

His nephews came out of the house, each bearing a picnic basket. Jack had his balanced on one shoulder and Douglas came out carrying his load in front at an awkward-looking angle. As the lad passed Emily, he checked out each of his biceps.

Ian couldn't help but give a faint smile. He probably would have done the same at that age.

"All right boys, let's have them," Claire said from the back door of the wagon. "Yours first, Dougie. It's the biggest."

Douglas scoffed. "It's not too big for me." The lad's chest swelled and he glanced in Emily's direction before hoisting his load into the car. Then he tried to relieve Jack of his burden, but Jack lifted the basket high above his head, also checking out the effect on his own muscles.

If Emily noticed the abundance of manliness surrounding her, she didn't show it. She seemed focused on making sure Aunt Grace was safely buckled into the front seat.

Douglas saw him approach. "Uncle Ian! Where's your fishing pole? I brought mine."

At the mention of his name, Emily looked up, cheeks instantly pink.

"No, Doog. He's coming swimming with *us*," Kallie said. "We're going to take turns dunking him under."

Hannah ran to Emily. "Will you swim with me?"

"I'm not ..." She glanced at Ian. "Sure, that sounds like fun."

"Shirrr." Kallie giggled.

Should Emily be swimming? Ian yielded to the tug of apprehension. Perhaps she should see a doctor before taking any risks. As soon as he could, he would find out more about the disease.

A wee frown creased Emily's brow. "Except I didn't bring a swimsuit."

Claire slammed the rear door, brushed her hands, and turned to Emily with a smile. "Good thing I brought an extra one. Although on you"—she pinched the sides of Emily's waist—"I'm afraid it might not stay up."

Jack nudged Douglas and leaned close. "Forget fishing. I'm going swimming."

Douglas frowned at his brother, then stared at Emily, his face neon pink.

Ian hid his smile while inspecting the roof rack. "Douglas, I'll go fishing with you next time. Bring your da and we'll take the *Seastrike* out."

Claire finished buckling Hannah into the car, pulled up straight, and spun to face him. "But you're coming today too, aren't you?"

"No, I have a story deadline and some new queries to send off."

She frowned. "Och! Take a break. Come with us."

Ian tugged on the metal rack to test it, rocking the whole car. When he didn't answer, Claire's fists flew to her hips.

Quietly, Emily broke in. "No, I'll stay here. Ian, you should go—"

Maggie tromped up to Ian with a hand thrust out, palm up. "Let's have it."

"What's that?"

"The key! I know ye're hiding it somewhere. It's still *my* truck. And dinna fash yerself—Jack can drive me."

"Oh no, Maggie. No." Claire had to shout above Jack's hooting. "I'm not falling for *that* one again. And besides ..." Claire turned to Ian with a pointed look. "Ian is going to drive."

He shook his head. "Sorry, Claire. If you need the truck, take it. Let Jack drive. Or Douglas. It's not that far."

"I can drive?" Douglas's voice rose to an unmanly squeak.

Kallie stomped over to Ian and tilted a frown up at him. "Why aren't you coming with us?"

Everyone seemed to be waiting for his answer, including Emily.

"I made a promise to finish what I started." When he looked up, he saw that he had Emily's full attention. "I always honor my promises. Perhaps another time."

CHAPTER TWENTY-SIX

In spite of the warm July sun, the chilly waters of Loch Lagan sent Emily back for her clothes the minute she finished swimming. After lunch, she stayed in the sun with the girls and tried to get warm again, which earned her a plastic bucket and the prestigious title of Sand Gatherer.

The girls didn't seem to mind being wet. Dirt clung to their damp swimsuits as they worked diligently on a palatial masterpiece of rock and sand, similar to the castles Emily had built with her mom and dad as a kid at the beach. Together, she and her mom would build a huge sandcastle while her dad packed in countless buckets of water for the moat.

She squinted against the sun's glare reflecting off the glistening water. If only her dad could be here and see the quiet majesty and beauty of this place. The protective Scots pines surrounding the loch, the green hills mounding in succession like pillows in the distance. The rich tones of greens, the splendor of God's magnificent creation. Her dad couldn't possibly deny the presence and majesty of God in a place like this.

Aunt Grace and Maggie packed the picnic things back into the baskets and didn't appear to need any help. Emily and the girls were sheltered from the wind by some low-growing bushes but still within easy distance of the loch in case they needed water for the moat.

Claire jogged toward them and dropped to her knees beside Emily. "The boys are on the bank fishing away. I guess one race across a freezing loch was enough."

Kallie reached for the bucket in Emily's hand, but frowned when she found it empty.

"Sorry, Kallie, I'm slacking off." She picked up the bucket and filled it quickly. "Here you go."

The girls worked steadily. Kallie mounded lumpy turrets while Hannah gathered pine cones. "These will serve me as my royal subjects," Hannah said. She formed a line with the cones in front of the palace.

Claire chuckled. "Bet you're glad you came. You'll not find fun like *this* anywhere else."

Emily filled another bucket and handed it over. "I am glad I came."

"But ...?"

Maybe Ian did have work to do, but he probably would have joined his nieces and nephews in a heartbeat, if not for her.

"What?" Claire gave her a probing look.

"Ian should be here spending time with your kids."

Claire gave her short hair a finger comb. "He sees more than his fill of them, trust me." She lowered her voice. "He seemed well enough today. You think he's avoiding you?"

Emily nodded and looked away. He was probably trying to make it easier on her. He must have overheard enough to know she couldn't handle being near him.

Maggie and Aunt Grace had been sitting on the large, plaid blanket where everyone had eaten lunch, but now they were slowly getting up. Or, at least, Grace was slow about it. Maggie hopped up, took hold of Grace's hand, and pulled her to her feet.

Emily raised her voice so they could hear. "Aunt Grace, do you two need anything?"

Maggie waved her off. The two of them headed away from the beach toward the meadow, a colorful sea of wild, brown grasses and purple heather against a backdrop of deep evergreen.

Emily squinted and looked closer. A bundle of paper poked out from under Maggie's arm.

"Daft." Claire chuckled, shaking her head. "Look at them."

The old women headed toward the meadow. Grace leaned on Maggie's arm, pointing out the clumps of grass and brush as they worked their way through the bank of shrubs separating the beach from the meadow.

An odd, heavy sensation fell on Emily as the two sisters worked together, helping each other.

"They're quite the pair, aren't they?" Claire's gaze followed their progress until they were out of sight.

"Are they okay to go off alone?"

Claire nodded. "They won't get far. It's been so good for Maggie, having Grace here. She's happier than I've seen her in a long time."

Aunt Grace seemed happy as well, but Emily wasn't ready to admit it out loud.

Claire chuckled. "Did you know Maggie's telling everyone that Grace is home to stay?"

Emily glanced at Claire. "I've heard."

"So what do you think?"

She poked a twig in the dirt, traced a series of connecting circles. What was there to think about? "I don't know. It's not what we planned."

"Right, but aside from a change of plans, what do you think of her living here? Have you thought about what's best for Aunt Grace if it turns out that you—you know—can't take care of her? What if she outlives you?"

The bluntness of Claire's words sent a new chill along Emily's already cool skin, and the hairs on her arms stood at attention. "I haven't really thought about it. But now that we're here, seeing them together gives me a lot to think about."

"She's happy here. After all, this is her home."

Is it?

"What does she have back in the States?"

Just me. Emily turned her attention to the girls. They had worked hard and steady and made quite a bit of progress on the castle, each one doing her part. Sisters working together without much fighting.

Whooping and laughter drowned out her thoughts.

Jack and Douglas appeared, each one jogging toward them with a fishing pole in one hand and a sloshing bucket in the other.

"I caught three. That's two more than Jack," Douglas said, breathing hard.

"But my one is bigger than the lot of yours combined." Jack set his bucket down near his mom.

Claire made a face. "Remember—you catch it, you clean it."

"Look at these." Douglas let his bucket drop next to Jack's, slopping water over the side.

The bucket moved and made more sloshing sounds on its own.

Emily peered at the fish and looked up with a smile. "Those are really nice, Douglas. What kind are they?"

He looked at her and stiffened, cheeks bursting with color.

Jack gave Douglas an elbow poke. "They're brown trout, but we call 'em brownies." He leaned close to his brother. "Race you to the honey buns." He took off running toward the picnic baskets.

Douglas dropped his pole and ran after him.

"A bonnie catch, boys." Claire's raised voice drifted after them. "Just don't forget what I said about cleaning them." Then she turned to Emily. "So, back to Grace. What concerns you?"

Emily frowned. How to say it gently? "Aunt Grace has trouble with her memory and sometimes she does things that are ... unsafe."

"I hadn't noticed."

"It happens a lot when she's tired or gets out of her routine. She needs to be with someone all the time. Someone who can keep an eye on her."

Claire's eyebrows shot up. "Don't you trust us, then? We Scots may be a lively bunch, but we're not all wild and reckless, in spite of what you may have heard."

"Oh, no, I didn't mean—"

"Fire!" Maggie's voice rang out from the bushes behind them. She burst into view, coughing, and croaked, "Fire! Get water!"

Fire? Where was Aunt Grace? Emily scrambled to her feet in spite of the numbing dread that raced through her.

Claire shouted at the boys to get their buckets, then disappeared into the bushes where Maggie had emerged.

Jack and Douglas came running.

Emily hurried after Claire, Hannah and Kallie trailing behind. She pushed her way through the bushes.

A whimper came from behind her and she turned.

Hannah was crying.

Emily scooped her up and ran on.

A cloud of gray billowed ahead, curling upward.

She reached a clearing and stopped. Still holding Hannah, she pulled Kallie close.

The fire wasn't big, but it had grown beyond a small, rock-lined pit and was spreading through the tall, dry grass.

Aunt Grace stood a few yards beyond the fire and waved, smiling at the blaze like a child over her birthday cake.

"Girls," Claire said, "stay with Emily." She ran to the beach.

With Hannah in her arms, Emily took Kallie's hand and skirted the fire toward her aunt. She let go of Kallie's hand to switch Hannah to the other hip, then reached for her hand again, but the older girl was gone.

"Kallie?"

Douglas came running with a bucket. With a garbled yell, he tossed the contents of his bucket into the fire.

Water and three brown trout flew through the air and hit the blaze dead center. The fish bounced on the smoldering spot doused by the water, flopping around and twitching like break-dancers on a charred, smoky stage, surrounded by an audience of flames.

Jack came next with his bucket. He set it down, took out his fish, and tossed the water at the fire. He slapped his brother on the back with a "way to go, mon," and sprinted off with his bucket.

Douglas stood there, shoulders drooping, watching his flailing fish through the smoke.

"I'm scared." Hannah wrapped her arms around Emily's neck. "Will it burn us up?"

"Oh, no, honey. We'll put it out."

"Will it cook Doogie's fish?"

As Douglas disappeared with his bucket, Emily threw a look over her shoulder. Were the others coming?

The water had put out the center of the fire, but the outer edges were still burning.

Kallie appeared with two pink plastic buckets of sand.

"Careful, honey," Emily said.

Kallie set one down and tossed sand from the first bucket onto the fire, then switched and did the same with the other one.

Claire appeared and threw water at the fire, but the outer flames spread farther.

Maggie came tottering along the path.

Grace made an exasperated sound. "Maggie, ye didnae use my good tablecloth to put out a fire again, did ye? The Buchanan plaid?"

The old woman frowned. "What else was I supposed to use? The fancy lace one?"

Claire frowned. "Tablecloth? What are you two talking about?"

"Och, Gracie," Maggie said, ignoring Claire. "Ye were always the smart one." She turned toward Kallie. "Run get the blanket we used for our picnic and bring it here. Quick, lassie!"

Kallie turned and ran.

"She's only eight, Maggie," Claire said.

"So help her instead of squawking at me like a chicken."

Claire turned and ran as flames crackled and spread to the dry grass.

Smoke drifted toward Grace and Emily. Aunt Grace coughed.

Within minutes, Claire returned with Kallie, Douglas, and Jack, all bearing the thick, plaid blanket. Dripping wet.

"Everyone, grab a corner," Claire called out. "Kallie, you be careful."

They spread it out and dropped it onto the burning grass, smothering the fire instantly.

Billows of smoke and the smell of singed fabric rose with a sizzle from the wet cloth.

They all formed a solemn circle around the smoking plaid. No one said a word.

Maggie wrinkled her red nose at the smoldering mess. Grace patted Maggie's shoulder and leaned close to her. "Thank you for the bonfire, dearie. I had a lovely time."

Claire shook her head.

Douglas stared at the blanket for a long time.

Jack clapped his brother on the back. "We're heroes, eh, Doog? We killed a fire."

"My fish," Douglas whispered.

Kallie giggled. Then Hannah got the giggles—in Emily's arms.

Tension-laughter bubbled up in Emily's throat.

Oh, no, not now ...

Laughing would hurt the boy's feelings. She covered her mouth and held it in. Bad idea, as usual. She snorted.

Hannah leveled wide eyes at Emily.

Emily burst out laughing, all hope of a dignified save gone. Then everyone was laughing, alternating with bursts of coughing, even Douglas.

Claire turned to Emily. "Well, as you can see, you have nothing to worry about. Aunt Grace should do very well here. She fits right in."

Emily looked at her great-aunt.

Grace nodded and smiled.

By the time they cleaned up the mess and gathered the picnic supplies into Claire's car, everyone was exhausted. Even Maggie, who climbed into the backseat without a word about driving.

Grace snuggled between Claire and Emily in the front and quickly dozed off.

"Aside from demented chickens and wild fires, Scotland isn't such a bad place now, is it?" Claire kept her eyes fixed on the narrow road.

Emily drank in the view. The endless hills, all in a bright assortment of green earlier in the day, had taken on deeper shades of green in the late afternoon. She gathered the colors in her mind. While she would have the photos she'd taken of the farm and their outings to remember this place, no photograph could fully capture the charm and beauty of Scotland.

"Grace may have friends in the States," Claire said, "but this is her home. Her family. And Maggie needs her."

"No," Emily said.

"No?" Claire shot a frown over the old woman's head.

"I mean, no, she doesn't have anyone in the States. Just me."

Claire navigated the narrow road for a while. "What about you? Do you have family to help you when you need it?

Family? Right. She definitely wouldn't be calling her dad. He made it clear that he wanted no part of going through the dying ordeal again.

"I have friends."

Claire puffed out a laugh. "So do I. But family takes care of each other."

In a perfect world, maybe.

Grace stirred against Emily's shoulder and suddenly the weight of Claire's words sank in. The MacLeans were Grace's true relatives, a connection Emily didn't have. Maybe Grace did belong with them. But did Claire and Ian want the responsibility of caring for her? And with Maggie bent on mischief, were Ian and Claire prepared to give Grace the kind of care she needed?

"The solution's simple. Both you and Grace move here."

"Me?"

"Aye. You could get a job in the village, if you fancy. Stay on the farm and keep an eye on the old hens. Then you wouldn't have to worry about her, and you'd be looked after. When the time comes."

When the time comes ...

Emily studied the side of Claire's pretty face. "That's really kind, but I couldn't possibly burden any of you. I'm not family."

"Pssh, of course you are."

Emily shook her head. "Claire, I can't—"

"Hey." Claire turned, dark eyes flashing. "You're not only Grace's niece; you've been like a daughter to her. She loves you. And Ian loves you. That makes you family."

Did Claire know what she was suggesting? Emily shook her head at the passing hills dotted with sheep, carefree little specks of black and white against gently rolling green mounds. How simple, their sheepy little lives. No concern for anything beyond moving from one grassy patch to the next.

"You do want to stay close to Grace, don't you?"

Emily glanced at her great-aunt, praying she wasn't hearing this. "I do, but—"

"And you love Ian." Claire shrugged. "So what's stopping you?"

"That *is* what's stopping me."

"How'd you figure that?" Claire frowned as she turned the car onto another narrow road. "You love him. He loves you. If he's going to lose you, what difference does it make if it's now or later?"

How could Claire ask a question like that? Claire was married. Wasn't there a deeper, more intimate bond between a husband and wife than there was for others? She'd seen it in her parents. Didn't that kind of bond bleed all the more when torn apart? "There's a huge difference, Claire."

"Not to Ian." Claire shook her head. "He's a MacLean. When we love someone, it's forever."

And I'd be thrilled to know that, if things were different. Emily swallowed hard. "He's free to begin again, to have a family of his own. That's what he wants."

Claire snorted. "Ian has plenty of family. Look round you."

It's not the same. "Claire, it's kind of you to offer to ... look out for me, but I have to think about what's best for Ian. And for everyone."

The car slowed and Claire turned onto the road that led to the farm. "What about Grace? Don't get me wrong, Ian and I can manage those two without help, but you've been with her a long time. She loves you."

The thought of being separated from Aunt Grace brought a twinge of sadness. Not knowing if she was okay. Not having her near. Living alone.

"If she *were* to stay here," Emily said quietly, "it would be better for her—and everyone else—if I wasn't around."

"Have you talked to Ian about this?"

Emily leaned a cheek against her aunt's soft, white hair. "No."

They crossed a small bridge and drove the remaining mile in silence. Claire turned the car in at the farm and climbed the slope.

They passed the cottage. No sign of him.

"This is Grace's home and Ian knows it." Claire pulled up beside the house. "As I see it, she has no other options. So there's really no question about it, is there?"

Sadness tugged hard at her heart. Emily tried to ease it away with a steady exhale. "I can't lay this burden on you and Ian."

Claire cut the engine and turned to Emily. "She's a *woman*, not a burden."

"I know." She looked Claire in the eye. "I need to think about it."

"Talk to Ian. See what he thinks."

Ian. "Okay, yeah. I should do that. I'll ... talk to him."

"Good. Get it settled now." Claire smiled. "Everything will work out, you'll see."

Emily returned the smile with a pang. What would it have been like to have Claire for a sister-in-law?

CHAPTER TWENTY-SEVEN

After Claire and the kids left, Grace settled in for a nap. Emily's gritty, sun-baked skin continued to cook inside her clothes, and the lingering heat of the day added to the irritation. She ran upstairs to change.

An envelope taped to Ian's study door caught her eye. It was addressed to her. She took out a single, folded sheet.

> *Emily—Please use whatever you like. The computer*
> *in my study is online now if you need one. And if*
> *there is anything else you need, anything at all,*
> *please ask and I'll make certain you have it.*

> *IAN*

With a sigh, she refolded the note and slipped it in her pocket, both touched and saddened by his thoughtfulness.

Since she and Grace had left home a week ago, she hadn't checked her email. She entered the study and slipped into the seat at the desk. Within minutes, she found a week's worth of messages cramming her inbox. Her swift scan of the subject lines stopped short on one from Oregon Health and Sciences University.

> *Dear Ms. Chapman,*

> *Thank you for your interest in clinical genetic testing for Hypertrophic Cardiomyopathy (HCM). Clinical genetic testing is provided for individuals to confirm a referring doctor's diagnosis. We are*

210

*accepting blood samples for clinical genetic testing
and for our FHC (Familial Hypertrophic
Cardiomyopathy) Research Project. Please contact
us with questions toll-free or by email.*

*Sincerely,
Rebecca Kerbs
Research Associate, OHSU*

A research project was better than nothing. Emily read the
message again before she typed a reply, telling Ms. Kerbs about her
family's connection with Freyer's and how she would be willing to
take part in whatever research her case qualified for.

After sending her that, she looked through the rest of her email,
answered a few messages, and wrote a lengthy letter to Jaye,
attempting to answer her multiple emails in one. Describing how Ian
had taken her news made the memory fresh again, made her heart
hurt.

Just as she prepared to close the server, she received a new
message from OHSU.

Ms. Chapman,

*The Project Director for the Freyer's Syndrome
Rare Disease Research Network is very interested
in meeting with you. Our program is gravely
lacking access to live case studies who can provide
human biological material and clinical data
necessary for biomarker identification and for
clinical studies that would help advance the care of
Freyer's patients.*

*Dr. Hanes wants to schedule an appointment to
discuss your participation. How soon can you come
in?*

Emily replied that she would be back in Oregon mid-August

and could meet then. Ms. Kerbs wrote back immediately saying she would forward a packet of forms and questionnaires to complete before her visit.

For the first time in more than a week, a bit of her burden lifted.

Maybe they were working toward a cure. And even if there wasn't a cure on the horizon, at least she had a chance to know more and to assist the study. Maybe she could volunteer for experimental treatments, if it would help the research.

Still feeling damp, she went to her bedroom and dug through her things, found a white, cotton sundress, and slipped it on. As she turned to head back downstairs, she caught a glimpse of herself in an oval freestanding mirror, one that hadn't been there before.

Ian must have brought it up for her, of course.

She met her gaze in the mirror. Her hair had dried into curling tendrils after swimming. She twisted it up and secured it with a clip.

Claire was right. She should talk to Ian about Aunt Grace.

But could she handle seeing him? Maybe she should wait, take some time to collect her thoughts. Put that kiss behind her.

Good luck with that.

So how long would that take? Three weeks? Right. Three *years* wouldn't be enough. The longer she waited, the harder it would be.

Taking a deep breath, she made a face at her reflection. "Quit making such a big deal out of this. It's simple. Just talk to him."

Emily headed downstairs. She would help Maggie clean up the picnic things while she collected her nerve.

But in the kitchen doorway, she stopped.

The old woman frowned at a gigantic bouquet in the middle of the kitchen table. A bouquet with an unmistakable scent. A bushel of honeysuckle blossoms and green leaves, stuffed into a metal bucket that could barely contain it all, spilled over in every direction.

"Well, lassie," Maggie said. "I dinna ken how this came here. Do ye?"

Good question. The sweet fragrance filled the kitchen, stirring up a mixture of memories, emotions, and questions. A pretty solid theory had instantly formed in Emily's mind, but it wasn't one she wanted to discuss with Maggie. "Maybe one of your neighbors stopped by while we were out at the loch? Or the reverend?"

Maggie snorted. "Havers. Why would anyone go to the trouble of bringing it into the house when there's loads of it up in the woods?"

So she knew about the hidden honeysuckle grove. Emily fingered a blossom, brought it to her nose. "Is that where you think this came from?"

"Aye. There's a lovely, wee woodbine thicket up on the brae. But this didn't march down and arrange itself on my kitchen table, now. Not without help." She cocked her head to one side and peered into the bouquet like a mother probing for the truth in the eyes of a child.

The old woman obviously suspected someone. Emily shifted on her feet.

"No matter. It smells well enough. Smells just like ye." Maggie shoved the picnic basket into a corner and took her apron down from a hook on the wall. "And yer letters."

Wow, good nose. And good memory.

The day's heat had collected and settled like a fog, low and dense, making wood-splitting a sweaty job. Ian peeled off his work shirt and hung it from a nail on a nearby post. He wiped his brow and continued bringing the axe down, splitting the dried rounds into smaller pieces.

How else could he persuade her to marry him? What did Emily want that he could appeal to? There had to be something. He'd gotten the idea for the flowers after everyone left for the loch. A dead-brilliant idea *that* was. As if a bucket of flowers could change her mind.

He stood another piece on the block.

A bit of movement crossed the corner of his eye.

Emily.

Coming toward him in a white dress that brought out the warm, sun-kissed look of her skin. A day of swimming with his nieces had been good for her, set her aglow. Her hair, glinting in the sun, was piled up in a pretty sort of knot, with a few curls falling loose along her cheek and neck.

Unable to breathe, Ian straightened, heart thumping. Had she changed her mind? Perhaps those flowers wielded more power than he'd given them credit for. "Hello, Emily," he said, voice unsteady. He cleared his throat, brought the axe down hard, sinking the blade into the chopping block, and rested his hands on his hips.

Instead of answering, Emily drew in a sharp breath and stared at him wide-eyed, cheeks pink. She turned away and focused her attention on the ground.

"Did you want something?"

It could have been his imagination, but it seemed she went a few shades redder.

"Maybe later, when you're not ... busy." She turned to leave.

"No, wait. I'm not busy."

She stopped. "Then would you mind ... um ..." She took a deep breath and frowned at her feet. "Could you please put your shirt on?"

Oh. "Sorry." But as he turned and reached for his shirt, his thoughts raced.

No. It was for the sake of propriety that she asked. Of course.

Unless ...

His hand paused mid-reach. Remembering her agonized confession the night before, he savored the sudden rush, the dizzying awareness that seeing him work bare-chested had an effect on her.

You wanted to appeal to her, here's your chance. Use this to your advantage.

Right. What kind of idiot would try to tempt a woman into marriage with bulging biceps and a sweaty, bare chest?

So it could work, then?

Only an idiot would ask. And even if it did, would you really stoop to doing it?

With a sigh, he lifted his shirt from the nail, slipped it on, buttoned it up, and turned round.

Emily's eyes remained fixed on the ground.

Did she know that the color of her cheeks, still quite pink, was the loveliest color he'd ever seen? A sudden urge to kiss her seized him. He took a deep breath and forced his lips into a polite smile. "Better?"

Emily checked with a wee, sideways glance. "Thank you."

"What's on your mind?"

She cleared her throat and faced him. "What do you think about ... Maggie driving?"

Maggie? Ian frowned. *You came out here to talk about Maggie? Looking like that?* "What do I think?" He let out a sharp laugh. "I think *not*. Why?"

"She's been talking about driving Aunt Grace around. They want to visit the place where they grew up. I don't know if she would actually try it. I just thought you should know."

Ian reached in the pocket of his jeans, pulled out the truck key, and dangled it from his fingers.

She stared at the key, then up at him.

"I keep it on me always. A lesson learned the hard way. She'd have to ... well, she won't get her hands on it, trust me."

Emily went pink again. "Right."

He slipped the key back in his pocket and waited. Dead cert Emily hadn't come out here to talk about Maggie.

She swept a loose strand of hair from her forehead and took a deep breath. "I've been talking to Claire and thinking about Aunt Grace. I'm afraid there will come a time when she'll need somewhere else to live. I'd like to know what you think about her relocating here. With you and Maggie."

There will come a time. He waited for the sinking-heart feeling to hit bottom, giving the pang in his chest a moment to subside. "Does she want to live here?"

"I don't know. She doesn't know about the disease. I've decided not to tell her yet. I know how much she's wanted to come back. Now that she's here with Maggie, she seems ... happy." The last word sounded hollow.

"Grace is family. She's always welcome here."

Emily turned her attention to the house. "It means you'll have not one but two old women needing supervision. Claire is willing to help—"

"She'll be well-looked after, Emily. Don't worry. I've given it

215

plenty of thought. I've arranged to do all my freelance work from home now. I'm not going anywhere."

"Good. Thank you," she whispered.

Tell her. "I'm here to stay, Emily. To take care of my family." He stepped closer, willing her to look at him, to see into his heart. "And that includes you."

A stunned look passed over her face, and she took a step back.

Ian drew a deep breath, held himself in check. "Wouldn't you be happier here? Close to Grace?"

Emily shook her head. "I'll be happy knowing she's being cared for. I'm needed back home. I have a chance to help with an important clinical study of the disease."

"What study? You mean a cure?"

She stood very still, eyes glistening. "There's no cure. But there is a Freyer's Syndrome research study in Portland, and they have no live cases of people with the disease. The director is eager to meet me as soon as I return. I don't know what impact my participation will have, but I have to try. Maybe I can help bring some good from all the loss my family has suffered."

Ian's chest tightened. He forced himself to speak slowly, to loosen the desperation taking hold inside. "Perhaps there's a way to help the study from here."

She met his gaze and held it for one breathless moment. Then she shook her head and looked away, searching the wooded hills behind the house. "I also have the Juniper Ranch kids. They have no family except each other and the counselors. They need continuity. I'd like to help at least one kid feel wanted. I need to finish what I started. Just like you." She drew a shuddering breath. "So there are a few significant things I can do with the time I have left. The kids and the study need me."

But I *need you.* "You have a family right here who loves you and wants to take care of you when you need it. It makes perfect sense."

"I can't marry you. You know that."

No, I don't know that. "Then stay as Grace's niece."

"I couldn't."

"Why not?"

She threw him a pleading look. "You know why," she whispered.

Heart pounding, he stepped closer, his voice falling to a rumble. "Because you love me."

Trembling, Emily stiffened and turned away. "I'm sorry, Ian. It would be best for everyone, including me, if I wasn't here. The less we see of each other, the better."

"But there must be something—"

She turned to him, pain filling her eyes. "Please, Ian, no more offers. No more notes or flowers."

He took another step, but her hands flew up as if to ward him off.

"No more ... us."

The words belted him like a sucker punch. Dazed, he just stood there staring long after she disappeared into the house.

CHAPTER TWENTY-EIGHT

Sunday after church, Emily parked the old truck next to the house and stepped out. The day had turned out gray and damp. A thick, aimless mist had moved into the glen and seeped into everything it touched, including her. *Dreich*, Maggie had called it.

While Emily reached in to help Aunt Grace out of the truck, Maggie slammed the passenger door and stomped away. Attending church had done little to improve the old woman's foul mood.

Grace moved slowly along the walkway to the house, and Emily hung close by her side, getting damper by the minute. But she was in no hurry to get inside and rejoin Maggie.

The old woman hadn't said a word to Emily since she'd come knocking on her bedroom door earlier that morning with a message from Ian.

"Grace and I want to go to kirk," the old woman had said. "Ian says he's not going and ye can take us. He says ye know where the truck key is." She just stood there with a hazy glare, her lips pressed hard and arms tightly folded. "*My* truck."

Fabulous. Yes, Emily knew where the key was kept, meaning not only was she caught in the middle of a feud between the two MacLeans, but she had to see Ian to get it.

Two days had passed since she'd spoken to him out by the woodshed. It still pained her to remember what she'd said, but it had worked. She hadn't seen any sign of him, no more flowers or notes. Then, when she'd gone to the cottage early this morning, Ian met her at the door with the key and a quiet warning about the clutch sticking in third gear, and nothing more.

Aunt Grace finally reached the house, and Emily helped her inside.

In the kitchen, Maggie slammed cupboard doors, muttering.

Grace shuffled over to get an apron from the wall but it was caught too high on the hook.

"Let me get that down for you, Aunt Grace," Emily said.

Maggie spun around. "*I'll* get it. She doesn't need yer help and neither do I. Ye can go now. We dinna need ye."

Emily pressed her lips tight as she watched the old woman stomp over to the wall and yank at the apron until it came down. Heat prickled up the back of her neck.

"Och, Maggie," Grace said softly. "That's no way to speak to the lass."

Maggie chewed her lip in silence, scowling.

If that was how Maggie felt, fine. Emily wasn't in the habit of arguing with blind, old women. She turned her attention to Grace and tried to think of an excuse for leaving that wouldn't make Grace think Emily's feelings were hurt.

Grace wrapped the apron around her waist, held it steady against her belly with her curled arm, tied it in a lumpy knot at one side, and inched it around until the apron hung in front. Then Grace turned to her sister. "Well?"

"Sorry," Maggie said with a sniff and a nod in Emily's direction. But the old woman made no effort to include her.

Emily stayed only so Aunt Grace wouldn't worry.

As they prepared lunch, the sisters argued and corrected each other over stories of growing up and which seasonings to use and how hot the oven should be. As Maggie rolled bread dough into circles, Grace mixed meat together with onions and seasonings. Talking nonstop, she divided the mixture evenly among Maggie's rolled-out rounds. Maggie folded each pastry over the filling and pinched the edges together. Grace placed them on a baking tray, then Maggie slid them into the oven and asked Grace why she hadn't started the tea. Aunt Grace filled the teakettle and set it on the stove without missing a beat in her story about the old neighborhood.

They made leek soup to go with the meat pies, and to Emily's surprise, lunch was delicious. Maggie was right—they hadn't needed her at all.

After the meal, Aunt Grace went to take a nap.

Grumbling, Maggie puttered around the kitchen, filling and arranging dishes on a tray, then headed for the front door.

Emily rushed to get ahead of her.

Maggie nudged her aside. "I can do it." She balanced the tray on one arm and opened the door.

Emily held her tongue and waited until Maggie was outside. "Is that for Ian?"

"Who else?" the old woman retorted as she shuffled away with the tray that held enough food for a small family. "Though I'll wager your plane ticket home the daft laddie's fainted away or dead of hunger by now."

A growing heaviness pressed on Emily's heart. Being useless and confined produced a restless energy that consumed her. She needed to get out and spend it, regardless of the damp. She ran upstairs and changed into jeans, a sweatshirt, and hiking boots, then headed out back.

The path Ian had used to take her to the honeysuckle grove led through beautifully rich, fragrant woods. Emily turned toward the hills and followed the trail up the brae to the line of trees where the sloped meadow ended and the woods began. The heavy air clung to her clothes and hair, but she didn't care. A native Oregonian would never let a little drizzle slow her down.

Emily drew in deep breaths, letting the moist air fill her lungs. Anxiety and sorrow and dread had been building all week like a pressure cooker, and when it finally blew, the force sent her adrift.

She followed the trail up the hill and into deeper woods. It took about ten minutes to reach the cluster of trees that hid the enchanting honeysuckle grove where Ian had so eagerly taken her that first day.

The sooner you forget that day, the better.

Emily hiked past the grove without slowing.

At the top of the next hill, the trail leveled out. A lush valley in varying shades of green stretched out below for miles in every direction. Ahead, where the trail sloped down, it was veiled by a low blanket of fog. Something stood fixed in the middle of the otherwise undisturbed meadow, a building of some kind, but the fog was too thick to see what it was.

By the time she reached the valley floor, the mist had shifted enough for Emily to make out an old, stone church. Standing in the middle of nowhere, it seemed a natural, timeless part of the landscape, a ruddy anchor in a misty sea of green.

The path took her through the meadow, the fog thicker on the valley floor. The view from the top of the hill was deceiving; the distance to the old church was a lot farther than she had first thought.

But she had nowhere else to be. No one needed her—Maggie had made that quite clear.

Emily wasn't sure what to make of Maggie, but it was obvious that she and Grace had quickly developed an odd but symbiotic routine in spite of their time apart and Maggie's temperament. Being together seemed to be good for them both. And keeping them together was probably best for them.

And ultimately, for Emily.

In Scotland, Aunt Grace would be surrounded by people instead of being left to fend for herself after Emily was gone. But out here, in the stillness of this meadow, Emily couldn't deny the phenomenon she'd witnessed since their arrival in Scotland. Aunt Grace was *needed* here. She not only enjoyed being with Maggie, she thrived. She had purpose. And that made her happier than Emily had seen her in a long time.

Wonderful. Perfect. More than Emily could've asked for. So why the growing distress, this awful feeling of panic?

She reached the stone church. The remains of a low fence around the churchyard enclosed an old cemetery. Wildflowers and tall grass grew between the headstones. The stones and the building crumbled at the edges and were crawling with moss. The church was probably centuries old, abandoned in favor of the more modern, conveniently located church in town.

She stepped over the fence and strolled around the headstones.

A section of the cemetery had graves dating back over a hundred years, but, moving amongst the stones, she discovered a much newer section.

The name MacLean caught her eye. She stepped closer to the

gravestone, holding her breath.

Kathryn Carmichael MacLean.

Heart hammering, Emily closed her eyes to block out the dates. The thought of Katy dying so young while she and Ian were so deeply in love paralyzed Emily with sorrow. Tears streamed down her face.

Stop it.

But she couldn't. As she stared at the headstone, the crushing sadness pressed deeper. Wiping her face, she spun around and bolted for the woods. The mist had become a light drizzle, flattening her hair and dampening her sweatshirt, but she didn't care. Getting far away from that cemetery was more important than being dry.

When she reached the woods, she slowed her pace and kept on. The structured layout made Emily wonder if it was private woodlands. The church was probably part of the same land, part of the local county parish. Hopefully, whoever owned it wouldn't mind her passing through. Maybe she'd get a glimpse of a laird's castle.

About fifteen minutes passed, and by then, the darkening sky hinted at more than a mere drizzle. The drizzle soon turned to rain, and as it fell, the sky darkened with the threat of more. She was going to get soaked. Good thing it was August—at least it wouldn't be cold. She tromped on.

The fog seemed thicker than before, which seemed odd with the rain. She kept walking, but instead of thinning and leading to a castle or a manor, the trees got thicker and all signs of the trail disappeared.

"Okay. Let's rethink this." Emily stopped, turned, and looked around her, listening. Nothing to see or hear but rain, which was coming down hard and heavy in places where the trees weren't as thick. She turned back and picked her way through the woods, toward the clearing and the old church. Wet ferns and tangled briars brushed against her clothes as she pressed through, completely soaking her boots and pant legs.

She should have reached the clearing by now. But the woods didn't look like anything she'd seen. Taking a deep breath, she tucked dripping clumps of hair behind her ears. She was lost, obviously.

Big surprise. She didn't know this place at all.

"Okay." It took the edge off her rising unease, thinking aloud. "Just go back the way you came."

She turned and trudged through a tangle of trees and rotting trunks and leaves for a while, pressing on until she had walked more than long enough to come out near the church—if she had been heading the right way. But the woods were no thinner here. And everything had grown darker.

Emily stopped and closed her eyes, her pulse racing. "Lord, help me, please."

Thunder rolled in the distance. And another steady sound, like radio static, filtered through the mix of rain and thunder.

Running water. A stream?

She strained to see through the trees, but it was too dark and the woods too thick to see anything. *If I can find a stream, maybe it will lead to a house, to civilization.*

A few times, while running or traveling to and from the farm, she'd crossed a wooden bridge spanning a large stream about a mile or so from the house. Maybe this was the same stream. It was hard to tell where the sound was coming from, but if she started moving, at least she might be able to tell if she was getting closer or farther away.

The dark slowed her pace even more. She stepped carefully over fallen tree trunks, feeling for tree roots beneath a boggy carpet of needles and rotting leaves.

What time was it? How long had she been gone? It must have been hours. Panic crept up her throat. Aunt Grace was probably awake by now, maybe even beginning to worry.

Worrying was something Grace wouldn't have to do for long. If she stayed here in Scotland with Maggie, she'd have no reason to worry about Emily. Once Emily was back in the States, she'd be out of sight, out of mind.

But first, she had to find her way out of these woods.

She pressed on, listening for the sound of water as she worked her way through trees and over roots and downed limbs. After a while, the sound grew louder. A heavy downpour soaked her clothes, drawing heat from her body.

And she was wrong about August—she was cold.

Finally the trees thinned and the sound of rushing water grew louder. The ground sloped downward and a stream came into view. A few more steps brought her to a rocky edge of the water. If this was the same stream she'd seen before, it would lead to the bridge and the road back to the farm.

But which way? Emily wiped rain from her face with a wet sleeve, then looked upstream and down for a clue. Pretty much the same both ways.

Which way had the stream flowed at the bridge? She hadn't paid close enough attention. Closing her eyes, she listened. Above the rush of water, the silence was deafening.

"God, which way?"

Maybe if you'd been listening to Him, you'd be able to hear Him now.

"I have been listening. Haven't I?"

She'd been doing exactly what God wanted her to do. With all that had happened in the last few weeks, she'd dealt with making heartbreaking decisions. What God wanted from her was a no-brainer. She needed to do what was best for everyone, do everything in her power to make sure everyone was okay. This had been her role for longer than she could remember. She didn't *have* to ask.

She was just a little stuck at the moment and needed some direction.

Emily wiped the rain from her eyes. Aunt Grace would be worried, maybe even distraught. Emily needed to get back—now. There was no telling what could happen to her poor aunt in that state.

In the stillness, her quickening pulse thudded in her ears, sending her heart pounding harder. What if she had a heart attack now? She closed her eyes, willing the panic to stay down. No. Not a heart attack. Not here. Not alone.

But she *was* alone.

Figure something out, Em.

Any sense of direction she had was useless here. If this stream flowed to that loch she'd visited with Claire, then the loch was probably downstream. Her best guess was that the farm was upstream from the loch.

"Upstream it is," she whispered, words falling flat in the rain. "Lord, I hope I'm right."

CHAPTER TWENTY-NINE

"She's gone." Maggie stood in the cottage doorway chewing her lip, empty-handed this time except for the old, scarred shovel handle she used as a walking stick.

Ian frowned. "Who's gone?"

She stomped her foot. "Och, are ye daft now too, laddie? The lass! The one that writes ye letters."

A burst of adrenaline shot through Ian's veins. Emily was *gone*? "What do you mean, 'gone'?" His voice thundered louder than he'd intended. "Since when?" He pushed past Maggie and rushed to the drive, trying to ignore the uneasy tingle creeping up his spine.

"Grace woke wanting to see her, but she wasnae there," Maggie said from behind him. "We looked everywhere. We waited and waited, but she's still not come round."

Ian sprinted to the middle of the drive, barely noticing the rain smacking his face.

The old truck was there, next to the house in the spot where Emily had parked it after church.

He spun round to Maggie, who had followed him and stood without flinching at the steady rain matting down her stiff, white hair, her hands clutched together in a knobby clump around the shovel handle. "She hasn't gone far. The truck is still here."

"I *know* the truck is here. I'm no gowk, Ian. I checked that first."

Ian? Maggie hadn't called him by name in some time. Something was definitely wrong. "How long has she been gone?" he called over his shoulder as he headed back inside for a raincoat.

Maggie followed. "I dinna know."

"When was the last time you saw her?"

Maggie frowned. "Lunch." She chewed her lip again, a quirk he hadn't seen since Granddad Liam was alive.

Inside, Ian checked the clock: it was nearly seven. Where would she have gone for so long, and without telling anyone?

"Have you checked the—never mind. I'll look." He grabbed a rain slicker and pulled it on as he headed for the door. "Tell Aunt Grace I'll find her and not to worry." He turned and stared hard at the old woman. "Can you do that?"

Maggie nodded, face downcast.

"What is it, Maggie? Is there something else?"

"No," the old woman said through pursed lips. "Just find the lass."

In a few long, brisk strides, Ian reached the paddock at the back of the house, forcing down the rising quiver of fear. Empty. Where would Emily have gone? And why? She couldn't have gone too far on foot, and yet she had been gone a very long time. It wasn't like her to let Aunt Grace worry. Not like her at all.

The rain fell harder.

He checked all the outbuildings, scanned the hillside, then glanced at the house. How thoroughly had the old women searched the house? Maybe Emily had fallen asleep somewhere they didn't think to look. He let himself in through the back door and checked the lower floor, but there was no sign of her.

What if—could she have left? Gone home?

Heart racing, he took the stairs two at a time. The door to his bedroom was open. He held his breath and went in. He stood in the middle and surveyed the room.

The bed was made. Her jacket hung on the back of the door. Her purse, her passport, and a few of her things were all laid out on top of the chest, along with the truck key, which he snatched up and stuffed in his pocket.

He yanked open the wardrobe. Her clothes hung there, soft and light-colored, resting against some of his. The faint scent of honeysuckle drifted out.

Honeysuckle. She must have gone to the glen.

In seconds, Ian was down the stairs and out the back door.

Heavy rain pummeled his head and shoulders as he hiked up the braeside. She must have gone to the glen and got caught in the rain, perhaps decided to wait it out there. He hit the wooded trail at a run, ducking through sagging branches and dripping leaves, and kept on running until he reached the grove. Gasping to catch his breath, he scanned the silent wood. She wasn't there.

"Emily!" His voice echoed in the thicket, mocking him.

Had she been here?

Still catching his breath, he stood in the center and looked round. Dripping leaves bounced under the heavy spattering of raindrops. The steady roar of rain grew, tightening the fist of panic clutching at his chest.

She had to be on foot. But where?

Drenched and dripping, he pushed his way back through the wet brush to the main trail, turned north, and hiked to the top of the hill. He scanned the meadow but couldn't see anything in the mist.

He yelled her name, listened, yelled again. His voice fell flat, grounded by the rain.

Heart pounding, he sprinted down the hill and across the meadow. His eyes searched over the valley on both sides of the trail. It took several minutes, even at a full-out run, to reach the church.

"Emily!" He doubled over to catch his breath, hands on his knees. Then he stood and scanned the building and churchyard, listening. He peered inside the church, then circled the cemetery and the building, calling her name.

No answer.

Standing at the edge of the cemetery where he'd begun, he raked both hands through his dripping hair and took a long, hard look across the meadow. "Emily, where are you?" he whispered.

Silence.

Was she injured? Or had she—

Panic thundered in his chest and sent him running back to the farm as fast as he could.

Her fingers, toes, and lips were numb. So were her thighs.

Emily shivered inside her clothes, which were thoroughly soaked and chafing against her cold skin. She had no idea how far she'd gone upstream. In the hour or more she'd been walking, it felt like miles, but now it was fully dark. The shore was rocky and the going slow. Nothing looked familiar, and nothing had changed.

Stupid idea.

Kicking herself was a waste of energy. She needed to think. She'd thought about turning back a few times. But by then, long after dark, Grace would probably have gotten worried enough to send someone out looking—that someone most likely being Ian—and if he or anyone was looking for her, doubling back would make it harder for anyone to find her. The best thing to do would be to find shelter and wait.

Rain continued to beat down on Emily's head and shoulders as she stumbled along the wet rocks. It was stupid to take off like that without letting them know. Stupid to let something a poor old, blind woman said get to her.

The sound of thunder grew closer and more frequent. It was too dark to see beyond the banks. She couldn't tell if woods, hills, or meadows bordered the stream.

A sudden crack of thunder overhead made her jump. *Lord, I'm tired and scared. Please help me out of this.*

A burst of lightning illuminated a dark mass looming ahead, upstream.

Emily worked her way toward it, stepping into the stream and tripping over slippery rocks when there was no shore.

The mass took shape, arching high over the stream. A bridge.

The rain fell in a sudden, heavy smattering of hard, wet bullets. Emily kept moving until she reached the bridge. Not the little wooden bridge she'd hoped to find, but a massively tall, narrow stone bridge, towering about twenty-five feet above the water. Which meant a road nearby, hopefully. And shelter.

Emily waded through shallow water until she was under the bridge. It was solid stone, but the arch was high, nearly as tall as the bridge. Inside, she found a flat rock that rose above the water. She crouched on it and leaned back against the cold stone.

Thunder rolled and crackled overhead.

Fatigue swept over her like a flash flood. She rested her forehead and arms across her knees. Every part of her body felt numb. Except her mind, which now raced with the thoughts she'd held back in the need to find shelter.

It was bad enough that Aunt Grace could be worried into a state of distress, but the whole household would be in upheaval. They would have to send someone out to look for her. How bad would it be? Would they call authorities, disturb their neighbors?

How could she have been so stupid as to get herself lost? She should have known better. She should have known a lot of things. Like what a mistake it had been to come to Scotland. She should have found someone else to bring Aunt Grace here. She should have done whatever it took to avoid seeing Ian in person. That was her biggest mistake.

Seeing him, talking to him, being near him—all a huge mistake.

And kissing him—colossal mistake. Didn't she have enough to battle? Longing was a creature awakened that should have been left alone.

"I wish I'd never met him." Angry tears welled up, but she choked them back. "I don't know why You're letting things happen this way, Lord. I don't get it." Frustration racked her body and she leaned back against the cold stone.

You're angry.

"Don't I have some right to be angry? I've lost everyone I care about. My mom, before I had a chance to really know her. My dad, when I needed him the most. I'll lose the group home kids, and I'm losing Aunt Grace to Maggie." She broke down sobbing and didn't care. There was nobody around to hear it. "And don't forget Ian. Did I ask You to bring him into my life? Did You do that so I could lose him, too?" Shivering, Emily lifted her soaked face. "I've lost everyone I've ever loved. And as if that's not enough, I'm losing my own life too. Why, God?"

Thunder rolled, drowning out her words.

✤✤✤

Sprinting back to the farm, his feet kept time with the hammering in his chest. He burst into the house, gasping.

Maggie and Grace sat at the kitchen table—but no Emily.

"Did she come back?" He dripped puddles all over the kitchen

230

floor.

"No." Chewing on her lip, Maggie set her teacup down with a rattle and turned away.

Grace looked up. "Ian? Do ye know where Emmy is?"

Ian drew in a shaky breath. "I'm looking for her, Aunt Grace. I'm taking the truck now. Don't worry, I'll find her." *God, help me, I have to find her.*

He took the large flashlight they kept in the kitchen from the shelf and rushed out the door, pulling the key from his pocket.

As he got the truck running, he phoned the Kirkhaven constable, told him where he'd looked and where he was going. Then he headed out, and once he turned onto the main road, he switched the headlights on high-beam and drove slowly, scanning the fields and hills on both sides of Craig's Hill Road.

He searched along the old drover road and headed for town. In the village, he asked the few people he saw if they'd seen her, but no one had. He scoured every road surrounding the village, all the while fighting paralyzing alarm and trying not to think the worst. But his panic continued to build. It was the same panic he felt as Katy lay dying, the same feeling of utter helplessness.

Where had Emily gone? Had something happened to her? Had she fallen and injured herself? Or worse? Was she lying in the rain unconscious? The image of her lying at the bottom of a cliff or in the Kirkhaven burn, famous for overflowing with every hard rain, gripped his chest with a surge of fear-laced adrenaline.

His foot slammed the pedal. "God, You have to help her. You have to keep her safe. Help me find her, please."

Think, MacLean. What would keep her from returning to the farm?

He swallowed hard, willing away the worst-case scenario.

Again, she couldn't have left for the States—her passport and clothes were still here. Even if she wanted to leave, she would never do anything to upset Aunt Grace. So she had to be out here. If she'd gone walking, she could be anywhere in the surrounding countryside.

He drew a deep breath, exhaled hard, and searched both sides of the old drover road as he followed it northeast, toward the motorway to Stirling. "God, please help me find her. I'll do whatever You want. I'll be kinder to Maggie. I'll spend more time with Davy. I'll spend more time with You. I'll go to church every Sunday."

The Dumhnall Road sign loomed ahead.

Ian turned south and followed the narrow, winding road that led into the hills. He crossed the bridge and drove on, straining to see anything or anyone along the road.

The hills, burns, and meadows were known for attracting hikers, with walking trails stretching out for miles in all directions. She could be anywhere.

He pulled the truck over to the edge of the road and stopped. "Emily ..."

There was too much ground to cover. If she was out here, he wasn't going to find her, not without help.

"God, if You're there, I need You."

Rain dumped more water than the ancient wipers could handle.

With a sinking feeling in his gut, Ian turned the truck around, crossed the bridge again, and headed back toward the village. He needed help.

Use the flashlight.

Ian stopped the truck in the middle of the road, engine rattling at an idle, grabbed the light, and jumped out. He shined the light ahead, then swept the beam slowly over the meadow and across the road to the other side.

Nothing.

Reaching into the cab, he switched off the motor, then stepped away from the truck. Rain pelted his head, spattered against his face. He walked along the road, shining the light back and forth on each side.

Nothing.

"This is nuts." He returned to the truck, the knot in his gut twisting tighter with every step. As he reached for the door handle, a faint sound broke through the rain. Pulse racing, he held his breath and turned, listening.

The sound again, faint, like a cough. From the burn far below the road.

Heart thudding, he ran back to the bridge and shined the flashlight down onto the gurgling burn.

Nothing but water and rocks.

He crossed to the other side and aimed the light down, rubbed the rain from his eyes, and searched up and down the stream, around every rock and bush.

Nothing.

"Emily!" He held his breath, listened. "Emily!"

A faint voice drifted above the babbling water.

Ian ran along the bridge and shined the light at the edge of the road until he found part of an overgrown trail. He scrambled over rocks, through thorny briars, tangled branches, and tree roots, hugging the bridge's mossy stone face down to the water's edge. "Emily?"

A voice echoed. "In here."

He aimed his flashlight under the bridge.

She crouched under the arch, hugging her knees, shivering.

Ian hit the stream with a splash and ran, slipping on the rocks. When he reached her, he grabbed her arms, pulled her to her feet, and held her close. Relief came in tidal waves, sending a violent shudder through him.

"Thank You, God," he whispered.

She trembled against him.

He held her tighter. "Are you hurt, love? Are you all right? What happened?" He pulled back to see her face. Even in the dark, she looked pale, hollows circling her eyes. "Are you ill? I'll take you to the hospital."

"I'm okay. Just cold."

"I can't believe I found you." She tried to pull away, but he kept her in a firm grip. "How did you get here?"

"I went for a walk, but I got lost." Her voice was hoarse. "Is Aunt Grace upset?"

"She's just worried, naturally. Maggie too."

"Maggie's worried?"

"Aye. They didn't know where you'd gone."

She groaned. "I'm so sorry."

He heaved a deep sigh and tipped her chin up. "Emily, if you want to go exploring, take someone with you next time. I'd be happy to show you round."

Emily broke free of his hold. "I'm sorry for causing so much trouble. Thank you for coming out in all this to find me." She turned and made her way toward shore. Her foot slipped.

Ian instinctively offered a hand, but she caught herself and kept going until she reached the slope and Ian's makeshift trail. He walked on, shining the light ahead of her.

Illuminated raindrops fell hard and steady in its beam.

"Emily."

She stopped and looked back. The flashlight cast an upward glow, deepening the shadows beneath her eyes.

"I can't stand round and watch you go on alone like this."

She studied his face, but her weary expression didn't change.

"Will you let me help you?"

Emily shook her head.

If she were a MacLean by blood, she couldn't be any more stubborn. "Why not?"

"You're not talking about hiking, are you?"

He stepped closer. "I'm talking about you leaning on me, Emily. For everything."

The sound of rain swelled to a steady roar and reverberated round them in the narrow ravine.

Emily shivered. "You can't help me, Ian. You can't fix this."

"I know that, but I love you, Emily. I'll be your strength."

The shivering increased, shaking her whole body. She hugged her arms. "Ian, I appreciate that you want to, but you can't." She shook her head slowly. "Not for me, not even for yourself. I'm sorry, but no one's that strong. There's nothing you can do, Ian. Just let it go. Please." She turned and climbed the trail.

Her words sliced through him, their aim razor-sharp. She was right. He was helpless, just as he had been with Katy.

And the sooner you accept it, the better.

Angry tears stung his eyes. He swallowed hard, fighting the ache in his throat.

They hiked up the trail to the road and walked to the old truck. The weight of defeat threatened to crush him, but he concentrated on getting Emily home as quickly as possible. They rode back to the farm in silence.

When they arrived at the house, Maggie leaped from her chair and forced Emily to sit. "Grace!" Maggie's voice sounded unusually tremulous. "Put the kettle on." Then she scurried out of the kitchen.

Grace took Emily's hands and rubbed them. "What kept ye away so long, child?"

Emily darted a glance at Ian. "I got a little turned around and lost my way." She squeezed Grace's hands. "I'm sorry for causing you worry."

Maggie returned with a towel and wrapped it round Emily. As she rubbed Emily's shoulders, she glanced up at Ian. Her expression was odd, like a clashing mixture of guilt and relief.

"We must give the child something to eat, Maggie." Grace peered at Emily, worry etched in her wrinkly brow. "The poor lass needs food."

Jaw clenching tighter with every passing minute, Ian watched the old women tend to Emily.

Emily caught his eye. "Thanks," she whispered.

He nodded.

She was safe.

He slipped out of the house without a word. As he reached the cottage, his foot caught a rock. He bent, snatched it up, and hurled it as far as he could. The growing heartache finally sank in, settling down so deep that no amount of fury could drive it out. All he could do was lift his face to the sky and let the frustration come, cascading down his face with the rain.

CHAPTER THIRTY

The downpour continued. At times, rain pelted Emily's window so hard it sounded as if a mob were trying to get in. The older women busied themselves storing heather honey, maintaining their bickering banter, and making a huge mess, but Emily kept to herself.

Getting lost in the woods had broadsided her with a numbing truth. She couldn't be there for any of the people she loved, so there was no point hanging around and dragging out the pain of separation. The longer she stayed trapped in the house with the old sisters, the stronger her certainty became that she needed to remove herself. Not just from Ian, but all of them.

The deluge persisted and the walls of the old farmhouse seemed to press in. Emily spent her time in the upstairs study, exchanging messages with Rebecca, the research associate in Portland, and filling out questionnaires.

On the day Ian went to town, she went down to the cottage and phoned Jaye. Emily filled her in on what had happened with Ian and what she'd learned from the university clinic but held back the part about getting lost in the woods.

Jaye was unusually quiet.

"What's up, Jaye? What's wrong?"

"I was still hoping things would work out with you and Ian somehow. You know, the two of you in a castle on a cliff overlooking the sea, with a boatload of kids and living happily ever after."

"Really?" If not for the girlish pout in her friend's voice, Emily might have felt a stab of loss at the comment. But as it was, Jaye's fantasies came as a sparkling ray of relief. "Sounds good. And what do you get out of this little fairy tale?"

The line went quiet again. "Seriously? Em, if it meant you'd get a guy like that, I'd take a travel trailer in a hay field with forty-seven cats."

Emily couldn't help but laugh. "Now that's a lovely, wee picture."

"See? I knew it. You already sound like a highland lass."

"With a castle on the sea, don't forget."

By Wednesday, the rain eased up enough to get out of the house. Claire came and took Maggie, Grace, and Emily to Glasgow, where they spent the morning touring the city and visiting the sisters' old neighborhood, then back to Claire's flat for tea.

Emily hovered in the background and let the sisters visit with Claire and her family, but, for some reason, Maggie insisted on including her in everything and she made Emily join them at the table. After a few minutes, an unsettling sense of frustration burned in Emily. She jumped up and went to the window.

Claire pulled Emily aside and tossed a nod toward the older ladies. "You need some time away from the old hens. I'll pick you up Saturday morning. And pack a bag—you're staying the night."

Later, back in her room, Emily reached for the Bible Ian kept on top of the chest.

It wasn't there. In its place was an envelope bearing her name in Ian's neat block print.

Maybe she could pretend she hadn't seen it.

Holding her breath, she opened the envelope and drew out the folded paper. Not a letter, but a map. Hand-drawn in remarkable detail, it showed several landmarks including the farmhouse, walking trails, honeysuckle grove, surrounding roads, and hills. Even the loch where she went swimming with Claire's family. It was labeled and marked with directions and distances, with walking trails in blue. The church and cemetery were in the middle, and far northeast of the meadow and woods, a tall stone bridge arched over a stream.

She put the map back in the envelope and left it on the dresser.

Saturday morning, while Aunt Grace and Maggie assembled pies, Emily hung around the kitchen window and kept a close eye on the driveway. At the sound of Claire's car, Emily grabbed her duffel bag and jacket and waited at the door.

Claire burst in and winked at Emily. "Hey, there!"

"Hi." Emily smiled.

Claire ducked into the kitchen. "Do you have a pie for my boys, Maggie?" She shook her short hair, sending droplets of water flying. "If they find out I've been here on pie day and didn't bring one home, they'll have my head."

Maggie muttered, "Do *I* have a pie. Humph." She turned to the bunker and came back with the requested dish. Handing it to Claire, she leaned close and nodded in Emily's direction. "Keep a keen eye on that one, now. Dinna let her wander off."

"Fat chance." Claire grinned. "Hannah won't let her out of her sight."

"I'm making a pie for the reverend," Aunt Grace said over her shoulder, smiling. "He's so kind. He brought us a chicken for supper last week."

"No, Grace, I told ye. He dinna bring us a chicken."

"Margaret Agnes, I know a chicken when I see it."

"Let's go, Em, before things get ugly," Claire said beneath her breath. She headed for the door and called back with a song in her voice, "Cheerio, you two. We're off for some girl time—we're going shopping!"

✛ ✛ ✛

Aside from slipping up to Emily's bedroom to leave the map, Ian had avoided the house all week. It wasn't until Emily was safely on her way to Glasgow with Claire on Saturday that he finally had a chance to venture up to the house to see if anything needed done.

Janet Anderson's call, which had come later the same night he'd found Emily, could not have been a coincidence. It bore the mark of some carefully timed, divinely executed plan.

Janet could always look past the initial blow and the ensuing turmoil that often blindsided others, and focus on the biblical perspective. When she phoned, Ian almost didn't take the call. He was still numb, still trying to swallow the bitterness of defeat. But before long, he was telling Janet all that had happened, from the beginning. Her calm, steady strength traveled across thousands of miles without the slightest pause.

"I'll pray for you, Ian, for both of you," she said. "We don't often get to know where God is leading us or why, but we do know He'll provide whatever we need to get there. Read Isaiah and let God's word speak to your heart. Commit Isaiah 41:10 to memory and remember it when you pray. When the plan is God's, He provides the means. He is faithful, Ian. All His ways are good. Always."

Always? Coming from anyone else, Ian might have scoffed. But coming from Janet, the words carried weight.

As he neared the farmhouse, Ian slowed his pace. He stopped and leaned against the truck. The air smelled clean and fresh.

The dark rain clouds had finally moved on, leaving only wisps of white parading past the sun.

"Lord, I don't question Your goodness. I do trust You. But I don't understand why You brought me into her life if I can't *do* anything for her. Why did You let me fall in love with her if I have to let her go?" He leaned his head back and closed his eyes.

A gentle gust stirred. He pictured Emily standing there, a lock of hair moving across her cheek in the breeze. "Why?" he whispered.

Why? Where were you when I laid the earth's foundation? Tell Me, if you understand.

"That's not fair," he muttered. "Even Job couldn't answer that one."

The breeze picked up.

He opened his eyes.

The clouds made slow but steady progress across the sky.

"All right, forget I asked why. Just tell me what You want from me. If You'll help me, I'll do my best. Your way, God, not mine." With a slow exhale, Ian pushed off from the truck and went inside.

The kitchen was a war zone every Saturday afternoon, and this day was no different. Scattered flour, crushed berries, heaps of crusted mixing bowls, and dribbling pies adorned the room.

At the center of it all sat two white-haired, old women, sipping tea and looking quite pleased with themselves.

"It was honey." From Grace's tone, this wasn't the first time she'd said it.

"It was bread." Maggie set her teacup down with a clank. "Tell her, laddie."

Too late for escape—they'd seen him. "What's this?"

"Manna," Grace said. "In the desert. God sent it from heaven every morning."

"Aye." Out of habit, he went to the bunker and swept a critical glance over the pies.

"They crrrushed it up and made porridge from it," Maggie said, her words rolling low and burry like an old storyteller.

"No, they made it into cakes. Honey cakes."

With a grunt, Maggie rose from her seat and padded to the cupboard, shaking her head.

Grace's voice rose. "It came with the dew every morning and all they had to do was go out and gather it up. They always had plenty."

"Not plenty," Maggie fired over her shoulder. "They were only allowed to take enough for the one day. If they took extra, it got maggots."

"When I said plenty, I meant enough. It's the same thing."

"Och, 'tis not." Maggie turned to Ian. "Have some tea, laddie. There's *plenty*." She snorted and pulled out a cup.

Grace set her cup down gently. "Can ye imagine going to bed every night without a crumb to yer name? All they had at the end of the day was the good Lord's promise to provide again in the morn."

"Sit." Maggie shuffled toward Ian with a cup and saucer.

"No, thanks. I think I'll leave you ladies to your stories," Ian said. "Two's company, three's a crowd."

Aunt Grace lifted a quick smile. "Ooh, no. You must stay."

Ian sighed. "For a minute then." He pulled out a chair, shoved the clutter aside, and sat down.

The week-old honeysuckle bouquet still sat in the middle of the table. Though beginning to droop, it still gave off that haunting scent.

This wasn't right—the three of them having tea without Emily. For more than two years, the four of them had exchanged countless letters over tea. Emily's absence sent a cool, hollow feeling over him, like a swiftly moving shadow.

God could heal her. He'd done far more amazing things.

You want a miracle, but have you taken a look at the one you've already been given?

As Ian mulled on that thought, Maggie set a cup near him and poured from her teapot. "We saw our old house in Baillieston. They turned that drafty old place into a fancy gift shoppe." She clucked and shook her head. "Ye believe me now, eh, Gracie?"

"Do they know about the tree in the backyard?" Grace's pale eyes danced with girlish delight. "Did they see what Liam carved in it for ye?"

Maggie snorted and plopped onto her chair. "Havers."

Ian's studied his grannie. "What's this, Maggie? Love notes from Granddad?"

"Hoo-hoo." Grace chuckled.

Maggie's nose and cheeks burst with bright splotches. "Ye're not the only MacLean who can swap secret letters."

Ian frowned into the murky contents of his teacup. What else did the old woman know?

"Thomas slipped me notes when we were at the University." Grace chuckled. "When we worked in the clinic."

"At Glasgow University?" Ian asked. He grabbed a scrap of paper, scribbled a note, and shoved it into his pocket.

Grace nodded. "We had a lovely time then." Her smile faded. "But it was a sad time, too. I wanted to be with Emmy. With her precious mum gone, Emmy's poor father ..."

A familiar twinge tugged at Ian's chest.

"So she was a wee child then?" Maggie asked.

"Fifteen," Ian said much too quickly.

Maggie smiled and slurped her tea.

"I did love being in Scotland, but I needed to go back for the lass."

Maggie poured more tea for Grace, but the pot clanked hard against her cup. "And go back ye did. I never saw ye again."

"Och, Maggie. Ye've had Ian here. And Claire and her lovely, wee family. Ye've not needed me."

"Who said anything about needing ye?" Rising from her chair,

Maggie took the empty scone plate and stomped to the stove for more.

Grace reached over and laid a hand lightly on Ian's arm. "Such a dear young mon. Maggie is blessed to have ye and Claire so close."

Ian put his cup down and turned to his aunt. "Did Claire take you to visit the university hospital when you went to Glasgow?"

Aunt Grace shook her head. "No. There was not enough time."

"I'll take you then, if you fancy a tour."

"Ooh." Grace patted his arm. "That would be lovely." She sipped her tea and smiled.

"Aye, lovely," Maggie chortled as she returned to the table. "A whole day footerin' about in a hospital." She thrust her pudgy, red nose close to her sister's face. "Best keep yer eyes open, Gracie. I've heard tales of old folks like ye going in for a visit and never coming out again."

"Never?" Aunt Grace lowered her cup. "Ooh, dear."

Ian stifled a chuckle. "I'll go with you."

"I'm going too." Maggie set the pot down with an exasperated grunt. "If ye'd stayed here where ye belong, Gracie, there'd be no need for all this foolishness."

"Margaret Agnes, I had to go back. Emmy needed me. Her dear mum wanted the lass properly cared for. Ooh, if Jess could see her now, she'd be so proud. Emily turned out so lovely."

"Aye, quite lovely." Maggie cocked her head at Ian. "Dinna ye agree, laddie?"

Ian swallowed scalding tea with a loud gulp and set his cup down hard enough to rattle the saucer.

"Jess named Emily after a Wordsworth poem," Grace said. "There was a heartsick young maid named Emily who ... ooh, dear, I can't mind the whole of it now, but there were some lines about those flowers. How did it go, now?"

The old woman's brow furrowed so deep that Ian grew half afraid she would have another stroke.

"I remember." With eyes closed, Grace smiled. *"She approached yon rustic shed/ hung with late-flowering woodbine, spread/ along the walls and overhead/ the fragrance of the*

242

breathing flowers/ revived a memory of those hours."

Maggie grunted. "Woodbine. There's no mistaking that scent." She reached out and plucked a blossom from the bouquet on the table.

Ian frowned. "Woodbine? I thought this was honeysuckle."

Maggie smiled and brought the blossom to her round nose. "Did ye now?"

"Woodbine *is* honeysuckle," Aunt Grace said. "Jess loved it, and so does Emmy."

"It turns up in such odd places." Maggie sniffed the flower so hard the petals almost disappeared.

"Thomas says,"—Grace's voice fell to a conspirator's tone— "'When words escape, flowers speak.'"

"Do they now?" The old woman leaned back in her seat and folded her arms across her bosom. "This bunch appeared on my table. I dinna ken how."

Maggie's hints didn't go unnoticed, but nailing down the thought that kept springing to mind was more important.

Grace's eyes grew round. "Maybe it was faeries."

Maggie cackled long and loud.

The idea stirring in Ian's mind suddenly took shape, like a painting when the key brushstrokes are applied. He sprang from his seat. "I've got things to do." As he headed for the back door, their voices trailed him down the hall.

"I've always wanted to see a faerie," Grace said.

Maggie chuckled. "I believe ye just did."

CHAPTER THIRTY-ONE

Claire and Emily strolled from shop to shop under only smatterings of rain in spite of overcast skies. By early afternoon, the clouds parted and the sun finally appeared, warming the streets and working to dry a week's worth of puddles.

Not that rain would have made any difference to Emily. Getting a break from the farmhouse felt like a long-awaited parole.

They stopped for lunch at a cozy, little chip shop tucked upstairs above a pub. The place housed a small gift shop with an assortment of Scottish souvenirs. Emily bought a drawing pad and matching pencil with a red and blue tartan design for Hector, and she picked up postcards for her dad, Jaye, and the rest of the kids at Juniper Ranch. After a lunch of fish and chips with fresh apple pie and cream, they toured the oldest house in Glasgow. Built in the late 1400s, the house had been renovated to give visitors a glimpse of what it might have looked like in centuries past. When they returned to Claire's flat later, Emily met Davy. With his burly build, bright, blue eyes, and quiet manner, he looked a lot like Douglas, but the dimpled smile was definitely Jack.

After dinner, Emily stood. "I'll do the cleanup."

"Sorry, love." Claire carried dishes to the sink where Davy was scrubbing and rinsing. "This handsome chap here offered to help me, and I hate to say it, but his offer tops yours. Besides, it looks like you've got bedtime-story duty." She nodded toward the doorway.

The girls awaited—Kallie clutching a book and Hannah hugging a cloud of purple, shimmery fabric.

Story time? But ...

Hannah stuffed the purple cloud into Emily's hands and

smiled.

Emily returned the smile. What had she expected? If she really wanted to distance herself from the farm and Ian, then spending time with his sister and her family probably wasn't the wisest choice. "Okay." She held out her free hand. "Lead me to my chambers."

One twin bed was ready for Emily and the other had been fixed up double so the girls could share.

"Tonight's a slumber party," Kallie said. She hopped onto a bed and bounced until it squeaked. Giggling, Hannah joined her sister.

Slumber party. Marvelous.

"So what bedtime story am I reading?" Emily asked.

Kallie shook her head so hard her hair whipped against her face. "I'm reading. But I'll hold it up so you can see the pictures."

"That's the best part," Hannah said. "Uncle Ian's pictures."

Emily sucked in a sharp breath. "Wait. What book is that?"

"*Daniel's Friends Face the Fire.*" Kallie giggled. "I couldn't say all those *f*s when I was wee."

Fabulous. What next—Ian in person?

Kallie flipped to the first page, but Hannah made her go back and start at "Jack's page." A handwritten inscription, slightly faded with time, sprawled across the inside cover.

Emily's heart tripped at the familiar print.

"Read it." Hannah nudged Emily.

Clearing her throat, Emily looked to Kallie for the go-ahead, then read aloud. "'To my little man, Jack. From your favorite Uncle Ian: May we men always stand up for what is right, play hard, and win the hearts of beautiful ladies. (If it's okay with your mum.) But most of all, may we have the courage to—'" Her throat tightened and the words wouldn't come.

Kallie dove in and finished. "'To stand in the fire and remember that God will always stand in it with us. Love, your Uncle Ian.'"

Emily stared at the ink standing out against the white space as Hannah spoke. "Jack was a wee baby when Uncle Ian made this book."

"He didn't make the book, only the pictures," Kallie said. "Wheesht! I'm reading now."

And very well for an eight-year-old.

While Kallie read, Hannah crept close, snuggled into Emily's lap, and leaned against her. The account of the three young men standing up to King Nebuchadnezzar for their faith in God, in spite of the fire that threatened to take their lives, took on a living heartbeat. It breathed, whispering words only her soul could hear.

"I'd be so afraid." Hannah said.

"Not me," Kallie said. "I'd take a sword from the guard and cut their heads off."

Emily winced.

"No, you wouldn't," Hannah said. "The guards got all burnt up and so did their swords."

"Still, I wouldn't be afraid. Shadrach, Meshach, and Abednego weren't afraid."

"Yes, they were. That's why they were brave." Hannah looked up at Emily. "Would you be afraid?"

The fiery furnace scene lay open on the floor. The three young men must have been terrified, and certainly had no idea how it would turn out. All they knew was to trust and obey God without question.

Would I trust God enough to surrender to the flames and stand firm, no matter what?

God, would You really ask me to do that?

Both girls waited.

A pulse-quickening urgency stole over her, as though her answer was somehow forever binding. A test.

My grace is sufficient for you, for My power is made perfect in weakness.

Emily drew a calming breath. "I think if the Lord wanted me to go into a blazing furnace, He would—"

Have to send her a text message. In all caps.

"He would go with me and give me the courage and strength I need to do it." *That's good, Em. You almost have yourself convinced.*

Kallie closed the book with a snap. "Uncle Ian is going to make

246

a book for me, too. Someday."

Emily studied the girl. "Is he really?"

"Aye. About Samson."

"And a beautiful princess," Hannah said.

"No. Samson was a super-warrior. He killed a thousand men with a donkey bone."

Hannah frowned. "Then I'll ask him to make me a book, too." She turned to Emily. "You forgot your princess frock. Here." She pulled the wad of purple from Emily's hands and thrust it at her.

Emily stood and held the tutu against her. "I'm not sure this will fit me, Hannah."

"It will. My da wears it when we play castles."

Emily bit her lip, but the image of stocky Davy in a purple tutu sprang to mind and a chuckle slipped out. She slipped the fabric over her head, stood up, and pulled it down around her waist.

Kallie giggled.

Hannah smashed herself against Emily's legs and hugged her tight.

Emily hugged her back, fighting the tug in her heart. *Good job letting go of Ian and his family.*

A creak came from behind them.

Claire stood in the doorway, head cocked to one side. "Join me in the kitchen in a bit?"

Emily finished up the bedtime rituals according to the girls' specific instructions and tucked them in before wandering to the front of the house and complimenting Claire on their manners.

"You have a fine way with kids." Claire set a plate of shortbread on the kitchen table and filled Emily's mug from a flowered teapot. "I'm impressed."

Emily sipped her tea.

Claire's kitchen was small, about the same size as the one Emily shared with Aunt Grace, but stuffed to overflowing with everything from cooking utensils and food bins to toys, books, and gadgets in various stages of disassembly. Colored drawings, notes, and photos covered nearly every inch of the refrigerator.

One photo caught Emily's eye—Hannah in a purple dress with glittery cheeks. Beside her stood a small, fierce-looking pirate.

"Is that Kallie dressed as a pirate?" Emily pointed. "I almost didn't recognize her."

"Aye. That was taken at the Summer Fair in Kirkhaven. The girls each won a ribbon in the fancy dress contest." Claire took down the photo and gave it to Emily. "The sparkles on Hannah's face were her Uncle Ian's doing. Faerie dust, he told her. We averted a scorching meltdown when a broken-hearted faerie princess lost her crown. A very noble rescue."

Emily's throat tightened as she stared at the painted faces. How like Ian to care about such a seemingly little thing. "That must have made her day."

"Och, you've no idea." Claire rolled her eyes. "He's quite the hero. But I suppose you already know that."

Emily nodded. Time for a change of topic. Ten ways to put out a grass fire. Anything.

"I heard Ian spent a weekend at the beach with you and Aunt Grace."

"Yes. That was a special treat for Aunt Grace. It meant a lot to her."

"And you? Did you have a good time, then?"

Emily swirled the tea around in her mug. The weekend she spent with Ian was one she would never forget. "Yes."

"Oh. So you do know how to have fun. Or at least you did."

Emily gaped at Claire.

"Can I be frank with you, Emily?"

Frank? She widened her eyes. *Good grief, what were you before?*

"You may be alive, but you're not living." Claire crossed her arms and leaned back. "Not like the woman you were meant to be."

Heat rose in her cheeks. How could Claire say that? Emily clasped her hands around the mug, but the cooling ceramic drew heat away from her fingers, leaving them chilled.

Claire lifted the teapot and filled Emily's cup. "You're a very gifted woman, Emily. Generous, caring. And loads of fun, I'll wager. You have so much to give. But since you've been here, all you've done is fash and brood about how you're going to die." A snort puffed from her nose. "As if you're the only one."

Emily's mouth gaped. Brood? She met Claire's dark gaze. "I'm trying to avoid causing anyone pain. Especially Ian. I just want to do what's best for him."

"Best for Ian? Well that's good and noble, love, but how do you know what that is? And what gives you the right to decide?"

The blunt force of Claire's words sent Emily's heart pounding. Claire had no idea how long and hard Emily had agonized over this decision.

"So you're throwing away what life you have left to avoid pain?"

"I'm not throwing away—"

"Has it occurred to you that you're being selfish?"

Selfish? Emily's mouth dropped open again. Did Claire think this was easy for Emily? That she enjoyed losing those she loved?

Emily cleared her throat, but the tightness wouldn't budge. "I'm not sure what makes you say that. I don't think you understand how much I'm giving up."

"Listen, love. I know you think you're sparing everyone you love by checking out of their lives, but you're wrong."

Ah. The real reason Claire invited her here. Emily should have known. She reined in a growing wave of resentment. "I don't have a choice."

"Oh, you have a choice." Claire nodded. "You just don't like your options."

"What do you mean?"

Claire leaned forward again, bracing her chin in both hands. "I'm going to tell you a story. Davy left us once. Did you know that?"

Emily shook her head.

"When Hannah was a baby, Davy lost his job and had to go looking for work, but jobs were hard to find. He would find something for a while, but then he'd get let off. He had to travel farther away to find work and send money home. It was hard on him, hard on us all, but he did it. And he kept it up for a while, but then a time came when there just wasn't any work. He went all the way to England and beyond, came back, went out again. But every time he came home without a job, it did something to him. It ate away at him. I had to get part-time work, get a sitter for the kids. He felt like a failure, like he'd let us down. He couldn't face his children, or me. The last time he went looking for work ..." She shrugged. "He didn't come back."

Perhaps Davy was one of those who also felt the weight of responsibility for others. "He must have felt terrible."

"Aye. Our children's faces were a constant reminder of his failure. He felt worthless."

"That's so sad."

"You want to know what's truly sad? Davy couldn't see there were far more valuable things he could provide us. Things worth much more than money."

"That must have been incredibly difficult for him," Emily said.

Claire's dark eyes locked onto Emily's. "It was incredibly selfish of him."

Selfish. There was that word again, parting the conversation like the Red Sea and leaving a silent gap. "How was he being selfish?"

"He wanted to provide for us, but only if he could do it on his terms. When it didn't work out the way he wanted, he couldn't bear the guilt from seeing us every day." Claire rose and took her cup to the sink. "He left because he didn't like the way being with us made him feel."

The words landed like a punch to her gut.

Claire washed and rinsed her cup, dried it, and put it away.

How could she possibly think Emily's situation was anything like Davy's?

After a few uneasy minutes of silence, Emily asked, "He's doing well now, isn't he?"

"Aye. And he finally found a good, steady job." Claire returned to her seat across from Emily. "But it took a long time, and that was hard. And yet it was the best thing that could have happened. Because during that time, Davy learned how much his kids needed him. They didn't care what he brought home, only that he came home." She leaned forward. "He's a good man, Emily. Coming home without a job took loads of courage. It's easy to stand there and do your part when times are good and everyone's pleased with you. But it takes real courage to stand up and do the right thing when it will cost something. Like your pride."

"Pride?"

"Or comfort. Whose pain are you really trying to avoid—Ian's? Or yours?"

CHAPTER THIRTY-TWO

Sunday morning, Emily awoke to dazzling light streaming in the girls' bedroom window. In spite of the promise of a gorgeous day, her heart felt heavier than it had in a long time.

The Kendals somehow managed to squeeze seven people into Claire's station wagon and get them to church. Theirs was pleasantly similar to her church back home.

Had Ian taken Maggie and Aunt Grace to church?

After the girls were dismissed to children's class, Claire scooted closer to Emily and tugged on Davy to follow.

A humorous video clip played on the screens, showing a guy dangling from the side of a cliff until he couldn't hold on any longer, only to discover he was just a few feet from the ground. Then the minister began his message by asking the congregation if they'd ever felt hopeless to the point of giving up.

As he delivered his sermon, Emily caught only bits and pieces. Her thoughts drifted to the hopelessness she'd felt about her dad. A growing sense of shame pressed on her heart.

Lord, I gave up hope that he could ever change. I gave up believing You could help him, didn't I? Please forgive me.

"Friends," the minister said, "when the children of Israel wandered in the desert, the Lord provided manna to sustain them, but they only received what they needed for each day. Did they wring their hands in worry over how they would survive the next day? Or did they believe God's promise and trust in the faithfulness He had shown so many times before?"

Davy reached an arm around Claire, leaned over, and whispered in her ear. She smiled up at him, and Davy gave her shoulders a squeeze. Claire snuggled close under his encircling arm.

252

A deep longing for that kind of loving support caught Emily off guard. She stared at her interlaced fingers, then smoothed the already smooth white suede of her skirt.

The couple's simple embrace didn't do justice to the story of Claire and Davy's struggles and the courage it had taken to bring them together as a family.

Swallowing the knot in her throat, she kept her eyes trained on her skirt.

Soft, steady music played as the minister drew his message to a close. "Saints, where are you today? Has the desert's heat stolen your hope? Have you surrendered yourself into God's ever-faithful hands? Let us pray."

The music increased. When the minister finished praying, he stepped down.

Emily looked around, but no one got up to leave.

A Celtic-sounding wood flute played a beautiful, poignant melody. The tune rose, then quieted, as a deep, male Scottish voice sang.

> *"I love the Lord, my Rock, my Strength*
> *He's with me even ere the dawn*
> *With peace and safety, love and grace*
> *His love will guide through every storm*
> *No trial's strain, no burden's weight*
> *No fear beyond all measure*
> *Can take away my hope, my joy*
> *His love for me, His pleasure."*

Emily gasped. That voice, rich and deep with a gentle burr, sounded like Ian. She scanned the platform.

The man stood near the back. Shorter and fairer in color, a few years older.

Emily closed her eyes, gripped by the words of the song and the shock of hearing a man singing them with such depth of feeling. Every nerve in her body tingled with a sense of awe at God's love, power, and presence. On the last verse, she held her breath to hear every word.

"Trusting in the cross of Christ
No longer all alone to stand;
No pain in life nor fear of death
Can take me from His loving hand."

Though her eyes remained closed, tears rolled down her face as the song ended with the final sweet strains of flute.

A thunderous silence filled the room.

In her mind's eye, she could almost see her Savior standing amid flames, beckoning to her to come and stand with Him and not be afraid.

Dear God, I thought I was being strong, but maybe I've just been afraid. I haven't been listening to You or depending on You at all. I've been trying to take care of everything and everyone on my own. I haven't been trusting You.

Why had she been trying to do it all on her own?

Head bowed in prayer, Emily fought her darkest doubts that surfaced from the depths. Did God really hold her in His hand? Did He truly care?

Can I trust You? Are You going to be there?

In the quiet of her heart, she heard, *Yes, I'm here, and I will hold you. Always.*

An overwhelming sense of love and peace poured over her like warm oil, surrounding and embracing her, unleashing a flood of tears from somewhere deep inside. She covered her face with both hands and wept.

After a while, Emily wiped her eyes and looked around.

Claire sat waiting nearby, her own eyes rimmed with tears.

Some people had moved to the rear of the sanctuary, but most had moved out to the foyer. Davy waited near the entrance doors with a giggling Hannah in his arms.

Claire handed her a tissue.

"Thanks," Emily whispered and took it. As she blew her nose and wiped her face, she braced herself for more of Claire's blunt remarks.

But none came. Nothing but a hand rubbing across her back,

gently stroking her hair.

Emily swallowed back tears and turned to Claire.

Her dark, inquiring eyes probed Emily's, her head cocked to one side. "You all right, love?"

She gave Claire a faint smile. "Yeah. But I think I need to spend some quality time in prayer. I'm sadly overdue."

"Well, too bad there's a queue. Get in line."

Emily's smile widened.

Claire stretched out both arms and wrapped them around her.

Emily hugged her back, long and tight.

By the time Emily returned to the farm, the sun was setting. Shadows seeping up from the earth turned heather-covered hills a deeper, dusky purple. Strokes of orange, purple, gold, and pink filled the enormous sky-canvas, painting the hills behind the house in glorious color.

I lift up my eyes to the mountains—where does my help come from? My help comes from the Lord, the Maker of heaven and earth.

Emily picked up her bags from the end of the walk and breathed in the sweet floral and pungent wood scents that mingled in the air after a full day of sun. She took a fleeting glance at the cottage, then headed to the house. As she passed the kitchen doorway, she stopped.

The kitchen was clean, no sign of the two old ladies. In the sitting room, she found a partially finished puzzle on the folding table and a note. Emily set her bags down and took a closer look.

The note was written in Aunt Grace's once elegant, now shaky scrawl.

> *Dear Emmy,*
> *Maggie and I are taking a walk. She says not to worry, we'll be back soon.*
> *Love from your Aunt Grace*

She laid the note down with a sigh. Two old women, one blind and one frail, venturing out together without a bit of fear in either of them.

You may be alive, but you're not living.

It wasn't the first time Claire's rebuke marched across the trail of her thoughts. Maybe she should join the two fearless, old ladies. Get out there and make the time she had left with them count. But she also wanted to spend a few more moments alone while God's quiet promptings were still fresh in her mind. She slung her duffel bag over her shoulder, gathered her shopping bags, and headed up the stairs. At her room, she held her breath, opened the door, and surveyed the room.

Exactly the same way she had left it. No notes, no maps, no sign of Ian.

She dropped her bags at the foot of the bed.

Where are you? Have you surrendered yourself fully into God's hands?

The words sung in that rich baritone continued to play in her head the way they had all day, echoing the last lines from the song.

No pain in life or fear of death can take me from His loving hand.

The room felt stuffy. She needed to clear her head, to think. She opened a window, knelt beside the bed, and rested her head on folded arms.

A gust of fresh air wafted in, a clean, cool contrast to the hot, thick air trapped in the bedroom.

Like a furnace.

The fiery furnace story seemed to follow her like a shadow. Emily had taught Sunday school students to trust God in all things, no matter the outcome. She was well acquainted with what the 'outcome' was in her case. Her mom's death had affected the lives of everyone, especially Emily's dad. Emily could never leave such a lasting scar on those she loved.

It was the right thing to do, wasn't it? To shield those she loved from pain?

But that wasn't what Emily's mom had done. Mom loved everyone, including the Lord, without holding back, right to the end. She'd had so much love to give, so much peace and faith-filled assurance. Her mom's love and peace in the face of uncertainty had touched Emily, left a deep impression on her. Her mom had trusted God with her life and had lived every day with His help and without fear. Like the three young men in the furnace.

"I'm not afraid of dying, Lord. But maybe Claire is right—maybe I *am* afraid of living. Or the pain that comes from it. And if loving fully and being there for the people around me is what You want from me, then please help me do that. One day at a time, if that's what it takes. Help me have the courage and peace that my mom had. Please forgive me for pulling away, Lord. Help me live the rest of my life the way You want me to." She leaned back on her heels and lifted her face, eyes closed. "And please, please help me know what to do about Ian. I want ... whatever You want for him. Please show me what that is, Lord. I need to know."

Emily drew in a deep breath and let it out in a long, cleansing sigh. Memories of her mom when Emily was a little girl filled her thoughts, memories she hadn't visited in a long time. Catching butterflies in the backyard. Gathering flowers. Watching hummingbirds together. The way her mom would always slip a few drops of honeysuckle oil into the laundry, a tradition that Emily had continued for herself. The way her mom smelled when she hugged—

Mid-breath, Emily froze.

The scent of honeysuckle had crept into the room and had been growing stronger, infusing the air with sweetness and surrounding her like a tender, warm embrace. Where was it coming from? The woods? Could it carry that far?

She went to the window and looked out across the yard and at the trees covering the hills behind the house. The grove had to be at least half a mile away. So how—

But there at the window, the scent was so thick and so sweet that she could almost taste it. She looked down.

Directly below her, along the wall, a new wooden trellis supported a massive cluster of honeysuckle.

Her jaw dropped. The dirt at its base was freshly turned and tamped down. Who—?

You know who.

For a moment, she couldn't breathe. But as she stared at the mass of blooms, her breath quickened. She turned and ran from the room and took the stairs two at a time. She threw open the back door and ran along the back of the house to the flowerbed. Yes. There, beneath her window, stood a gigantic mass of freshly transplanted honeysuckle. She covered her mouth and blinked her blurring eyes. Since she still couldn't see, she closed her eyes and just breathed.

CHAPTER THIRTY-THREE

When Ian heard Claire's car pull up, he stopped cleaning the shovel and listened, pulse racing.

A car door opened and closed, then the car backed round and left.

He went back to cleaning. *Lord, just one last chance to change her mind, that's all I ask. Just one.* He forced himself to concentrate on what he was doing, even though cleaning garden tools didn't require much thought. He'd lost track of how many times over the last twenty-four hours he had pulled out his mobile and began to ring Claire's number.

And how many times he had sensed the need to wait.

So I guess this is the part where I lean on You. Ian scraped the mud from the shovel and put the tool away. Then, one by one, he cleaned the rest of the tools and put them back in their places.

The back door opened and slammed against the house, followed by the patter of rapid footsteps.

Ian dropped what he was doing and ducked out of the shed.

Emily stood at the honeysuckle with her back to him, trembling.

Adrenaline surged into his chest, sent his heart pounding. *Steady, MacLean. Don't blow it.* Ian let out a slow breath.

There would be no burst of passion this time, no raw emotion, just a solemn promise. If she refused again, he'd press her no more. He'd let her go.

As he walked toward Emily, she turned round. Her eyes widened at the sight of him.

He stopped a few feet from her.

She searched his face. "Did you bring this here? From the

woods?"

"Aye."

Emily stared at the flowers, then up at her bedroom window. When she faced him again, she whispered, "Why?"

He shrugged. It was an impulse, a flash of inspiration. "Thought you'd fancy it."

She stared at him for a long moment, eyes glistening. "I love it. I can't believe you did this, Ian." Her voice fell to a whisper. "Thank you."

A lump formed in his throat that stung when he swallowed. "Emily, what you said to me the other day, beneath the bridge ... you were right. I can't be your strength. Or mine." He shook his head. "I can't hold us both up. Not on my own."

Her tears spilled and trickled slowly. She brushed them away with a trembling hand.

He took a deep breath. "I want you to know I've given this plenty of thought. I remembered how God once helped me overcome things I couldn't on my own. He gave me strength before, and I believe He will again. You don't have to be afraid for me, love. I'm putting my life in God's hands. I've been praying and trusting Him. And I'm going to keep praying every day for the strength to face whatever comes. And not just what you have to face, but everything. I believe that's what He wants from me. He'll provide what we need to get through each day. Like manna in the desert."

She gasped. "Manna?"

He sought her eyes, her heart, and hoped she could see into his. "I'll look to Him every day, one day at a time. That's all I can do. I mean, that's what I *will* do. I promise."

Emily's face was unbearably difficult to read.

He drew a shuddering breath. "I love you, Emily. Nothing will ever change that. So if you're not going marry me, I just want you to know that no matter where you are, I will always—"

Wait—was she *nodding*?

Something squeezed his chest so tight he couldn't breathe.

"Yes," she whispered.

"Yes?"

Emily took a step toward him.

His arms opened for her as if on cue, but like an idiot he just stood there, heart racing, numb with disbelief. "You'll marry me?"

She slipped her arms round his waist and rested against him. "If you're willing to stand in the fire with the Lord's help, then so am I." She raised a tearful, little smile. "I love you, Ian. I want to spend the rest of my life with you."

Relief flooded over him like a tidal wave, nearly knocking him down. He crushed her close and held her tight.

Thank You.

Eyes closed, Emily savored his embrace. She would hold onto every moment, every second from now on.

Ian pulled back a fraction and looked into her eyes, his arms still encircling her. "You're sure?"

Emily met his gaze. "Yes. Absolutely."

His focus went to her lips. He cupped her face with one hand and bent his head slowly.

Emily closed her eyes, every nerve tingling with anticipation.

His lips touched—

A blaring car horn made them both jump and turn toward the drive.

Claire slammed her door shut and marched straight for them. Behind her, Maggie and Grace fumbled to get out of the car.

Ian groaned.

"Well, and what's this?" Claire reached them, eyebrows cocked as high as they could go.

Maggie's door slammed. "We were not lost! I know my way round my own farm!" The old woman stomped to the other side of the car where Grace was getting out.

Aunt Grace called out to Emily, "Ooh, dinna fret, lassie. We went for a long walk, but then Claire came and said we'd gone far enough."

"Aye." Claire grunted. "The old hens were halfway to Stirling."

When the older women reached them, Ian said, "Aunt Grace, Maggie, Claire; Emily and I have something to tell you." He grasped Emily's hand. "We're going to be married. As soon as possible."

Claire's mouth formed an *O*.

Maggie chuckled.

Grace sent a dazed smile around the circle. "Who? Who's getting married?"

"Ian." Maggie's smile turned her cheeks into rosy mounds. "And yer bonnie lass."

"Och, a wedding!" Claire squealed. "I'll start a guest list." She grabbed Ian's arm. "Ian, you'll have to find a way to bribe Kallie into wearing a frock. Maggie too, for that matter. I'll help Emily find the perfect one for the wedding."

Maggie's smile fell. She sputtered and coughed. "Ye're not putting a frock on me."

"There's going to be a wedding, dearie," Aunt Grace said. "Ye can dress up this once."

"No." She crossed her arms and shook her head.

"What shape is that cottage in?" Claire asked Ian. "Oh, never mind. It does no good to ask a man. I'll take care of it. We'll fix it up cozy for you two."

"The cottage?" Ian said.

Claire snorted. "Well, what else? You'll be newlyweds. You didn't think you were going to live in the house with those two, did you?"

"Aye, they can have the cottage," Maggie said. "And that eejit telephone."

"But is it big enough for the wee bairns?" Grace asked.

Claire turned a worried glance at Emily.

Emily frowned. "Bairns? You mean kids?" She glanced away to hide the disappointment in her face. That was a topic she and Ian would discuss, and it wouldn't take long. Having children was out of the question.

"Well, let's not get ahead of things," Claire said quickly. "First things first. We need to set a date. Ian, find out what you need for a marriage license and see how long that takes."

"Two weeks."

Everyone fell silent and stared at Ian.

He cleared his throat. "I checked." He met Emily's gaze. "Do you have a birth certificate?"

"It's at home. I'll have to get my dad or Jaye to send—" Emily gasped.

"What is it?" Ian asked.

Dad. How could she tell him she was marrying Ian after everything he'd said?

"What's wrong?" Claire laid a hand on Emily's arm.

"I have to tell my dad," she whispered.

"If it's all right with you, I'll tell him," Ian said quietly. "I'd like to speak to him."

Emily shook her head. "He's dead set against—" She glanced at Aunt Grace and shot a meaningful look at Ian. "He's not going to give his blessing."

"Do you need it?" Claire frowned. "Is this some sort of American thing?"

Emily lowered her voice. "It's more than that. It's complicated."

"Och, how hard can it be?" Claire snorted. "Let *me* talk to him."

Emily bit her lip and looked to Ian.

He turned to his sister. "It should come from me. Man to man."

"Fine." Claire shrugged. "Maybe he'll change his mind." Her eyebrows shot up and she smiled at them both. "Emily did. Maybe it runs in the family."

CHAPTER THIRTY-FOUR

Emily expected a certain amount of crazy to erupt with a wedding about to take place, but she wasn't prepared for Claire. Ian's sister moved in like a small tornado, scrubbing, painting, hauling stuff out of the cottage, sending Ian for supplies, and making the cottage tidy.

While Ian was gone, Emily spent some time looking online for a doctor. She could see Dr. Fletcher for an exam when she went back to close up the house in Juniper Valley, but she needed a prognosis now. Though she felt fine, HCM could be asymptomatic until a person experienced a sudden heart attack. She needed to know what to expect and what precautions to take, if any. And whether or not she could be running or doing anything strenuous.

During her search, she made a surprising discovery: Glasgow University had published articles about Freyer's Syndrome written by Dr. Thomas Clark.

Uncle Thomas? Why hadn't she remembered his work in Scotland?

And not only had he studied there, the genetics department at GU had a current study devoted to researching the disease.

She contacted the hospital and set up appointments for a full exam and DNA testing. With that done, a little of the weight troubling her lifted. This was good. She could accomplish something of significance, at least. But the rest of what tugged on her heart would remain unfinished. Maybe time would ease the guilt of abandoning the people she had been responsible for. She could only pray that her dad would be okay. Maybe, in time, he would be able to accept her marrying Ian. But what about the kids at Juniper Ranch? How would Hector and the others feel when they got the news that Emily wouldn't be returning? Would they feel abandoned

264

again?

Ian returned just after lunch. He thundered up the stairs to the study, pulled her into his arms, and kissed her. "The sun is calling, love. Let's take a walk."

They went through the back gate and headed for the woods. The sun had dried up the last of the rain, bringing the grass on the meadow and hillside springing to life.

Emily breathed in the mingling woodland scents.

"Your dad sent what you need. Global express. It should arrive tomorrow."

She stared at him. "Really? How did he sound? Was he upset?"

He shrugged. "He agreed to send it, that's all I know." He took her hand as they climbed the hill. "Emily, how do you feel about leaving your life in the States behind? Your dad, the kids at the home, the study in Portland. You're okay with letting all that go, then?"

She gave his hand a squeeze. "I'll keep in touch with my dad as much as he'll let me. And I've been thinking about the kids." She shrugged. "I would've had to say good-bye to them eventually. It's just they've been through a lot."

Hector's face came to mind, and a weight of sorrow pressed on her.

"I'm just afraid my leaving will only add more to the sting of being abandoned."

He drew a deep breath. "When we go back to close up your aunt's house, let's spend some time there. Give you a chance for a proper good-bye with the kids. And your dad."

"I'd like that." She turned to him with a smile. "And it looks like I'll be able to take part in research here. I found a Freyer's Syndrome clinical study in Glasgow." She explained what she'd discovered. "I have an appointment next week."

"For what?"

"A full exam and official prognosis. Then they'll start blood work for genetic tests."

"I'm going with you." He stopped and looked at her, hope dawning in his eyes. "Maybe we'll find out if they've made any progress on a cure."

She kept walking, pained by his expression. How long would he hope for a cure that wasn't coming?

They reached the glen and Ian led her to the center of the clearing. Honeysuckle, warmed by the sun, filled the air with a powerful, sweet scent.

Inhaling, Emily drank in the beauty of the quiet sanctuary.

"Will this do for the wedding then?"

She spun around. "Really? We can have it here?"

"If you fancy."

She wrapped her arms around him.

He searched her face, her hair. "I dreamed of you. The same dream, again and again. You're always coming to see me, just like you did that day in your white dress with your hair up and a few curls sneaking down. In my dream, you're coming to say you'll marry me. But then I'd wake and find ..." He let out a sigh, then smiled lightly. "It was just a dream."

A tear trickled down Emily's cheek. Perhaps one day she could make him understand that she'd had a dream of her own, and he far exceeded it.

CHAPTER THIRTY-FIVE

Emily adjusted the strap around her heel and stood for one last look in the full-length mirror. Maybe if she stood here staring at the woman in white long enough, she could convince herself the day had really come, that this was truly her wedding day.

Thank You for today, Lord. This day is all I can hope for. All I need.

The simple, white dress brought out the warm tone of her skin, but the glow came from within. Her hair shone with coppery highlights, swept up in the back with tendrils cascading down around her neck and shoulders. Maybe not exactly the way Ian remembered it that day, but close, hopefully.

A knock rattled the door and Claire burst in, draped in blue and out of breath. She stilled, eyes shining. "Oh, Emily. Look at you; you're so beautiful. You're absolutely glowing. Poor Ian is going to faint dead away." She grasped Emily's hands. "Everything is set. Davy took the last of the guests up to the glen and he'll be back for you next."

"Aunt Grace and Maggie made it up there okay?"

Claire dabbed at her eyes and snorted. "Barely. Ian got the log trailer rigged up with a bench, so getting them up there wasn't the problem. The problem was Maggie battling over who was going to drive the tractor. But Aunt Grace set her straight."

Emily chuckled. She had no trouble picturing that.

"Oh, I almost forgot. Our parents send their congrats and apologies. Da is laid up sick and can't make the trip. They're sending the Peruvian coffee and chocolate they meant to bring as a wedding gift."

A triple rap on the door made Emily jump.

"Perfect timing," Claire said with a grin and raised her voice. "Come in."

Emily stilled. Ian wouldn't try to see her before the wedding—would he?

Short, magenta hair poked around the door.

Emily caught a sharp breath. "Jaye?"

With a squeal, Jaye rushed into the room and pulled Emily into a hug. She squeezed her long and hard, then stepped back and stared. "Oh, Emily." Tears filled Jaye's eyes. "You're stunning!"

"But—I thought you couldn't come."

Jaye shrugged with a grin. "Surprise? But really, how surprised could you be? You're the girl who swore you were never getting married. No way was I going to miss this!"

Emily wiped her eyes. "I hate to tell you this, but there's no castle."

"No castle?" Jaye winked at Claire and leaned close to Emily's ear. "No worries. I've seen Johnny and it's all good. Besides, I'm allergic to cats."

The hum of a tractor drifted in through the open window.

Claire craned her neck and looked out it. "And here's my husband with your chariot." Her smile beamed. "Ready, love?"

"Ready?" Emily met Claire's gaze. She drew in a deep breath and glanced toward the hills. "Marrying Ian is a dream I never dared hope for." She turned to Claire and Jaye, unable to contain her joy. "I couldn't be more ready."

The approaching growl of the tractor stopped.

Emily drew a deep breath. "Claire, there's something I want to ask you. Because you've become like a sister to me."

Claire let out a little snort, a feeble cover for a fresh batch of tears. "I am your sister now. Your older sister and you'd better not forget it."

Emily smiled. But as the sound of footsteps on the stairs drew closer, her smile faded. "It breaks my heart to think about all those years Ian was alone. Claire, I want you to promise me something. Don't let him go back to being alone after I'm gone." She swallowed back the rising ache in her throat. "Promise me?"

Claire dabbed the corner of her eye. "Well. I suppose I could do that. For you." She aimed a look at Jaye. "Though I make it a strict rule never to meddle in my brother's business."

Emily burst out laughing and hugged her.

A knock parted them.

Emily stood and ran her hands along her dress as Claire went to the door and swung it wide.

It took three heartbeats to realize the man standing there wasn't Davy.

Dad?

Ray Chapman stood in the doorway, stiff, unmoving, and staring at Emily.

A wave of numbness spread through her chest and flooded her, pooling at her knees. He wouldn't come this far to try to stop her, would he? Heart racing, she could only stare at him and wait.

Jaye took hold of her elbow and leaned close to her ear. "You all right?"

Dad cleared his throat and took a step into the room. "Congratulations, Emily."

Her dad was ... congratulating her? "Thank you."

He drew a deep breath. "I came to apologize."

Claire and Jaye looked at each other and slipped quietly from the room.

The shock of his words sent Emily's heart racing, oddly magnifying the slowly passing seconds.

Dad looked her over again, then cleared his throat. "This is your special day and I don't want to spoil it. I just want to say it was wrong—no, unpardonable—to keep such a secret from you." He cleared his throat again, but the words still came out strained. "But what I'm most sorry for is all the time I threw away that you and I could've ... been a family." He stared at the framed pictures on the dresser. His jaw worked and struggled, as if he had more to say.

Emily waited in silence, throat too thick to speak.

"I can't make up for what you've lost. I can only tell you that I'm truly sorry and ask if you can ever find it in your heart to forgive me." His gaze stayed fixed on the dresser.

Love and sorrow and relief filled her with an almost dizzying force, bringing on a swell of tears. "Of course I forgive you, Dad. I love you. I always have."

Dad nodded but just stood there, breath held, frowning at the pictures.

Emily went to him.

He was stiff but he allowed her to hug him. Though he trembled, she held on.

With a deep sigh, he relaxed, then wrapped his arms around her and hugged her back. Tightly. "I'm sorry, Em," he whispered, voice choked. "So sorry."

"All's forgiven, Dad," she whispered back. "Really."

They held each other for a long time.

When he finally let her go, he cleared his throat again, wiped his eyes. "I know it's way too late. I don't expect any—"

"No, it's not too late. It's never too late. We'll start fresh today." She smiled and took his hand. "I'm so happy you're here. I couldn't ask for a better wedding gift than having you with us."

"That's another thing I wanted to say." He took in her dress, her hair, then shook his head. "You and Ian know as well as I do that there will be pain down the road, and yet you're not letting that stop you. Your courage to face this thing together is inspiring."

Emily wiped her cheeks. "Thanks, but I don't have the courage. Not on my own. The only way I can face the future is to look to God and depend on Him every day for strength."

Dad took a long look at her. "You sound like Ian."

"Ian?" Emily stared at him. "When did you hear that from him?"

"He called. We've talked a couple times."

"Really." Emily smiled. Would Ian ever cease to surprise her?

With moist eyes, Ray studied Emily again. He lifted his chin, as if bracing himself. "I wish I'd found that kind of strength a long time ago. When you needed me."

Emily laid a hand on his arm. "I still need you." A sudden idea sent a burst of joy through her. "Dad, will you give me away?"

He looked straight into her eyes for the first time in years. "Emily, I'd be honored to walk you down the aisle. But"—he shook his head slowly—"please don't ask me to give you away."

When the tractor came to a stop a short distance from the grove, Emily asked Davy and her dad to go on ahead. She followed on foot, wanting time to collect her thoughts.

Lord, I'm trusting You to keep Ian close to You. Please be his strength and bring him through whatever comes. And be with me. Help us to look to You for our every need.

The path into the grove was much wider than before, with strands of white flowers adorning either side. The sun warmed the little sanctuary, filling it with the lovely, sweet scent of honeysuckle. A small crowd of people filled a circle of chairs.

Aunt Grace and Maggie sat together talking, Jaye beside them.

A few of the faces, she didn't recognize—probably church friends and the MacLeans' neighbors.

My neighbors now. She smiled.

Her dad waited at the edge of the clearing and Emily went to him, too thrilled to speak.

The chairs formed a circle around the clearing with an opening near the big Scots pine. Next to the tree, the minister was speaking to Ian with one hand on his shoulder.

Ian nodded.

The sweet, lilting sound of a wood flute fluttered and danced above the murmur of guests.

Emily held her breath to quell the excitement rippling through her.

Ian looked stunning in a black waistcoat and plaid kilt, crisp, white shirt, and black tie. Stopping in mid nod, he turned, saw Emily, and froze.

She froze too, but only for a second. With a hand resting on her father's arm, she urged her feet forward. The sound of the wood flute floated over the thicket as she locked eyes with Ian. The rise and fall of his chest and the way his eyes took in every inch of her sent Emily's heart pounding.

When she reached him, Ian's mouth opened, but not a sound came out.

Emily turned to her dad and kissed his cheek.

With trembling fingers, Dad squeezed her hand and took a step back.

Then Emily looked into Ian's eyes.

He found his voice. "I'm not dreaming, then?"

The depth of his tone unleashed a wave of joy through her. She smiled. "Is this anything like your dream?"

His gaze swept over her again as if capturing every detail. He shook his head slowly. "No. My dreams don't even come close."

The minister welcomed everyone and invited Emily and Ian to join him under the big pine.

"Wait!" Maggie shooed Kallie and Hannah over to join them.

Emily tore her eyes away from Ian long enough to wink at Jaye, then she turned to him and whispered, "So you've met Jaye?"

Ian glanced over her shoulder at her friend. "Aye. But she keeps calling me Johnny."

Emily grinned and glanced over the crowd.

A slightly familiar-looking woman was seated beside Jaye.

Reverend Brown addressed the guests. "Friends, we're here today because Ian and Emily have formed a very special bond. But that bond is about to change." He turned to Emily and Ian. "The Bible tells us that a cord of three strands is not quickly broken. Marriage joins two people together to form a new bond. But a marriage centered on Christ creates a much stronger bond. Your love for one another, woven together with God at the center, will form a three-part cord of tremendous strength. Cling to the Lord daily, for God is faithful. Storms will come, but you will weather them all if you keep your hearts and eyes on Him. God's love, strength, and faithfulness will carry you through. Let us pray." He prayed and blessed them, and when he finished, he invited them to exchange vows and rings.

Ian grasped her hands. "Emily, I ..." He cleared his throat. "You believed in me though I'd given up on myself, and you led me back to God, where I found strength to do the impossible. You brought my heart and my faith back to life. Because of you, I can be the husband you need me to be. With God's help, I'll be at your side through everything—the good and the bad."

Smiling, she let the tears fall.

His voice fell quiet. "Every time the sun rises, the first thing I'll do is thank God for the gift of a new day and another chance to love you. I promise."

The touch of his hand as he slipped a ring on her finger sent a tingle along her arm.

The reverend turned to her.

Gazing into Ian's eyes, she said, "Ian, you've given me so much, and all I have to offer is my heart, one day at a time. But each new day, I will love you like there's no tomorrow."

His eyebrows shot up and he spoke low. "Is that a promise?"

Blushing, Emily nodded.

"What was that last bit?" Maggie shouted. "I couldnae hear."

Emily's fingers trembled as she slipped the ring on his hand.

Reverend Brown pronounced them husband and wife.

Heart racing, Emily looked up at her handsome husband.

Ian's eyes shone. Taking her in his arms, he bent close and met her lips in a sweet kiss.

A warm surge of love and joy swept through her.

As they parted, the guests rose and clapped.

The wood flute played a cheery tune as Ian and Emily crossed the circle to the center to receive their guests.

Aunt Grace's voice rang out above the music. "Ooh, isn't she the loveliest bride ye've ever seen? She looks so much like her dear mum."

"Yes, she does," her dad said.

Emily turned and smiled at them.

The woman who looked vaguely familiar stood beside her dad, smiling, her eyes glistening.

Ian slipped an arm around Emily's waist. "Emily, I'd like you to meet someone." He turned to the woman. "This is my good friend from Portland, Janet Anderson."

"Of course. Hello, Janet." Emily offered her hand. "I'm so glad you could be here. I've heard so much about you."

"And I'm very happy to meet you." She smiled. "I've heard a lot about you, too."

Emily sneaked a glance at Ian, who was gripped in a firm handshake with her dad.

Something seemed to pass between the two men. For a moment, neither of them said a word.

Janet took a step closer and spoke quietly to Emily. "I can't tell you how happy it makes me to see you and Ian together. I've prayed for this for a long time."

A twinge of sorrow tugged at Emily's chest and her smile fell. She whispered, "Has he told you about my condition?"

With a smile, Janet laid a hand on Emily's arm. "All any of us really has is today, Emily. You vowed to love him and live each day by the grace of God. I couldn't ask for anything more for our Ian."

Emily looked at Ian, but noticed that her dad appeared very interested in what Janet was saying.

"Every day is a gift." Janet turned to Emily's dad and smiled. "Don't you agree, Raymond?"

A flush colored his face. With a nod, he looked Janet in the eye. "I do now."

Emily stared at Janet, then at her dad. "Have you two already met?"

Dad glanced at Ian. "Maybe you should ask your husband about that."

Frowning, Emily turned to Ian. "What did you do?"

Ian just shrugged and tugged her close to his side.

Emily looked at Janet.

"Ian introduced me to Raymond by phone a few weeks ago," Janet said. "We've been swapping battle stories. And we had a chance to get better acquainted on the flight over." She studied Emily's dad with a trace of a sparkle in her eye. "I'm looking forward to getting to know him better."

Dad turned a shade redder.

Numbing joy washed over Emily. She turned to Ian. "I don't know what you did, but thank you. Not only did I gain a new family today, I also got my dad back."

Feigning an innocent look, Ian shook his head. "I don't know anything about that. I'm just here for the girl." But his eyes shone with something else, a glowing mix of pride and pleasure.

She slipped her arms around his neck.

Ian swept her up and hugged her close. "I'd do anything for you, Emily MacLean," he whispered in her ear.

Emily held on tight, too happy to speak. *Thank You, God.*

EPILOGUE

A brisk February wind blew through the farm before sunrise, seeping into cracks in the old cottage. This was the coldest morning yet.

Ian bundled up and went to the main house to stoke the fire for Aunt Grace and Maggie. Then, as the sun rose, he hiked over the brae to the cemetery. He stepped over the fence and crouched low near Katy's stone, his breath coming out in big, white puffs. "If You could, please tell her I don't hate him anymore. I hope he makes things right with You and everyone else, for his own sake. Tell Katy I'm grateful for the time she and I had together. It taught me to value each day. I suppose You knew I'd need that."

The sun's first light broke over the hills to the east—a new day. He reached out to brush frost from the gravestone, but then stopped. He rose instead and left the stone untouched.

On the way back to the cottage, Ian continued to pray. First, thanks for the gift of a new day, then to ask for direction and the strength to follow, for Emily, himself, and their family.

Their growing family.

A slow smile spread across his face. With their foster-parent paperwork approved, and the adoption petition in the works, he and Emily were finally realizing what they had only dreamed of—the day they could bring Hector home.

The lad was crazy for fishing. He and Ian could work on art together. Or anything he liked to do—Ian was ready to try new things. Whatever it took to make the lad feel at home, like part of a real family.

A gust of wind ripped the door from his hand when he entered the cottage, slamming it into the wall.

Emily came out of the bedroom to meet him, a grin lighting her face.

He checked his watch. "Sorry, love, but Hector's flight doesn't land for several more hours. We have to wait. But if you insist, I suppose we could go early and pace the runway. I'm sure the airport staff will understand."

Still grinning, she held something behind her back. "Funny. Guess what came by courier while you were gone?"

He opened the wood burner, stirred the fire, and latched the door. "A warrant for Maggie's arrest? Ah, I knew it. It was bound to happen."

"No." She pulled out what she had hidden.

A book. A shiny, new children's storybook.

"So it came." He took *Samson, the Super-Warrior* and ran his fingers lightly over the bright, glossy cover. Examined the pages. Tried but couldn't hold back a smile.

"It's beautiful, inside and out." Emily beamed. "Look at the cover. Isn't it gorgeous?"

"Not bad."

"Not bad?" Emily huffed. "I'm sure the artist-slash-author would be deeply flattered to hear *that*."

Ian met her gaze and held it. Love welled up, filling him with gratitude. "Aye," he said softly. "The artist-slash-author *is* flattered. And honored." He reached for Emily's hands and wove his fingers through hers. "But most of all, he's thankful."

She held his gaze for a long moment. "Well, maybe you could tell him—if you see him—that I'm thankful too."

"I think he'd say ... he couldn't ask for anything more."

Emily leaned close and planted a swift kiss.

The telephone rang.

She turned to get it, but Ian grabbed her and tugged her close. She laughed. "We should get that. It could be important."

Ian shook his head and held her tighter. "That's what answering machines are for. It's more important to stay right here. Keeping warm." He kissed her neck.

The phone continued to ring.

She wiggled free. "It could be Hec's case worker."

276

As Emily took the call, Ian waited, listening to her half of the conversation.

"That's excellent news, doctor ... Of course, you're very welcome ... Yes, it's my pleasure to help." Emily pulled the receiver away from her ear and whispered, "The Freyer's Syndrome study at Glasgow University received full grant renewal because of my participation!"

Ian moved close to her side.

She tilted the phone toward his ear.

"—extremely indebted to you. I'm also calling to answer your question, Mrs. MacLean. Tests indicate that you are positive as a carrier, which means you run a fifty-percent risk of passing on the gene."

Emily inhaled sharply and looked up at Ian. They already knew this, but wanted to make sure.

"As you know, your test results have given us reason to pursue new possibilities in our study. Based on our findings, we have been able to reclassify the heritability of this disease. Specifically, we have recently discovered that patients with a variant result such as yours can fully express the disease, or experience partial expression."

Ian frowned. "Partial?" he whispered. "What does that mean?"

"It's also possible for the disease to never express at all."

Emily's mouth hung open. "Never? Is there a way to know for sure?"

"I'm afraid only time will tell," the doctor said.

The room spun.

Ian closed his eyes.

The voice on the other end went on. "Mrs. MacLean, you're very healthy today. We will continue to monitor you and help you stay as healthy as possible for as long as possible."

"Thank you." Emily said something about her next visit, ended the call, and turned to Ian.

He couldn't speak. Couldn't think. Couldn't decide how to process the information.

Emily grasped his biceps. "Ian."

He could only stare at the telephone. There was a chance that what his wife had wasn't fatal.

"Listen, Ian, it doesn't matter. Every day is a gift. Whether it's one day or twenty days or twenty-thousand days. We only have one day at a time, any of us. If we're doing everything we can with the gifts we've been given—like your beautiful storybook, or making a lonely child feel loved—then I can't ask for anything more." Eyes glistening, she caressed his face. "We're already so blessed, Ian."

He pulled her close and held her. "You're right. None of us knows how long we have." He brushed a lock of her hair from her brow and kissed her forehead.

Emily's eyes closed and she smiled. "You will be an amazing father."

He kissed her temple and murmured, "Aye. If I can manage Maggie, it's a dead cert I can handle one young lad."

Emily chuckled softly. "*You* manage Maggie? That's funny, I thought it was the other way around."

"Did you now?"

She rested against him. "He'll know he's wanted?"

He nodded "Every day."

"Is that a promise?" She looked up at him.

"Aye." He kissed her cheek. "Now do you remember what you promised when you married me?"

She feigned a look of strained concentration. "Um, that I'd laugh at all your dorky jokes?"

Ian frowned. "Hey. I thought that was a given."

"Yes, I remember," she said. "I promised to treasure every minute with you."

"And ...?"

"And ..." she said, her expression softening, "to love you like there's no tomorrow."

He pulled her closer, held her tight. "Is that a promise?"

Emily nodded. "Aye," she said in her best Scottish brogue. "That's a promise."

The End

Aunt Grace's Lemon Shortbread Cookies

Preheat oven to 325°

1 cup butter, softened
1 cup powdered Sugar
2 cups white flour
Zest from 1 lemon

Cream butter and sugar until smooth. Add lemon zest. Stir in flour and mix until a dough forms. Knead slightly on a floured surface, then roll to a rectangle ½-inch thick. With a long knife, cut into 1" x 3" bars. Poke shallow holes in 2 rows lengthwise (like a twelve-dot domino).

Place 1 1/2 inch apart on a cookie sheet. Bake at 325 for 20 minutes until still light in color but golden on the bottom. Remove to cool. Makes about 3 dozen.

Discussion Questions

1. How many times does honeysuckle appear in the story? What does its increasing presence symbolize?

2. God is the Master of irony. How many instances of irony can you find in this story?

3. Ian's inability to forgive affected his relationship with God. How might praying for an offender or an enemy bring you closer to God?

4. When Ian and Emily met, they felt an instant attraction to each other. But was it truly instant? How did years of correspondence affect Ian and Emily's ability to fall in love? Is it possible to know a person and their character through letters/email well enough to engage in a relationship? Why or why not?

5. Though Emily's fears kept her from getting involved in romantic relationships, she hesitated to find out if she had the illness. Why did Emily avoid learning the truth?

6. Emily vowed to save her first kiss for her husband out of a desire to keep her heart from feeling "tied" to someone she might not marry. What harm is there, if any, in engaging in physical intimacy and creating emotional bonds with multiple people?

7. Could you relate to Emily's fears? Ian's bitterness? Do they remind you of yourself or someone you know?

8. How did getting lost in the woods symbolize Emily's life? What impact did that realization have on her choices later on?

9. How does Ian's attitude toward Maggie change? Did she acknowledge this change?

10. How did Grace and Maggie's physical or mental limitations affect their relationship when they were reunited? How did

being together bring out each woman's strengths?

11. What part did Emily's faith in God play in her decision to withdraw from her loved ones? How would you respond in Emily's situation?

12. Ian believed he could be strong for Emily and that she should lean on him, but that belief changed. What caused that change? What affect did it have on Ian's desire to win Emily?

13. Have you ever been challenged to let go of your greatest desire, or to face your worst fear? How did you handle it? After reading this story, would you do it differently?

14. Did any part of the story make you stop and think about your own life or your faith in God? If so, what part and why? Did this lead to an awareness of some aspect of your life you might not have thought about before?

Bio

Camille Eide lives near the Oregon Cascades. She blogs about God's amazing grace at Along the Banks (www.camilleedie.wordpress.com) and inspirational fiction, TV, and film at Extreme Keyboarding (www.camilleeide.blogspot.com) and writes faith-inspiring love stories with sprinkles of wit. She is also the author of *Savanna's Gift*, published by White Rose Publishing, a Christmas romance set in a snowy ski lodge with the sweet promise of cinnamon, spice, and second chances.

Look for her next novel …

Sandcastles in Snow

When she finally surrenders her heart, is it too late?

A social worker-turned-surrogate mom to a mismatched bunch of outcast teens fights to save the group home she's worked hard to build. Her only hope lies with the last person she'd want help from: a beefy handyman with a guitar, a questionable past, and a God he keeps calling Father.

Coming **Spring 2015** from Ashberry Lane Publishing!

Acknowledgments

Though writing is a solitary activity, a book is never birthed alone. I couldn't possibly list all of the people who helped bring me and this story to where we are today. But there are a few I must mention:

My agent, Rachelle Gardner, who gave the first version of this book a revision "memo" that grew both the story and me as a writer. The amazing team at Ashberry Lane who made "delivering" this book an absolute pleasure. My first critique group: Kellie Coates Gilbert, Cheryl Linn Martin, and RanDee Hill. Faithful writer friends Karla Akins, Linda Glaz, Jessica Nelson, Emily Hendrickson, April Strauch, Larry Topliff, Leslie Gould, and the incomparable Carla Stewart. Thank you for holding me up and walking me through to the finish line.

Thank you to my amazing husband, Dan, and kids—Shane, Ben, and Janae—who ate a lot of frozen lasagna and plugged their ears to late-night key-tapping so I could write. I also owe thanks (plus one exploding helicopter) to Randy "The Snowflake Guy" Ingermanson for never letting me off easy, as well as Patty Slack and the rest of the CRCW crew. I owe a very special thanks to Kim Moore, Harvest House Senior Editor, for championing me and for her love for this story. Many thanks to Robin Jones Gunn for inspiring young women to guard their hearts and their first kiss for the man they will marry; my English teacher, Mrs. Gano, who loaned me books because she believed there was a writer in me; and Mom and Dad, who always believed.

Like There's No Tomorrow would not exist if not for Lisbet, my beautiful Viking friend, who believes in international love stories and told me I should just write one.

More Books from Ashberry Lane

The **Journey** of **Eleven Moons**

Northern LIGHTS — BOOK ONE

Bonnie Leon

A successful walrus hunt means Anna and her beloved Kinauquak will soon be joined in marriage. But before they can seal their promise to one another, a tsunami wipes their village from the rugged shore … everyone except Anna and her little sister, Iya, who are left alone to face the Alaskan wilderness.

A stranger, a Civil War veteran with golden hair and blue eyes, wanders the untamed Aleutian Islands. He offers help, but can Anna trust him or his God? And if she doesn't, how will she and Iya survive?

ASHBERRY LANE

ASHBERRYLANE.COM

Winner of the 2014 Oregon Christian Writers Cascade Award!

On the Threshold

Sherrie Ashcraft &
Christina Berry Tarabochia

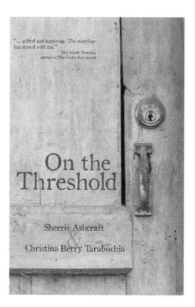

Suzanne ~
a mother with a
long-held secret

Tony ~
a police officer with
something to prove

Beth ~
a daughter with a
storybook future

When all they love
is lost, what's worth
living for?

ASHBERRY
LANE
ASHBERRYLANE.COM

BROKEN *Wings*

THE
Thistle
SERIES
BOOK ONE

DIANNE PRICE

He lives to fly—until a piece of flak changes his life forever.

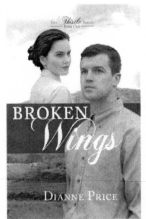

A tragic childhood has turned American Air Forces Colonel Rob Savage into an outwardly indifferent loner who is afraid to give his heart to anyone. RAF nurse Maggie McGrath has always dreamed of falling in love and settling down in a thatched cottage to raise a croftful of bairns, but the war has taken her far from Innisbraw, her tiny Scots island home.

Hitler's bloody quest to conquer Europe seems far away when Rob and Maggie are sent to an infirmary on Innisbraw to begin his rehabilitation from disabling injuries. Yet they find themselves caught in a battle between Rob's past, God's plan, and the evil some islanders harbor in their souls.

Which will triumph?

ASHBERRY
LANE
ASHBERRYLANE.COM

Wing
AND A
Prayer

DIANNE PRICE

Confronting death isn't the
most difficult challenge he will face.

When Colonel Rob Savage
recovers enough from a near-
death accident to resume
command of the demoralized
Heavy Bomber Group at
Edenoaks Air Base in England,
he faces many challenges. As
Rob labors to make his group
best in Wing again, his bride,
Maggie, works long, exhausting
hours as an RAF nurse, all the
while fearing for Rob's safety
during bombing missions.

The unthinkable happens. Rob and Maggie return to their
Scots island of Innisbraw, battling to keep alive their dreams
for the future. Rationing, blackouts, and the threat of
German U-boat invasions conspire against the newlyweds.

Can Rob and Maggie cleave to their faith in God through
such hardships and trials as the devastating war goes on
and on and on?

ASHBERRY
LANE
ASHBERRYLANE.COM

Constant fear, piercing sirens, the darkness of
war ... all that fades with

The Promise of Dawn

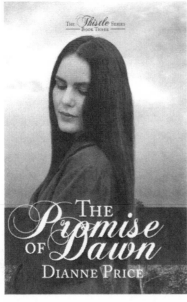

World War II is
over, but there's
much rebuilding
to be done on the
wee Scottish isle
of Innisbraw. Now
a wife and mother,
Maggie Savage longs
for other lasses to
return to their island
home, but how can
they when there is
no way to provide
for themselves and
their families? Her
husband, Rob, driven
by his unrelenting
dream to build a
rescue boat for the
local fishermen, continues to be plagued by nightmares of
impending disaster.

Will their simple faith in God and love for each other
help them find a new dawn for their beloved community?

ASHBERRY
LANE
ASHBERRYLANE.COM

And for the Younger* Readers!
*and the young at heart

The Water Fight Professional

I, **Joey Michaels,** am the Water Fight Professional.

Basically this means that customers pay me to soak other people. But my super-competitive best friend is sucking all the fun out of summer. All because I made a secret bet with him.

Winning the bet wouldn't be so hard if I didn't have the following three problems:

1) My dramatic mother who feels the need to schedule every moment of summer

2) A surfer-dude mailman who can't keep deliveries straight

3) The annoying neighbor girl who all my friends have a crush on

If I lose ... ugh, I can't even tell you what I'd have to do. I'd rather lick a slug!

ASHBERRY LANE

ASHBERRYLANE.COM